CW00531423

ROMANS
ON
THE SILK ROAD

A novel spanning two continents and two empires

Brian Shane McElney &
Andrew Hoste Primrose

Romans on the Silk Road

By Brian McElney and Andrew Hoste Primrose

ISBN-13: 978-988-8552-24-5

© 2018 Brian McElney and Andrew Hoste Primrose

Cover design: Jason Wong

FICTION / Historical

EB114

All rights reserved. No part of this book may be reproduced in material form, by any means, whether graphic, electronic, mechanical or other, including photocopying or information storage, in whole or in part. May not be used to prepare other publications without written permission from the publisher except in the case of brief quotations embodied in critical articles or reviews. For information contact info@earnshawbooks.com

Published by Earnshaw Books Ltd. (Hong Kong)

NOTE

READERS MAY WELL want to know the extent to which this story accords with history, and the authors have decided to make a few comments to help the reader appreciate the background.

The extant Roman sources for the history of the final days of the Roman Republic are quite prolific and detailed insofar as the lives of the great Romans of the time are concerned. (Gaius) Julius Caesar, (Marcus Licinius) Crassus, and Pompey (Gnaeus Pompeius Magnus) were not only the triumvirs but the leading players at the time, and their actions, recorded in this novel, follow very closely the facts recorded about them. Not only was Crassus the richest Roman of his day but despite his years he had an overweening ambition for military glory. Julius Caesar in his Gallic Wars, a contemporary record, describes in detail the events leading up to the revolt of the Veneti and the involvement of Publius Crassus (younger son of Marcus Licinius Crassus). Caesar also describes the building of ships at the mouth of the Loire to combat the Veneti at sea and the battle in which the Veneti were crushed and its aftermath. The manoeuvre involving the cutting down of the sail and the calm that occurred appears in that report. The situation in Rome and the meetings of the triumvirs at Lucca and Ravenna as described and the ensuing results are historically recorded.

The actions of the tribune Aetius, Crassus's eastern adventure and the bad omens that dogged Crassus are drawn from historical records; as are the various phases of the famous Roman defeat by Surena at the battle of Carrhae. The battle and its aftermath, including the gruesome method by which the victory was announced to the Parthian King, when he was entertaining the King of Armenia at a performance of the Euripedes's play 'The Bacchae', are much as described in the ancient texts (see notably Plutarch's Lives). The Parthian commander known as Surena (Surena is probably a title rather than a name but his real name is unknown) was later assassinated by the Parthian King shortly after Carrhae.

Under the Shanyu Zhi-Zhi, the vast Xiongnu territory stretched across the steppes from Western Manchuria, across Mongolia, the Pamirs and as far as the Lower Volga and the Ural foothills. The Xiongnu territory was a loosely-connected federation of tribes who were united under one leader. It required a powerful and assertive Shanyu to unite the different factions and tribes for any concerted aim, the tribes spent most of their time raiding and fighting amongst themselves. The various nomadic Turkic tribes were first unified into a powerful federation under T'ou-Man who was the leader of the Xiongnu (ruled c.225-209BC) and Zhi-Zhi was a descendant of that great leader. The linking up of various walls to create the Great Wall of China by the First Emperor Huang Ti (221-210BC) had been primarily been designed to keep these nomad tribesmen out of China. The construction of the Great Wall was a drawn-out process, with work continuing for many decades as different sections were built, re-enforced and connected to form a composite barrier. With the Great Wall blocking them to the east, T'ou Man and his successors had turned to the west and driven the Yuezhi, another powerful nomadic people of Turkic origin, further west. The Yuezhi had in turn conquered the Bactrian Kingdom (c.130BC) which had been established by Alexander's successors. Following this conquest, the Yuezhi lands bordered

Parthia, and some Yuezhi are recorded as having served under Surena at the battle of Carrhae.

The tombs of the high nobles of the Yuezhi have revealed that they practised head-binding at this time. During the attacks on the Yuezhi by the Xiongnu, the Xiongnu killed the Yuezhi ruler and in accordance with Xiongnu custom made a cup of the Yuezhi ruler's skull. We have mentioned this cup being used at Marcus's meeting with Zhi-Zhi. The Yuezhi appear to be the same people referred to as the Tokharians and as Kushans in later history. The Xiongnu practice whereby a warrior who recovered a dead colleague's body from the battlefield inherits the dead warrior's wife and property is one of the strange customs recorded of the Xiongnu by the Chinese.

It is also a historical fact that a decree of Ptolemy III Euergetes confiscated for the Great Library at Alexandria the original of any book that arrived in the port of Alexandria, not represented in the Library. These books were marked in the Library's index "from the ships". (Official scribes replaced the original with a copy given to the owners.)

Interestingly it is also recorded that this Ptolemy borrowed from Athens the official copies of all three tradegians (Aeschylus, Sophocles and Euripedes) in order to correct the texts in the library. He had put up a considerable deposit for this loan, yet once he had his hands on the originals, he decided to forfeit his deposit and keep the originals.

Lucretius died c. 55BC but the bequest of the manuscript of his famous work to Crassus has been invented for our story, though the paying off of lifetime favors (in this case the putting out of the fire at Lucretius's house by Crassus's fire brigade is also invented) by legacies was very common at the time.

It was also a fact that many Roman soldiers, captured at Carrhae (recorded to have been 10,000 in number and to have included 500 of the Gallic cavalry), were settled at Merv, then known as Antiochus Margiana, but history does not record what became of them. The legionary standards captured at the battle were later recovered diplomatically by the Emperor Augustus.

Roughly contemporary Chinese historical sources record the career of the Chinese General Gan Yan Shou, and his successful expedition against the Xiongnu Shanyu Zhi-Zhi, in 36BC. The Chinese account states that Chen Tang was the deputy commander, and it provides the reasons for the expedition, namely the murder of the Chinese envoy Guji. The Chinese histories record the attack on the town of Zhizhi, a city which only started to be constructed in 46BC and was entirely destroyed by the Chinese in 36BC, so it was a somewhat ephemeral city. The Chinese sources tell how the Xiongnu Shanyu, Zhi-Zhi, was beheaded by a Chinese soldier named Du Xun. The Chinese account also records the capture of 145 soldiers, and their ultimate settlement at Li-qian (otherwise spelt Li-chien or Li hsien) now in the county of Yongchang, in the Kansu corridor. In 9AD the town of Li-qian was briefly renamed Jie-lu by the Emperor Wang Meng. 'Jie-lu' means "prisoners taken in storming a city". A skeleton exhibiting European features has been dug up at the site. The skeleton came from a very tall man, quite unlike a Han Chinese.

The exact location of the city of Zhizhi is unknown but working from the Chinese records it appears to have been near Taraz in southern Kazakhstan on the west bank of the Talas River.

The identification of these 145 captives as Romans relies on.

1. The description of the wooden palisade protecting part of the wall at Zhizhi, described in the Chinese texts; this palisade is similar to that normally erected to protect a Roman camp.

2. The description in the Chinese records of the maneuver performed by the troops later captured. The Chinese

description suggests that the troops formed up in a testudo, a distinctive Roman infantry formation.

3. The fact that Li-qian was the only town in China where bull-baiting was practiced, and this was the town where these prisoners were settled confirmed by the name given by the Emperor Wang Meng as mentioned. Bull-baiting was a known Gallic practice in Transalpine Gaul and this fact lends weight to the possible Gallic origin of some of the prisoners.

4. A small number of the inhabitants in the area of Li-qian still exhibit markedly European characteristics, such as straight big noses, light eyes and curly hair. These people are thought to be the descendants of the original Roman captives. Limited DNA testing suggests that 20% of the persons tested show traces of European ancestry.

5. The original name Li-qian uses the character 'li' in its name. The Chinese character was also the name given to the Roman empire and all things Roman during the Western Han dynasty.

Joseph Needham in his great work *The History of Science and Civilization in China*, took the view that these captives were Romans, (see volume 5 Abridgement page 14.)

The Oxford Professor, Homer H. Dubs in his lecture to the China Society in 1955 suggested that these captives were escaped Roman prisoners from Carrhae. Other commentators, however, have suggested they were Parthian mercenaries but have not advanced any evidence for this idea. At this distance in time whether they were Romans is probably impossible to prove but, from the recorded facts, their identification as Romans seems a reasonable supposition.

We must emphasize, however, that this book is a historical novel and should be treated as such.

ROMANS ON THE SILK ROAD

1

Transalpine Gaul, Mediterranean Sea and Rome, 64 BC

SOME WINDS HAVE names; Marcus could feel the familiar hot gusts against his back as he stood on the prow of his father's galley, and he knew that is was the Mistral breathing down his neck. He had grown up with the Mistral and he knew that today it was only blowing gently, despite this the wind was strong enough to stir up the waves and make the deck buck beneath his feet. He resisted the urge to reach out and hold his father's toughened hand for support. He was a young man now, well into his fifteenth year, and he must behave like one. This was his first proper voyage at sea and they were going all the way to the port of Ostia, and then on to Rome. The prospect of seeing the famous city known as *Caput Mundi* or the 'Head of the world', made Marcus's youthful heart pound with excitement. Marcus and his father were on the Albatross, a new trading galley owned and built by his father. It was the finest of his galleys and it was on this sleek craft that his father, Lucius Frontinius Marcellus, ship-builder and timber merchant, had decided to make the journey to Rome. Lucius was nearly three times as old as his son, yet he noted with a wry smile that Marcus was almost as tall as him, although he did not yet possess the powerful build and muscular arms of his father. Both father and son shared the unruly blond hair, which was a family trait, although Lucius had begun to develop grey tints which lent an air of gravitas to his affable countenance. Father and son also shared similar piercing blue-grey eyes; both pairs of which were now focused intently on the horizon and the approaching wonders of Rome. The clear blue of the Mediterranean surrounded them and cast flickering reflections of sunlight across the galley as it cut through the waves.

Lucius had begun life in the family trade as a timber merchant, felling the white oaks from the family forests in the Luberon region of Provence and then transporting the timber to the flourishing shipyards in Massalia. The busy port was an important Greek city famed all around the Mediterranean as a cultural and legal center. After the Greeks of Massalia had aided the Romans in the Second Punic War, the city was recognized both as an independent colony and as an ally of Rome. Roman forces had first arrived as allies, in response to a request for support from the Greek colony. For three years from 125 BC to 122 BC, a Roman force had fought alongside the Greeks against the Ligurian tribe of Salian Franks. After their victory the Romans had settled and remained in the area. The Romans went on to found the colonies of *Aquae Sextiae* and *Narbo Marius* in the new province of Transalpine Gaul which was created from their newly conquered territories, and introduced the *Pax Romana* to the region. Roman influence soon spread through the whole region, and the city of Massalia was no exception. The weight and power of the expanding Roman world played an important part in the life and politics of the city, although Massalia still retained its Greek heritage.

As a young lad accompanying his father on the deliveries to the shipyards Lucius had displayed a marked interest in the practical details of ship-building. A friendly ship-wright had shown the young lad around the yard, and impressed by his enthusiasm he had suggested Lucius stay on as an apprentice over the summer. The summer was a quiet period for Lucius's family; they did all the logging in the winter months when the trees were not burdened by the enormous amounts of foliage that doubled their weight. So Lucius was permitted to remain in Massalia and earn his keep by helping at the shipyard. Under the ship-wright's guidance Lucius had worked hard, exulting as the crafts of carpentry and ship-building were slowly revealed to him. It ceased to be a mystery to Lucius how the long cumbersome oak logs from the family forests were transformed into the graceful galleys which filled the port and ploughed the seas with such ease.

As Lucius's understanding and skill increased he had moved to Massalia permanently and left the forests to be managed by his cousins. It wasn't long before Lucius set up in the ship-building business for himself. Using his family connections and first-hand knowledge he always managed to buy top quality seasoned timber at favorable prices. With the best raw materials it was no surprise that his business flourished and he acquired something of a reputation as a masterful shipbuilder. His skill and efficiency also brought him to the attention of the Roman *praefectus* who commanded the local fleet. Lucius worked with extra care and attention to fulfil a minor order for the *praefectus* to produce two small delivery launches for the fleet. The other carpenters had scoffed at him, pointing out that such detail was wasted on mere launches, and with the amount of effort he spent on the order it would not prove profitable. In one sense their comments were accurate; Lucius calculated that he made a net profit of ten *asses*, not even an entire *denarius*, a paltry sum for ten weeks hard work; but in another sense it had proved the most profitable venture of his career, for when the *praefectus* came to commission a new fleet of twenty galleys it was to the maker of such fine launches he decided to award the contract.

Lucius had worked with the same level of attention to fulfil this larger order and the final result had greatly impressed the *praefectus*. In gratitude he had recommended Lucius to the Governor of Transalpine Gaul for the award of Roman citizenship. So it was that Lucius became a Roman citizen in addition to receiving the large payment for the order. The rank of Roman citizenship was hereditary and it conferred a number of important privileges. Roman society was divided into the three strata of slaves, freedmen and citizens; this honor had elevated Lucius to the highest class. Freedmen were subjects rather than citizens of the Roman Empire, and as such were only able to join the *alae* or auxiliary regiments rather than the ranks of the famed and feared Roman legions. The *alae* received half the pay of the legions and upon completion of their service the auxiliaries did not receive the grant of land which provided the legionaries with a secure retirement. Serving in the legions was the surest way of securing social advancement, for the constantly expanding Empire rewarded those who protected it, and the scope for advancement within the Army was considerable. Thus it was with some pride that Lucius was able to reflect on the inheritance he would leave his two sons; thanks to Lucius's efforts both Flavius and Marcus were born as Roman citizens and wealthy ones too.

Some seventeen years earlier, with his newly acquired status of citizenship and flourishing shipyard, Lucius had found himself one of Massalia's most eligible bachelors. It had been with a mixture of awe and pleasure that he had agreed to marry Eugenia, the beautiful daughter of a wealthy Greek merchant, when the latter had suggested the match. The marriage had not been a success, for Eugenia took offence that her father had not found her a husband from amongst the established Greek upper class and she had found comfort only in the excessive quantities of wine she consumed. She withdrew into self-imposed isolation where she nursed her resentment and fed her wrath to keep it warm. Despite this, her new husband treated Eugenia with honest affection and tender concern, so it was only in isolation that Eugenia could remain disdainfully aloof and embittered. Refusing to be won over she had, however, provided him with two sons who were as different in temperament as could be. The first was Flavius, tall, graceful and elegant with black hair like his mother; he had also inherited her stubbornness and haughtiness. The second was Marcus, who resembled his father both in his blond hair, blue eyes and rugged features as well as his friendly demeanor. Finally frustrated by the rebuffs of his embittered wife, Lucius had eventually ceased trying to win her over. They had settled into an uneasy relationship in which they avoided each other and Lucius feigned ignorance of her worsening alcoholism. The young entrepreneur found emotional comfort in the company of his sons, and he spent as much time with them as he could. Eugenia had brought her personal slaves with her to run the household and so both boys had grown up speaking Greek as well as Latin. Flavius, with his grace and elegance was a source of pride to the ship-builder who marveled at his eldest son's refinement and sophistication; yet Flavius also displayed traits of excessive pride and greed. He disdained manual work and only ventured into his father's shipyards when he needed funds to settle the bills at his fashionable tailors. In contrast Marcus was a firm favorite at the shipyard, known and loved by all the carpenters and shipwrights. The laborers and craftsmen had adopted him as a mascot and they indulged his interest in archery by fashioning him simple bows and arrows in their spare time.

The current voyage was to deliver a cargo of timber to the port of Ostia, where the Tiber reached the sea some twenty miles from Rome. Lucius could quite easily have sent a subordinate, but he had chosen to combine business with pleasure as he wanted to see Rome in all its splendor. Although he claimed that it was to show his sons around Rome, the boyish gleam in his eyes revealed that the excitement and pleasure would not be only theirs. One astute carpenter had observed with a laugh, that Lucius had promised to take the boys to the Games, before they had even thought of asking him! Lucius wanted to see the capital of the Roman world, to which he and his family now belonged as full citizens. He had also hoped the trip would impress on his two sons the world of opportunities, which lay open to them as Roman citizens.

Lucius recollected a recent discussion with the two boys when he had mooted the option of joining the legions, an honorable career open to them both. Marcus responded eagerly, with a somewhat childish conception of heroic deeds and adventures in unknown lands. The boy had long cherished a fascination with the East; of all his mother's precious ornaments the piece he admired most was an Oriental brooch made from lapis lazuli depicting a leaping tiger. However, this was far from Lucius's mind as he remembered Flavius's alarming response. The young man had smiled sweetly whilst replying that he would rather cut off his own thumb, simultaneously bringing his elegant left hand down swiftly onto the right as it lay on the table as if to illustrate the amputation. Lucius had heard about this practice amongst the more effete circles of young nobles who preferred this mutilation to serving in the army. Without their right thumb it was impossible to hold a sword or javelin and thus they would be refused entry to the Army. Indeed, some young nobles even boasted of their shameful amputation, flaunting their disfigurement as a badge of ingenuity. Whilst Lucius could not be certain if his eldest son was in earnest or not, he knew from bitter experience how stubborn and precocious Flavius could be. This journey had provided yet another example; Flavius had resented the fact that two whole weeks of his precious holiday would be consumed by the trip, and it would mean missing one of the elaborate parties, which were the highlight of his calendar. Flavius had flatly refused to accompany his father, and it was only by withdrawing Flavius' credit at his tailor that Lucius had coerced him into coming on the trip.

Sighing deeply, Lucius allowed the sea breeze to blow away these concerns as he filled his lungs with the freshness of the sea air. Standing beside him Marcus subconsciously mimicked his father, filling his youthful lungs and enjoying every moment of the voyage. The two stood there till long after the sun had passed its zenith, and the smaller shadow of Marcus extended beside that of his father in front of the galley, pointing towards their destination Ostia. The boy's actions and barely concealed excitement brought a half-smile to the weather-beaten face of Petrus, the venerable captain of the Albatross, a man as rugged and scarred as the galley was smooth and sleek. Turning towards him, Marcus approached to greet the revered sailor, for the two were firm friends. Petrus's smile spread across his face and he delivered a report to the boy with mock seriousness;

'Well Captain Marcus, the wind is blowing well and the sail has been set so I have given the slaves a rest from their oars, the weather looks set to hold till nightfall at least and the cargo is all securely stowed in the hold.'

'Thank you Petrus', replied the young boy, 'and what about my brother?'

'Um...well sir... he was feeding the fishes, Captain,' replied Petrus after creasing his brow in the search for an appropriate euphemism.

'What do you mean Petrus?' asked the boy, nonplussed at the sailor's attempt to be polite.

'That is to say he was being sick over the stern, sir. He has retired to his cabin now. It seems he hasn't the stomach of a sailor, though he has certainly acquired some of a sailor's language! From the curses he was heaping on my fine Albatross and these little ripples of waves you'd take him for a veteran of twenty years! Quite where he learnt such language I'd not like to guess.'

'Oh…, yes, well, best say nothing of it to my father,' remarked Marcus.

'Of course not Captain,' replied Petrus with a grin.

'Now, tell me about how you got that one', asked Marcus, indicating one of the silvery white scars which crossed the broad tanned chest at his eye level. For Petrus spent half the year bare-chested, he took off his shirt on the last day of spring, and refused to put it back on till the first winter rains came, claiming ruefully that his long-suffering wife was so tired of stitching up the tears and washing out the stains that she could only be brought to do so for half of each year. The result was that his powerful torso was tanned a deep mahogany, off-set by the silver-white of his many scars and the greying hair which seemed to match the color of the scars.

'Oh, that was where I caught myself on a nail in the shipyard', replied Petrus as his face creased into another large grin, for his modesty was as famed as his scars, and he always gave the same reply when asked about the origin of his wounds. It was left to others to point out that all the injuries he had sustained were on his chest and arms, with none on his back, just one indicator of the bravery for which he was also well-known. Resigned to that fact that he would have to ask the other crew for the story behind that particular scar, Marcus went to check on his brother in their quarters.

A shout of alarm reached Marcus just as he was descending the ladder to their small cabin. He scrambled back on to the deck to see what had caused the commotion that was erupting all around him. The Albatross had rounding a headland with the wind filling her sail to find a large ship with a flotilla of smaller craft waiting in ambush. The boat's darkened hull marked it out as a pirate ship, only the pirates painted their hulls dark to help them camouflage against the shoreline and hide from the Navy patrols. Around it there lurked the scavengers who accompany any large predator. This pack had probably been tipped off about the Albatross's departure, for the water rats had informants in all the major ports and this was a carefully planned ambush. The ship and the small rowing boats were waiting 50 yards apart. They were positioned so that when the galley turned to its port and tried to flee out to sea the pirates could simultaneously approach on both sides and swarm over their victim. The pirates would be able to use the wind, which was channelled down the valley and blew out into the bay to catch up with the heavily laden galley.

The large patched sail of the pirate ship had been unfurled as soon as the galley rounded the point, and it was clear that the off-shore wind would soon bring the pirates in towards the galley. Meanwhile the smaller craft were manoeuvring to approach the galley on the other bow. It was much harder to repel boarders from both sides, so the pirates always tried to attack in unison. It was precisely to avoid this trap that Petrus steered the galley in towards the coastline; as he shouted to the overseer to calm the panicking slaves. Petrus used the vessel's momentum to plough into the smaller boats. Caught unawares by this aggressive move, the scavengers were suddenly on the defensive against a much larger craft charging headlong into their midst. Although the Albatross did not have the submerged iron-clad beak which the military galleys used to ram enemy craft, it was still a sturdy boat built from the dense oak of the Luberon forests, and with a hold full of timber the Albatross had a considerable amount of momentum. As the galley charged into the first skiff it crushed the light boat under its keel with almost no discernable check to its progress. The others boats scattered as swiftly as they could, withdrawing out of range of the arrows which Lucius was loosing from his position high on the prow. As the Albatross had a full crew, Lucius did not have to command the galley so he had quickly strung his bow and taking a quiver full of arrows he had positioned himself on the prow to defend his boat, cargo and sons.

Although the scavengers had scattered they refused to disperse, their greed kept them hoping for plunder, even though it had become apparent that this would be no easy prize. Around the Albatross's prow floated the remains of the destroyed skiff and the bodies of two pirates pierced with arrows. The bucking deck had made a mockery of Lucius's normally fine marksmanship; for when a wave lifted the prow it sent his arrow flying high over the target and correspondingly each trough caused his arrows to fall short, harmlessly plunging into the sea. Despite this difficulty some of his shots had found their mark, as evidenced by the red pools slowly spreading out from the floating bodies in the water.

Meanwhile, the pirate ship was busy turning in response to this unforeseen charge by its prey. On board the Albatross, the panic-stricken slaves had been quietened and set to working their oars; back-paddling furiously the galley was able to decelerate enough to avoid crashing into the rocks, for the pirates had been waiting close to the shore to conceal their position for as long as possible. Expertly steering the craft to hug the coastline, Petrus started to take the galley back out of the bay. The pirate ship had now altered its course and was bearing down on them. Even with the slaves rowing at maximum tempo, the heavily burdened galley could never outrun the lightly-laden pirate ship, which possessed a much larger sail as its sole means of propulsion. Meanwhile Lucius had moved to the stern and was waiting with an arrow already cocked on his bowstring for the pirate ship to come within range. The slaves pulled fervently at the oars, all too aware of the terrible treatment they could expect if the pirates captured them. Stories of the cruelty and maltreatment of slaves in the slave markets outside the Roman Empire were well publicized. It was even suggested by some that they were exaggerated in an attempt to prevent Roman slaves from trying to escape. Yet despite their best endeavors the Albatross could not outpace the pirates, for although the galley was expertly built it was burdened with a hold full of timber and stores, goods that were too bulky to be jettisoned to buy the craft any extra speed. The great weight which had enabled the Albatross to charge into the smaller craft now proved a disadvantage as the galley endeavored to flee from the pirate ship.

The scavengers had regained their courage as it became clear that the pirate ship would overhaul the Albatross. The small craft entered the chase and moved forward in a pack; none were sufficiently audacious to venture ahead of the group, yet their greed forced them to keep level with the others lest they should miss any loot. As the pirates closed to within range, Lucius began shooting in earnest. He was all too aware that he was fighting for his craft, his life and a valuable cargo which included his beloved sons. By this time Marcus had run to join his father. The preceding action had taken place in a matter of minutes and Marcus had been so shocked he had stayed rooted to the spot. Now seizing a spare bow, Marcus struggled to fit the string; but even with his full weight leant against the bow he could not bring the loop at the end of the bowstring into place. Lucius saw his son's efforts and stopped to help him, taking the bow in his calloused hands he fitted the string with one controlled movement. It had crossed Lucius's mind to send his son below deck out of the way of any danger yet he was painfully conscious of what would happen to the handsome boys if they were captured, and every hand on deck would help prevent that dreadful eventuality.

'The deck's moving with the waves so it's hard to aim,' shouted Lucius above the grunts of the slaves and the loud beat of the drum going at full tempo to give the time for the oar strokes. 'Wait till we're on the crest of a wave then shoot before we drop down,' he instructed.

Marcus's first few shots plunged into the sea in front of the ship, or soared too high, making small mocking rents in the sail and rigging of the ship. With concentration he quickly learned to feel the rhythm of the waves beneath his feet, taking up the tension in the bowstring as each wave lifted the galley and then firing in unison with his father when they were poised momentarily on the crest of the wave. The timing was crucial and the strokes of the straining rowers would sometimes disrupt their rhythm when the oar stroke happened to coincide with the crest of a wave.

The gap was closing fast when one such piece of timing occurred; just as the galley rose up on the wave's crest the rowers heaved on their oars and pulled the galley down the wave. As the prow dipped down and the stern rose, both Lucius and Marcus shot too high and their arrows sped harmlessly into the ship's sails. The pirates had soon become wary of the pair of archers and were planning the tortures they would inflict on them once they had captured the galley. Looking up with the next arrow already notched onto his bowstring Marcus noticed something had changed. The pirate ship's sail was flapping loosely and uselessly on the port side. It appeared that an arrow had cut one of the stays which attached the sail to the yardarm. The square sail was now only fastened in three of the four corners, while the remaining corner was flapping uselessly in the wind. With the sail still attached on both corners of the starboard side but only one corner on the port, only half of the sail was being filled by the wind. With the unbalanced force from the damaged sail, the pirate ship was veering off course. The pirate captain spotted the problem and shouting to his men to repair the rigging, he took control of the steering and tried to compensate for the drift off course. Father and son both realized the advantage this fortuitous shot had given them; Marcus continued to take aim at any of the pirates who attempted to reattach the sail, whilst Lucius now took deliberate aim at the rigging. With the full force of his powerful arms behind each arrow, his shots thudded into the mast and bored neat holes in the sail, yet none of these shots managed to disable the sail or further slow the pirates. Lucius pulled out one of the three feather fletches which guided each arrow, this made the arrow spin in its flight. These spinning arrows did greater damage to the sails, but it was not until they were running low on arrows that one lucky shot caught the main stay and sent the entire yardarm and sail falling onto the deck of the pirate ship. The chase had taken them out of the bay and as the other pirates saw the disabled ship withdraw from the pursuit they immediately lost their eagerness and hung back.

Once out of range of those dreaded arrows the pirates set about hoisting the yardarm and replace the rigging, but by this time the Albatross was clear of the bay. It was obvious that Petrus had understood the significance of this and he steered the galley back towards Massalia. The crew had lowered the sail on the Albatross, and under the power of the oars the galley was able to head directly into the wind, a course which the pirates were unable to match as they were totally dependent on sail power.

With an overwhelming sense of relief, Lucius watched the pirate sails diminish into the distance as the rowers settled into a steady monotonous rhythm which took the galley away from the bay. As this relief settled, Lucius reflected just how much had been at stake, and he resolved never again to risk his sons, his business and himself all in one venture. With Marcus safe and standing beside him Lucius turned his attention to check on Flavius, who had not been seen throughout the engagement. Both father and son climbed down into the hold to ascertain what had become of him. The cabin door was locked fast and no answer came to their hammering. At first their calls had been good-natured and jocular, but as no answer was made they became increasingly alarmed. Lucius was about to force an entrance when the sound of a loud splash was heard distinctly. Marcus climbed back onto the deck and ran to peer over the side. The sight that beheld him caused his face to split into a mix of amusement and concern; with a puzzled shout to his father he stooped and took off his sandals. When Lucius reached the top of the ladder it was to see his youngest son dive gracefully over the bow and strike out towards something on the port side. Petrus had seen the boy dive over and had ordered the rowers to stop, the galley continued away from Marcus for a short while but it was soon drifting back with the wind. Marcus had reached the colorful object by this time, and it proved to be the curious spectacle of Flavius floundering in the water with his most treasured cloaks and tunics in his arms. These were of bright and vivid hues and the thrashing about of the young man was creating a riot of colors as the clothes became tangled together.

Flavius was not a strong swimmer and it was clear that he was having difficulties as the sea water soaked into his bundle and pulled him down; yet he obstinately refused to let go of the clothes and as a result he was being pulled down with the water-logged garments. With the assistance of Marcus the two were able to secure the clothes and tread water until ropes were thrown from the galley and they were pulled back on board. Flavius's subsequent explanation, that he thought the galley had been taken by the pirates and he had tried to escape, merely confirmed Lucius's notion that Flavius resembled his mother in character as well as appearance. With a wry smile he thanked the gods that Flavius had not known about the bag of gold coins hidden in the cabin, for the boy would certainly have taken that with him and his tenacity and avarice would have caused him to drown before he would relinquish his grip on such a large sum.

With the boys safely back on board, and Flavius's treasured clothes spread out to dry, they were able to continue on their journey. After rowing for a few more hours Petrus swung the galley round and steering a course far out into the sea they headed east again, giving the bay a wide berth as the sun set behind them. After such an action-packed start the rest of the voyage passed in comparative tranquillity; some rough seas on the third day caused Flavius to provide some more fish food, but otherwise they had an uneventful trip. In the eyes of Marcus their arrival and disembarkation at Ostia failed to overshadow the excitement of the pirate attack, and he spent hours discussing every details of the encounter with anyone who was willing to listen. After registering with the port authorities and reporting the incident to the Navy, they hired horses and left for Rome. The journey of nineteen Roman miles was easily accomplished along the straight paved road, which followed the Tiber upstream to Rome.

They had three days to explore the city whilst the Albatross unloaded its cargo of timber and filled the hold with wines and cloth to be sold in the market of Massalia. Lucius chose an inn and lost no time in depositing their luggage and taking the boys out to explore the city. The journey in from the countryside past the factories and workshops around the city's limit had somewhat prepared them, but the shock of entering the heaving metropolis was still considerable. Multitudes of people thronged the streets as Lucius lead the boys towards the city center. They were going to the Games, to see the famed gladiators and the other wonders which were organised to entertain the people of Rome. Whilst work had only just started on the Coliseum, the existing arenas were still far larger than any of the buildings in Massalia, and the trio marveled at their size. In subsequent years cynics, priests and philosophers alike were to declaim the fact that Rome's greatest architectural achievement was dedicated neither to religion nor learning, but to entertainment for the masses. Yet the Games and horse races were also an important cohesive factor for the diverse population of Rome. The same spectacles were enjoyed by people of all ranks, from the lowest auxiliary soldier to the wealthy tribunes and consuls, for the arenas were open to all and at a price that made them easily affordable.

After buying their tickets and queuing with the jostling and excited multitudes, Lucius and his sons found seats in the banked arena. As the final preparations were being made jugglers and acrobats entertained the crowd; a knife-thrower and an archer competed to impress the audience with their accuracy. A brief hush fell as the trumpets announced the first spectacle; from one side or the arena rushed a pack of fifteen hunting dogs, barking and leaping with excitement. Dogs and audience alike waited eagerly to see what beasts they were to be matched against; then from the opposite side of the arena a drum roll preceded the release of a pair of lions. The pack rushed in unison at the first lion, ignoring the second as it skulked around the edge of the arena. With its back against a wall the first lion roared and its mane rose in a circle around its fearsome jaws. The crowd tensed with anticipation as the pack rushed across the sand to attack the lion. The first bold dog leapt rashly at the mighty beast. It met a swift end as the lion caught it in mid leap and crushed its neck with one bite. It was now the crowd who roared as the blood spurted from the dying dog, showing darkly against the tan of the lion and the light sand of the arena. The fight continued with the weight of numbers finally telling, and the first lion was brought down. The second lion lasted longer, and a fresh pack of hounds had to be released before the required result was secured to the delight of the spectators. The barbaric lions had been vanquished by the familiar hunting dogs and thus after the exciting prospect of disorder, the *status quo ante* had been re-established. There was an unwritten rule in the Games which decreed that the familiar must always triumph over the alien, thus if the dogs had failed to kill the lions, archers and hunters would have been sent into the arena to secure the ordained outcome.

Exotic and savage animals were highly sought after at the Games and the ceaseless demand had created a market which astute merchants had been quick to exploit. Along with the spices, cloths, furs, perfumes, timber and grain which were imported to Rome, there now came a steady string of exotic creatures. Large predators were the most highly sought after; wolves and bears from the forests of Danubia and Germania, leopards and lions from North Africa and crocodiles from the Nile. Novelty was also a significant factor, hence it was not only the large predators which the crowds loved; giraffes and camels were brought to be attacked by dogs or hunters. Elephants and rhinoceroses were also popular features, their tough hides ensuring that the spectacle was drawn out for some time because of the vast number of arrows or spears which were required to bring them down. However, it was unquestionably the gladiators who remained the most popular feature; the more successful combatants built up a cult following amongst the fans, who transferred their support to the next hero when one was cut down. The fickle nature of the fans' support had even become a contemporary byword for infidelity amongst the citizens of Rome.

The inn was a very noisy place in the early evening, and Marcus tossed and turned repeatedly in the unfamiliar bed. After the cramped quarters on the Albatross his bad in the inn was spacious, but the ceaseless drone of conversation and raucous laughter was a far cry from the gentle lapping of the waves against the boat's hull. Marcus could hear the shouts and jeers as the revelers returned from the Games, and noisily relived the excitement of the gory events. Despite his exhaustion after such a long and exciting day, sleep eluded him even as the twilight shadows on the walls continued to fade and soften. As dusk fell, the familiar odor of burning oil rose from the numerous small terracotta lamps that were being lit around the inn. This seemed to be the signal for the first of the raucous guests to make their way home before the darkness closed in, and Marcus listened with interest as the assorted population bade each other good night in a host of languages. Before long both the inn and the streets outside were wrapped in an unaccustomed silence.

However, the silence did not last for long. Once darkness had fallen a distant rumble could be heard approaching the city, as if a storm was rising in the surrounding hills. As Marcus strained to identify the unusual sound it grew louder and closer. Then against this curtain of noise, he made out the clatter of wheels on the paved streets and the clash of horses' hooves. The streets were soon filled with carts and carriages as fresh supplies were delivered to the booming city. In his sleep-befuddled mind, Marcus recalled that he had not seen a single cart throughout the day, and he now remembered hearing about the ordinance which forbade wheeled traffic from entering the city walls during daylight hours. This drastic measure had been adopted by the Senate as a solution to the permanent traffic jams which had grid-locked the city streets. All deliveries within the city walls were now made by night, and the din which filled the air was created by the rumble of thousands of wagons as they moved about the city streets.

The persistent drone of wagon wheels rumbling across the stone slabs was a world away from the city streets during the day where the soft patter of sandaled feet mingled with a range of exotic languages as the cosmopolitan population went about their business. Marcus lay in bed thinking about the two different worlds which operated within the same city. The contrast between the nocturnal and diurnal life of Rome was as great a shift as the change from the secluded life on board the Albatross to the hustle and bustle of the city. Yet there was another contrast in Rome of which Marcus could not possibly be aware. It was the contrast at an entirely different level, and one that in many ways steered the future destiny of Rome and all its citizens; it would even come to have a profound and significant impact on Marcus himself. It was the gulf between the everyday life of the Roman population and the extraordinary machination of the political elite.

2

THE ROMAN WORLD, 1ST CENTURY BC

BY THE MIDDLE of the first century BC, the Roman Republic had been severely destabilized by the ambitions of its major politicians. These men thirsted ardently for glory, gold and the good opinion of their contemporaries. It had always been a Roman's ambition to procure social advancement for himself and his family, as well as to secure a personal fortune. Advancement and social recognition was best achieved by obtaining one of the annually elected magisterial posts within the Government, post that carried with them membership of the Senate for life. The three ranks of magistrate within the civic administration in ascending order were Quaestor, Praetor and Consul. In 82BC the dictator Lucius Cornelius Sulla (138BC-76BC), the victor in the Civil wars of the 80sBC, had abolished the tribunes' power to initiate laws in the assembly, and had set age limits for each post as well as other eligibility criteria. He also fixed the number of magistrates at 20 Quaestors, eight Praetors and two Consuls and he decreed that only after serving as Quaestor and Praetor was one eligible to run for Consul. The Consuls were supposedly barred from holding the office for consecutive terms. Since the Republic's early days the powerful figures in Rome had formed factions to achieve their goals and assist one another in their political machinations. Initially the influential figures had played by the rules and the struggle for power in Rome had been orderly, even if it was not always decorous.

However, by 60BC, however, this was no longer the case and a secret triumvirate of Gnaeus Pompey Magnus, Marcus Licinius Crassus and Gaius Julius Caesar took effective control of Rome and all its provinces. These three men formed an unlikely alliance, united solely in their interest in furthering their political aims. Pompey was Rome's most successful general and had just celebrated his third triumph in 61BC. He had first risen to prominence in 82BC when, at the age of 23 he had led an army in support of the dictator Sulla . Pompey had ruthlessly defeated an army of the Marian faction in the civil wars, earning himself the nickname "teenage butcher". He had at the time just inherited the largest private estate in Italy from his father Pompeius Strabo, who was notorious for switching sides whenever it paid him to do so. Tis aptitude was inherited by the son, though by 60BC Pompey was enormously popular with the Roman people, who loved him as much as they had loathed his father. Pompeius Strabo had been so hated that his body was dragged from the funeral pyre and desecrated before it could be burnt. The younger Pompey was unique amongst Roman generals in securing a major victory in each of the three continents known to the Romans, namely Europe, Africa and Asia. His exploits in Africa had earned him the title of 'Magnus' or 'the Great', although even this had not satisfied his vanity.

After a successful campaign against the barbarian tribes in Spain, Pompey had returned to Italy with his legions. On his return from Spain his forces fortuitously ran into some 5,000 rebel slaves who had escaped from Crassus's defeat of Spartacus and the slave army in 72BC. Pompey annihilated the rebel slaves, and then wrote to the Senate reporting his achievement in quelling the slave revolt. It was an action that rankled with Crassus, who felt that the actual suppression of the slave revolt had been his achievement, and that Pompey had robbed him of the glory. Crassus and Pompey at Crassus's suggestion both stood for Consul on a joint ticket and both were duly elected Consuls in 70BC. Pompey was awarded a triumph for his victories in Spain, whereas Crassus was merely awarded a second class parade for defeating Spartacus and the rebel slaves. It was considered less meritorious to defeat slaves than barbarians. Pompey was only 36 at the time, far younger than was permitted for a Consul under Sulla's reforms, nor had he served as either Quaestor or Praetor so there were question marks over the validity of his appointment. Crassus on the other hand was of the legal age required and by this time he had also served by this time in the other junior magistracies. Pompey and Crassus duly proceeded to roll back some of Sulla's reforms and in particular restored the right of the tribunes to initiate laws in the people's assembly over which they had greater control than the Senate, and they were soon to take advantage of this alteration.

Meanwhile the exponential increase in the population of Rome had put a great strain on the local food supply. Many of the poorest citizens relied on free corn distributed by the government, since the huge numbers of slaves meant the poorest Romans were forced out of jobs. Corn was imported to the capital from the Roman provinces and North Africa and Egypt in particular. Although Egypt was still ruled by the Ptolemy dynasty, the Romans had a strong influence in Egypt. The fertile black silt which was deposited each time the Nile flooded had made Egypt a very productive and wealthy country as well as providing the country's first name as, 'The land of the black mud'. The ruler Ptolemy XII had used Egypt's vast wealth to purchase the might of Roman arms to reclaim his throne after three years in exile.

The deal tacitly ended Egyptian independence as the Pharaoh had relied on Roman arms to secure his throne. Egypt served as the bread-basket of Rome; but before the corn could reach Rome it had to cross the Mediterranean, which was plagued by pirates.

The corn trade was highly lucrative, not least because the pirate menace served to keep the market price of corn high. Many powerful merchants thus profited indirectly from the nefarious activities of the corsairs. One result was that no concerted action was mounted against the pirates and they were able to develop into organised and established groups, often with lavish lifestyles and luxurious boats. The pirates grew increasingly bold, and as time went on and they no longer restricted their activities to attacking ships in the open seas but they even seized towns and ports as well. Tributes were extracted from many ports and cities and important Roman officials were regularly captured and held for ransom. At one time even Julius Caesar was a victim and held for ransom. During his captivity, Caesar reportedly laughed at the pirates and told them he would return to kill them. He even insisted they increase his ransom, protesting that they did not appreciate his true worth. The pirates apparently tolerated his haughty manners. The increased ransom was duly paid and Caesar was released. When Caesar did return, he crucified the captured pirates as he had promised, although their throats were apparently cut first in an act of mercy.

In 68BC the pirates, who had already defeated one pro-Consular fleet sent against them, became so bold as to enter the harbor at Ostia where they burnt the Roman fleet as it lay in dock. This was not only a dramatic act of aggression occurred a mere 19 miles from Rome itself, but it also disrupted the corn threatening the city with starvation. With the populace alarmed and close to rioting agitating, a tribune proposed in 67BC that Pompey, the people's hero, be given a sweeping license to deal with the pirates now that his year in office as consul was completed. The tribune's proposal quickly gained popular support, and in this volatile climate the Senate was forced to appoint Pompey as proconsul with full powers to destroy the pirate menace and secure the food supply of Rome. Pompey's appointment was exceptionally made for three years instead of the normal one, and his mandate embraced the entire Mediterranean with all its islands and up to 50 miles inland. There was very little Roman territory which was not included in this extraordinary mandate. The Senate also provided an unprecedented force of 500 ships and 120,000 men, with the power to levy more should Pompey decide that they were needed. Never before had the resources of the Republic been so concentrated in the hands of a single man, and most of the Senate were concerned at this breach in custom. However, Julius Caesar voted in favor of the Commission this was decisive in securing the mandate that was so urgently needed. Pompey successfully and efficiently ended the pirate menace within a mere three months. After defeating the pirates, Pompey recognized the social problems which were behind brigandage and in some cases he bought the pirates plots of land and settled them as farmers. Following his victory over the pirates Pompey was accorded his second triumph in Rome.

The Senate in 67BC, impressed with Pompey's success and efficiency, then proceeded to invest him with further unprecedented powers. Not only was he given command of the largest force ever sent to the Eastern Mediterranean, he was given the right to make war and peace without consulting the Senate. Over the next five years Pompey settled all Rome's affairs in the East, finally dealing with Mithradates of Pontus, who had long been a thorn in Rome's side. Armenia became a dependency of Rome, with its King Tigranes left with little power, Syria became a Roman province (64BC), Herod was set up as a client king, and a peace treaty was made with the King of Parthia, with the Euphrates marking the border of Parthian territory. Pompey returned to Rome in late 62BC, fabulously rich with the treasures of the East. In Rome he started building a magnificent theatre on the Campus Martius near the Forum to rival those he had seen in the East. He also asked the Senate for ratification of the various treaties he had concluded and for grants of land he had promised to his veterans, which were the normal rewards on completion of their service. Both of these requests were denied by the Senate who were alarmed at the power Pompey now exercised. It was this refusal that ultimately led to the creation of the unannounced first triumvirate of Pompey, Crassus and Caesar working together to obtain their respective political ends. In Pompey's case this was to coerce the Senate to ratify his promises to his veterans.

Marcus Licinius Crassus was a 'political fixer and millionaire', his father and brother had been executed by Gnaeus Marius (157BC-86BC) and the family's estates seized during the Civil wars at that time. Crassus first rose to prominence through his support for Sulla who became dictator of Rome. From relatively humble beginnings Crassus had amassed a huge personal fortune as a landowner, money-lender and speculator. He began to build his fortune when he purchased the properties which Sulla confiscated from his enemies and then sold at bargain prices. Crassus was reputed to have added an innocent man's name to the list of proscribed men solely because he coveted his estate. Crassus had also acquired large parts of Rome by purchasing properties that were in danger of being burnt down. He maintained a private fire brigade and whilst a building was burning he would bargain with the owners, if they refused to sell he would stand with his firemen and watch the building burn. If they sold the property to Crassus he would send his firemen to work and extinguish the blaze, but only within the properties Crassus now owned; they left the fire unchecked in neighbouring properties. Crassus also used this method to buy the adjacent properties from panicking owners, for Rome was a densely populated city and fires quickly spread from one building to the next.

In addition to his fire brigade, Crassus kept a force of 500 masons and builders on standby to repair the damaged properties he acquired. Indeed the bulk of his fortune was said to subsist in the thousands of slaves he owned and trained. Understandably there was some resentment at the way in which Crassus profited from public disasters. With the huge gain that each fire in the city could generate for him it was even rumored that Crassus was behind some of the blazes. Whether there was any truth in the matter or not, it was recognized that the manner in which Crassus had made his fortune was not to his credit. His many virtues were obscured by his avarice; this greed was identified as his only vice for it was said to be so great it obscured any others.

Crassus used his immense fortune to gain power and influence in Rome. Through his tireless efforts he acquired a huge support base amongst both the upper and lower classes. Throughout his career he feasted the people of Rome at his own expense. He kept an open house, and his hospitality extended to aiding all those who might conceivably be of use to him in future, whatever their status. In this manner he acquired a large following in Rome despite the fact that he did not have any brilliant military victories to his name. Although in his youth Crassus had achieved some competent military successes he had never acquired the fame or recognition of such brilliant generals as Pompey or Caesar. In addition to his material wealth, Crassus yearned for military trophies and public glory. There had been a long-standing rivalry between Crassus and Pompey since the time when they had both served under Sulla, and it had taken all of Caesar's insight and skill to bring the two together and form the coalition, which constituted the first triumvirate.

Crassus was an early supporter of the dictator Sulla, and he first rose to prominence by raising an army of 2,500 men and joining Sulla during the latter's bid for power in 82BC. During this power struggle a Samnite force attacked Rome itself, but Sulla pinned them down outside the Colline Gate, and in the ensuing battle Crassus and his force shattered the left wing of the Samnite forces, ensuring victory and earning Sulla's gratitude. Under Sulla's dictatorship Crassus became the wealthiest man in Rome through his mercantile activities, speculating and dubious business practices. With his wealth he built up a party of senators who supported him. At the same time Crassus also acquired considerable influence with the plebeian leaders who were becoming so important on the Roman political scene.

When a group of gladiators lead by Spartacus started a revolt amongst the slaves (73BC-71BC), Crassus saw his chance for glory. Although this was by no means the first or last slave revolt it developed into a serious internal threat. The rebellion started in Capua thirty miles north of Naples and it spread quickly. The rebels had defeated several Roman forces sent against them before the Senate gave Crassus an army and the task of crushing Spartacus. The revolt had now continued unchecked for nearly three years, during which time Spartacus and his forces had marched the length and breadth of Italy undefeated. Many slaves had escaped and joined the rebel force, so by the time Crassus went to fight them there were over 100,000 rebels. Pompey was campaigning in Spain and so Crassus had the ideal opportunity to gain the military glory and recognition he so eagerly desired. Crassus once declared that no man should be considered wealthy who could not afford to raise his own army; so in addition to the forces which the Senate gave him he raised and equipped two legions at his own expense.

The rebels fought and routed part of Crassus's army which had been sent to scout the territory with strict orders not to engage the rebels. In response Crassus resurrected the feared punishment of decimation, which had not been used for over two hundred years. The Roman cohort which were held to be the most responsible for the shameful rout were made to draw lots, and one in every ten men were then beaten to death by their comrades in front of the whole army. This punishment was deeply shameful and the most dreaded end a legionary could meet. Crassus demonstrated his ruthless resolve when he decimated soldiers from a force which he had raised and equipped at his own expense. After some manoeuvring Spartacus and his army were finally forced to face the legions in a pitched battle. Spartacus dramatically called for his horse before the battle and slew it in front of his army, declaring that if they triumphed he would have many more better horses, whereas if they lost he would have no need of a mount as he refused to flee. The rebels were defeated and Spartacus was slain, although his body was never recovered. Crassus demonstrated his merciless efficacy a second time when he crucified the 6,000 prisoners at intervals of forty yards along the length of the Appian Way from Capua to Rome. Pompey's annihilation of the surviving slaves escaping from the battle meant that Crassus did not achieve the military recognition he so ardently desired, and this further stoked the enmity between Crassus and Pompey.

The rivalry between Pompey and Crassus was brought to public attention during their year as Consuls in 70BC. During the period of Pompey's eastern commission, Crassus continued to wield his influence on the Roman scene building up his power base and protégées, of whom Julius Caesar was only one. The return of Pompey with his vast wealth in late 62BC meant that Crassus then ceased to be the wealthiest man in Rome, and he was ambitious to remedy this and to achieve great things and surpass Pompey.

Gaius Julius Caesar, 'the Gambler' the remaining Triumvir was the scion of an extremely ancient Roman family. His father had been Praetor in 92BC and went on to be Governor of Asia. Following his father's death in 84BC, he became a priest of Jupiter at the age of sixteen. He started his career as a supporter of the Marian faction and he even married Cornelia the daughter of Cinna, the head of that faction. Sulla subsequently required that he divorce Cornelia, which he bravely refused to do. Sulla thereupon deprived him of his priesthood and he was forced to flee Rome with a price on his head. It was only because some of Sulla's main supporters were related to Caesar's mother that his life had been spared and a pardon was later obtained for him. Caesar, well aware that whilst Sulla was in power he was in danger, went to the East as a staff officer and with his charm and stylish dress was an immediate diplomatic success. He also joined the assault on Mytilene, Asia Minor in 80BC and with conspicuous bravery won the civic crown, a wreath of oak leaves. This award, Rome's highest award for bravery, meant that even Senators had to rise to their feet and salute him when he entered the circus to watch the Games. After this, Caesar stayed in Asia for a couple of years, studying how provincial administration worked. It was during the course of his time in Asia that he was captured by pirates and ransomed. When Sulla had died in 78BC Caesar returned to Rome.

He soon came to public notice as an orator whilst his extravagance and flamboyant dress quickly made him the leader of the smart young set in Rome, at the same time he became a notorious womanizer par excellence. In 69-68 BC he was elected Quaestor; in 65BC he became an aedile at the age of 35. The aedileship, a junior magistracy, was not obligatory to those seeking the Consulship but it was advantageous as the post included responsibility for staging the Games, and thus the opportunity to gain great public support. Caesar's Games were so lavish that legislation was rushed through limiting such extravagance in future. In 63BC the prestigious post of Pontifex Maximus fell vacant. This office, exceptionally was held for life, and carried with it a house in the Forum of Rome. Election to this office was traditionally the preserve of patrician former Consuls. Although he was a patrician, Caesar had not served as a Consul, however, he flouted the traditions and stood for the post of Pontifex Maximus. With massive bribes and his popularity among the electorate from the staging of such lavish Games, it was no great surprise that he was elected to the post. His gamble had paid off but he was left with enormous debts, which he could only recoup by serving as governor of a province or as a general in a war. In 63BC he was elected as Praetor and in late 62BC he went to Spain as Governor. There, to the surprise of his enemies, he made a great success, proving himself a natural and gifted commander during the war in Lusitania, modern day Portugal, which not only enabled him to repay many of his debts but also earned him a triumph from the Senate. He returned to Rome in the spring of 60BC.

The elections for Consul that year were a turning point in the Republic's history and they led to the First Triumvirate. Pompey was still agitating for the ratification of his treaties and land grants for his veterans. Caesar immediately recognized the opportunity this presented and rushed back to Rome, even before his successor was appointed as Governor of Spain, to stand as Consul. To do so he had to declare his candidature before the start of July and he made it just in time. As a General he was not allowed to enter Rome until his triumph, so he applied for the right to stand by proxy, but opposition from Cato and other senators prevented this. Caesar had to choose between entering the race for the Consulship or celebrating his triumph. Knowing the substance of power he chose the former and stood for election. Pompey's money and veterans swung behind Caesar's candidature. Cato tried to neutralize matters by putting up a plodding senator named Marcus Bibulus as a rival candidate supported by Pompey's many enemies. Caesar won by a landslide and Bibulus just scrapped in, extensive bribery by both candidates having been evident in the election.

Early in his Consulate, Caesar presented a bill in the Senate for the settlement of Pompey's veterans. This was opposed by Cato and Pompey's enemies there, and Caesar was unable to get it through in the Senate against such opposition. He was therefore obliged to back down. He then decided to take the measure to the Forum, which, when the measure came up for discussion, was filled with Pompey's veterans. Caesar also paraded his heavy-weight supporters in the persons of Pompey and Crassus. No one was surprised at Pompey's presence but the support of Crassus was indeed ominous and the opposition was at a loss to know what it might mean. Crassus normally was opposed to anything Pompey wanted, but he never did anything without a reason and his support seemed out of character. Bibulus the other Consul was so flustered that he told the voters he cared nothing for their opinion. When the measure came up for a public vote Bibulus in a desperate rearguard action announced that he had observed unfavorable omens in the sky and proposed that the voting should be postponed. The response of Julius Caesar, the Pontifex Maximus, was to have a bucket of dung emptied over Bibulus's head, with Pompey's veterans beating up his lictors and smashing his symbols of office. Bibulus then invited Caesar to cut his throat, which Caesar contemptuously refused to do. After this the bill was duly passed and Caesar made the senators swear that they would obey the law. Bibulus went into a sulk and refused to leave his house for the remainder of his term as Consul.

The First Triumvirate, initially secret, was now in the open and the divided opposition could do nothing to withstand the combination of the General, the Gambler and the Millionaire Fixer. Pompey's Eastern settlements were quickly ratified and Caesar was granted Cisalpine Gaul and Illyricum as his pro-Consular provinces. Crassus contented himself with amending the tax laws to his profit. Suddenly in the spring of 59BC the governorship of Transalpine Gaul fell vacant on the death of Metellus Celer, and this province was also added to Caesar's pro-Consular territories providing ample scope for his ambitions. Exceptionally the period of his appointment as Governor to these three provinces was to be for 5 years. Pompey was then awarded control of Spain and the western Roman provinces, whilst Crassus gained the post of Governor of Syria. The Roman Republic was now controlled by the three Triumvirs and each had their designated sphere of influence.

3

Transalpine Gaul, 57 BC

WHEN THE MESSENGER arrived he was ushered straight into the atrium, still wearing his mud-stained tunic and dripping cloak he handed over the sealed letters he had rushed so urgently to deliver, before going in search of food and a change of clothes. The letters were taken directly to Julius Caesar as he sat in post-prandial ease, enjoying the melodious tones of a lute being strummed by a young slave. A fire of fragrant cherry-tree logs burnt brightly at one end of the room to ward off any winter chill. Abruptly dismissing the musician, Caesar beckoned for the letters. His attendants knew to only interrupt him with matters of the utmost gravity, so these letters would certainly require his full attention. It was only permitted to use the legion's couriers to send official messages and anyone caught misusing this vital communication system was severely punished. After a cursory glance at the superscription, he broke the wax seal and opened the letters. They came from Publius Crassus, son of Marcus Crassus, in Armorica, the recently pacified province of north-east Gaul. Caesar had left Publius in charge of the VII Legion *Macedonica* in their winter quarters near the mouth of the River Loire. Within the camp, the Romans held hostages from the recently subjugated tribes, and so no further trouble was anticipated. Scanning over the preliminaries, Caesar focused on the main content of the letter. This reported how the Veneti tribe had taken two Roman officers hostage with a view to exchanging them for the Veneti hostages held by the Romans. The situation was worsening as winter set in, and the Veneti were becoming increasingly rebellious, refusing to pay taxes and openly flouting the terms of the truce which they had agreed with Caesar.

The VII Legion was short of supplies, and it was in order to replenish their depleted granaries that Publius had sent out envoys and tribunes to collect the *annona*, a tax paid in wheat, which was used to feed the legions. Two of these envoys, Quintus Velanius and Titus Silius, had been sent to the Veneti. There, in defiance of the accepted sanctity of envoys, they had been seized as hostages. Whilst it was only the Veneti who had taken Roman hostages, the other tribes were exploiting the opportunity to delay or withhold the tributes they owed the Army, and the problem showed signs of spreading. Publius reported that there were rumors of the Veneti and the normally disparate Celtic tribes exchanging oaths to join forces against the Romans. The threat of a unified Gallic revolt was something to be taken seriously. The Roman conquest of Gaul had been greatly facilitated by the lack of cohesive opposition from the feuding tribes, who were too embroiled in their internecine conflicts to unite against the Romans.

Caesar paused to determine his priorities. A scribe had been summoned and waited patiently to take down Caesar's orders. In the courtyard outside, there were already messengers standing by their horses to deliver Caesar's instructions. After two tough seasons campaigning in the region, Caesar knew the Veneti tribe well. They were expert sailors with strongholds on the islands and headlands around the north of the Bay of Biscay. They were a sea-faring people who made a profitable living from fishing, trading and charging tolls for safe passage across their territory and for the use of their ports along the south coast of Armorica. As the alternative to paying this tribute involved crossing the Bay of Biscay and braving the formidable storms for which it was famous, most merchants begrudgingly paid the toll demanded by the Veneti.

With their large fleet, it had previously proved impossible to engage the Veneti on land; at the approach of any formidable force, the Celts simply took to their ships and sailed to a different stronghold. The Veneti's craft possessed a flat wide keel permitting them to approach close to the shore, thus they could land or embark from numerous points along the coastline and were not restricted to the ports. Their maritime strength and focus on fishing also rendered the tribe almost impervious to reprisals on their homelands. The Veneti relied much more on their fishing grounds than on their few farms for sustenance. Sedentary tribes could normally be punished by burning their crops, fields and orchards, even nomadic tribes could be subdued by slaughtering their herds and burning any pasture, but fishing grounds were invulnerable to such reprisals. After assessing the situation, Caesar concluded that a fleet would be necessary to subdue the Veneti. To this end, he sent orders for all allied vessels in the region to assemble in the town of Portus Namnetus at the mouth of the Loire. Caesar also ordered the shipyards of the Mediterranean to move their operations there, and to commence the immediate construction of a fleet of war-galleys. Caesar was vexed at the delay, which building a fleet would necessitate; it set a bad example to leave rebels unpunished for such a long period. He also sent additional orders to the *Praefecti* at the port of Forum Julii, for the dispatch of all available sailors, helmsmen and overseers from the south coast of Gaul to Portus Namnetus. As the evening progressed, and Caesar's plan developed, he dictated additional instructions; orders for galley slaves to row the new boats, regular reconnaissance reports to be made of the Veneti's positions, wheat supplies to be delivered to the VII Legion from the Army depots, and cohorts to be stationed in the villages of Armorica to prevent the spread of the revolt.

In Rome it appeared that the remaining two triumvirs had fallen out. The political opposition hoped that the coalition was breaking up. However, this did not prove to be the case, and in the spring of 56BC Crassus travelled to Ravenna for a meeting with Caesar. Ravenna lies just within the province of Cisalpine Gaul in northern Italy, a region that Caesar was governing. Accompanying Crassus was a Roman called Appius Claudius, who exercised considerable political power and influence in Rome. After the meeting Crassus returned to Rome, whilst Caesar and Claudius proceeded to Lucca where they met Pompey. News of Pompey's intended trip to Lucca got out and many ambitious young Romans travelled to Lucca at the same time. The result of these conferences was to revive the triumvirate for a then undisclosed purpose.

When the news had reached Lucius in Massalia, he soon secured a very profitable order for six war galleys to be built and delivered at Portus Namnetus. The order specified an extremely tight time scale for its completion and required the galleys to be fitted with a submerged iron-clad beak on the prow, designed to sink enemy craft by ramming them below the water line. The Roman Navy also wanted boarding ramps and planks and grappling irons to be supplied with each galley. Lucius immediately set his younger son Marcus to work on the designs of the new galleys, for Marcus was now his chief designer and engineer. Marcus listened to the specifications required, then fell to adapting the design they had used for the Albatross. That galley had proved such a reliable vessel that eight years later they still used the same basic design in their shipyard. Marcus now added a submerged iron-clad beak to the plan for the Albatross and he strengthened the keel to cope with the additional weight. With the alterations to the design complete, the father and son compiled a list of the wood and materials they would need. The most important timbers were the heavy trunks for the keel and beak. Each beam was hewn from a single oak trunk, and would require several yokes of oxen to transport each one to the river bank, from whence they could be floated down the Loire to the port. Amidst the uproar of their preparations for departure, Lucius had written to some cousins involved in the timber trade in the forests near Anjou in the Loire valley. He informed them of the new market they find for their timber in Portus Namnetus in the upcoming months, and ordered the necessary seasoned timbers for six galleys.

After he had arranged for the delivery of the necessary timber, Lucius hastened to organise his departure for Portus Namnetus. He decided to take Marcus and his entire team of carpenters and shipwrights from Massalia. It was seven years since the two boys had accompanied their father to Rome and Lucius reflected that time had merely accentuated the differences between his two sons. Lucius barely saw Flavius nowadays. The latter was almost nocturnal as a result of his fashionable revelry, so he rarely crossed paths with his industrious father or younger brother. Lucius did not bother to invite Eugenia or Flavius to accompany him. He knew that neither would care to leave the comforts of the family villa in Massalia.

The ageing shipbuilder reflected that the trip would be a welcome occasion to enjoy the company of his youngest son, and he tried once again to quell his preference for Marcus over Flavius. Through his professional contacts, Lucius had managed to apprentice Marcus to the best engineers in the region, and the young man now possessed an extensive knowledge stretching far beyond carpentry and ship-building. From the engineers of the VIII Legion, Marcus had learnt the theory of bridge-design, aqueduct-construction and fortress-building. The finest engineers of that time were in the Army, and the legions carried out a large number of civic projects as well as building the forts and roads, for which they had already become famous. Whilst working with the Legion, Marcus found that his interest in horses and archery had provided topics of mutual interest with the men, and he enjoyed riding and shooting with them whenever he had the chance. From the legionaries, Marcus had learnt the practicalities of the various civic projects in which he and the Legion's engineers had been involved; for the amicable young man made friends easily, and he got on well with the soldiers and engineers. His father had impressed upon him the importance of practical as well as theoretical knowledge, so Marcus often spent evenings drinking and relaxing with the legionaries who were employed on the projects he had helped design. He listened attentively to their grumbles and complaints, whilst in his mind he differentiated between the usual grumbles and the occasional constructive piece of criticism. From this reflective process, he had been able to draw much useful information, and in many areas he was experienced far beyond his 22 years of age.

Caesar needed a fleet in the Atlantic before he could put his plan into operation and he was vexed by the delay this inevitably required. His frustration had resulted in high wages being offered to those carpenters and shipwrights willing to work the long hours needed to complete the work. The timescale for Lucius's contract was tight, but with the generous premium the *Praefecti* were paying, Lucius knew his men could be persuaded to work the long shifts the task would require. As Lucius was one of the first ship-builders to arrive in Portus Namnetus, he succeeded in establishing his workmen in a prime location, between the main road and the edge of the port. Thanks to Lucius's foresight in ordering the timbers before he left Massalia, little time was wasted. His cousins in Anjou had despatched the necessary beams as quickly as possible; consequently, the workmen had barely finished setting up their workshop in Portus Namnetus when the first timbers arrived. At the portside, the timbers were hauled out of the water using a system of pulleys and stays. The port had not been built to handle these heavy and cumbersome deliveries. Although the stone quay and harbor areas were sufficiently strong and large, temporary frames had to be erected for the pulleys needed to raise the large beams. The unloading ropes in the port had also proved too short, and several of them had to be joined together before they were long enough. The tight timescale made every hour valuable and the carpenters and ship-wrights waited impatiently for the beams to be in place, so the real work of building the galleys could commence.

With their minds on the large rewards and profitable contracts at stake, the men had worked eagerly, laboring through the night to set up their workshop. However, the completed workshop was too small to build all six galleys simultaneously, so Lucius and Marcus decided to complete the order in three parts, producing two galleys at a time. The shipyard soon became a constant hive of activity from sunrise till sunset and the cacophony of hammering, sawing and chiselling soon drowned out the usual town din. Even more impressively, the scent of fresh saw dust, wood shavings and chippings managed to mask the harbor's residual fishy aroma.

Lucius had taken lodgings for himself and Marcus at an inn behind the workshop. The wily shipyard owner had decided to lodge his workmen across town, far away from the temptations of wine and women in the many taverns around the port. However, Lucius's precautions could not prevent the innkeeper's young wife taking an instant fancy to Marcus when they arrived at the inn. Her flirtatious banter and overtly attentive care proved a mixed blessing, for it did not go unnoticed by the jealous innkeeper. Whilst the young lady's attentions ensured that Lucius and Marcus received the best cuts of meat and freshest linen, these were accompanied by dark scowls and menacing mumbles from the inn-keeper. The tensions in the inn meant that Lucius preferred to dine with the *Praefecti* who were in charge of the amassing Navy.

The first four galleys were quickly completed and the men were exhausted by the long shifts. They joked and shouted less as they now worked on the last pair of galleys. The carpenters were operating as efficiently as possible and could not spare the time or energy for idle banter. One cloudy day Marcus was supervising the positioning of one of the large trunks in the ship-yard, when he heard a great tumult behind him in the port. He went to investigate and saw a crowd gathering around the quay where his father's team had been hauling up the last trunk. A dreadful sense of foreboding came over Marcus as he pushed his way to the front; the groans emanating from the center of the crowd reached his ears despite the noise of the crowd, and they produced a cold ball of fear in the pit of his stomach; they were disturbingly familiar in tone. Frantically barging past the last few workmen, Marcus's worst fears were confirmed as he beheld his father trapped beneath one end of the beam. The great weight of the trunk had pinned him to the stone floor, where he now lay writhing in agony. The other end of the trunk was still suspended and men were rushing to stabilize it before the rope gave way. The accident had occurred when the knot joining two of the ropes had caught in a pulley and snapped, releasing the end of the beam which had come crashing down onto Lucius. Exhausted as the carpenters were, they rushed to the assistance of the injured man. All around men were working fervently to secure the trunk, whilst others struggled to replace the broken rope so that it could be lifted.

Meanwhile, Lucius lay trapped beneath the trunk; it had caught him across the legs as he tried to dive out of the way. The beam was still suspended from one end and the remaining rope would not be able to hold the additional strain for long. The shipwrights rushed to stabilize it with anything they could find. A nearby cart was wheeled under the trunk to support it, whilst assorted crates and spars were hastily employed as levers to raise the beam and allow Lucius to be pulled to safety. Marcus knelt by his father's side and he raised Lucius's tunic to assess the injury. The sight caused him to let out an involuntary gasp, the beam had crushed both Lucius's thighs. The lower half of his body was a darkened pulp of torn muscle and shattered bone in a pool of blood. Mercifully Lucius was still in shock, and the glassy look in his eyes showed that the pain had not yet registered. Whilst working on various engineering projects Marcus had seen some serious injuries, but this was one of the worst. He knew the first priority was to slow the bleeding, Lucius had already lost a lot of blood and if it continued unchecked he would soon die. Steeling himself to the task, Marcus cut away the tunic and raised his father's ruined legs onto a crate. This elevation slowed the bleeding but there was nothing else Marcus could do until a surgeon arrived. He sent instructions for the slaves to boil water, fetch bandages and a stretcher and to prepare a couch in the adjacent workshop.

The surgeon arrived promptly; and under his supervision they managed to move Lucius the short distance into the workshop without worsening the bleeding. The surgeon had noted the quay-stones awash with blood and he recognized the most immediate danger was from further loss of blood. He set to work applying dressings and bandages to stem the bleeding. The surgeon's fervent endeavors succeeded in slowing the bleeding, but the vital trickle would not stop. Lucius had lost consciousness shortly before they moved him, sparing him any further pain at this point. When the steady flow of precious blood failed to stop, the surgeon ordered the furnace to be stoked. Two slaves worked the bellows furiously whilst the surgeon placed a nearby poker in the glowing coals.

'You're father's lost a lot of blood, I'm going to cauterise the injury', explained the taciturn surgeon as he removed all the blood-soaked bandages.

'It will be painful but we need to stop the bleeding,' he continued, 'I need someone to hold him down. Tie his chest and arms down and then hold his legs for me.'

Marcus carried out the surgeon's instructions quickly: the limp body of Lucius was easy to secure whilst he was unconscious but the bindings had to be secure in case Lucius awoke during the process. By this time the iron poker was glowing red and the surgeon used a pair of blacksmith's tongs to remove it from the coals. With a steady hand and grim determination he applied the glowing poker to each of the points where blood still seeped. At the first contact the smell of burning flesh filled the room and Lucius awoke with a scream of agony, the pain had caused him to regain consciousness and he thrashed against the ropes that bound him. Undeterred, the surgeon continued and each hiss signaled another wound successfully sealed. With tears in his eyes, Marcus struggled to hold his father down as the sickening smell of burnt flesh surrounded them both. After the fourth application Lucius lost consciousness again and the surgeon was able to finish his work in a few minutes.

When the treatment was completed the surgeon anointed the burns with a salve and wrapped fresh bandages around the wounds. Next he gathered the used bandages and tossed them all into the furnace where he paused to watch the flames take hold. With his work complete the surgeon let out a deep sigh and sat down with Marcus to discuss the situation. He was a military man who saw no benefit it talking around a topic.

'He's lost a lot of blood; it's hard to say if he will recover. If you had not raised his legs he would be dead by now,' concluded the surgeon.

'Oh!' muttered Marcus. The shock of the accident was only now settling in and he forced himself to confront the possibility that Lucius might not survive.

'Is there anything we can do?' asked Marcus.

'Only wait, pray, and change the dressings daily,' was the reply, 'and give him plenty to drink when he wakes up', added the surgeon.

The days passed and Lucius remained unconscious. Work continued on the remaining galleys, though Marcus refused to use the beam which had crushed his father. He ordered it to be chopped into logs and a replacement trunk procured. The whole team of carpenters worked on one galley whilst they waited for a replacement trunk. The fifth galley was complete before the replacement arrived, so the shipwrights cut and shaped all the other timbers whilst they waited for the vital beam. When it did arrive they worked through the night to assemble the final galley and ensure that the entire order was completed in time. Marcus had moved Lucius to a warm corner beside the furnace where he was able to tend his father whilst continuing to supervise the workshop. It was essential that the galleys were completed on time, for the contract included harsh penalties for late delivery.

Marcus wrote to inform his mother and brother of the accident but he was not surprised to find their response was nothing more than a formulaic expression of grief and concern. On the fourth day Lucius awoke, he was very weak from the loss of blood but after drinking some watered wine he revived a little. Marcus called a halt to the work on the galleys as his father's whisper was barely audible above the noise of the carpenters. Father and son talked for over an hour before Lucius went back to sleep. It was five days later when he next awoke, and the galleys had been completed. Lucius managed to drink some soup, although his frame was visibly withered and he had appeared to have aged a lot. He sent for a scribe as soon as he finished eating. When the scribe arrived he dictated his will; Lucius explained to Marcus that the shipyard must go to Flavius as he was the eldest. Lucius left his younger son his horse and the large payment for the six galleys. Once the testament had been witnessed and sealed Lucius sighed with relief. He was a man who liked to keep his affairs in order. Lucius awoke one final time the following day, he chatted peacefully with his son before sinking into a deep sleep which eased him out of this world.

Marcus spent the rest of that day and night in mourning, numb to the world as he fought to accept the reality that his father had died. Marcus was deaf to the consolations and commiserations of those around him, and he sought solitude. The smothering attentions of the innkeeper's wife now vexed him and he could not understand how anyone could joke or laugh after such a tragedy. He returned to his lodgings only to wash, eat and sleep. Marcus tried in vain to escape the pain of his bereavement by riding his father's horse along the shore line each morning, cantering in the edge of the waves, and feeling the strong Atlantic breeze clear his mind as he gave full rein to the fine thoroughbred. The salt spray which splashed up around him and soaked his cloak was cold, for although spring was approaching the Atlantic retained its winter chill.

Marcus was accustomed to having the beach to himself on

these early morning rides, so it was with some annoyance that one clear day, he perceived another rider come into view. The other rider was a slim, lithe man in his thirties. He rode with control and precision, each movement demonstrating his experience and poise in the saddle. He approached on a fine tan gelding, and beneath his cloak Marcus recognized the insignia designating a *trierarch*, or captain, of one of the galleys. The title was Greek as were many of the captains, for the Romans made poor sailors and they relied heavily on foreign seamen, particularly Greeks. The captain's upright riding posture had made him appear taller than he was, and on closer inspection Marcus found the captain to be of small stature, with a typically Hellenic complexion, a round face and dark eyes. The young man admired Marcus's white stallion, and fell into place beside him. Marcus felt his initial chagrin disappear in the affable company of the captain, who introduced himself as Dimitri. In the days that followed, they regularly rode together, testing each other and their mounts over various distances and jumps as they raced along the beach. In the end, they concluded with wry smiles that both the riders and horses were equally matched. Marcus had noticed the Greek accent in Dimitri's speech, and the latter had been delighted to have an occasion to use his native tongue. Since joining the Roman Navy he had been obliged to use Latin, and whilst he was competent in that language, he missed using his mother tongue. They chatted in a relaxed manner each morning as they met for a ride, enjoying the break from their respective duties.

One rainy afternoon, Dimitri came to find Marcus at the shipyard and invite him to a dinner. A number of the galley captains had been boar-hunting that morning, and they were gathering that evening to roast and enjoy the spoils of their chase. Marcus gratefully accepted, curious to meet the men who would be commanding the vessels he had built. At dinner, the conversation had begun with accounts of the day's hunt, but it soon turned to the approaching campaign against the Veneti. One of the captains pointed out that the design of the Veneti vessels would cause problems for the Roman galleys. Traditional Roman naval tactics involved either ramming with the iron beak, or grappling with irons and then boarding the enemy with legionaries. The Romans were inept sailors, and their naval victories were largely secured by boarding the enemy vessels. This tactic enabled the naval engagement to be treated as a land battle, with the galleys effectively providing a floating platform for an infantry engagement, and once on board, the superior legionaries could defeat any opposition. The problem was that the Veneti's Atlantic boats were of a very different design to those the Romans had encountered in the Mediterranean. The former had to contend with the rough winds and waves of the Bay of Biscay, whilst the latter remained in the relatively sheltered Mediterranean, and consequently there were marked differences in their design. The captains were worried that neither of the traditional approaches would prove effective against the Atlantic boats. As there were some craft of similar build amongst the allied fleet already in the port, it was proposed that various exercises should be attempted to establish the best means of attack.

The captains were universally impressed with the young shipbuilder and engineer, and they invited Marcus to join them whenever his work permitted. It was only a few days later that Marcus went to dine with them again. He inquired about the exercises and heard with dismay that their suspicions had proved accurate. Their investigations had revealed that the Atlantic vessels were built entirely of oak, with cross beams a foot wide, and all fastened together with iron bolts as thick as a man's thumb. This meant the boats where too sturdy for the galleys to ram. They had even put the matter to the test when one local captain had boasted that his craft could withstand being rammed at full speed by a Roman galley. The boat had survived, earning its captain an amphora of wine and the grudging respect of the Romans. The trials had also revealed another problem, for the Atlantic craft were much higher at the bows and stern than the Roman galleys. The boats were designed to withstand the extreme buffeting of the Atlantic, and the high sides prevented the large waves from breaking over the decks. A side effect of these high sides was that boarding the boats from the galleys had proved much harder, as it was difficult to use boarding planks between the different craft on account of the disparity in height. The legionaries had been obliged to climb up grappling ropes and cargo nets, putting them at an immediate disadvantage while boarding the Atlantic boats.

Marcus listened attentively to the problems, questioning the captains in detail about the Atlantic vessels. The rigging was essentially the same as that used in the Mediterranean, but the Atlantic craft used leather sails, instead of the flax or linen that was used in the Mediterranean. The leather was beaten thin and heavily worked with tallow to prevent it stretching when wet. The Gallic captains refused to trust flaxen sails in the gales which they frequently encountered, and they preferred to use leather which was more durable. In his mind, Marcus was replaying the lucky escape from the pirates whilst aboard the Albatross with his father all those years ago. The memories brought back the pain of his recent loss, but he forced himself to focus on the information he was now being given. The Atlantic boats relied entirely on wind power as had the pirates. The difference in material for the sails did not alter that. The Roman galleys possessed both sails and oars manned by slaves, as had the Albatross.

Dimitri had observed the look of concentration on Marcus's face, and he now enquired what his friend was thinking about.

Marcus declined to reveal his train of thought until he had all the information he required about the rigging of the Atlantic craft. Like the pirate ship, these boats were rigged with one yard attached to the top of the mast, from this was suspended the large sail which formed the vessel's sole means of propulsion. Marcus told the story of his escape on the Albatross, and asked if similar tactics could not be used against the Veneti. One dismissive voice remarked it was not possible to rely on lucky arrows during a pitched sea-battle.

'That's missing the entire point!' cried Dimitri with excitement, his exasperation evident as he raised his voice above the din of the tavern. 'The whole concept is that our galleys are more manoeuvrable than their boats. With our rowers, we are not dependent on the wind.'

'So the great Roman navy can escape directly into the wind, is that what you are so excited about?' asked the first man, his question loaded with scorn.

'No, that's still not the point', replied Dimitri, 'We just need to find a way of disabling their sails, then our galleys can surround them and board each boat from both sides at once. That should make up for the differences in height and give the legionaries a chance of boarding more easily.'

All agreed that the theory was entirely valid but as had been pointed out, they could not rely on lucky arrows to disable an entire fleet of several hundred boats. With this *impasse* ending the conversation, the talk passed on to other topics, and they started to plan their next hunting trip. Dimitri refused to be defeated so easily, and withdrawing to another table with Marcus, the two of them continued to discuss ways of disabling the rigging of an Atlantic boat. They worked from the premise that it was necessary to detach the entire yard, rather than merely make holes in the sail. As the sails were made of leather they did not even have the option of trying to ignite them with flaming arrows, an unorthodox tactic which was still occasionally employed. They also accepted it was not possible to rely on archers in any way since the Bay of Biscay was renowned for its choppy waves and volatile weather, thus the archers would be unlikely to have a stable position from which to aim. By the end of the evening, they had come up with a number of possible methods which they set out to test the following day.

The two young men used Marcus's workshop to construct and adapt the various devices they intended to test. Dimitri then bribed the captain of one of the Atlantic boats to lend them his vessel for their trials. It was the same captain who had won the wine, when his boat had survived being rammed by a Roman galley, and he consented to some more easy earnings. The first device they tried was a discus with sharpened edges. Whilst practising in the shipyard, Marcus had been able to cut several ropes with each throw. However, it proved impractical at sea and after all of the discuses had been lost to the sea-bed, they abandoned that option and moved onto the next. Their second idea involved using a grappling iron to entangle the main stay of the enemy's rigging and then pull it down. The concept received its first modification almost immediately; standing on the prow Dimitri had succeeded in hooking one of the stays with a grappling iron, but when the galley rowed backwards, instead of pulling down the ropes, Dimitri had been pulled off the front of the galley and into the sea. The incident had amused the galley slaves and captains alike but the impromptu plunge into the ice cold waters of the Atlantic had in no manner cooled Dimitri's enthusiasm. Climbing back onto the galley, he seized Marcus in a big wet hug which failed to quell the latter's laughter. After Marcus's recent loss, it felt good to laugh again and the young man appreciated the companionable support of the captain.

Marcus was also impressed by the *camaraderie* which united the legionaries of all ranks and he was giving some serious thought to enlisting.

'There, now you're wet too', said Dimitri, 'and I have some improvements to make. Instead of pulling down the rigging, we need to cut through the main stay holding the yard to the mast. We could easily manage that by sharpening the inside edge of the grappling iron. And secondly, the rope needs to be attached to the galley, not just to me!' He added with a hearty laugh.

Whilst Dimitri went down to his cabin and changed into some dry clothes, Marcus carried out the modifications. The next trial proved much more effective. Standing on the galley prow, Marcus and Dimitri both threw the customized grappling irons into the other boat and hooked its main stay. Then they attached the ropes to the galley and as the rowers back-paddled, the customised grappling iron cut through the main stay. With the main stay cut, the boat's yard had fallen uselessly onto the deck bringing the sail down with it and paralysing the vessel. They carried out several more successful trials, after pacifying the aggrieved captain and persuading him to replace the main stay and raise the sail again. On each occasion the customised grappling iron proved equally effective, and both men thought they had perfected the device until the captain observed that in battle all it required was for him to cut the rope attaching the modified grappling iron to the galley.

After further consideration and revision, they managed to preclude this eventuality by placing the sharpened hooks on the end of wooden poles rather than ropes. Their first response had been to replace the rope with a metal chain. However, this had proved too heavy to throw into the rigging from the galley's prow. Whilst the wooden poles could still be cut, that process would take much longer and it only required a very short time back-paddling to cut through the main stay and bring down the enemy's yard and sail. The poles also possessed the advantage that they could be manoeuvred more easily for they did not have to be thrown, but merely swung into place. As trials with the hooked poles proved equally successful, it was decided to demonstrate the device to the *Praefecti,* who commanded the fleet.

Whilst the boats returned to harbor, Marcus and Dimitri discussed how they should approach the *Praefecti* with their idea. They were saved the decision when they reached the port and found the *Praefecti* waiting for them on the quay. The *Praefecti* had been riding along the cliff with their staff, and had stopped to watch the peculiar experiments taking place in the bay beneath them. Once the *Praefecti* had seen the yard come crashing down they had been quick to applaud the potential of such tactics. From their vantage point, they had not been able to make out what had been used to perform the feat and they listened with interest as Dimitri explained the device and credited Marcus with the innovation. Congratulating them on their resourcefulness and ingenuity, they invited the young men to join them for dinner and expressed an earnest desire to hear more about Marcus' engineering ideas.

4

Roman Armorica and Bay of Biscay, 56 BC

As soon as the spring sun had rendered the roads passable, Julius Caesar travelled to Portus Namnetus to review his forces. He split the seventh Legion into its ten cohorts, and ordered each cohort to move from village to village in a long line until they had surrounded the rebellious area. A cohort comprised six centuries and each century comprised between eighty and one hundred men, so each cohort contained at least five hundred fighting men, and this was sufficiently large to deal with any isolated pockets of resistance. The sight of the advancing cohorts acted as a powerful deterrent for the neighbouring tribes so the Romans were able to encircle the rebels before the problem spread. The Veneti soon realized this manoeuvre was designed to contain the revolt and isolate them from any support, yet they dared not risk leaving their familiar waters and territory. The tribe's chieftains decided to fortify their strongholds, gather in whatever early harvest they could, and rely on the power and size of their fleet for protection. Reports had reached them of the Roman fleet assembling at Portus Namnetus, yet they were confident they could outpace and out-sail any boats the Romans could send against them. Caesar advanced the cohorts as the spring rapidly progressed, bringing the legionaries into an ever tighter ring around the Veneti. The rumored oaths of solidarity between the tribes had proved exaggerated and the legionaries encountered only minor resistance as they advanced. The centurions used the occasion to extract triple the normal amount of wheat as tribute, and they burnt any villages that resisted. This practice emphasized the price of disobedience, as well as providing supplies for the town of Portus Namnetus. The sailors, shipbuilders, carpenters, galley slaves, staff and camp-followers who were gathered in the town meant there were a lot of extra hungry mouths to feed.

As the new galleys were completed, the whole port hummed with the preparations of the massing naval force. Sailors, helmsmen and galley slaves poured in from all over Romanised Gaul, and the small town of Portus Namnetus was soon stretched to its limits to accommodate them all. The captains of the new vessels signed up their crews and then took the boats and men out into the Bay for training. For the first few weeks the galleys jostled and bumped as the crews familiarised themselves with the new boats. The galley slaves also required some time to become accustomed to the turbulent waters of the Atlantic. They still had to take each stroke in unison despite the rough waves. The long oars were so close that any mistiming caused the oars to clash. The Romans were highly experienced at training recruits, and under the rigorous tuition and watchful eyes of the instructors, the assembled boats were soon transformed into an ordered fleet.

The command of each galley was split between two men. Each galley had a captain, who was usually Greek. His role was to sail the ship and command the crew. The second commander was a centurion who was in charge of the contingent of legionaries which were on each galley and who were used to board enemy vessels. The crew and rowers could fight when necessary, but the legionaries were the main offensive force on a galley, and they were of higher standing than the sailors. A squadron of ten galleys came under the command of a *navarch*. This was the highest rank a sailor could achieve as the higher post of *praefectus* was only open to Army officers of the equestrian class. Each *praefactus* was stationed in a different harbor where they commanded a fleet of anything from six to twenty galleys. One senior officer was in overall charge of the amassed naval force for any particular campaign. In this campaign to suppress the revolt by the Veneti, Caesar placed Decius Brutus in command of the fleet, while he commanded the forces on land.

Once the galleys had been delivered, the ship-builders and carpenters were encouraged to leave Portus Namnetus; having fulfilled their part in the great Roman war machine, their continued presence was an additional strain on the limited resources of the small town. The experienced officers also knew that keeping idle workmen with money to spend in a busy town was asking for trouble. Marcus had given his workmen a few days holiday in reward for the long hours they had labored on the galleys, but they were all set to return to Massalia at the end of the following week. Their final job had been a commission from the *praefecti* to equip each galley with the customised hooks that Marcus had designed and demonstrated. The *praefecti* had been so impressed with the new device that they had ordered all the captains to attend a trial and then to practise the manoeuvre as soon as they had the hooks. The instructions also specified that the manoeuvre was to take place out in the Bay rather than in the sheltered port. This served the dual purpose of familiarising the crew with the procedure in rough conditions as well as concealing the new device from any prying eyes on the shore.

After the accident, Marcus had written to tell his brother and mother. A few days later he was obliged to write again, with a heavy heart, to inform them of Lucius's death and the details of his will. Marcus had also told them of the funeral arrangements although he knew the letters would not reach Massalia until after the event. The first reply from Flavius had shocked Marcus; for along with his condolences and protestation of grief, Flavius had included a second letter with specific instructions about the next job for the carpenters. Flavius refused to let emotion interfere with business and directed the carpenters and shipwrights to return to Massalia where they could be actively and profitably engaged without further delay. As Marcus complied, the realisation dawned on him that there was no reason for him to return to Massalia and he was now effectively rootless. There was no love lost between the two brothers and Flavius had made it abundantly clear in his correspondence that Marcus's services would no longer be required at the shipyard. This realisation was intensely liberating yet also bewildering in the array of decisions he now had to make. Marcus was a young man, a Roman citizen and a competent engineer. He also possessed a fine horse and a large purse full of gold as payment for the galleys. He could find employment anywhere in the vast Roman empire.

One fine evening Marcus was discussing his options with Dimitri as they trotted back from a gallop along the shoreline.

'If you were a citizen, I would advise you to join the legions, but as it is, you could still join the *alae*. The pay is not as good as the legions, but they have some good cavalry divisions', remarked Dimitri.

'Oh, but I am a citizen', announced Marcus, for Gallic citizens were still sufficiently rare that Dimitri had assumed his new friend was a *peregrine* and therefore ineligible to become a legionary.

'Then the best thing you can do is enlist.' concluded Dimitri, 'You could join the legions and try to get transferred to a cavalry cohort. Or you could become a military engineer – Mithras knows they never seem to stop building roads and forts, so you'd have plenty to do. Alternatively you can join me in the Navy. The service is three years longer than the legions, but you have the advantage of being at sea.'

This last comment had brought a sparkle to Dimitri's eye, for the Greek captain loved nothing better than the feel of the bucking deck beneath his feet and the salt wind in his face. Indeed his daily rides along the edge of the sea were an attempt to recapture this sensation whilst he was on land. For Marcus the opposite was true. He enjoyed sailing only as far as it reminded him of horse-riding. With his friend's frank advice, Marcus found it much easier to narrow down his options. After discarding the Praetorian Guard and the Navy, he was left with the choice between serving as a military engineer or joining the legions and trying to gain a place in the cavalry. Both options seemed equally attractive, so he deferred the choice and allowed himself to get caught up in the final preparations for the campaign.

Marcus was still reflecting on this choice when he heard shouts of excitement in the inn where he was staying. His enquiries soon established that the order to depart had finally been given. On the following morning Caesar was sending his new fleet into action under the command of Decius Brutus. The rest of the day was employed in last-minute preparations by the excited galley crews and captains; whilst in the temples, sacrificial victims were examined for auspicious signs. Although privately Caesar believed that each man made his own luck, he also knew the advantage of having a motivated and optimistic force. To this end he had sent numerous sacrificial animals to each of the religious orders and cults in the town. The large number of animals politely implied that the priests and augurs were to continue sacrificing until they found the appropriately auspicious omens! Some of these sects met in mobile temples which travelled with the legions; for the Roman Army was a tolerant employer and as long as it did not interfere with a soldier's duties, the legionaries were free to worship as they chose.

The wide-ranging reforms carried out by Gaius Marius(157-86 BC), had turned the Roman Army from a civil militia into a professional standing army open to all citizens of Rome whether they were landowners or not. Marius was a veteran commander and highly successful general; he was elected Consul an unprecedented six times between 108 BC and 100 BC. His reforms were intended to increase recruitment to the Army, and they duly achieved this end. However, the consequences of these reforms were considerably more far-reaching than Marius had imagined. The professional legionaries now looked to their general to provide them with a grant of land at the end of their service and this required new territories to be conquered. The profound changes which followed the reforms led to the Army's irreversible entry into politics and ultimately contributed to the end of the Republic, as Rome became an Empire. The Marian reforms also provided each legion with an eagle standard. This was the *aquila* which was treated with immense respect and used in a variety of ceremonies. Whilst these eagles were not actively worshipped, they soon became the focal point for numerous sects and superstitions, as well as permitting the development of a strong *esprit de corps* centred on an established symbol.

When the sun rose the following morning it was a clear and bright summer's day. The ships of the fleet were fully prepared and they set out with an off-shore wind filling their sails and whipping at the tops of the waves which rolled in from the Atlantic. These waves had built up over the vast fetch of thousands of miles of ocean, and the off-shore wind was unable to check their progress as they continued to drive in against the shore. On land, the cohorts of the VII legion had advanced far into the territory of the Veneti. They had succeeded in storming a few of the coastal strongholds but each time the Veneti had escaped by sea, depriving the Romans of any decisive victory. The shallow draught of their boats enabled the Veneti's fleet to come in close to the coast and carry the rebels away to another stronghold. Caesar was neither surprised nor deterred by the course of the campaign on land, for he had long ago determined that a naval defeat would be the only way to subjugate the Veneti.

On the day of the battle, Caesar accompanied by his guard and his staff took up their position on a hilltop, overlooking the expanse of the Bay of Biscay. Beneath them they could see the entire Veneti fleet. It had been anchored in scattered groups in the sheltered pockets around the islets of the rugged coastline that formed the heartland and principal defence of the tribe. As word of the approaching Roman galleys spread, the Veneti boats began to set sail, their leather sails filled with the off-shore breeze as they grouped together to meet the forthcoming attack. The Veneti boasted a vast fleet and from the hilltop the Romans counted 220 boats amassing to challenge their 160 war-galleys. Caesar had every confidence in his fleet and he had already deployed the half the cohorts of legionaries along the coast to catch any rebels who tried to flee overland. The other legionaries were deployed on the galleys where they formed the heavily-armed boarding parties upon which the Roman Navy relied to storm and capture enemy boats. On board the galleys the legionaries' heavy armour was a dangerous advantage; once they had boarded an enemy ship they were well-protected against the lightly armed Veneti sailors, yet the very weight of the armour was a potential threat as it would drown any unfortunate legionary who fell into the sea. This death was considered much worse than dying in combat, and the fear of falling into the sea was one of the main reasons the legionaries rushed to board an enemy craft with such alacrity. Each soldier was desperate to spend as little time as possible on the unprotected boarding planks or nets. Once on board, the men could form up behind their large shields and advance on the enemy in unison, sweeping the deck clear of any resistance.

Out in the Bay the morning breeze continued to blow. As on every sunny morning, the land had absorbed the heat from the sun's rays more quickly than the sea, causing the customary off-shore flow of air. The Veneti were now sailing with skill and control to meet the approaching galleys. The largest vessel took the lead and initiated the conflict by charging into the Romans and separating a few galleys from the rest of the fleet. This allowed the other boats to move in and fire volleys of arrows at the isolated Romans before withdrawing. The Veneti sailed masterfully, keeping their boats out of range of the grappling irons which they knew the Roman employed. Initially the Veneti's tactic was proving successful, for whilst the armoured legionaries were protected from the falling arrows, the same was not true of the exposed galley slaves. In previous naval engagements the Romans and their opponents had relied on the tactics of ramming or boarding the enemy and so the vulnerability of the galley slaves had never previously been an issue. This weakness was now being adeptly exploited by the Veneti who concentrated their archery on the unprotected slaves with devastating effect. In several galleys this caused panic amongst the slaves, and the captains had to use their legionaries to force the mutinous slaves to continue rowing.

Dimitri's galley was amongst those which had been separated, and the dismayed captain watched in alarm as he lost half of his rowers to one volley of arrows. He ordered the legionaries to protect the slaves as best they could, and then he directed his galley to follow the large Veneti boat which had just swung away from them. With the reduced number of men at the oars, the galley could not move as quickly as normal and their pursuit was slow to gain momentum. Nonetheless they turned in chase and were surprised to see their target slow as it waited for them. The Veneti captain had decided the opportunity to fire a second volley into the sluggish galley was worth the risk of the Roman grappling irons; consequently he was waiting for the Romans to approach. Dimitri directed his helmsman to bring them alongside the Veneti's boat, whilst he moved to the galley's prow. Throughout their approach, the Veneti rained down arrows mercilessly into the galley slaves. The legionaries tried to protect them as much as possible but their *scuta*, the standard issue curved infantry shield. However, the shields were designed to cover one man only and were insufficient to protect the rows of slaves, many more of whom fell victim to the Veneti's arrows. At the prow, Dimitri swung Marcus's device into position and ensnared the enemy's stays. With desperation in his voice, he shouted to the remaining rowers to back-paddle; their very survival depended on this device working. Even with its greatly diminished crew, it only took a few strokes for the galley to pull away and the hook to cut through the stays causing the yard and sail to come crashing down onto the Veneti.

The leather sail and falling yardarm entangled the enemy archers and the vicious arrows ceased immediately. Dimitri was now able to bring his galley back into boarding position alongside the disabled boat without any further arrows being fired at them. As they pulled alongside, the legionaries rushed aboard and captured the boat whilst most of the Veneti were still entangled beneath the fallen sail. With their ears still ringing from the screams of the injured galley slaves, the legionaries showed no quarter to any of the Veneti. The fight was brutal and swift. Once they had secured the vessel, Dimitri and the legionaries returned to their galley. Marcus's device had proved as effective in battle as it had in the trials.

Meanwhile, the other galleys had also taken full advantage of their superior manoeuvrability by rowing up to engage the Veneti whenever a lull in the wind had slowed the latter. In close quarters the Romans were vastly superior, though frequently the heavy price of approaching the Veneti was paid by the unprotected galley slaves. Several of the captains realized that by approaching the Veneti head on, rather than from the side, they were still able to bring down the sail by using Marcus's device to sever the stays. This tactical approach was advantageous as it presented a much reduced target for the Veneti archers. The legionaries could protect the rowers against this narrowed field of fire more effectively by interlocking their shields to form a roof in much the same manner as they did to form the famous *testudo*. Once a boat had been disabled and the threat from the archers temporarily removed, the Romans were able to approach in safety on both of the enemy's bows. Then the legionaries swarmed onto the boats, competing to capture each craft.

The Veneti fleet was homogenous only in basic design, for there were craft of many different sizes with corresponding variations in the number of men and weapons on board each boat. The battle continued throughout the day with the slow but steady capture of the Veneti fleet. One of the Roman galleys took an unexpected prize from a large boat which had put up a particularly fierce resistance; the boat's deck was awash with blood before the legionaries had secured the vessel. The Roman captain had fixed on that boat as his target because it appeared to be moving slower than the rest and lying lower in the water. When the legionaries searched the boat, they discovered the hold was packed with the tribe's treasure. The Veneti knew that none of their strongholds on land could withstand a Roman attack and so they had loaded their treasure hoard into the boats, relying on their vast fleet for protection. This prize was not to prove the only one captured that day; although the Veneti succeeded in scuttling one richly laden vessel taking the treasure and the legionaries on board to a watery grave.

The unexpected prospect of more booty spurred on the legionaries and each galley hurried to engage with the enemy. The battle of attrition continued as the day wore on. Although the Romans were still outnumbered, their superior tactics and mobility gradually continued to wear down the Veneti. The Romans lost a galley when one of the larger Veneti boats used a brief strong wind to charge into the weak bow, snapping the oars and puncturing the hold with its momentum, despite not being equipped with an iron clad beak. The bulk of the Veneti fleet were too small to imitate this practice, but several succeeded in sailing into and destroying the vulnerable oars which projected from the galleys. While this did not disable the Roman galleys, it greatly impaired their mobility. Even after half the oars from the surviving side had been transferred to replace the broken ones, the galley was only able to move sluggishly. A further loss was sustained by the Romans when one of the boats managed to pull away as the legionaries were boarding. The screams of these doomed legionaries were swiftly cut off by the waves as their armour dragged them down; but those brief shouts were indelibly etched on the minds of the other legionaries.

Despite these occasional setbacks, the tide of the battle was flowing irreversibly in favor of the Romans. The galleys continued to work in pairs. They targeted a single boat, and then boarded it from both sides simultaneously. During the morning, Marcus's device was employed several times with great success. As the afternoon wore on and the wind died down, it was no longer necessary to disable the Veneti boats before boarding them. The wind decreased to a mere breeze, and the Veneti lost the advantage of speed as their means of propulsion diminished accordingly. As the rebel chieftains realized that the conditions were becoming increasingly unfavorable for any further engagement, they ordered a withdrawal. They intended to disperse the fleet and hide the boats amongst the islands and coves of the rugged Brittany coastline, relying on the shallow waters to protect them from pursuit by the Roman galleys. The word to disengage was passing through the fleet when the wind abruptly ceased altogether. This total lull was an exceptionally rare occurrence for the normally tempestuous Bay of Biscay. The Veneti fleet was virtually helpless as it sat becalmed, entirely at the mercy of the Roman galleys. Along the shore the Veneti could see the waiting legionaries cutting off any possible escape route by land. Faced with such a hopeless situation, the chieftains made the decision to surrender. They knew Caesar would exact a terrible price for their rebellion, but they hoped that this course of action might at least ensure the survival of the tribe.

High on the headland, Caesar nodded with satisfaction as news of the surrender was brought to him. The group of officers returned to their camp, whilst the legion's blacksmiths commenced the Herculean task of fitting chains to the thousands of prisoners who were being brought off the captured boats. Later that evening Caesar dined in his tent with his staff as they discussed the events of the day and celebrated the victory. From their vantage point the staff had enjoyed an excellent view of the battle, and even the smallest action had been noted by these important men. They now discussed the conduct of each captain and galley, interjecting laudatory and depreciating comments as appropriate. This review of the battle was interrupted by the arrival of an armed guard bringing the Veneti chieftains to submit to Caesar. He ordered the chieftains to be kept under guard within the camp until the fate of the captured Roman envoys was ascertained, warning them that they and the original Veneti hostages would share the fate of the two Roman officers. After dinner a messenger arrived to report the news that the Roman envoys, Quintus Velanius and Titus Silius had both been beheaded at the start of the battle. The news had been delayed as when the battle was nearly over the Veneti had attempted to conceal their treachery by mutilating the corpses almost beyond recognition. Caesar then summoned the chieftains and ordered the Veneti hostages to be beheaded in front of them. Next he ordered the chieftains to be executed in public the following morning as an example to all those who disrespected the sanctity of Roman envoys. Caesar then decreed that all the prisoners were to be sold as slaves. This total dispersion would effectively end the existence of the Veneti tribe. After they had broken their bond once, Caesar had no intention of giving them the opportunity to do so again. Julius Caesar was a man who firmly believed that if a man tricked you once, the shame fell on him but if he tricked you twice the shame fell on you.

The review of the battle was not solely an occasion to meet out punishments. Caesar listened with interest as one of the *praefecti* explained the device which they had used to cut the stays on the Veneti vessels. It was Dimitri's galley which had been the first to use the hook in the battle, and the Greek captain was summoned to provide his personal verdict of the device. After he had heard about the efficacy of this tactic, Caesar asked if the Roman vessels were similarly vulnerable. Once he had been reassured that the presence of rowers ensured the Roman galleys would never be similarly disabled, he inquired about the origin of the device. The *praefecti* recounted their ride along the cliff, and the experiment they had observed in the bay beneath. All acknowledged that the device was Marcus's innovation and they credited him with the full honor for its success. Caesar was impressed with the account and summoned the resourceful ship-builder; he had decided to endow the young Gaul with Roman citizenship in gratitude. When Marcus arrived and heard of Caesar's resolution, he humbly protested that the honor was superfluous as he was already a citizen. The awkward silence was broken by Caesar's hearty laughter as he asked what favor he might confer on Marcus as nobody could be made a citizen twice. The pressure of the moment brought clarity to Marcus's mind and he requested Caesar for a post in the legion's cavalry.

The orders were duly drafted and by the time sun set the following day, Marcus was a centurion of the fifth cohort of the VII Macedonica Legion of the Roman Army, or *quintus hastasus prior* as the Latin title said on his enrolment documents. Marcus received his enrolment[enrollment] pay of 75 *denarii* and swore the oath of allegiance. The enrolment[enrollment] money was intended as travelling money for a recruit to reach his legion, yet as Marcus merely had to cross the town to reach the Legion's camp, he was free to spend the money on a farewell feast. At his right hand sat Dimitri, while the tavern was filled with the carpenters, galley captains and assorted friends whom Marcus had made during his stay at Portus Namnetus. The evening concluded with numerous toasts to Marcus before they all stumbled back to their lodgings. As first rays of the sun light the morning sky, Marcus stood at the place where he had buried his father's ashes and implored Lucius to bless his future with the Legion.

5

ROME AND MASSALIA, 54 BC

IN THE ROMAN capital, the agreements which the Triumvirs had reached in Ravenna and Lucca slowly became evident in the proposals made in the Senate. Caesar's tenure as Governor of both Cisalpine and Transalpine Gaul was extended for an additional five years, despite some opposition. As a Roman Governor, Caesar enjoyed immunity from prosecution for the duration of his term in office. For a governor who had finished his term in office, the danger of prosecution was very real and an extension of his term in office granted Caesar more time to forestall this eventuality. Previously, Cicero had greatly increased his reputation and standing by prosecuting Gaius Verres when the latter completed his term as Governor of Sicily. The law courts of Rome provided an ideal forum in which an aspiring politician could gain public attention, and successful prosecutors were awarded the privileges of the person they prosecuted. In this way Cicero gained precedence in Senate debates as if he was a Praetor even before his eventual election to that magistracy.

Meanwhile the city of Rome was rocked by riots, and the elections for Consuls of 55BC were postponed as a result. The riots had been organised by Clodius, the brother of Appius Claudius, who had been promised the consulship for 54BC in return for his assistance to the Triumvirs. Clodius was the leader of one of the most powerful plebeian gangs which were playing an increasingly significant role in Roman politics. The delayed elections allowed Caesar to fill the city with his supporters, including his veterans who were given special leave to come to Rome for the elections. Pompey and Crassus both stood as Consuls for 55BC and they were duly elected after the opposition had been attacked and intimidated. Cato had been attacked and wounded, and his torch-bearer murdered before the election in an act symptomatic of the parlous state of Roman politics. Since the murder of the Gracchi brothers some 60 years before a dangerous precedent had been set which meant even the elected representatives of the government were not safe from attack.

The power of the Triumvirs and their secret agenda, was soon revealed when a tame tribune proposed a law to give Pompey a five year term as Governor of Spain with a similar five year term as Governor of Syria for Crassus after their year in office. In each case the Governors were to have proconsular powers including the right to levy troops and make war or peace in the territory as they saw fit. As Governors they would also enjoy the same immunity from prosecution which protected Caesar, this opened the possibility for each man to extract vast personal fortunes from the provinces they controlled. Despite some opposition in Rome, the law was passed. The Triumvirs had effectively carved up the Roman world between themselves. The three men now controlled 20 Legions and Rome's most important provinces and were safe from prosecution for a minimum of five years. Despite the fact that Crassus was a sexagenarian when he set out to take up his governorship in Syria, he made unseemly boasts about what he would achieve in the East.

Within Rome it was well known that Crassus intended to use his governorship of Syria as a base from which to pursue his quest for martial glory. Despite his advancing years, Crassus still yearned for military success, and he hoped to achieve this in the East. Crassus desired to emulate Alexander the Great, and he rashly boasted he would conquer the eastern world as far as India. Pompey and Caesar both knew that Crassus intended to invade Parthia, and they supported his plan for their own ends. However, within the Senate there was some opposition to this plan as the Parthians had remained at peace with the Romans and were protected as allies by a valid truce. On behalf of the people, the Tribune Ateius undertook to consult the augurs and sacrifice to the Gods to determine the appropriate course of action. Roman society was deeply superstitious, and the people and politicians regularly consulted the priests before making any important decisions. On this occasion, the chief augur of Rome personally marked out the observation square using the hooked staff which was the symbol of his office. From this square, a state official carried out an observation of the omens to learn what outcome an invasion of Parthia would portend. The augur's role was to interpret and explain the signs but it was a state official who performed the observation, for the results could determine Roman policy.

The augury duly took place and the official observed the ominous sign of a dark hawk flying to the left; this evil omen was compounded when the hawk hovered over a field. It was considered a premonition of treachery to see any bird hover; whilst observing any dark bird on the left side was an ill omen in itself, and a bird of prey was even worse. Ateius next consulted the other seers in the temple where he had sent animals to be sacrificed. The priests reported that one of the three sacrificial cockerels had a diseased liver but the other two were found to be healthy. In these circumstances the overall verdict would normally have been positive. However, an attendant had slipped whilst carrying wine to complete the sacrifice. The spilled wine was found to have splashed the second two cockerels but not the first. Accordingly, it was only the first sacrifice which was to be considered accurate. The dark pool of wine on the altar of the sacred temple also signified that a lot of Roman blood would be shed if the omens were not observed. The message from the Gods was clear; for the good of the Roman people, Ateius must prevent the invasion of Parthia.

The opposition to Crassus and his plans to invade Parthia was led by Ateius, but Crassus was one of the three triumvirs who controlled Rome, and he was supported by the other triumvirs along with his many powerful friends. Consequently, Ateius's attempts to stop Crassus met much resistance. The other tribunes refused to arrest Crassus in order to prevent his departure from Rome. Pompey's intervention and his popularity in the city, were crucial in securing public acceptance of Crassus's departure for the East. In desperation, the frustrated Ateius ran to the city gate as Crassus was leaving. Over a hastily kindled fire in a sacred dish, Ateius publicly cursed Crassus and his expedition. The Tribune called upon strange and horrible deities in these dreadful imprecations, which were observed by Crassus and all the men who were departing from Rome with him. The curses Ateius used were very seldom employed, as the Romans believed they contained so much nefarious power that the person who invokes them is also adversely affected. There were even those who declaimed Ateius for uttering the curses within Rome; they feared the city would suffer ill portents as a result of being the location where such dreadful forces had been summoned. The augury's results and Ateius's curses were the first of a long list of ominous portents and disasters which were to dog Crassus's campaign in the East.

In accordance with the unofficial agreements which the Triumvirs had concluded previously, both Pompey and Caesar were to support Crassus in his invasion of Parthia and Caesar was to release Publius and his crack Gallic cavalry unit to join Crassus's forces. In return, Caesar was to have a free rein to continue his campaign in Gaul, whilst Pompey remained in Rome. Pompey's intervention and popularity were crucial in overcoming the opposition to Crassus's departure from Rome. From Gaul Caesar duly sent out orders for Publius to depart with his unit of Gallic cavalry to join his father in the East. The cavalry were to sail from Gaul to Egypt where they would proceed to meet Crassus and his main force. Publius was commanding the cavalry of the Seventh Legion at the time, and these were the troops he took to join his father. The men were largely Romanised Gauls, and they had been moulded into a fearsome fighting unit.

After Crassus had succeeded in leaving Rome with his forces, he set sail from Brindisium to cross the Adriatic. He ordered the army to set sail immediately despite the rough seas, and several ships were lost in the crossing. Meanwhile, the Gallic cavalry were to take ship from Massalia, where vessels were waiting to take them and their mounts to Alexandria. Marcus was a centurion in this cavalry contingent and by now he had served with the Legion for the best part of a year. After defeating the Veneti tribe in Brittany, the Seventh Legion had continued the campaign south along the Atlantic coast. They conquered the entire Aquitaine region and further enlarged the province of Transalpine Gaul. The indomitable Legions only stopped when they reached the Pyrenees, the *Pax Romana* now stretched across Gaul as far as the Danube, and Caesar was Governor of all the newly conquered territories. The cavalry of the Seventh Legion were in peak condition, experienced and toughened from the campaign without being fatigued or weakened from spending too long in hostile territory. Crassus was aware that his army in the East lacked experienced cavalry and he relied on this contingent to make good this deficiency. Mounted scouts and skirmishers could be easily employed from amongst the Syrian natives, but Crassus also required experienced cavalry on which he could rely for shock charges and mounted combat.

The Roman army contained a number of different types of cavalry to fulfil the varied functions for which mounted troops were used. Horsemen in heavy armour were employed as shock troops for charges; lighter cavalry were used to chase routed infantry as they fled; other horsemen carried messages and acted as scouts. Horses were also used by a type of mounted infantry who dismounted for combat, combining the speed and mobility of cavalry with the Roman preference for fighting on foot. Barbarian tribes such as the Gauls rode with a simple rope rein and a blanket as a saddle, disdaining even a fixed saddle as effeminate. The Romans used more advanced saddles with raised posts in each corner giving a greater degree of stability. In the absence of stirrups, the Roman cavalrymen were trained to vault into the saddle in full armour, for they could not rely on finding convenient mounting blocks on a battlefield. This impressive method of mounting was possible as the animals used were much smaller than modern horses, and would be termed ponies by later standards. Roman cavalry were equipped with javelins and a long slashing sword instead of the short stabbing weapon used by the infantry. The cavalrymen were protected with a helmet, body armour and a shield, whilst their mounts were not protected. The armour was largely made of bronze or toughened hide, though some iron was used. The Gallic cavalry which were going to join Crassus were heavily armoured by contemporary Roman standards, and the Roman cavalry was the best in Europe.

The Army's rigorous training ensured that even with the full weight of their armour, a Legionary's manoeuvrability was not reduced. The cavalrymen could dismount to fight on foot and then remount even in the midst of a pitched battle. This level of mobility was achieved by the Legionaries training with heavier practice weapons and equipment, so that when they came to use the real weapons they found them light in comparison. These drills continued throughout a Legionary's service, consequently the men were always in fighting condition whether they were on campaign or not. After receiving his appointment as a centurion from Caesar, Marcus had successfully completed his training with the Seventh Legion in Gaul. He had proved himself proficient with the sword and javelin; however, it was his skill at archery and horse-riding which had excited the greatest admiration and respect of the other men. Marcus was already an accomplished archer and could regularly bring down a bird on the wing. In their free time, Marcus and the other centurions often went hunting. When their location permitted, the men took their light birding bows to the marshes and wetlands in search of the delicious plump waterfowl

Through serving and fighting with the Legion, Marcus had developed his previous skills and adapted them to combat. From his commanders, he learnt the importance of military tactics and discipline within the ranks. The senior officers were happy to explain the strengths and weaknesses of the different formations used by the Roman Army to the bright and attentive centurion. Marcus retained all this new knowledge and eagerly sought additional information about military manoeuvres, from anyone who could help him. From the Legion's armourers and blacksmiths, Marcus learnt about the assorted weapons in the Roman arsenal. The Legion's mobile armoury including some of the heavier siege weapons, and these piqued his engineering interest. In addition, the Legion's arrow-smith showed him the various types of arrow head and impressed upon Marcus the importance of selecting the appropriate one. Different tips were used for hunting or fighting, and there were special designs to pierce armour or to bring down horses. As Marcus acquired this theoretical information, he also saw the practical results in the Legion's frequent clashes with the barbarian tribes. The promising young shipwright and engineer evolved into an excellent soldier, and his foresight and popularity made him a natural leader and popular centurion. Marcus developed into a model Legionary as he united courage with craft, and craft with courage. His craft was made bolder by the vehemence of his courage, and his courage more circumspect by the awareness of craft. As the unit travelled to Massalia, Marcus looked forward to a new campaign and the variety of challenges it would offer. The whole force was blissfully unaware of the political machinations in Rome and the foreboding omens and terrible curses invoked by the Tribune Ateius.

When the cavalry heard they were to depart for the East there was a buzz of excitement and anticipation around the camp. Marcus was particularly enthusiastic about the prospect of seeing the fabled Orient, which had long appealed to his imagination. He recalled his mother's tiger brooch and wondered if he would have the opportunity to see one of the fabled animals. The combined knowledge of the officers and troops about their destination was so confused and fantastical it only served to further fuel their imaginations. Truth and rumor intermingled, and stories promptly circulated about the fabulous wealth which was there for the taking, with stories of gold and precious stones littering the desert sands. Others spoke of the dangerous beasts and bizarre animals they would encounter. It was soon asserted as fact that man-eating lions, tigers, crocodiles, phoenixes and elephants all co-habited in the East. The camp reverberated with interest and excitement as several men revealed themselves as impromptu authorities on Oriental matters and willingly shared their knowledge with their comrades. Soon, lewd and lascivious tales were circulating about the beautiful women and concubines whom the Eastern potentates enjoyed. This caused further excitement amongst the men and murmurs of indignation and disdain amongst their local girlfriends.

A number of the troops were disheartened at the prospect of leaving their partners in Gaul, although one or two were relieved that duty dragged them away! Roman soldiers were not permitted to marry, though many had local girlfriends and families who moved with the Legion. This prohibition was designed to ensure the Roman forces remained mobile and could be sent to different regions whenever necessary without the additional encumbrance of families. However, if strictly adhered to, this practice would have robbed the Army of a future generation of Romanised recruits. The children of the Legionaries would grow up in a martial atmosphere and were all *de facto* Roman citizens eligible to join the Legion, furthermore they made excellent recruits. This situation resulted in the tacit compliance of the generals, who permitted the partners and families of the Legionaries to travel with the Legion and settle outside the forts. The Army acquiesced with this unofficial state of affairs, and there were even official regulations about where the camp-followers were allowed to set up camp. From a strategic point of view, it was necessary to keep the surroundings of any fort or camp free from buildings which could offer cover to an attacking force. To this same end the Legionaries regularly felled the trees along the principal roads. However, the Army's tolerance did not stretch to transporting the unofficial families of the Legionaries across the Mediterranean. So the cavalrymen were obliged to leave their partners and children in Gaul when they departed for Alexandria.

Marcus was pleased to learn the cavalry would be sailing from Massalia. It was over a year since he had seen his home town and he was pleased to have the opportunity to bid farewell to his friends and family there. The two brothers had exchanged letters, but as each pursued their own career they found they had less and less in common. Marcus retained an affectionate interest in the shipyard and the men who worked there. However, Flavius now left the entire supervision to an overseer and consequently he had minimal news from the shipyard to tell Marcus. Their mother continued in her self-imposed seclusion, though unexpectedly she had now taken the stance of a bereaved widow. Flavius reported that she issued forth from her quarters to voice sporadic panegyrics about her departed husband. Indeed, it appeared she now resented his death more than she had resented his plebeian origins when he was alive.

By the time the cavalry unit arrived in Massalia, the port was a noisy bustle of preparations; the fleet of transport galleys which would take them to Alexandria lay at anchor in the harbor. The logistics of accommodating, feeding and transporting 1,000 men and their mounts were considerable, yet the experienced port authorities rose to the task admirably. Using the port's small launches and one quay, it would take several days to board the whole contingent and their mounts as well as load the necessary supplies for the voyage. They began the process by boarding all the supplies and equipment, this allowed them to minimise the amount of time the mounts spent at sea. Meanwhile, Marcus took the first available opportunity to visit his mother and brother in the family villa. The two brothers greeted each other cordially. Flavius was enjoying the significantly increased income which the inheritance had provided him, and he now lived in even greater opulence and idleness. He expressed sympathy for Marcus and the hardships of military life, although this sympathy was tinged with incomprehension as to why Marcus had chosen such a career. Conversely, the rigours of army life had toughened Marcus and his tastes had adapted to the Spartan routine. As a result of this he found Flavius's luxurious lifestyle overindulgent. Rather than revel in the excesses which Flavius enjoyed, Marcus found the sight of such surfeit sickened him and he preferred the simplicity of Legionary life. Whereas Marcus would stop eating when he his hunger was satiated, his brother preferred to induce vomiting in order that he might continue to feast. At the table, Flavius now kept a number of long feathers, or 'throat-ticklers', expressly for this purpose. Despite this unpleasant practice Flavius had put on a lot of weight in the relatively short time since they had last seen each other. When Marcus left, the two parted on cordial terms, although they both recognized they now had nothing in common.

When Marcus went to see his mother he found her crying in her room, he knelt beside her and held her trembling hands. Whereas Flavius's body was softened by the additional layers of fat, his face had not changed greatly. In contrast, Eugenia's whole countenance had changed, although her body had not altered. She still drank heavily and the make-up she applied could not conceal the prominent red capillaries in her nose and cheeks or the shaking of her hands. Nonetheless there was an unmistakable softness about her face; very different from her visage which had previously been remarkable for its acerbic expression. The simmering resentment which had characterised the unhappy matron had now died down to quiet despondency and regret. Through her tears she told Marcus of her remorse at how she had treated her husband during their married life. Posthumously, she recognized Lucius as the kind, courteous husband he had been. Eugenia then took her youngest son's face in her hands and with drunken sincerity she implored him to never let conceit or pride ruin his life in a similar fashion. It was only after solemnly swearing an oath to this effect, that Marcus succeeded in putting her to bed where he left her to rest. He was troubled to see his mother in this condition, for whilst her face no longer showed the lines of resentment and ire, she was visibly weaker and her hands shook uncontrollably. As Marcus walked back across town in a reverie, he marveled at just how much could change in such a short time.

On the way across town Marcus was hailed by Gaius, a fellow cavalry officer who was also returning to the officers' quarters. The centurion immediately realized that Marcus was troubled; as the two walked back together he stopped Marcus at a small roadside shrine and made an offering on his behalf. Marcus showed some surprise at this for the other officers knew he did not share their superstitions and beliefs.

'We have enough enemies to fight already, so I always think it's wise not to offend the Gods,' explained Gaius, who made offerings to all the deities he encountered as a form of insurance.

'But you know I don't believe in any of that,' protested Marcus. 'And you can see the Gods have done me no harm.'

'Maybe that's because other people appease them on your behalf,' suggested Gaius elusively.

His curiosity was now piqued and Marcus did not let up questioning his companion until Gaius reluctantly revealed that the other centurions regularly made offerings on behalf of Marcus. The interrogation had continued throughout their walk back and Gaius was pleased to observe that Marcus's surprise and interest had awoken him from his initial gloomy reverie. Before he turned in for the night, Marcus questioned several of the other officers about the veracity of this information. After he established that it was true, he went to bed with a mixture of gratitude and amusement lightening his thoughts. Whilst in public Marcus continued to profess his disbelief in the superstitions and charms of the other soldiers, he was touched by the concern for his welfare which his companions showed.

When Marcus awoke early the next morning, he recognized the tell-tale cuttlefish-shaped clouds in the sky to the north west of Massalia. He rushed to tell the other centurions to prepare the cavalry for the arrival of the Mistral. This was a strong seasonal wind, with which the inhabitants of Massalia were very familiar. The movements of the air currents inland were blocked by the Alps, and subsequently the dry, cold air was funnelled south along the Rhone valley until it reached the ocean around Massalia. The pressure changes which accompanied the wind caused animals to become agitated and many of the local residents suffered headaches when the Mistral blew. The headaches and shortened tempers were worsened by a lack of sleep, for the Mistral created a lot of noise as it whistled through the tiled roofs of the Mediterranean houses and kept everyone awake. Headaches were just one of the many things which were blamed on the Mistral; the wind was also held responsible for the flighty temperament and irascibility which were considered typical traits of the inhabitants of the region. The wind's name was derived from the word for 'master', a reflection of the power which many believed the wind exercised over the people in its path. The Mistral could blow for up to a week and occurred most frequently during the winter months. Its arrival was always heralded by the indicative warning clouds in the north west. The locals knew well how to prepare for the wind before it arrived, and consequently it did little serious damage other than fray tempers.

The following two days were very busy, and Marcus was unable to visit his family again. The horses were becoming restless and agitated even before the wind had started and they had to be checked frequently. Marcus used his initiative and local knowledge to direct the laden ships into the most sheltered part of the harbor, whilst he ordered the boarding to be postponed until the Mistral had blown over. The restless horses and whistling of the Mistral were causing alarm and unease amongst all of the cavalry. Marcus did his best to reassure them that it was an entirely normal meteorological event and not the work of aggrieved gods, but only when the local inn-keepers and dock hands confirmed this explanation did the cavalrymen relax and continue the task of securing their mounts and equipment.

Whilst the Mistral blew, Marcus was constantly employed checking on the men and their mounts, and organising additional provisions. Fortunately the wind did not blow for long and they were able to recommence boarding two days later. The ships were to make their first stop at Ostia, where fresh provisions could be obtained and the mounts could be taken on to the land. The journey to Egypt had to be broken into sections so the horses could be properly fed and exercised. This was essential to allow them to acclimatise and maintain their condition throughout the long voyage. It was pointless to transport a crack cavalry unit across the Mediterranean if they arrived so sick and unfit they would be useless for months. As he supervised the boarding, Marcus reflected with nostalgia on his first trip to Ostia with his father and brother aboard the Albatross. He had enquired about Petrus when he arrived in Massalia and had been saddened to learn the scarred old captain had died. Marcus had sent his condolences to the long-suffering widow.

After the initiative and experience Marcus had shown in coping with the Mistral, Publius placed him in charge of supervising the boarding. Consequently, Marcus was permanently occupied at the port; his labors were only interrupted by the regular trickle of visitors who came to seek him. Once word spread that Marcus was back in Massalia, the shipwrights and carpenters from the family shipyard came to pay their respects and offer their condolences for Lucius's death. All concurred that the lad had grown into a fine young man. One carpenter was even bemused to find that on the days when he went to visit Marcus, both his elder daughters were unusually eager to accompany their father and partake of his company. Their sudden burst of filial piety even extended to dressing in their best tunics, and they were additionally attentive to their hair and appearance on these occasions. Many of the shipwrights now worked elsewhere, and those that remained in the family shipyard did not speak favorably of Flavius's overseer who was only concerned with maximising profits. Marcus was delighted to see the workmen and his liberal nature extended to buying them drinks and sending gifts to their children. Marcus had accumulated his pay over the previous year and with minimal living costs he was pleased to find a worthy outlet for his wages and the large payment he had received for the construction of the galleys in Portus Namnetus.

Publius Crassus was impressed by the efficiency with which Marcus supervised the boarding process and he made a mental note to inquire about the young man. However, at present his thoughts were more occupied with a letter he had just received from his father. In the letter Marcus Crassus instructed his son to collect a number of personal items from Rome, whilst the ships were in Ostia. The chief item was a book which had been left to Crassus in a will, and the triumvir was impatient to read the work in question. The bequest was from the author, a respected philosopher and teacher by the name of Titus Lucretius Carus who had recently taken his own life. The book in question was his magnum opus entitled *De Rerum Natura*, an epic investigation of Epicurean philosophy written in verse. The work had been seen by very few, because although it already filled six books, it was unfinished and there were no other copies in existence. The extant text still represented a comprehensive analysis of Epicurean philosophy masterfully conveyed using poetry. Publius was surprised at the bequest, for his father and Lucretius had been acquaintances rather than intimate friends, and the two men certainly had different values. Publius suspected the pacifist and idealistic author would not be pleased if he knew his book was being taken on a military campaign.

As Publius read the remainder of the letter, he found an explanation for the unexpected bequest. Some years previously, Crassus had sent his private fire brigade to extinguish a blaze in Lucretius's villa, without obliging the owner to sell him the property. This instance of goodwill had not prevented Crassus from employing his standard practice to purchase the neighbouring villas, so he had still made a large profit from that particular fire. This action was so contrary to Crassus's avaricious nature that Lucretius felt greatly indebted to him. Now, Lucretius had manifested his gratitude and discharged the debt in his will. In Roman society, it was an accepted and common practice for wills to be used in the discharge of any debts or repayment of favors, which an individual had incurred during their lifetime. Publius was well aware that his father would have preferred Lucretius to have left him his villa instead of his writings, and he smiled as the irony of the situation became apparent. The deceased had viewed his home as merely a location in which he could study, teach and write his epic; as such it was valuable to him only as a shelter for learning. Lucretius considered this book to be his most valuable possession and as such he had bequeathed it to Crassus to clear his debt of gratitude. Conversely, Crassus had fully expected the philosopher to leave him the villa which his men had saved, and he was now nonplussed as to what the legacy signified. Lucretius had not included any valuables or other goods with the bequest, and Crassus was now deeply curious to see the book in question. He was intrigued as to what book somebody could value more than a villa in Rome.

In Massalia, Marcus was busy supervising the final stages of loading the men and equipment. On board the ships, the captains were anxious to depart and make full use of the favorable off-shore breeze which was blowing. The cohorts who had already boarded were waiting impatiently. The previous evening, Marcus had made a final visit to say goodbye to his brother and mother. He had left the family villa feeling even more disappointed and disillusioned with his elder brother. The sound of Flavius retching in order to continue his gluttonous gourmandising had re-enforced to Marcus just how alien this environment was to him and how different the two brothers were. Eugenia had been comatose in her quarters and her personal attendant had been unable to revive her, so Marcus had been obliged to depart without her blessing. A slave brought Marcus's personal baggage along the quay to the launch. Marcus hesitated to get into the launch and depart for an unknown length of time, from his family, native city and homeland. He scanned the jostling quayside a final time, and after a moment's hesitation he climbed into the launch which would convey him to his transport ship. A smile crossed his lips, as he realized it was one of the original launches his father had built all those years ago. Traces of the fine workmanship could still be seen on the boat, even though the years of tough service had removed much of the ornate workmanship.

Before the launch cast off, Marcus heard a shrill cry which rang out above the background noise, and he looked up to see his mother running along the quay. He climbed back up the ladder and reached her in a few bounds. Marcus encompassed her frail form in his large arms and supported her as she panted for breath. The captains were signalling that they must depart with the favorable wind. Marcus was oblivious to them; with tender consideration Marcus knelt and took leave of his mother. Tears welled in her eyes as Eugenia placed her quivering hand on his head and blessed her son. Then she pressed a small leather pouch into the palm of his hand. He thanked his mother and his throat tightened with a confusing mix of emotions; he was glad she had come and he was relieved to have her blessing on this trip, yet he was simultaneously forced to see how frail Eugenia was, and this worried him. The bright sunlight showed how pallid and weak Eugenia had become, something which was less evident by the subdued light of the lamps and candles in her quarters. The exertion of her frantic rush to the dockside caused her to wheeze and pant as she blessed her younger son. Eugenia clasped her hands together in an effort to restrain herself and conceal her tremors. Marcus returned to the launch with the parcel in his hand, and his brows wrinkled in a concerned frown.

As the launch pulled away from the quay, Marcus looked back. His blond hair, sun-bleached whiter from the recent days on the dockside, could not lighten the darkness which crossed his face as he realized that his mother's health would not last much longer. Once on board the ship, Marcus was caught up in the final preparations for departure. As a result it was several hours before he was able to withdraw to his cabin and inspect the parcel his mother had given him. Inside the dark leather pouch he found his mother's blue brooch. The brooch showed a leaping tiger and Marcus felt the familiar thrill as he held the lapis lazuli and admired the variety of blue hues which were created as the sunlight reflected on its polished surface. The color always reminded Marcus of his father's eyes and an observer would have noted how closely the blue matched Marcus's own eyes.

His mother had evidently remembered his childhood fascination with this brooch, and he was touched that she had presented him with such an appropriate talisman. The brooch combined the magic and mystery of the Orient, with a memento of his native country. The blue tiger on the brooch was both enticingly exotic and inherently familiar. With this fascinating and beloved object tightly fastened inside his tunic, Marcus returned to the deck and went to join the captain of the ship.

Publius had been greatly impressed with Marcus's efficiency and resourcefulness when he had supervised the boarding. Consequently, he had invited the centurion to join him and the other senior officers on board the lead ship. Marcus had first seen to the ship on which his own century and their mounts were to make the voyage, then he had left them in the able care of his deputy Titus, whilst he went to join Publius on the lead vessel. Titus was the *signifier* or 'standard bearer' for that century and the wolf-skin headdress which he wore complemented his fierce battle-scarred face. He was a veteran Legionary, who had acquired a wealth of experience during his time with the Legions, and Marcus knew he could trust the old man to run a tight ship in his absence. Titus had watched over Marcus since the fresh-faced new recruit had bested him at sword drill. Marcus remained the only man in the century to have achieved this feat, and Titus had been even more impressed by the dignified manner in which Marcus had handled his victory than by his fancy sword-work. Marcus had never boasted of his triumph, and his calm modesty had won him the respect of his second-in-command.

Marcus was flattered by the Publius's invitation, and the prestige it implied, however he was even more pleased to have the company of experienced officers from whom he could learn much during the long trip. Whilst he was content with the company of the Legionaries, Marcus knew he would soon tire of playing dice and gambling with his men during the voyage. The invitation to join Publius aboard the flagship was welcome news to Marcus, for the company of the officers would make the voyage much more interesting. There was a secondary advantage to this invitation which Marcus was only to appreciate later. The flagship was the only vessel which did not carry any horses and consequently it was not dogged by the odor of stale horse sweat and dung which hung around the other boats no matter how strong the wind blew, or how hard the men scrubbed the decks. Publius had given the order to set sail as soon as Marcus was on board, and now the convoy of vessels stretched out in a long line behind the flagship. As the sun descended behind the last vessel, the other officers were preparing to dine, whilst Marcus was making a final tour of the ship. Before going to join the others for dinner, Marcus went forward to speak to the captain. The two men stood on the prow with the salt air blowing in their face and the sun setting behind them. This time Marcus's was the larger of the two shadows which stretched out in front of the galley as the two men stared into the horizon and their destination in the exotic East.

6

ALEXANDRIA, 54 BC

THE NUMEROUS DIFFICULTIES of transporting a cavalry contingent across the Mediterranean disappeared from Marcus's mind when he discerned the faint glimmer of Alexandria's famed lighthouse. He had got up early in the pre-dawn, to complete his daily exercises on the deck, and to enjoy a brief moment of solitude whilst the rest of the men slept below. After finishing his exercises, Marcus stood on the stern and washed himself in a bucket of fresh seawater. As he poured the last of the cold salty water over his lean torso, he discerned the distant glimmer for which they had all been waiting eagerly. The light came from the Pharos, the wondrous lighthouse of Alexandria. In the early pre-dawn light, the outline of the famous monument was soon identifiable. The Pharos was visible long before the city could be seen, as the magnificent lighthouse dwarfed the city around its base. At night the light of the Pharos against the pitch black Egyptian night was often mistaken for a star by approaching ships. Rising over 400 feet into the sky the Pharos was one of the Seven Wonders of the Ancient World.

This welcome sight signified the end of their sea journey for the Roman cavalry and the men rejoiced to hear the good news. On board the lead ship, the lookout in the rigging had fallen asleep, and the crew of the morning watch were crouched around the forward lantern playing dice. Thus Marcus was the first person to spy the flickering light which shone from the flames at the top of the tower. The light was just discernible against the morning clouds and Marcus had savoured the sight in solitude for a moment, before he went to wake the captain and inform the men. The fact that it was their centurion who had made the auspicious sighting instead of the lookout, served to further establish Marcus's reputation amongst the cavalrymen as a man favored by the Gods.

As the sun climbed above the horizon, the fleet of ships approached the great city of Alexandria. This Alexandria was just one of the sixteen eponymous cities, which had been founded by Alexander the Great in his awesome campaign of conquest across the East. However, none of the other Alexandrias had prospered as well as this one. The great general had arrived almost three centuries earlier, and although he had not stayed to see it built, the city was now home to the earthly remains of its founder and tutelary God. Following Alexander's death, his short-lived Empire had fallen apart with his generals seizing portions of it and setting themselves up as rulers. Egypt, Cyprus, Palestine and parts of Asia Minor fell into the hands of an able Macedonian General named Ptolemy. Ptolemy founded a dynasty which adopted the title of Pharaoh and was to rule Egypt for over three centuries. As a Mediterranean port, the Egyptian Alexandria formed a natural center for the new ruler with his Hellenic roots and euro-centric views. It has long been remarked that Alexandria is a city which faces the Mediterranean and turns its back on Egypt and the African interior. The emerging city became the capital of the dynasty which Ptolemy founded. The city possessed two excellent natural harbors and it was into the Western Harbor that the fleet now sailed. Homer had named this harbor *Eunostos* or 'Port of Safe Return', and the cavalry were certainly relieved to reach their destination. The fleet had stopped at Crete to take on fresh water and provisions but that was over a week ago and the men rejoiced to reach Alexandria and dry land after the slow sea voyage.

Large parts of the Egyptian coastline were alluvial, especially near the mouth of the Nile, and thus it had proved necessary to have some form of beacon to mark the harbor around which the city of Alexandria grew up. The lighthouse served this purpose in addition to providing a useful point of reference to guide incoming ships through the limestone reefs which lined the shore. Work had commenced on the Pharos under the rule of Ptolemy I (323-285 BC), although it was not completed until 283 BC, in the reign of his son Ptolemy II (285-246 BC). The finished lighthouse towered over 400 feet above the port, and the light from the beacon was visible up to 25 miles away. Pharos Island was now a misnomer as a causeway had been built linking it to the mainland; over the years this causeway had silted up and became a narrow strip of firm land. Despite this, the Alexandrians continued to refer to the isthmus as 'the Island', to the confusion of many new arrivals. The lighthouse was an architectural development of enormous significance. Centuries later the Arab invaders called it 'El Manarah', and it became the basis both architecturally and etymologically for the Islamic minaret. Subsequently all the European Romantic languages derived the word for 'lighthouse' from the name for this great monument. Whilst to contemporaries the Pharos became a secular symbol for the great city and the two ports which it watched over.

Alexandria was a truly cosmopolitan and polyglot city; the mix of its inhabitants along with the vast volume of trade which passed through its ports all combined to spread its reputation as a royal city and *anus mundi (spirit of the world)*. The Pharos was an outward expression of the great advances in science, engineering and architecture which took place in Alexandria under the patronage of the Ptolemaic dynasty. The center for all intellectual activity within Alexandria was the complex of The Mouseion, a vast collection of lecture halls, laboratories, observatories, libraries and forums which grew up beside the Royal Palace and is the origin of the English word "Museum". Since its foundation by Ptolemy I, The Mouseion had received generous funding from the Ptolemies, in return for which the resident scientists, scholars and literary men were expected to turn their full intellectual might to any tasks set by the Palace. The design and construction of The Pharos had involved many of the academics from The Mouseion, and they were justifiably proud of this achievement, which watched over the entire city.

The official in charge of The Mouseion was the librarian, who controlled the great Mother Library which constituted the most famous part of the intellectual center. The Library contained an enormous collection of over 500,000 scrolls and manuscripts. This immense collection was unsurpassed in the world; it had been greatly enriched following an unusual and particularly astute decree from Ptolemy I Soter. The decree empowered customs officials to impound any books the Librarian or his assistants desired from any ship or caravan arriving in Alexandria. A team of scribes then worked day and night in the Library to reproduce these confiscated texts, and the owners of the original book were then provided with these copies as replacements, whilst the Library kept the originals. Alexandria was a thriving trade center and the volume of shipping which passed through its ports was considerable. At that time, the city was close to the Canopic branch of the Nile which remained navigable for many centuries before it silted up and forced trading vessels to use the Eastern branches of the Nile. Further upstream a system of canals built by the Pharaohs connected the Nile with the Red Sea via a number of salt lakes. Thus Alexandria sat on the key maritime trade route between East and West as it connected the Mediterranean and Indian oceans. This soon enabled the Library to acquire an unrivalled collection of writings combining the knowledge of the Orient and the Occident. However, this vast collection did not include a copy of Lucretius's *De Rerum Natura*.. Consequently, the six volumes of the poem were duly confiscated from the arriving Romans, despite the blustering protests and threats of Publius. The Librarian's assistant ignored the Roman officers and departed after issuing an official receipt for the books he had confiscated.

This dilemma of the confiscated books weighed on Publius Crassus's mind as the cavalry disembarked; his father would be furious at the delay in receiving the bequest. After the trouble which Crassus had taken to instruct his son to collect the books from Rome, Publius knew he would be vexed at any further delay. Publius also suspected his father would be particularly aggravated to learn that the book in the author's own hand he had inherited would now be in the Library and would not be returned. As Publius was occupied in mulling over how best to deal with the situation, Marcus was busy assisting with the mooring and disembarking of the ships. The Ptolemaic dynasty was of Macedonian origin and there was a considerable Greek community in the city. With his fluent Greek, Marcus had been of great use in completing the formal registration and disembarkation, and the senior officers had frequently summoned the aid of the bi-lingual centurion. The Roman convoy had become strung out during the voyage, and the remaining vessels could still be seen along the horizon making their way towards the port. As the ships arrived, they all anchored in the Western Harbor; the Great Harbor to the East was reserved for the Egyptian Royal Fleet.

Marcus took an immediate liking to the polyglot city and he was pleasantly surprised how many people spoke Greek. He had no problem in getting directions to the area where the cavalry where to be quartered. Some of the horses were a little skittish from the barrage of new and unfamiliar odors which the city contained, but the cavalrymen soon calmed them. As the men led their mounts through the streets, they were amazed at the size and opulence of the city. Alexandria far surpassed Rome in wealth and the city was correspondingly more ornate and elaborate. Unlike the Romans, the Alexandrians saw no virtue in austerity, and consequently they built in more elaborate and ornate styles. Much of the city was built from marble and the bright Mediterranean sun reflected off the white stone, making the city radiant with light.

Like all new arrivals, the Romans turned constantly to marvel at the Pharos as it towered over them. The men felt the need to check on the lighthouse every few minutes, as if it might disappear or collapse. As they passed along a street each cavalryman would turn his head to peer up every few hundred yards, half expecting a new perspective to reveal the Pharos as an elaborate façade or hoax, for they had never seen anything that tall.

'The top must burn in the sun,' volunteered one legionary named Flavius.

'I doubt that, but you could probably see off the edge off the world from there,' replied another.

'Or into some lovely lady's dressing room,' joked Titus, eliciting a chuckle from his companions. Titus was the most experienced legionary in Marcus's century, and his dry humour was appreciated by all the men.

The walk through the town had been accompanied by the tantalising aromas of spicy food cooking at street stalls, and so it was with rumbling bellies and necks stiff from craning to look at the Pharos, that the cavalry moved into their new quarters. As the

Gallic cavalry rode through the city, the sight of so many blond and red-haired men attracted the attention of the Alexandrians. However, the city received a constant flow of exotic arrivals and the Romans did not remain the center of attention for long. The new arrivals were billeted with the two Roman legions that were stationed already in Alexandria.

Shortly after they had arrived in their quarters, a messenger arrived to deliver several important letters and documents to Publius. Amongst them there was a letter from Crassus, he was still in Syria and he instructed his son to bring the Gallic cavalry and join forces with him there. The letters also contained an elaborate account of the battles and triumphs which Crassus had won so far. Caesar had personally written a masterful account of his Gallic campaigns, which had generated considerable prestige and publicity for him back in Rome. Crassus was determined to ensure the Romans heard about his victories and to this end he had taken two scribes with him. These slaves had the unenviable task of maintaining a laudatory record of the campaign for the benefit of the people in Rome and for posterity. Crassus was so determined to enter the history books for his military prowess that he attentively supervised the writing of these accounts.

At the start of the campaign, the scribes had a particularly difficult time as the Romans had encountered no opposition. Publius read with interest how his father had crossed the Euphrates with his infantry forces and auxiliary cavalry; they had then marched south and east into Mesopotamia. The Euphrates River technically marked the boundary of the Parthian empire, and the scribes made much of the ease with which Crassus had 'invaded'. Although the area was technically Parthian territory, it was far from their center of power and the Parthian Army. When Crassus arrived at the head of a large army, the inhabitants of the cities had prudently welcomed him and swore allegiance to him as their new master. These regions bordered existing Roman provinces and vassal kingdoms, so they knew the advantages of accepting Roman rule rather than resisting the indomitable legions. The sole city to offer any resistance was Zenodatia, and the legionaries had stormed it with relative ease. The triumphant Romans had then looted the city and sold the inhabitants into slavery. Upon entering the city, Crassus had been hailed with the lofty title of Imperator despite the insignificance of the city and the battle. The scribes had dutifully described how the men had foisted the honor upon their unwilling and modest commander, though this was far from the truth. Subsequently, many of the legionaries had viewed the action as inauspicious and unwise. In assuming such a magnificent title after a minor victory it appeared that Crassus despaired of achieving any greater successes.

The early engagements had provided the unfortunate scribes with minimal material for the heroic panegyrics which they were required to produce. Publius was now reading the result of their combined efforts, and whilst he knew the style of writing was not his father's, he was neither aware of its true provenance, nor how exaggerated the accounts were. Publius was delighted to read how easily and successfully his father's campaign was going, the news allayed his worries. Publius knew of the Parthians' reputation as fine soldiers, especially on horseback, yet it appeared that in the face of Roman legions they had not even put up a fight. Publius silently hoped that the campaign would not be finished and won, before he arrived with his Gallic cavalry. In Gaul, Publius had been awarded several decorations for his bravery in the field, and he was keen to increase his collection. Publius had learnt from his father's incessant complaints, that an illustrious military career, however brief, was an essential pre-requisite to become a successful politician in Rome. Both father and son hoped that the Parthian campaign would provide them with the necessary victories to establish the military reputation of the Crassus family.

Publius continued reading the accounts of the campaign so far. They detailed how Crassus had left garrisons of 7,000 foot soldiers and 1,000 auxiliary cavalry in the Mesopotamian cities he had 'conquered', before he returned to his winter quarters in Syria. Auxiliary cavalry were locally recruited and were far less reliable than the Gallic cavalry, which Publius was bringing. They fought using the traditional weapons and techniques of their tribes. The auxiliary forces did not receive the vigorous training of the legionaries, and were consequently, much less dependable. Thus Crassus had elected to winter in Syria and wait for Publius to join him there with the Gallic cavalry before invading Parthia fully. Crassus used his powers as Governor of Syria to summon soldiers from the cities and regions under his control. He then rescinded these orders upon the receipt of large bribes from each of the cities or regions. In this method Crassus was able to extort a large amount of money from the region he governed, although his army was in no way improved. During the winter, Crassus also neglected the opportunity to improve his forces by training and exercising the legionaries. Instead, he spent his time calculating the value of the various regions he now controlled, and weighing the treasures he had acquired. However, the accounts Publius was now reading did not refer to these matters, and Publius was only to learn the truth when he joined his father in Syria.

In Alexandria, the problem of the confiscated book remained unresolved when Publius went to meet Ptolemy XII (117-51 BC), in the Palace. Publius had sent an impertinent letter to the Mouseion, forbidding any copies to be made and demanding the original book be restored to him immediately. He had also demanded an immediate audience with the Pharaoh. The Palace officials responded with a lavish gift and an elaborate excuse and fixed an appointment for two days time. The Librarian had stalled for time whilst he waited for the Palace officials to pronounce judgement on the matter. Although the Pharaoh ruled Egypt in theory, his position was effectively that of a vassal or client kingdom. The current Pharaoh was Ptolemy XII, who had only been restored to his throne a few years previously by the might of Roman arms, and he was still paying the price both figuratively and literally. Rome purchased the entire surplus of Egyptian wheat each year, and the recent past had shown the legions were willing and able to interfere in Egyptian politics. The Roman legions garrisoned in Alexandria were stationed there to protect the Pharaoh from any internal threats whilst simultaneously ensuring the payment of the vast debt Ptolemy XII had accrued in financing his restoration to the throne. The Egyptians knew that the new taxes being levied were going to pay off the Romans, and the legionaries were tolerated with ill grace by the Alexandrians. Tensions ran high in the heaving city and the fresh sea air could not alleviate the conflicts which simmered between the different groups and threatened to flare up over the slightest pretext.

Inside the Palace complex, the Pharaoh had discussed the matter with his advisors but no compromise or solution had been suggested. The Librarian had already informed the Palace officials about the complaint from the Romans, and the insolent letter which he received the day after the Romans had arrived. The Librarian reported that whilst work on the book had been commenced, it would take at least another five days to complete the copying. The wily librarian had specifically referred to the 'calligraphic study' which the scribes from the library were rushing to complete; thereby he tactfully avoiding any explicit mention of copying. After serving as an official in the Palace for thirty years, the Librarian knew the value of such diplomatic nuances. He had set scribes to study the text and faithfully reproduce the calligraphy of each word. Should the occasion arise there would then be a loop hole permitting the Egyptians to claim the poetry had not been copied, as it was the calligraphy not the poetry which the scribes had been told to reproduce. The text was in Latin which made the work slightly slower as the scribes were more accustomed to use the Greek alphabet, but they still labored diligently.

Publius was unaware of the machinations of the Alexandrian Court as he made his way across the city for his audience with Pharaoh. Marcus was amongst the officers who accompanied the Roman commander as they walked through the streets towards the Palace. They were also accompanied by Aurelius and Gaius, the commanders of the two Roman legions which were stationed in Alexandria. Aurelius and Gaius had both impressed on Publius the weak-willed nature of the current Pharaoh. They told Publius how the real power and influence lay with the palace eunuchs who ran the government from behind the scenes. There had been a number of minor confrontations recently between the Romans and the Egyptians. Aurelius and Gaius were itching for an opportunity to assert their authority. Upon re-reading the letters from his father, Publius had decided it was imperative that he procure the original master copy of the book. Consequently, he was pleased to hear that Ptolemy XII was so feeble and irresolute and Publius intended to demonstrate his power. Publius was focussing on this thought as they entered the Palace complex, passing the imposing Nubian guards who flanked the doorway in silence. The visitors were unaware that the guards' silence was ensured by the drastic measure of cutting out their tongues.

Before the Romans had even entered the Palace, they were

enveloped in the fragrant floral aroma which wafted up from the gardens and flower beds. The fresh sea breeze stirred the air, as it did throughout the city, and prevented the heavy scent from the numerous flowers becoming overpowering or cloying. The Palace consisted of a compound of many different buildings; each Ptolemy had added new structures, and the complex now stretched over a large area. The Palace stretched as far as the Royal Harbor to the East of the city, housing and employing a huge number of officials, eunuchs, slaves and guards. The Mouseion ran along the South side of the Palace, its physical proximity demonstrating the source of its patronage. Between the Palace buildings there were a host of elaborate gardens and pools, each one created in a different mode and adorned with the plants and flowers most appropriate for that style. Indeed, the level of horticultural and architectural refinement which the Romans now observed was far superior to anything in Rome. As the visitors followed the palace eunuch who guided them to the reception hall, they were suitably amazed at the sights they beheld. This was the intended purpose of the circuitous route which the eunuch was taking to reach the Royal reception room. Much of the artwork they passed was of pure Hellenic style and the Romans saw statues and sculptures which were even more exquisite examples of this style than the works of Greece. In many matters the Ptolemies still exhibited their Macedonian roots, yet the vast wealth of Egypt and the superior materials available had resulted in many enhancements of the original Hellenic style. This new refined style was to be known as Hellenistic.

Although Ptolemy XII was not an assertive individual, he still cut an imposing figure when the Romans entered his presence, and Publius had second thoughts about the dictatorial approach he had decided to employ concerning the confiscated book. The spacious reception hall was richly adorned beyond anything the newcomers had ever seen and the whole room glittered with jewels and gold. The walls and floor were covered with mosaics and murals showing the ancient Pharaohs in various symbolic poses. Behind Ptolemy an elaborate engraving depicted a victorious Pharaoh beheading the three captives he grasped in one hand. The three prisoners were markedly different, each representing one of the traditional enemies of the Egyptian people. The giant-sized representation of Pharaoh held a dark Nubian, an armoured Assyrian and a nomadic Bedouin in one hand, the other held an uplifted sword frozen in its downward sweep. The stay in execution had frozen the looks of horror and panic on the faces of the victims. Ptolemy XII wore a similar headdress to the depicted Pharaoh, to ensure the symbolism would not be lost on the visitors. Publius steeled himself as he approached the throne, Aurelius and Gaius had told him many stories of the indecisiveness of this irresolute ruler, and Publius was determined to regain his father's book. The usual ceremonies and courtesies were performed on both sides, with Publius exercising his utmost reserve and frigidity. He resented having to perform the ritual genuflections before a barbarian ruler, however rich they might be, and consequently Publius rushed through the motions.

The Romans found it difficult to be domineering and assertive when their interlocutor was seated above them on an ornate throne. Furthermore the conversation was all in Greek, which put most of the Romans at a disadvantage as they could only converse stiltedly. Like all patrician Romans, Publius had studied Greek as a boy but he was far from fluent and often had to employ Marcus as a translator. The Romans called for couches to be brought into the reception hall, to the shock of the Palace household. Ptolemy graciously indicated that their request be fulfilled, and he took this extraordinary breach in etiquette with good grace. The new seating arrangements were hardly any better as the Romans still had to crane their necks to look up at Pharaoh. However, they were pleased to have asserted their position and power so visibly. The group now began to discuss the general state of affairs in Alexandria. Both sides knew that the issue of the confiscated book would prove the key point of contention and they manoeuvred for position and leverage before the topic was raised. Publius inquired innocently about the recent riots in Alexandria, which had only ended with the timely intervention of the legionaries. After downplaying the incident, one of the palace officials retorted by asking about the Romans' sea voyage. It was well known that the Romans were inept sailors, and that Caesar himself had been captured by pirates whilst at sea. The Egyptians mocked the fact that the Roman commander was held captive within the territory he claimed to have conquered. These exchanges and comments continued for some time, and the Romans were surprised at how well-informed their hosts were. The Egyptians knew of all the latest scandals and plots in Rome, and they made numerous barbed references to the intrigues and corruption within the capital.

After some time Publius and his officers rose to their feet, as if to depart. The interview had been a battle of wills between the Romans and the astute Palace officials who spoke on behalf of the Pharaoh. Ptolemy had sat silently throughout most of the exchange, despite the fact that the comments were addressed to him, and the responses delivered in his name. He indicated with a practised regal nod, that his ministers spoke for him to prevent the irksome need for the Pharaoh to be involved in such minor matters. As Publius was turning to leave, he casually mentioned that he had still not received his book, which had been unlawfully confiscated. However, the clench in his jaw and the tone of his voice revealed that this was anything but an offhand remark. One of the officials opened his mouth to deliver an appropriately evasive response when he stopped in shock. Publius had actually approached the throne. He now stood in front of the Pharaoh with his hand outstretched. The demanding pose almost implied he thought the Pharaoh had concealed the book in question under his chair, like a naughty school boy. The room vibrated with tension as the Egyptians stood aghast at the full severity of this breach of custom. The Pharaoh's body was sacrosanct, being simultaneously divine and regal. As such, it was forbidden to touch the Pharaoh or to point at him in any way. A normal visitor would have had his hand promptly lopped off for daring to present it to the Pharaoh in such an impudent manner. The captain of the royal bodyguard had loosened his sword in its sheath as he waited for the order.

All eyes watched to see what would happen next. Marcus whispered a warning to Publius about the gravity of the *faux pas* he had just committed. Sweat broke out on Publius's face as he realized he had breached an important protocol. The moments seemed to draw out in agonising suspense. Powerful as Rome was, the visitors were still guests in a nominally independent kingdom. Behind the Pharaoh there stood menacing armed guards, whilst the Romans had left their weapons at the entrance of the Palace and they waited defenceless in front of the throne. The other Romans now cursed the couches they had so pompously requested; it put them at a disadvantage if the guards were to attack. They were obliged to recline in feigned comfort as the whole room watched to see how the *impasse* would be solved. The tension broke when the Pharaoh's younger daughter rose to her feet from a couch by her father, and took Publius's outstretched hand in her own. Cleopatra was seventeen years old and she moved with fluidity and grace, which captured the attention of all. Her young body retained the vitality of childhood and she glowed with health. As she crossed the room, a gentle breeze blew the sheer fabric of her light tunic against her body and revealed the shape of the womanly curves which she had recently developed. She appeared to glide across the floor as she approached Publius, placed her dainty hand in his sweaty paw and effortlessly led the muscle-bound Roman away from the throne. Cleopatra had been watching the proceedings from the luxuriant couch on which she was seated to one side of her father. Her deft touch and astute intervention succeeded in averting a disastrous political situation.

Publius felt an overwhelming sense of gratitude rise within him as his saviour led the Romans out of the reception hall and into one of the gardens. Cleopatra had recognized the significance of the dilemma, and she had intervened to pointedly insist on showing the visitors around the magnificent Palace gardens before they departed. From the look of relief which showed on the faces of the Romans one would have thought that they were ardent horticulturalists who had travelled so far solely in order to view these gardens. The officers assented to the proposal in unison, each endeavoring to mask their unease with smiles and comments as they went outside. Publius had seized on Cleopatra's hand and the escape it offered with alacrity, and he was still holding the young lady's hand tightly in his own when they got outside. She winced as Publius's powerful grip started to bruise her fingers, and deftly withdrew her hand at an opportune moment.

Cleopatra was fascinated by the Romans. They were so uncivilised and barbaric yet they controlled the entire Mediterranean and the very future of Egypt lay in their hands. The Princess was amazed that men who could not even speak Greek without stumbling over every third word, had still managed to conquer most of the known world. Their legions seemed unstoppable and their greed insatiable. Cleopatra had realized that the very survival of the Ptolemies might lie in Roman hands. It was in order to satisfy her curiosity about this brutish race that Cleopatra had chosen to be present with the Pharaoh when the Romans arrived. She had swiftly become bored by the political bickering and she ignored the exchanges in favor of studying Publius. He was a powerfully built man, and Cleopatra was fascinated to see the soldier who famously once impaled two Gauls with one thrust of his sword. The Princess had found herself wondering what it would feel like to hold one of his gigantic hands in her own. When Cleopatra's reverie was broken by Publius's unwise and foolhardy gesture it was as if Isis had answered her prayers. The Princess was provided with an ideal occasion to satisfy her curiosity and she took it without hesitation.

The Romans were so relieved to have left the meeting without any open confrontation occurring, that it was not until they were leaving the Palace that Publius realized no agreement had been reached about the book. Cleopatra had accompanied the visitors to the gateway, and she saw the frown of concern darken Publius's brow. How childishly simple these Romans are, she thought to herself. They do not even have the foresight to conceal their thoughts, their faces reveal everything. Cleopatra had grown up in the world of Palace intrigues and conspiracies. From an early age she had understood the necessity of retaining an opaque mask no matter how tumultuous her emotions were inside. In response to Cleopatra's polite enquiries the Romans revealed that the matter of a confiscated work belonging to Publius's father still remained unresolved. The Princess was aware how narrowly a diplomatic crisis had been averted and she wanted to ensure the Romans left the Palace forthwith. She made excuses for her father's busy schedule and arranged another meeting in six days time.

Cleopatra knew that six days would be ample for the scribes to complete a copy of the confiscated book, and she personally intended to see it was lavishly bound and boxed. She had observed the glow of gold-lust in the eyes of the Romans when they drunk from the solid golden goblets in the Palace. With the vast wealth of the Pharaohs stored in the Palace treasuries it would be easy to order an ornate golden container for the book, and the price was a small one to pacify the rapacious Romans. So Cleopatra had confidently assured them the matter of the book would be resolved to everybody's satisfaction at the next meeting. The Roman officers duly departed without the faintest inkling how masterfully the diplomatic young princess had manipulated them. Cleopatra was particularly adept at thinking on her feet, a skill which was to serve her well in the volatile world of the Ptolemies. As it was, Cleopatra was pleased to have had the opportunity to converse with the Romans and examine more closely the fascinating race who ruled so much of the world.

The Pharaoh and his advisors were impressed with Cleopatra's timely intervention and the regal manner in which she had handled the situation. They all approved of her actions and her foresight in stalling for time before the next meeting. One eunuch pointed out that the letter to the Library had demanded no copies be made of the confiscated book. However, it was out of the question to accede to that demand now and they must make the best of a difficult situation. Cleopatra chuckled to herself as she imagined the choice she intended to present to Publius. On one hand he could accept the copy of the book, complete with the valuable bejewelled box; or he could retain the original and forego the container. To this end, Cleopatra sent instructions to ensure that the box be made to fit the copy but not the original. She wondered with a wry half-smile if the Roman's greed or principles would prove the stronger when offered the choice between the two.

Whilst she waited for the next meeting, Cleopatra found herself thinking about the Roman officers who had come so close to starting an open conflict between Alexandria and Rome. She had been impressed with Publius's physical presence and strength, her hand was still bruised from his grip. In Egypt the Nubian guards were the only men Cleopatra knew who could match the Romans in height and physique. Her attention had also been caught by the coloring of the officers. Marcus's blond hair and blue eyes had interested her, but there were blonds amongst the Macedonian and Greek population of Egypt so Cleopatra was accustomed to such colors. What had interested the Princess more was the red hair of Caius, another of the Gallic officers who had accompanied Publius to the Palace. But of all the Romans, it was their hulking leader which Cleopatra longed to see the most. She found herself inexplicably drawn to Publius, even after he had left. Cleopatra viewed him as adorable in his childlike simplicity yet dangerous in the power he commanded. Publius was the highest ranking Roman officer in Egypt and thus could command both the legions stationed there, in addition to his cavalry. This awesome power appeared to be mirrored in his muscular physique. The Roman officers all wore moulded breastplates which exaggerated their contours, yet Cleopatra had seen beyond this. The Egyptians were past masters at using clothes to disguise or enhance the gifts of Nature, and Cleopatra was not fooled by the bright armour. The Princess's interest and excitement led to an impatient wait before the next meeting with the Romans.

Throughout the Orient the Romans were mocked for their hypocrisy, in public they proclaimed the virtues of austerity, yet in private their greed was known to be insatiable. The situation was further emphasized by the Oriental disdain for Roman art. With the exception of a few notable crafts, the Orientals viewed Roman art as primitive and undeveloped. To many it seemed ironic that the race who controlled so much of the world, knew so little about how to appreciate the finest things it had to offer.

When the six days had passed and the Romans returned, the whole Palace waited with interest to see which copy of the book Publius would choose. The officers had entered through the same gate as previously, now they hurried through the gardens determined not to feel any awe or interest. The previous visit had alerted the officers to the dangerously seductive qualities of Ptolemy's Palace and they were resolved to complete this visit as quickly as possible.

The officers were shown into a different hall, as opulent as the previous one, but with more subdued lighting. One small window high in its East wall shed a bright beam of light on the Pharaoh and the only other source of illumination were the few oil lamps which flickered in alcoves along its walls. The Romans immediately suspected an ambush and were on their guard as they scanned the shadowy recesses. Both guests and hosts observed the customary formalities, although this time the Romans did not even attempt to alter the balance of power by demanding seats. Their previous boldness and assertive arrogance had totally disappeared, and now they only wished to get the book and leave the Palace without incident. At a signal from the Pharaoh two covered tables were brought into the Hall. The silent attendants placed them in front of the Romans and then withdrew. An official from the Library then summarised the great tradition of scholarship which had flourished in Alexandria, and the importance of the Library in facilitating the record and advancement of knowledge. The Romans waited impatiently as the official cited the original Ptolemaic decree entitling the Library to confiscate any books they wished and replace them with copies. The official then explained that in special deference to the Romans, and because the book in question was the author's own copy bequeathed in the author's will, the Pharaoh had decided to allow them to choose between the original and the copy. At a signal from the official, slaves then withdrew the coverings from the tables. The dim light revealed the fantastically ornate box of the copy, contrasted with the plain leather of the original. As the Romans approached the books, the official suggested they might appreciate more light and signaled again to the slaves. With a gentle rustle of cloth and a stirring of air, they drew back the large heavy curtains which lined both walls of the Hall. Light now flooded into the Hall in a myriad of different colors. The top half of each wall was an enormous window made with stained glass. The bright and multi-colored lights disorientated the Romans, who had never seen anything similar before. They were amazed and gaped in awe, to the amusement of the Court. Gaius was the first to regain his composure and he whispered to Publius to take the original book and leave. However, Publius was enthralled by the golden casket of the copy, the sunlight reflected off the inset jewels and the gold gleamed brightly. The other officers were also fascinated by the golden casket and they had no doubt that Publius would choose that one. The Court waited with interest as Publius battled with his greed and his sense of duty. This inner turmoil continued for some time as he vacillated between the two books. Finally, he took up the original master copy and left the Hall, muttering a formulaic salutation to the Pharaoh as he departed. At the doorway to the Hall he turned to take one final look, though it was hard to tell if the covetous look in his eye was directed more at the golden casket or the smiling princess who stood majestically behind it.

7

Alexandria, 54 BC

Marcus was sitting alone by the sea shore late one evening. Nearby the light of the Pharos outshone the moon as both gleamed bright against the deep black Egyptian night. Marcus had climbed down over the rocks which lined the causeway linking the Pharos to the mainland, and he was now seated on a boulder by the water's edge. He was lost in thought as he savoured a rare moment of solitude. Although Marcus enjoyed the camaraderie of the legionaries and officers, there were times when he required some privacy and the chance to be alone with his thoughts. The legionaries were united by a very close bond; they ate together, trained together, lived together and in many cases died together. This companionship was a crucial feature of the legions as it ensured their cohesion in battle, and their loyalty as a unit. Normally the men chose to spend their free time together, riding or hunting by day and drinking in the taverns by night. However, on this particular occasion Marcus had left his comrades and gone for a walk by himself. Within the bustling streets he had not found the solitude he desired, so he had made his way along the deserted causeway towards the 'Island'. The noise of the city was still audible, but out on the causeway the force of the sea breeze was not broken by any buildings and it cleared Marcus's mind. Marcus stared at the moon, intrigued by its uncanny appearance. The crescent of the moon actually looked considerably different in Egypt. Whereas in Gaul the moon's crescent formed a large 'C' shape against the night sky, in Egypt the change in latitude meant the crescent was observed differently, forming a large 'U' shape. Marcus had noticed the gradual change in the moon's crescent during their voyage, but now he had the occasion to admire and examine the difference. He resolved to ask the astronomers in the Mouseion for an explanation the following day.

Marcus was scanning the night sky for any other astronomical differences when he heard some scuffling and muffled grunts coming from nearby. The breeze carried the noises along from further up the causeway and the Marcus assumed the groans came from an amorous tryst. He was about to depart when he heard a scream. The cry was swiftly followed by the thud of someone being hit hard, and after the blow there was another groan. There was no way these noises could be mistaken for anything amicable and Marcus was instantly up and running along the causeway. As Marcus ran he heard more muffled noises and he altered his course accordingly, peering into the dark shadows all the while.

Marcus clambered over the rocks in the direction of the sounds he had heard. He had contemplated shouting for assistance, but his cries would not carry to the busy city streets, and it would rob him of the element of surprise. The Roman soldiers went lightly armed whenever they left the camp, for the accord between the Egyptian population and the Romans was fragile at best. Standing orders required a legionary to carry his sword at all times in any overseas posting. Marcus, like most of the men, chose not to wear his heavy and cumbersome armour when he left the camp. Marcus had already loosened his sword in its sheath as he ran along the causeway; his hand rested on the pummel as he stole from boulder to boulder checking each dark recess before moving on. Marcus climbed over some driftwood and approached the next small beach, the waves lapped at his feet as he strained to hear any further cries carried on the whistling breeze. The wind was stronger further along the causeway and the waves splashed noisily against the rocks. Marcus froze as he heard a thud and a grunt just ahead of him. He approached cautiously, and looking round a boulder he saw several people moving. There were at least two men, but the shadows cast by the moon and the lighthouse were confusing.

Marcus noted their position and then moved around to approach from the other side. The rank smell of cheap alcohol reached his nostrils and Marcus saw one of the men drinking from a leather wineskin, before passing it to his companion. Marcus was deftly slipping between two rocks when he saw a third man crouched low over a prostrate female figure. The young woman lay bound and bleeding as the man wrenched off her tunic, exposing her white breasts to the light with an animalistic snicker. She was gagged but still attempting to call out. Each sound earned her another vicious slap from the man leaning over her. Without a moment's hesitation Marcus leapt over the rock and charged. He had intended to approach quietly and establish how many people were involved, but his outrage propelled him forwards and he shouted with fury as he charged the rapist.

The three men were caught by surprise and they barely had time to reach for their weapons as they beheld Marcus burst from between the rocks. Marcus slashed at the nearest man who was reaching for a staff, and then rushed towards the young victim. Marcus crashed into the man who was stooped over the young lady, and bowled him over. Marcus and the assailant tumbled over in a heap of struggling limbs; the force of his charge had carried them both well past the terrified woman. As the two men grappled in the sand, Marcus dropped his shoulders and pushing with all his might, he heaved the man away from him. This provided the space necessary for Marcus to use his sword and as the rapist charged, Marcus thrust the blade deep into the man's torso. The assailant's momentum impaled him yet further on the short sword and he gasped in surprise as the blade passed right through his chest and he sank dying to the sand.

The handle of the sword was warm and wet with blood as Marcus wrenched it free and turned to face the remaining two men. One man had picked up the staff he was reaching for when Marcus had slashed at him. His limping gait showed that Marcus had made contact, but the man was still capable of fighting and the fierce look on his face showed he had every intention of doing so. The other man was armed with a large ugly knife, a weapon that was none the less dangerous for its filthy condition. The two men now circled around Marcus, wary of his sword yet determined to attack him, now that they realized he was alone. With thrusts and feints they attempted to manoeuvre Marcus into a position between them, Marcus was constantly turning and parrying to avoid this trap. He changed his sword from right to left hand in a ploy to disorientate the attackers, but they merely altered their stances accordingly. The attackers had been drinking, but they were by no means drunk, and Marcus had a serious situation as he faced them both.

The stand-off continued as neither side could find any weakness in the other's defence. The men were clearly experienced fighters and they worked in tandem to make the most of their number. As Marcus's initial adrenalin rush subsided, his rage turned to cold hatred and he realized the danger of the situation. He stood in an isolated spot, facing two armed men who were determined to kill him. They were emboldened by alcohol but they had not drunk enough to impair their co-ordination. Each time he moved to attack one man, his fellow would strike or stab at Marcus from behind. There was no way Marcus could summon help, and the rapists were now grimly determined to avenge their dead friend. On the sand the maiden had initially stared, frozen with awe and fear as she watched Marcus fighting for both of their lives. Now she struggled against the ropes that bound her and began working her hands free. The noise of her struggles distracted the knife-wielding attacker, and as he turned to see what it was, Marcus lunged at him. The man's swift parry only partially succeeded in diverting Marcus's thrust. The sword passed through cloak and tunic as it sank into the man's shoulder and cleaved his collar bone apart. Marcus ducked and rolled to the ground after the stroke, he knew that the other attacker would have swung at him from behind with the heavy staff he was wielding so competently. The gamble paid off and the staff whistled harmlessly by as Marcus rolled out of range. He had now injured both his opponents and had the temporary advantage of facing them both.

As he crouched and rose to his feet, Marcus scooped up a handful of sand. With a final effort he charged at the two men, throwing the sand into their eyes. The ploy gained him a moment's advantage but that was all he required. With dexterity and the unerring accuracy that came from months of training, he stabbed the knifeman in the throat and moved to block the swinging staff. The remaining assailant was quick, however, and the blow passed under Marcus's arm and caught him in the chest. He winced as the broken ribs dug into his side, and he pivoted to face the last man. Staying close to reduce the room for swinging a staff, Marcus struggled to draw in his breath as he thrust and lunged at the man. Under the flurry of blows the attacker backed away from Marcus, blocking or avoiding each thrust. Abruptly, his retreat was stopped as he collapsed, poleaxed from behind. The girl had freed her hands and now stood over her former assailant with a large rock in her grasp. She had crept up behind him as Marcus drove him back, and straining every muscle in her young body she had brought the rock crashing down onto her would-be rapist. The blow had crushed his skull and he was dead before he hit the ground.

Marcus now faced the young lady, who stood over the fallen assailant with the rock still in her hands. Her torn tunic flapped in the breeze and she dropped the rock as she fumbled to cover herself. The rock landed with a dull thud on the corpse at her feet and then rolled onto the sand. Marcus was still wincing from the pain of each breath and he leant on a boulder for support as he felt the pain wash over him and black spots blurred his vision. The girl's hands were still shaking from the shock and adrenalin, and she was attempting to fasten her tunic and smooth her hair. These actions were reassuringly familiar after her ordeal and she continued the impossible task of attempting to fasten the torn pieces of cloth. Marcus offered her his cloak and then sank exhausted to the sand. His vision had cleared but the pain still shot through his chest with each breath. Neither of the two had spoken a word, but now Marcus reassured her in Greek. The comfort of familiar words got through to the traumatised young woman, and as she took the cloak she began to sob. She wrapped herself in the cloak and cried with relief. Marcus now noticed that the girl was injured; she had been beaten as she fought her attackers. Her lips and nose were bleeding freely and her face was swollen in several places. The young lady sat on a rock opposite him, quivering and whimpering as she wrapped the cloak around herself. In the moonlight, she looked across at her saviour and thanked him between her sobs. Marcus found himself immediately captivated by the warm brown eyes which were looking up at him. The girl tried to say her name was Rebecca, though from her swollen lips it had sounded more like 'Memecca'. Marcus then tried to introduce himself. However, he followed his name with an involuntary wince as speech hurt his chest. Thus Rebecca thought she'd been saved by a man called 'Marcus-ee', whilst Marcus thought he'd rescued a girl called 'Memecca', a confusion the two were to laugh about considerably later.

As the young pair recovered from their ordeal, they helped each other wash off some of the blood and clean their wounds. The salt water stung as it cleaned the cuts and bruises but it also reduced the chance of any infection taking hold. Marcus had checked on the prostrate attackers, all three were dead and he left their bodies where they lay. Next Marcus and Rebecca helped each other over the rocks onto the path along the causeway. Marcus lent on the very staff which had injured him, and arm in arm the couple staggered towards the lights of the city. Marcus soon learnt that Rebecca was the daughter of a wealthy Jewish merchant who was based in Alexandria. Rebecca was his only daughter and she assured Marcus that her father would reward him handsomely for rescuing his beloved only child. Marcus demurred quietly, stating that meeting her was sufficient reward for his actions. As the pair talked Marcus found himself intrigued by the delightful young Jewess with her natural grace. The beating she had received from her attackers had done nothing to impair her innate elegance, and even as the injured young pair walked towards the town, Marcus was struck by her bearing and poise.

They soon found and hired a wagon to take them out to the villa where Rebecca lived. The night was well-advanced and outside the city center the streets were almost deserted. With the faint sound of music drifting from the opulent villas they passed, the slow journey was relaxing and peaceful. Rebecca was wrapped up tight in Marcus's cloak even though it was not a cold night; she enjoyed the smell of the garment as she snuggled into its reassuring folds. Once the ordeal was over and Rebecca felt secure, she soon realized how tired she was. With a sleepy voice she just managed to direct the wagon driver as she leant against Marcus's uninjured side and fell asleep. When the wagon pulled up at their destination Marcus paid the driver and carrying the sleeping Rebecca in his arms, he kicked at the door. There were still lights burning in the house and footsteps hurried to answer his summons. The door was opened by a large man wearing a black gabardine who almost filled the doorway. In between his long black beard and ringlets Marcus recognized the same soft brown eyes with which Rebecca had looked at him. The man's face was furrowed with anguish and concern as he raised a lantern to peer into the darkness outside the villa. As the light fell on Rebecca, he let out a moan of relief and pain and took the young lady tenderly in his arms as she began to wake. Ushering Marcus into the atrium, the rotund Jew called for slaves to fetch water and salves.

With one arm still supporting his beloved daughter, Reuben muttered prayers of thanks for her safe return as he directed the household entourage. He gently turned Rebecca's face towards the light and winced when he saw her injuries.

'My God, what have they done to you?' he gasped in shock.

'I'm alright father,' replied Rebecca, still wrapped in Marcus's cloak but now seated by a fire.

'It could have been worse,' she continued, 'this brave Roman rescued me. What you see is mostly just scratches and cuts, they will soon heal.'

'Send for a physician immediately,' instructed Reuben as he gently embraced his beloved daughter.

The household slave soon returned with a physician, and both Reuben and Marcus were much relieved to hear him confirm Rebecca's assessment that the injuries were only superficial. The physician examined and dressed each wound, as the two men watched wincing sympathetically. Marcus was surprised to catch glimpses of the very comely face emerging from the mass of cuts and blood.

'My name is Reuben bar Ezra, and I am forever in your debt,' announced the large Jew solemnly and simply as he turned to thank Marcus and embrace him.

Marcus gave a sharp intake of breath as further pains shot through his chest. Reuben had not realized the young Roman was injured, and he now called the physician to tend Marcus immediately. The efforts of the two young people to wash their injuries in the sea had been rudimentary at best. Now, with a chest full of ointments and salves the household slaves were able to perform a much more thorough job. The effect was incredible; Marcus soon beheld a beautiful young woman instead of the bloodied and battered victim he had rescued earlier. Meanwhile the physician was fastidiously examining Marcus's broken ribs and listening to his breathing. The firelight flickered brightly as the couple stared at each other, oblivious to the presence of the slaves and physician who were attending to their injuries. Rebecca blushed slightly as the physician lifted off Marcus's tunic, her pupils dilated and she felt the blood rush to her cheeks as her eyes ran over his muscled torso. The left side of his chest was already darkening into a mass of blue and black bruises with the contours of the broken bones clearly visible beneath the skin, but fortunately the broken ribs had not punctured his lungs.

Reuben had left the room to call off the various search parties he had organised since his daughter had gone missing that afternoon. Rebecca had last been seen leaving the synagogue in the afternoon and her father had raised the alarm when she failed to return that evening. He now returned to the room and found the young pair in much better shape. Cleaned and anointed with medicinal salves, the couple now sat in fresh clothes and recounted their experiences. Rebecca told them how she had stopped to pet a stray puppy in the street. She had naively followed the puppy into an alley, where she had been seized by the three drunken men and dragged through a warren of back alleys until they were on the causeway. In his turn, Marcus explained how he had gone along the causeway in search of some solitude and then heard the sounds of Rebecca struggling. All three now silently gave thanks that Marcus had been there to rescue Rebecca.

Marcus was wearing one of Reuben's billowing gabardines as the household servants cleaned his own garments. The long black robe was much too large for him in width but it was the right length. As they talked, the three sipped strong wine and drank hot milk, sweetened with honey. Food was brought and set down beside Marcus. Reuben explained that as the sun had set it was the start of the Sabbath so neither he nor Rebecca could eat anything. In response to Marcus's nonplussed expression, Rebecca explained that for Jews a day began when the sun set the previous evening. However, Reuben was also a practical man and he permitted both himself and his daughter to partake of the restorative drinks after their ordeal. The spirit of youth and the kindling flames of romance ensured that the couple were soon oblivious to their injuries as they became engrossed in each other. Reuben had retired to his room for a few hours sleep after the rigours of the exhausting night. The slaves had also been dismissed, so Marcus and Rebecca were alone as they sat and talked, losing themselves in the fascination of discovering each other. Rebecca felt herself irresistibly drawn to this gallant

Gentile and she no longer felt tired at all. Their conversation never seemed to dry up and they were still going strong when Reuben descended some hours later and the household began to stir as the Sabbath sun climbed in the sky.

The blood and dirt had been skilfully sponged from Marcus's tunic and it had been left to dry by a stove. Marcus now changed back into his Roman attire and he prepared to take his leave. Rebecca still had his cloak wrapped around her but Marcus chose not to ask for it, thinking that it would make an excellent excuse for at least one more visit. His simple machinations proved unnecessary as Reuben insisted he return to join them for dinner the following evening. Thus it was a jubilant and exhausted Marcus who staggered back to his quarters in the bright morning sunshine. The other officers teased him boisterously about his nocturnal absence and the big smile on his face, until they noticed his injury. After a brief explanation, Marcus went to see the legion's surgeon and get a second opinion. The surgeon declared that the injury had been expertly treated and should heal quickly. It was impossible to make a cast for broken ribs, but he did bandage Marcus's chest to ensure he restricted his movements whilst the bones reset.

Marcus waited impatiently for the time to pass so that he could go and meet Rebecca again. He made some discreet enquiries about Reuben and these merely served to further whet his curiosity. Apparently the Jewish merchant traded in rare and valuable goods from all over the Orient, supplying numerous luxuries for the wealthy Romans. These exotic products could earn profits of one thousand percent for anyone who was brave and resourceful enough to transport them from the Orient to the markets of Rome. Rich Roman matrons paid small fortunes for Chinese silk or fragrant spices, as they vied to surpass their social peers. However, the trade routes were dogged by numerous dangers, including bandits, hazardous weather and wild animals, so demand always exceeded supply. There were so many fantastical tales surrounded the exotic Orient that few ordinary people knew where fact ended and fiction began. An air of mystery surrounded the tough and resourceful merchants as the hard-bought details about the safest routes and the practicalities of travel were only passed from father to son.

When the following evening finally arrived, Marcus rushed across town to the villa. In his eagerness and impatience, Marcus found that he arrived far too early for dinner. Reuben had not even returned from his work-place. It was left to Rebecca to entertain him whilst the servants finished preparing dinner. Both Marcus and Rebecca welcomed the opportunity for some more time alone, and as they walked in the villa's verdant garden they cast longing looks at each other. In the short time since they had last met, the medicinal salves had done wonders and Rebecca's face was regaining its former beauty. Marcus was entranced by her vitality and charm as they strolled in the verdant arbours of the garden. As they passed behind one particularly lush bush, Marcus pulled Rebecca towards him and cut off her conversation with a kiss. It was simultaneously so expected yet so surprising that even when he broke contact with her lips, Rebecca was lost for words. In silence she pulled him towards her again and their lips met again, silently fulfilling the promises which their eyes had been making all the while. Carried away in their passion, they both ignored their injuries in the heat of the moment. Their first kiss had been a bold declaration, now they kissed each other with an insatiable desire. Each contact inflamed, rather than satisfied the young pair. They were interrupted by a call from Reuben as he returned to the house and came into the garden looking for his guest and daughter. Through the leaves of the arbour Marcus saw him approaching, and he quickly kissed

Rebecca once more before they broke off to hurriedly sort out their disarrayed clothing and hair.

Rebecca had already explained to Marcus that her father was an Orthodox Jew and he would never countenance her marrying a Gentile. Yet Reuben was also a worldly wise man and he knew the importance of compromises. When he travelled with a caravan of goods, Reuben would never oblige the rest of the company to halt their journey because it was the Sabbath nor did he prevent his men eating pork. However, on a trip Reuben always choose a route that passed towns with synagogues, even if it lengthened the overall distance of the journey. Over dinner, Marcus was fascinated by Reuben's tales of the East. He listened in rapture to the merchant's accounts of crossing deserts by camel train, resting at oases, enduring sandstorms, fighting bandits and dealing with corrupt officials. Reuben declared that he infinitely preferred the former to the latter. When the nomadic bandit tribes spotted a baggage train they would approach cordially, assess its size and the escort that guarded it, and then withdraw to make their decision. If they thought the guards were insufficient or inexperienced they would swoop down in a raid, relying on the fury of their onslaught to drive away the guards and leave them in possession of the goods. Alternatively, if the train seemed orderly and the men experienced, the tribesmen would offer their services as guides and huntsmen. Reuben explained that this simplicity made his work much easier than dealing with corrupt officials. The latter were constantly angling for larger bribes or commissions and they were infamous for their duplicity.

As Marcus listened intently, Rebecca smiled to realise that their kissing had brought up the color in the Roman's tanned face. He looks good with some more color in that handsome face, thought Rebecca. She sat opposite him and was determined not to let her father's dull business talk spoil the evening. They ate at a table in deference to Marcus's Roman habits, but nearby there were couches on which to recline for the wine and sweetmeats which would conclude the meal. Rebecca stretched out one svelte leg under the table and searched for Marcus's foot. In accordance with eastern custom, Marcus had left his heavy sandals at the door, and he now gave a slight start as he felt Rebecca's toes playing with his foot. She smiled coyly at him as he endeavored to focus on the conversation with Reuben. Rebecca chuckled with satisfaction as she saw the color return in his cheeks. Throughout the rest of the meal, whenever she saw the blood begin to subside from Marcus's face, Rebecca would run her foot up his calf, or suggestively wiggle her toes against his knee. In this manner the meal progressed, with father and daughter vying for Marcus's attention in very different ways.

They were served dainty roasted desert quails stuffed with dates, the sweet juice from the fruits flavouring the light meat and keeping it moist. Then there were rich tagines which had cooked all day with the flavoursome juices condensing inside the conical lid and dripping down into the dish. A huge grilled perch fresh from the Nile formed the center-piece of the banquet, basted with olive oil and lemon juice. Side dishes of hummus, olives and deep-fried falafel balls fragrant with cumin accompanied each course, but between the three of them they only made small inroads into the mountains of food. The meal was a veritable banquet, for Reuben was determined to express his gratitude. The young Roman had politely declined all Reuben's generous presents, explaining that as he was shortly to depart on campaign it would be imprudent to take additional baggage with him. Reuben was quietly impressed with the young man's self control. From his merchant voyages he knew the problems and risks of transporting costly gifts. Many a rich present had brought its recipient additional problems or even a premature death, though few were the men prudent enough to decline a valuable gift. The meal was interrupted when a frantic messenger arrived for Reuben. The man hurriedly informed his master that there was a fire raging by the docks and one of his warehouses was in danger. Reuben excused himself and instructed his daughter to entertain their guest as he rushed from the house.

Across the table two pairs of bright eyes glimmered with passion. It was impossible to tell how long this providential opportunity would last. For the benefit of any nearby servants, Marcus volubly declared that Rebecca looked fatigued and must have not yet fully recovered from her ordeal. He announced he would depart and let her rest. Rebecca was about to protest that she was far from tired, when a large wink from Marcus told her to play along. Equally loudly she announced that she would retire to her room, and she pointed upstairs to her quarters. As the two rose to their feet and moved away from the table, their hands brushed each other and an electric frisson of excitement shook them both. Marcus hastily opened the front door and then shut it with a bang whilst he remained inside holding Rebecca's hand. He then took her hand and led the way swiftly upstairs. As soon as a bend in the stairway sheltered them from view, the eager couple began kissing again. In the half-dark their lips sought each other and their bodies pressed hard together. Marcus lifted her in his arms and carried her up the rest of the stairs, without breaking off the kiss. At the top of the stairway Rebecca had no need to indicate her private quarters. Marcus instinctively followed the scent of her perfume which issued from the rooms to his left.

Oil lamps burnt inside, and the flickering light fell on soft furnishings illuminating a room decorated tastefully yet simply. There was a large low divan against one wall above which two niches contained lamps of polished brass. Opposite the divan was a balcony which overlooked the garden behind the villa. Marcus headed for the divan as he held Rebecca in his arms. She had one arm around his shoulder whilst she ran the other through his hair and twisted his blond locks between her fingers. As Marcus laid Rebecca down on the divan she refused to release him, and pulled him down on top of her. They kissed fiercely and silently. Throughout the evening they lay together in half darkness, whispering and kissing. Their reverie was interrupted by Reuben's return. Marcus silently gave thanks that Rebecca had thought to call to the servants that she was retiring and would see her father in the morning. Reuben did not disturb them, but Marcus knew he would have to leave soon. His presence was too great a risk to Rebecca's reputation. The couple shared a final tender kiss on the balcony and then Marcus climbed down a vine into the garden. He left his cloak with Rebecca and told her he would call again the next day on the pretext of collecting it. She smiled as she wrapped herself in the warm folds and watched Marcus climb over the garden wall and drop quietly into the street beyond.

Marcus gently probed his ribs as he made his way back to quarters, the surgeon's bandage had been somewhat dislodged during the evening. Momentarily forgetting his professed atheism, he offered a coin to a road-side shrine, grateful to Fate, the Gods or the providential arsonist who had called away Reuben at such an opportune moment. However, at the back of his mind Marcus still vaguely resented any supreme power that did exist. He had met a wonderful girl but his unit would have to leave Alexandria in a few days and he might never see her again. Furthermore, he could never marry Rebecca as he was not Jewish. Marcus could not stay down-hearted for long. However tragic the circumstances his innate optimism buoyed up within him and he reprimanded himself for thinking of his departure rather than enjoying the moment. This attitude was to characterise the brief but intense relationship the two enjoyed. They seized every day, and night, that they could. In between military duties and training, Marcus spent as much time as possible in the company of Rebecca and her father. The young love-birds took any opportunity they could to be alone, but they also cherished their public friendship and they both enjoyed Reuben's company.

Marcus enjoyed hearing about Reuben's travels, and he was fascinated with the exotic paraphernalia which the merchant had collected. Reuben showed him one of the huge bows which the tribes in north India used; it was so large it required two hands to pull the string whilst the bow was held by a raised foot. Reuben also showed him the hide of a tiger which had attacked one of the pack animals on one of his caravans. There was a long rent along one side where Reuben had killed the animal with a spear. The hole made the skin almost worthless as a pelt, but Reuben would not have sold it anyway. The villa also contained a secure store room where the most valuable commodities of silk and certain spices were storied. Marcus was amazed to see entire sacks full of nard, precious peppercorns, pungent spices and fragrant incense along with parcels of costly saffron, the latter more valuable than gold. The saffron came from the stigmas of the crocus flower and the stigmas had to be plucked from over five thousand flowers to produce a single ounce of the orange spice. Similarly, there were entire bolts of lustrous silk, a material which doubled in value with each territory it passed through on its long journey from the East. The taxes and restrictions on the export of silk ensured that only a very limited supply reached the markets of Rome and this kept the prices extraordinarily high. Reuben explained that it was always prudent to keep a large reserve of capital as the

Eastern trade business was a risky one. If a merchant lost one caravan he needed enough stock in reserve to finance another venture or he would be ruined. Similarly it was also wise to have sufficient ready funds to pay a ransom, should a merchant be captured by pirates or bandits.

Reuben did not have a son, and he found it a pleasure to impart some of his professional knowledge to the young Roman. He touched on the intricacies of trading in each product and the importance of acquiring a balanced caravan. One product might be harmed by the cold mountain air, whereas another might be ruined by the desert heat. There were also considerable fluctuations in some markets, and the value of a commodity could rise or fall considerably during the time it took for a merchant to reach the East and return with his cargo. For this reason a wise merchant selected a balanced cargo, so that the success of his venture did not depend entirely on any one product. It paid to diversify, and Reuben discussed the various new markets he was investigating. The popularity of the Games and horse races in Rome meant that Reuben was now looking into the logistics of transporting exotic beasts from the East, such as the famous 'blood-sweating' horses of the Ferghana Valley.

Marcus enjoyed all the time he spent with Rebecca and her father, so it was with a heavy heart that he went to see them, with the news that the Romans' departure had been fixed for the following day. The men and horses were fully rested and now Publius had retrieved his confiscated book, orders had been given for the cavalry to depart at dawn. Both Marcus and Rebecca knew this moment must come, but they were still upset and shaken by the news. They tried to make light of the matter as they strolled in the garden where they had first kissed.

'I'll miss you Memecca,' said Marcus with a sad smile. Her cuts had healed well, and were barely visible against her delicate skin.

'I'll miss you too, Marcus-ee,' she replied with the same simple frankness.

As Marcus took his leave from the villa where he had spent such a short, but intensely happy period, Reuben insisted on presenting him with a gift. It was a small silver pendant showing a tiger. On the reverse of the pendant was an inscription in Hebrew, it read 'Chaver' simply meaning 'Friend'. Reuben explained that the scattered Jewish community in the East was not without influence and Marcus merely had to show the pendant to secure their aid. Rebecca had noticed his interest in tigers and the brooch he wore depicting one, so it had been her idea to have the pendant made. Marcus accepted gratefully and it was with an ache in his heart that he said goodbye to Reuben and Rebecca.

8

SYRIA AND MESOPOTAMIA, 54-53 BC.

IN SYRIA, Crassus waited impatiently for the arrival of Publius and the Gallic cavalry. The aged Triumvir had extorted all the riches he could from the province he governed, and now he was anxious to pursue his military plans. On the journey from Italy to Syria the Romans had passed through the land of Galatia, ruled by King Deiotarus (c.105-40BC). Crassus had mocked Deiotarus who was starting to build a new city even though he was far advanced in years. The King had pointedly replied that Crassus was no longer a young man, and that building was more suited to old age than campaigning. This retort continued to nettle Crassus and he was anxious to prove his vitality and dispel any rumors of his frailty, although he was already a sexagenarian.

During the winter Crassus had received occasional reports from the Roman garrisons he had left in Mesopotamia. The soldiers reported fearful tales of the Parthian cavalry; they told of Parthian arrows which pierced any armour and travelled so fast that they hit their mark before the victim could even see who fired them. The soldiers also reported that it was impossible to catch the Parthians for their horses were much swifter than those of the Romans. In addition the legionaries reported that the Parthians rarely had to retreat, as their armour was impervious to Roman arrows, whilst their swords cut through Roman armour with ease.

At this news there was some dismay amongst the men, many of whom also were reminded of the unfavorable omens which had dogged their journey from Rome. Until this news had arrived, the soldiers thought there was no difference between the Parthians and the Armenians or Cappadocians. In a previous campaign, the Roman General Lucullus had grown weary of routing the latter two tribes, and reported that the main difficulty of the war had been the tediousness of marching and the trouble of chasing such cowardly opponents. Lucullus had defeated forces which were over twenty times the size of his Army, before he was relieved of his command and replaced by Pompey. The soldiers now amassed under Crassus were expecting a similar campaign in Parthia, and they were certainly not pleased at the prospect of fighting fierce opponents with impenetrable armour and awesome weapons. However, Crassus chose to ignore such stories as exaggerations and dismissed the men who had travelled from Mesopotamia with scant thanks for their perilous journey. Although many were alarmed at these tales, the soldiers looked at the thousands of legionaries camped around them and took reassurance from the sheer size of the Roman force. However bad the stories or omens, it was impossible to remain discouraged for long when surrounded by such a vast body of men. It seemed inconceivable that the combined might of so many men could be opposed.

Crassus met with his officers several times to discuss the invasion plans, despite his extensive powers he still thought it wise to identify a *causus bellum* as justification for the invasion of Parthia. When his term of office was complete, Crassus would be vulnerable to prosecution for any of his actions whilst in office. Crassus knew that success in this venture would be the single safest and surest justification for invading Parthia, but he wanted a reasoned argument in addition. The fickle Roman populace cared more for victories and celebrations than they did for political rationale, and with the vast wealth of Parthia at his disposal Crassus would also be able to buy as much political support in the Senate as he required. Even the august senators who constituted that eminent body were not immune to bribes. After he had amassed and transported such a large force, there was no way that Crassus would return peacefully to Rome. However, he still required a political justification for his actions. As the Romans had already breached Parthian sovereignty and disregarded the terms of an earlier treaty by crossing the Euphrates River, they required a symbolic explanation for their current belligerence.

Through an appropriately selective reading of the recent historical events, Crassus was able to identify his force as a punitive expedition to avenge the death of Mithradates III, who had been recognized and protected by the Romans in an earlier treaty between Parthia and Rome. In 57BC, King Phaartes III of Parthia had been assassinated. Phaartes had previously entered into treaties with Rome, these treaties had fixed the Parthian border at the Euphrates River and were intended to ensure the rival empires of Parthia and Rome did not clash. On their side, the Parthians had respected the terms of the accord scrupulously and they had not interfered with affairs in the neighbouring Roman provinces. However, Pompey had violated the agreement and in connivance with princes from the vassal states he had seized provinces from the west of the Parthian Empire. When Phaartes had protested against this contravention of the treaty, Pompey had insulted Phaartes and relations between the two nations had cooled considerably, although the terms of the treaty still stood in theory. Following the assassination of Phaartes, the Romans intrigued to assist Mithradates III to become King of

Parthia. Their machinations proved unsuccessful and Phraates's son became King Orodes I in 56BC, executing Mithradates in 55BC. Although the Romans had previously breached their side of the agreement, Crassus now seized on this treaty and the execution of Mithradates as a pretext for his campaign. It was also advantageous to identify the Roman force as a punitive expedition as it justified extensive pillaging of the Parthian lands.

By the time Crassus and his officers had finished their debates about the most advantageous political justification for the expedition, Publius and his cavalry had arrived. They had travelled fast, carrying minimal provisions and requisitioning food from the towns they passed through. These vassal states were anxious to minimise the unexpected expense of feeding 1,000 men and their mounts, and they did all they could to speed the Roman cavalry on their way. Although during the journey the first spring buds were visible in the sheltered glades, there was still snow on the mountain tops. They completed the journey at full pace, covering upwards of 50 miles a day. Marcus admired the spectacular scenery they passed through, although the bouncing of the pendant against his chest continually reminded him of the wonderful girl he was leaving behind in Alexandria. The motion of the horse and the cold nights outdoors made his injured ribs ache, but with a hundred men under his immediate command Marcus had much to occupy him. He focused on the needs and wants of his men as a distraction from the pain of separation. With the demanding routine of a legionary and the rigours of travel Marcus found that thoughts of Rebecca only troubled him briefly before he fell into an exhausted sleep each evening.

The invading Army would be the largest force Rome had ever mobilised in the Orient. The amassed force of over 36,000 men made an impressive spectacle as they camped at the marshalling ground. With the arrival of Publius and his 1,000 cavalry, Crassus now commanded a huge composite force. He had already massed seven legions, 4,000 auxiliary infantry and 3,000 auxiliary cavalry in addition to the garrisons which had been left in Mesopotamia. King Artavasdes of Armenia had also arrived at the head of 6,000 troops and with the promise of a further 10,000 cavalry and 30,000 infantry. The 6,000 troops were magnificently equipped and were said to be merely his personal bodyguard. Artavasdes advised Crassus to lead his force on the more circuitous route into Parthia through the foothills of southern Armenia. He pointed out that in the hills along that route, the heavy Parthian cavalry would not be able to operate, and the King could guarantee there would be adequate water and supplies for the men and beasts. However, Crassus declared that he had left brave Roman soldiers in Mesopotamia and he was would not countenance invading by any other route. Crassus was mindful of the glory he intended to achieve on this campaign, and a direct drive into the heart of Parthia would provide a more noble record than a circuitous route via Armenia.

The main body of the Army was camped outside the city walls of Antioch, for there was insufficient space to accommodate all the men within the city. The soldiers had been outside of the city throughout the winter, and the camp had developed into a small town. Antioch was watered by the Orontes River which also connected it to the Mediterranean some thirty miles downstream. Behind the city there rose Mount Silpius which sheltered the location from the worse desert winds. When Pompey invaded Syria and made it into a Roman province in 64 BC, Antioch was the largest city and it was the natural choice for the Roman provincial capital. However, Antioch had not always been the capital of Syria. Originally the capital was on the Mediterranean coast at Seleucia, but the same advantage which had attracted the Macedonian rulers to its location also proved its downfall. The rival Ptolemies arrived by boat and seized that city on several occasions, precipitating the move to a more secure inland city. As a provincial Roman capital the city developed considerably. It soon boasted a basilica, an amphitheatre, an aqueduct, and no less than five public baths.

By the time Marcus arrived the Roman camp already boasted the full infrastructure of a large barracks, right down to the pair of busy brothels, and crude graffiti adorning the communal latrines. The arrival of some 36,000 additional men adjoining the provincial city had placed a huge strain on the city's existing brothels. The madams who ran the brothels had sent for more girls and opened two establishments in the camp, with the tacit support of the officers. The whorehouses boasted a wide range of girls, for the assembled army came from diverse backgrounds and had different tastes. Amongst the women there were busty brunettes and blondes from the Celtic tribes in the north, svelte women from Arabia with jet black hair and entrancing almond-shaped eyes, and tall dark Nubian women who moved with regal grace. Throughout the entire camp there was one courtesan who was admired above all the others. Her name was Luana and she was a whore par excellence. Although there were other girls who exceeded her in beauty, Luana had the reputation of being very selective about her clients. She only entertained officers, and even amongst them she only chose those that pleased her, these few men were then treated to an extraordinary sensual experience. Luana ensured the night in question was unique as she never slept with the same man twice. This tactic meant she was never discarded by a man who was bored of her, and it ensured that her past customers had only good things to say about her. This cunning policy had worked to enhance her reputation and like any elusive commodity her price remained correspondingly high.

Like all the new arrivals, Marcus soon heard about Luana when his century had reached the camp ground. One of the other centurions pointed her out to Marcus on his second day, as she was carried along in her luxurious sedan chair. The artful harlot was draped in a mysterious diaphanous fabric, which concealed whilst pretending to reveal. The novel fabric was a costly gift from one of her past lovers and it had been tailored into an elegant yet provocative dress. However, she did not lower the curtain around the chair for she wanted the rank and file to see and admire her beauty, which they could never hope to enjoy. As the sedan was passing, Luana instructed her bearers to halt. Looking up through her artfully thickened eyelashes, she had smiled coquettishly at Marcus as he rode slowly past. With a practised flick of her head she then dropped one of her pearl ear-rings. Marcus dismounted to retrieve the jewel and courteously returned it to the lady as she reclined in her chair. Marcus accepted her thanks and cordially remounted his horse and rode to his tent without giving the matter any further consideration. When he was not engrossed in the demands of looking after his men, Marcus's thoughts were entirely devoted to Rebecca. The other officers had noticed his low spirits and were a little concerned, the young centurion was normally buoyant and upbeat, but since they had left Alexandria a faint melancholy seemed to underlie his every action. Titus made every effort to cheer up Marcus, but even the grizzled old man's dry wit and jovial banter could not entirely remove the frown from Marcus's brow. Marcus appeared to have matured and no longer displayed the same boyish traits.

The following evening, Marcus was surprised to see a pair of lanterns stop outside his tent. The flap was drawn aside to reveal Luana standing in the dark night, flanked by two large guards. These men held the two lanterns which Marcus had noticed, and he was amused at the incongruous sight of such burly men holding the dainty lanterns adorned with fine filigree patterns which Luana insisted her escorts bore. With the innate confidence which came from never being refused, the bold harlot strode straight into the tent and approached Marcus as he sat alone cleaning his armour. Most officers let their attendants care for their weapons and armour, but Marcus preferred to maintain the tools of his trade personally. He reasoned that it was his own life which depended on these weapons and no attendant could ever have a similarly strong motivation to care for them as assiduously. The guards let the flap fall shut behind Luana, and then turned their backs to the tent, standing as silent sentinels whilst their mistress was within.

'Well aren't you going to unwrap your present?' asked Luana as she pirouetted in her fine tunic in front or Marcus with her hands raised above her head. The cloth shimmered in the lamp light and Marcus saw that it was almost transparent.

'I'm sorry, I think there must be some mistake,' replied Marcus, stunned by her direct approach. She is certainly an attractive woman thought Marcus, the little turn she had artfully executed had caused her musky perfume to drift towards Marcus, and the scent was intoxicating.

'I am a gift from the Gods,' explained Luana. 'They have sent me to show you pleasures you never imagined possible,' continued the self-assured new arrival.

Luana had approached Marcus during the brief exchange, and she now ran her soft hands through his blond hair as she stood in front of him. Marcus tensed as the familiar sensation brought back memories of Rebecca and their recent separation. The experienced courtesan noted the contractions in his muscles and stepped gracefully to stand behind him. As she moved, one trailing decorative sleeve brushed across Marcus's face, enveloping him in the enticing fragrance which Luana knew to employ so effectively. The mysterious material was cool and soft to the touch, as it glided over Marcus's face. With adept fingers she massaged his shoulders and ran her hands appreciatively over his powerful shoulders. Marcus was still nonplussed at the unexpected and unexplained arrival of this artful woman, but despite himself he began to relax. He let out a contented sigh as her practised hands pummelled his aching muscles. Luana then lent forward to remove the brooch from Marcus's tunic. One moment her hand was closing deftly around the tiger brooch with its bright lapis lazuli stone, and the next she found herself flipped onto her back staring up at the man she had been trying to seduce. Her wrist was clasped in an iron grip and Marcus was fully alert. His eyes were fixed on the brooch which Luana still held in her hand.

'I was removing your tunic, not stealing your tawdry trinkets,' she explained with an angry spark of pride burning in her eyes.

Marcus apologised and raised the stunned courtesan to her feet, his response had been so fast she did not realise what had happened until she was lying on the carpeted floor. He offered no explanation for his reaction but calmly assured the girl that he meant her no harm. However, Luana was still very startled and her hands trembled as she returned the blue brooch to Marcus. She was evidently shocked and Marcus led her to the couch before he poured out some wine. The reversal in roles had been so quick and so unexpected that Luana was still dazed as Marcus passed her the wine and continued to reassure her. She was so startled by the shock of what had happened that Luana now began to cry. Marcus sat beside her and consoled her as she cried daintily against his broad chest, too daintily thought Marcus. As her sobs receded and her caresses became increasingly affectionate, Marcus had his suspicions confirmed. The resourceful harlot had adopted another guise and was now trying to seduce him with her injured innocence. The angry spark of wounded pride in her eyes had been a much more accurate reflection of her personality than the crocodile tears she now employed.

The process continued for some time, with Luana adopting different guises in her attempt to seduce Marcus. Whilst he admired the skill with which Luana played each part, Marcus had no desire to sleep with her. His heart was still fixed on Rebecca and he parried and rejected each of the advances Luana made. In the end she sighed with frustration and scooping up the wine she sank into the couch pillows and stared at Marcus.

'You're the first man I have not been able to seduce, and it's driving me wild,' she declared frankly.

'Do you not find me attractive?' she enquired, stretching out one smooth leg out from underneath her translucent gown.

'You are certainly an impressive woman!' replied Marcus, admiring both her beauty and her forceful character.

'Well then, what is it?' Luana demanded.

'You know,' continued the courtesan, before Marcus had the chance to reply to her question, 'I am discovering what it must be like for all those drooling legionaries, gaping at me as I pass. Thanks to you, Marcus, I will now know what it is like to long for something unobtainable. I suppose I should be grateful, but I'm annoyed instead.'

Marcus thought of telling her about Rebecca and the place she occupied in his affections, but he decided the details should be kept private and merely told Luana that he loved another. Luana finally accepted this answer, and the two then spent many hours in conversation. Marcus was fascinated by the artful and bold lady, and she was willing to share the experience she had gained from her many adventures. Frustrated at being unable to seduce Marcus, Luana talked about her past conquests, as a substitute and consolation. In her conversation she paraded her previous conquests before Marcus, describing how she had seduced each of them. As the night progressed, and Luana continued drinking Marcus's wine, she revealed to him some of the secrets of the oldest profession in the world. Luana taught Marcus the art of reading subconscious body signals. She showed him such details as the barely discernible flaring of the nostrils when someone breathed in deeply as they were aroused with lust or anger, or the typical eye movements when someone was preparing to lie. Marcus also took the opportunity to ask the courtesan about the fabric of her dress, she explained that it was silk which had been especially woven to ensure it was translucent. Marcus had encountered this fabled material in Reuben's storeroom, but this was the first time he had seen it made into garments. Now he appreciated why it was so valuable, for the dress was certainly alluring, and Marcus still remembered the soft cool feel of the cloth as it had brushed across his face. Luana gave a tipsy giggle, and brushed her sleeve across his face a second time as if she could read his thoughts.

In that one night, Marcus learnt much about his fellow men and the wiles of these working women along with the skills they employed to survive in their dangerous occupation. As the faint glow of the pre-dawn sun heralded the start of a new day, Luana rose to leave. She kissed Marcus lightly on each cheek and ran her fingers over his tiger brooch with a mischievous flicker in her eyes.

'I want you to promise me something,' said Luana.

'What is it?' asked Marcus.

'Promise first,' insisted Luana, 'I assure you it will not be to your detriment.'

Indebted and fascinated by this marvellous lady, Marcus promised, silently hoping it would not be a pendant or ring she wanted him to wear. He did not like wearing jewellery and the brooch and pendant were ample.

'I want you to promise you will never tell anyone what has happened tonight, or rather not happened,' said Luana, a faint pout accompanying her final words.

With relief and a smile, Marcus complied. Upon which she spun imperiously on her heel and departed, outwardly as confident and triumphal as when she arrived. Marcus proved as discrete as his word, and Luana's reputation as an irresistible harlot remained intact.

After the cavalry had arrived, Crassus swiftly organised a public offering to the Gods and requested their blessing on the expedition. Although he was not overly concerned with Divine Will, Crassus knew that it would ease the minds of some of his men who were still disturbed by the curses of the tribune Ateius and the accidents which had hampered their naval crossing from Brundisium. Crassus was far more interested in completing the reading of Lucretius's book, which Publius had duly delivered. The old miser was determined to find what made the book so valuable in the author's eyes, however to placate the legionaries he went through the motions of sacrificing to the Gods. In front of the large temple which faced the forum Crassus and Publius made offerings at the altars of Venus and Juno. As Venus Genetrix, the former was worshipped as the mother of the legendary Aeneas, the founder of the Roman people. Venus also possessed the titles Venus Victrix, the bringer of victory, and Venus Felix, the bringer of good fortune, making her a particularly appropriate deity to invoke before a campaign. Furthermore Venus was a goddess of Nature, and was closely connected with the arrival of spring, which also commenced the campaigning season. Juno was the patron goddess of Rome and the Roman territories, so her protection was invoked both for the Roman forces in Syria, and the garrisons which had been left in Mesopotamia. The principal feast-day for Juno was called the Matronalia and occurred on the March 1st. The priests had indicated that this would be an opportune day for the Army to leave Syria and Crassus had finalised his plans accordingly.

Crassus and his son duly performed the required sacrifices, unconcerned about the outcome as the priests had strict orders to 'find' favorable omens. The soothsayers had privately warned Crassus of the unfavorable omens they had observed. However, he had made clear his determination to continue and warned the priests of the dire consequences for those who failed to support his invasion. The ceremonies were complete and Publius walked in front of his father as they left the temple. They were exchanging observations about the farcical nature of these ceremonies as they progressed. Outside the forum was packed with legionaries and auxiliaries who had come to witness the sacrifices. They filled the square and were crowded onto the steps of the basilica and even the bases of the fountains and statues which adorned the forum. As Publius left the temple doorway he tripped and fell, in full view of the crowd of spectators. Crassus was following close behind him, and stumbled over his son, collapsing right on top of him. A smug look crossed the high priest's face briefly before he joined the aides and acolytes who rushed to assist the men as they regained their feet. But by then the damage had been done. The soldiers who had gathered to witness the offering were by nature the more superstitious members of the Army, and they now gasped in shock at such an ill omen. Few of them were convinced by the subsequent announcement issued by the officers declaring that a loose slab in the temple doorway was the cause of the incident. The temple priests were coerced into performing a very ostentatious 'repair' to the stone floor, but the theatrical repairs did little to reassure the worried men, and when the Army set forth on March 1st there was a palpable sense of unease amongst the men.

The army proceeded without incident for the first two days. On the third day they reached the Euphrates River, without any sign of the Parthians. The men were beginning to forget their fears and talk once again turned to the loot which they hoped to acquire in Parthia. The army camped by the River that night and then progressed downstream to a place called Zeugma the following day. The crossing commenced in the morning and was initially progressing well. The army and its full supply train constituted a large body of men and beasts, so the crossing was a sizeable military operation in itself. The engineers had worked through the night to construct a bridge, and as soon as the sun rose they put the final touches to the wooden structure. Once the bridge was in place, the army began to cross. Marcus was amongst the first to cross as the cavalry formed an advance guard. The Army still followed defensive military tactics, despite the apparent absence of any opposition. An army was particularly vulnerable when crossing a river, for a sudden surprise attack could split the force in two, and this could mean men were separated from their supplies and in the worst case even their weapons or officers. The rest of the force continued to cross, bringing up the supplies and beasts whilst the cavalry scouted the area and marked out a camp ground on the far side of the river. As the afternoon progressed the brisk morning breeze developed into a strong wind. The bridge was still usable but it began to shake a little as the wind whipped at the wooden structure. Crassus refused to halt the crossing and instructed the officers to hurry their men across as quickly as possible. These orders had scarcely been issued when dark clouds were discernible forming over the hills to the north east.

The thunderstorm which ensued was as intense as it was unexpected. The dark clouds swept down over the plain and fierce winds whipped up the River. On both sides of the bridge the horses and other animals were panicking and struggling to break free. Thunder and lightening arrived shortly after the first drops of rain. The first two bolts of lightening struck the provisional campground which the advance guard had marked out. The terrified men stared in amazement as the lightening also threatened to cause a stampede amongst the horses and pack animals. The drovers and cavalrymen struggled to control their charges as the storm raged. An unfortunate groom was crossing the bridge with one of Crassus's war horses when the lightening struck. The horse was a large stallion, magnificently apparelled and caparisoned with costly trappings. At the first bolt of lightening the stallion reared and tugged at its reins. The second bolt caused it to panic and it charged along, dragging the terrified groom with it. Finding its way blocked by a wagon, the stallion leapt over the side of the bridge, in full view of the army, both groom and horse were drowned in the waters, which were a seething torrent by now.

The storm was mercifully brief, and after it had subsided the army were able to complete the crossing. The bridge had been damaged during the storm, but it was swiftly repaired. On the Parthian side of the river, a new campground was selected and the more resourceful officers set about preparing things as best they could. They knew that a dry bed and a hot meal did much to quell the worries of superstitious men, and consequently they began setting up the camp and distributing the food. As the baggage train had become confused the officers had to improvise with whatever supplies they could find in the disarray. The first food supplies to arrive were promptly opened and distributed. As chance would have it, these consisted of lentils and salt. The zealous Macedonian officer in charge thought nothing of this as he distributed the rations to his Roman legionaries. He was a little perturbed at their strange expressions but put this down to the shock of the storm and continued his work. To Romans salt and lentils were foods appropriate only to a funeral as they are given as offerings to the dead. The Macedonian officer was unaware of this custom and he had unwittingly committed a grave error in his attempt to improve the situation. The Romans were on the verge of despair and it took the swift intervention and all the persuasive assurances of the other officers to restore their spirits.

Crassus was vexed by the difficulties of the crossing. He refused to pay heed to the omens, yet he was simultaneously forced to take them into account as so many of his men were influenced by them. He was riled that something, in which he had no faith, was able to alter his plans and influence his decisions. Crassus was in the new campground, debating his next move with mounting ire, when a report arrived from the priests. After the storm, they had gone to collect the seven silver eagles which constituted the most important standards of the seven legions in the invading force. The eagles were always amongst the last parts of a force to cross a river, for if they fell into enemy hands the legions in questions remained in disgrace until their standard was recovered. If a standard was permanently lost, then the legion to which it belonged was disbanded, never to be reformed. The officer in charge of the eagle was the *aquilifer*, who wore a lion skin headdress in recognition of the great honor which came with the position. One of the *aquilifers* had summoned the priests earlier that afternoon. When he had gone to pick up the eagle, he found that the pole on which the eagle was mounted was stuck fast in the ground. It had taken six men to pull the pole out, and further rumors were circulating about the portent of this ill omen. The priests now informed Crassus that it was imperative to publicly sacrifice to the Gods before the soldiers became irreversibly down-hearted.

Crassus reluctantly recognized the truth of their assessment, and with ill grace he accepted their advice. Personally, he reasoned that the problem was likely to have occurred by the heavy rain softening clay deposits in the soil, which in drying then set around the standard's pole. However, the intricacies of alluvial petrology were not likely to reassure the superstitious legionaries and so Crassus duly ordered the sacrifice. An ostentatious offering was hastily organised to thank the Gods for the safe crossing, despite the terrors of the storm the entire army had only lost a few animals and one groom in the crossing. By any standards this was a successful operation, and a public spectacle was called for to focus the men's attention on this, rather than the bad omens which had accompanied the crossing. A large platform was duly erected, high enough to ensure that the event would be visible to all the men. Then in front of the amassed Army, Crassus attended the priests as they officiated over an elaborate offering for their safe passage into Parthia. After the preparatory rituals, the high priest handed Crassus the entrails. The bloody organs slipped out of his hands and the crowd let out a gasp. Crassus endeavored to recover from his blunder; he laughed nervously and quickly called out;

'See what it is to be an old man, but I shall hold my sword fast enough.'

After the offerings were complete, Crassus took the opportunity to address the Army. He encouraged the men and spoke of the wealth they would acquire, the weakness and innate inferiority of the barbarians and the invincible might of the Roman legions. Crassus informed the men that they would return via Armenia rather than cross the Euphrates again. This decision had been prompted by the high waters of the River, overnight the sudden torrential rainfall had drained into the

River and it was now a raging torrent. The bridge had been severely damaged, and the River would be difficult to cross for some time. Crassus had decided to use this to his advantage, and he announced that he was going to destroy the bridge. This move was designed to show the men that retreat was not an option, and only after defeating the Parthians could they return via Armenia. As Crassus was encouraging his soldiers and outlining his plans, he made an unfortunate slip in his choice of words. After indicating the bridge that was in the process of being destroyed he announced that this action was designed to ensure none of them returned. Although it would have been a simple matter to explain that he meant none of the soldiers would return by that route, or that none could desert, Crassus was too stubborn and he refused to correct himself despite the gasps and groans of the soldiers.

The next day the Romans broke camp early, they were eager to leave the scene of such ominous occurrences. The Army marched south along the banks of the River. The convenient water supply and the flat terrain made their journey easy, and after a few days their spirits rose again. On the fourth day after crossing, the scouts reported envoys from the Parthians were approaching. Crassus hastily arrayed his force to make a daunting impression on the envoy and set up a luxurious tent in which to receive the Parthians. The Parthian ambassador declined Crassus's hospitality and delivered his message after the most cursory of formalities. King Orodes declared that if the Army was sent by the Roman Senate then he announced there would be war. But if, as he understood was the case, Crassus had invaded Parthia for his own private profit against the wishes of his countrymen, then the King would take pity on his senility and allow the Romans to depart unhindered. Crassus boastfully retorted that he would make his reply in the Parthian capital of

Seleucia, once the Romans had captured the city. In response, Vagises, the senior Parthian ambassador laughed and showing the palm of his hand he declared;

'Hair will grow here before you will see Seleucia.'

In this bold reply, Vagises was mindful of the fate which had befallen a previous Parthian ambassador. In 95BC, Sulla had received an ambassador from Mithradates II who wished to conclude a peace treaty. Sulla had arrogantly assumed the overture signified the submission of the Parthians and agreed to a treaty with such contempt that Mithradates executed his own ambassador for failing to uphold the honor of Parthia. After their brief exchange the Parthian ambassadors returned to King Orodes and told him the Romans chose war.

9

PARTHIA, 53 BC

THE SIGHT OF the unstoppable Roman force marching into Parthia was truly impressive, and Crassus felt a sense of elation as he surveyed the large Army which he commanded. Crassus had ridden onto a small mound accompanied by his aides and bodyguard, and he now remained in this elevated position whilst his Army marched past below. A surge of pride and vanity flushed his wrinkled cheeks and the wind played with his greying hair as he sat in the saddle and he picked out the glittering armour of his son. Publius rode at the forefront of the Gallic cavalry, and his embossed breastplate sparkled in the sun. Despite the wrinkles in Crassus's face, it was still easy to observe the lines of determination and the square jar which reflected his stubborn character. Both Publius and Crassus were in fine physical shape, they trained regularly and maintained the same high level of fitness which they expected from their men. Due to their wealth, prestige and physique both father and son possessed a remarkable physical presence which struck all those who met them.

Crassus now breathed deeply and squared his shoulders whilst he overlooked the powerful body of men filling the plain beneath him. Despite his great wealth, Crassus had never given himself over to the lavish indulgencies of the richest Romans.

In his private life, he chose simple fare and he maintained his body with a regime of exercises and cold baths. It was only to impress his fellow Romans that Crassus spent such sums on his costly villas and celebrated chefs which bolstered his reputation. His tastes remained austere and he was enjoying the campaign, untroubled by the minor hardships of life on the move. Unlike his last campaign against the slave army of Spartacus, this expedition was in an entirely new environment and Crassus admired the rugged beauty of the landscape. It struck him as incongruous to see such fecund fields border on the barren desert; his eye followed with interest, the clear green line marking the fertile region in which water was available.

The soldiers advanced in orderly formation, with each distinct unit maintaining its place in the column, whilst the auxiliary cavalry scouted the surrounding territory. The auxiliary cavalry had been recruited from tribes who lived in similar terrain and they were well-equipped and adapted for the Parthian environment. They were much less heavily armed than the Gallic cavalry who formed the vanguard of the advancing force. If the occasion arose, this cavalry screen was ready to engage any attacking force they met, whilst the rest of the Army closed ranks and moved into battle formation. However, the terrain was so flat that there was insufficient cover to conceal an enemy force, and there was little chance of an ambush or surprise attack. The River protected their right flank as well as providing a ready water supply, and the Army progressed with relative ease and confidence. Provisions were brought by boat, and the soldiers only had to forage the surrounding countryside for fuel. The confidence of the troops began to mount as they encountered no opposition, and the rigours of the journey were far less than they had feared. They began to despise the Parthians as cowardly barbarians who would not face the legionaries in combat.

Marcus was glad that the Gallic cavalry were providing the vanguard. It was the most honorable and prestigious position to occupy and Marcus was eager to excel in this campaign and put into practise the military theories he had learnt. He had responded well to the demands and challenges of life in the legions and his superiors had remarked that his conduct could soon earn him a promotion. The vanguard also had the advantage of being the most comfortable position to occupy during a journey as it did not mean marching in the dust raised by the other units. The progress of 36,000 men and the cavalry mounts over the plain stirred up a considerable amount of dust. At the rear of the convoy, the baggage train was covered with a layer of thick dust each day, to the extent that the wagons were unintentionally camouflaged against the brown earth. As each day brought a fresh blanket of dust, the wagon drivers soon stopped trying to remove it, and the wagons soon adopted a uniform color and appearance as the dust obscured any differences.

Unlike some of the other officers, Marcus was relatively unconcerned about the appearance of his men whilst on campaign; he only insisted that they maintain their equipment assiduously and took good care of their mounts. With the dry desert conditions and omnipresent dust, it was necessary for the legionaries to clean and oil their armour more regularly. Once grains of sand became imbedded in the armour they swiftly caused it to stiffen and this restricted the mobility of the soldiers. Ingrained sand also rubbed at the saddles and bridles, so these had to be meticulously cleaned on a regular basis to ensure their reliability; otherwise the sand would weaken the bridles and straps. Once a grain of sand was embedded in a rope or strap, the continued movement would cause the grain to wear away the internal fibres and the rope would soon snap under tension. Whilst some officers maintained that their soldiers were only as good as their commander, Marcus believed that a soldier's equipment and weapons were equally important. He knew that weary legionaries on campaign were often reluctant to clean and maintain their equipment diligently. Yet when they came to battle it was on these very weapons that they relied for their survival, consequently Marcus carried out regular inspections and punished those who failed to meet his exacting standards of maintenance.

The numerous ill-omens on the campaign to date had no effect on Marcus; he maintained his atheist views and amicably teased his superstitious men. Over an extended period of service it is remarkable how much any group of soldiers comes to reflect the officer who commanded them. Through a barely discernible osmotic process the men gradually took on the character of their commander, and occasionally the centurion acquired traits from his legionaries. Marcus had now served with this century for over a year and a strong bond had grown between the legionaries and their centurion. Marcus was privy to their jokes and when he was in conversation with his fellow officers he had to refrain from using any of the nicknames employed by the legionaries. The century had lost three men in Gaul, but since then there had been no fatalities. When one of his legionaries named Gnaeus, had fallen ill during the voyage across the Mediterranean, Marcus had personally tended the sick man. When they landed in Alexandria, Marcus had summoned a physician and paid him out of his own purse. Gnaeus duly recovered before they left Alexandria, and he was currently riding in the cavalry screen to the left of Marcus.

This simple act of consideration had furthered the cohesion, which was forming amongst the century who now obeyed their commander out of respect rather than fear. Roman officers were legendary for their disciplinarian ideals and the severe punishments they employed. Many of the more conservative commanders openly declared that it was necessary for the legionaries to fear their commander more than the enemy, as this was the surest was to ensure they did not retreat, desert or neglect their duties. Marcus disagreed, and he commanded with a different approach; he believed that mutual respect was the surest basis on which to deal with his legionaries. The men obeyed Marcus, just as all the legionaries obeyed their officers, but Marcus's unit worked with a greater sense of unity and satisfaction.

As Crassus sat on the mound surveying his Army, the scouts returned to report that the surrounding area was deserted, although they had found the tracks of a large number of horses. These tracks all lead away from the Romans, and the overly-confident officers readily interpreted the tracks as evidence of a Parthian retreat. Rumors to this effect soon spread through the ranks, and the legionaries were once again buoyed with optimism. The legionaries' morale was a strangely fickle thing, and it could swing either way by the smallest chance occurrence. The next day, two Arab chieftains called Ariamnes and Alchaudonius arrived at the Romans' camp bringing 6,000 light horsemen to join the Roman force. The swollen Roman convoy was now huge, and the soldiers together with the camp-followers and supply train numbered well over 50,000 people. The two chieftains came from the Arab kingdom of Nabatea which had its capital at Petra. Ariamnes had served with Pompey previously in the same area and some of Pompey's veterans now recognized him, Ariamnes made much of this and he portrayed his unexpected arrival as a reunion of old comrades. The cunning and duplicitous chieftain now set about his mission of persuading Crassus to march across the open desert, rather than follow the River. The desert route was the shortest and quickest way of striking at the Parthian capital of Seleucia. However, without the River protecting the Romans' flank, the Parthian cavalry would be able to surround the invading force in the open plains, and the desert route necessitated a much tougher journey. Ariamnes was a wily and persuasive man; he commended Pompey as his friend and benefactor, whilst professing his desire to fight against the oppressive Parthians. Crassus and his aides welcomed the chieftains and listened attentively to their advice.

Gaius Cassius Longinus was serving as Crassus's quaestor, and the ambitious Roman was eager to gain as much as possible from the campaign. The only thing noteworthy about Cassius's appearance were his restless eyes, he was perpetually glancing from one thing to the next as if searching for a more advantageous object to behold. Despite his flighty eyes, Cassius was an astute and practical man who knew that it would greatly benefit his career in the Senate if he could establish a successful military reputation. Cassius was an intelligent man and he now cautioned Crassus against leaving the relative security of the River for the unknown hinterland, especially as the nature of the nearby horsemen had not yet been established. At this point Ariamnes intervened to explain that the tracks which the Roman scouts had found were those of the Parthians in full flight. He furthered his claims by stating that the Parthians were encumbered with all their most valued goods and chattels, as they endeavored to save their possessions from the advancing Romans. Ariamnes offered to lead the Romans after the fleeing Parthians and confidently announced that the Roman Army would easily be able to overtake the heavily burdened Parthian horsemen. Cassius argued against this proposal, pointing out that the Romans were already travelling in unfamiliar territory and the reports had not yet arrived from all the scouts. The bulk of the Roman Army consisted of the heavily armed legionaries who fought and travelled on foot. Cassius counselled against attempting to pursue any mounted force across open terrain with infantry, however burdened the horsemen might be with possessions and baggage. In his ardent desire for glory, Crassus refused to heed the advice of his officers and chose to pursue the unknown Parthian horsemen with his foot soldiers. He accepted Ariamnes' offer to act as a guide and promptly gave the orders to follow the Arab chieftain. With this decision the Roman Army left the cultivated riparian countryside and they marched away from the Euphrates and into the inhospitable desert.

At first the terrain was relatively pleasant and the route was easy, but as the amount of vegetation decreased, the barren landscape made it increasingly difficult for the infantry to march. The soft sand, shortage of water and lack of vegetation or fuel made for a gruelling journey. Six days after the Army had left the River; morale amongst the legionaries began to drop as the soldiers struggled further into the desert with evident reluctance. The following day messengers arrived from King Artavasdes reporting that the additional troops he had promised could not be sent to join the Roman Army, due to the pressure of unexpected Parthian attacks in Armenia. The Parthian King Orodes, had taken the bulk of his forces into Armenia where he was harrying the population and laying waste to the countryside to punish the Armenians for supporting Crassus. Crassus was strongly advised to join forces with Artavasdes in Armenia, or failing that, to proceed into Parthia via the Armenian foothills where sufficient water and supplies could be guaranteed. The messengers specifically warned Crassus against taking the route directly through the open country which was ideal terrain for the Parthian cavalry. However, Crassus took no heed of the warnings and declared he would make Artavasdes pay for his treachery once he had dealt with the Parthians. With these bold words

Crassus proceeded even deeper into the desert. The Roman commander did not even deign to reply to his Armenian ally, but continued the march with his characteristic stubbornness and arrogance. Publius fully supported his father in this decision, the bold young man had declared that it was unbecoming for a Roman Army to take such a circuitous route rather than strike directly at their target.

The silver-tongued Ariamnes had been artfully praising the Roman forces which constituted Crassus's Army and now he began to taunt the Romans for the slow speed of their progress. Ariamnes implied that the Roman officers were deliberately stalling in order to avoid conflict with the fleeing Parthians. He needled the commanders for the inability of their men to march quickly through the unfamiliar terrain and jokingly questioned their virility. At the same time, Ariamnes skilfully deflected the questions and accusations from the disgruntled Roman officers and made ostentatious efforts to cheer up the troops. Next Ariamnes declared that he would proceed in front of the Romans in order to harry the retreating Parthians, and hamper their flight. Before he rode off, Ariamnes publicly counselled Crassus to proceed with all haste, lest the Parthians be defeated and his Arabs seize all their goods as booty before the Romans caught up with them. The day after the wily Arab had departed with his 6,000 horsemen, Crassus was seen inadvertently wearing a black cloak instead of the scarlet garment proper to Roman generals on campaign. The superstitious legionaries made much of this momentary lapse, even though Crassus changed as soon as he noticed the effect it had caused. After the latest taunt from Ariamnes, Crassus increased the speed of the Army and ordered his tired infantry to march at cavalry pace, despite the inhospitable climate and arduous terrain. Even the cavalry were finding it hard to travel at their normal pace due to the shifting sands and the large dunes. For the heavily armed infantry the pace was gruelling and they were soon extremely weary.

As the fatigued Roman force neared the town of Carrhae, the scouts began to return in a state of alarm and panic. They reported that some of the auxiliary cavalry, who had been scouting the plain in front, had been attacked and killed by the Parthians. The scouts also reported that the main body of Parthian horsemen were even now deploying ahead for immediate battle. This information was totally unsuspected, and it threatened to throw the exhausted Roman forces into disarray. Crassus initially opted for an open order formation, and he ordered the Army to split into a number of columns leaving a gap between each column, with the auxiliary cavalry occupying the wings. The Gallic cavalry were to be held in reserve, either to charge a weak point in the enemy line, or re-enforce a beleaguered Roman unit. In this open formation the Roman forces would extend across much of the plain; this classic military procedure was appropriate to the open nature of the battlefield and would ensure that the Romans could not be easily surrounded. The Romans were busy manoeuvring into this open formation, when Crassus changed his mind and ordered the forces to be drawn up in a closed formation. The Romans now formed a large square, with twelve cohorts supported by cavalry and light infantry protecting each side. Whilst this formation would not prevent the Romans from being surrounded, it was designed to ensure that their forces were evenly distributed with no weak flank or rear which could be taken or turned by the enemy. The square was large enough to contain the baggage train, which was securely positioned within the walls of soldiers. Crassus took up position in the center of the square, whilst his son Publius commanded the left and Cassius commanded the right.

Marcus and his century were drawn up on the left of the

square. They were in position behind the rows of legionaries and could rapidly move to aid any weak points in the wall in the event of an attack. Publius was disappointed at being in a reserve position; he publicly voiced his determination to avenge himself on the Parthians for the recent rigours of the journey. In Gaul, Publius had led his men with the heart of a lion and his courageous charges had always carried the field. Fortunately the imprudent nature of his tactics had never been revealed, and few realized that he commanded with the brain of a mule. Publius had never studied military tactics, and relied entirely on bravery and boldness to carry him through each engagement. Now Publius loudly joked that he intended to slay one Parthian for each of the many blisters he had acquired in the long journey, and the other officers followed suit with similar boasts. The Gallic cavalry had enjoyed a highly successful campaign against the barbarian tribes in Transalpine Gaul. They were more heavily armed than the cavalry of the barbarian tribes and had managed to rout most opponents with one concerted charge. Publius was now eager to employ this tried and tested technique against the Parthians. Publius was impatient to engage the enemy and he kept drawing his sword and then returning it to its sheath as he shifted in his saddle and controlled the nervous fine stallion he rode.

Meanwhile, Marcus was attending to the small details which ensured his century would be able to function promptly and efficiently when their orders came. The Gallic cavalry were unaccustomed to the hot and arid environment, however Marcus was still determined to ensure his century were fully prepared for battle. He ordered all his men to carry out a final check on their weapons, armour and saddles. Next he announced a temporary amnesty whilst he inspected the horizon, and any non-essential baggage or equipment they were carrying was to be left in a supply wagon. Standing orders prohibited the carrying of non-essential equipment whilst on campaign, but Marcus turned a blind eye as the wagon soon filled with wineskins, spare food, gambling dice and a variety of souvenirs which had been 'liberated' from the territory they had passed through. There was even a pair of fighting cocks which had somehow been smuggled along by one artful legionary. Marcus told the wagon driver he held him personally accountable for the contents of the wagon and then sent him back to his position in the baggage train. With their lightened loads the Gallic cavalry proceeded inside the closed formation, eager for action and tense with excitement.

Unbeknown to the Romans, the Parthian forces were equally adept at attacking forces in both open and closed order. They had developed very simple tactics which exploited the strengths of their two types of cavalry with lethal efficiency. Blissfully unaware of this, the Roman Army marched on until they came to a small river called the Balissus. The soldiers were greatly relieved to see a source of water after the difficulties of their desert journey and they eagerly filled their water-skins. Cassius and the other senior officers suggested that the Army should halt by the River and camp there for the night, whilst the scouts were sent to ascertain further information about the Parthian forces. The officers reasoned that the men would be in much better condition to fight after they had recovered from their arduous forced march. The adrenalin rush which had flowed through the Army at the prospect of action had soon given way to fatigue when no Parthians appeared and the legionaries were dragging their feet. However, Publius continued to urge his father to proceed and engage the enemy at the earliest opportunity. He argued vociferously that the River would still be there after they had defeated the Parthians, whereas the Parthians could escape if they stopped overnight at the River. Crassus was swayed by his son's argument, and he willingly accepted the advice which concurred so neatly with his own desires and intentions.

Crassus ordered the Army to maintain their formation, and all those that wished were to eat and drink as they stood in their ranks. This was an unusual procedure and generally avoided because of its inefficiency. The process of feeding an Army was complex enough when the soldiers were in camp, but to perform the same feat whilst they maintained ranks was extremely impractical. The standard staple ration for the Roman legionaries was wheat. Each century received its ration and they would then grind the corn to bake their own bread. They baked unleavened loaves, and each one was then stamped with an insignia to show the century to which it belonged. On campaign the baking was done in keyhole shaped field ovens, which were constructed from stone and mud. However, on this occasion the men did not have time to construct ovens and bake the round loaves. Instead the corn was coarsely ground and then cooked into a thick gruel, along with any available meat or vegetables. Marcus had secured a pair of goats for his century, and tough though the meat was, it made a welcome addition to the gruel. Beef and pork were the preferred meats of the legionaries, but it was impossible to transport cows or pigs in such dry and barren terrain so the soldiers had to settle for mutton and goat meat.

Before all of the men had received their rations, let alone cooked or eaten them, the orders came to advance until the enemy were sighted. There were grumbles of discontent from many soldiers and from their empty stomachs, as the men reluctantly obeyed. Crassus led the Army on at full pace, as if they were in pursuit of a routed foe, or rushing to relieve a beleaguered unit. Normally an advancing force would stop for frequent breaks to ensure that the men arrived fresh at a battle, however in his impatience Crassus relentlessly rushed his Army onwards. Marcus and his century retained their position on the left of the square. The consideration and efficiency of their centurion had ensured that all of the men had eaten something, however hastily. Marcus was annoyed that the cavalry had not been given sufficient time to rest their mounts. The horses had been watered while the men ate, but there had not been time to distribute any fodder to the hungry beasts, and their fat reserves had been depleted by the harsh desert march. In the first week of the campaign the men had also marched off any excess fat from their sedate life in camp. The Army that crossed the Euphrates had been a force of lean and fit men; whereas now the desert journey had weakened both men and mounts considerably.

The Army maintained their square formation as they waded across the shallow River and climbed the other side. As they reached the crest of one large dune the Romans finally beheld the force they had pursued so ardently. The Parthians were arrayed in battle order across a small dry plain. There were no infantry in evidence and the battle-hardened legionaries were confident they could rout the Parthian cavalry. The Romans scoffed with delight when they saw that the Parthian force numbered less than a quarter of the Roman Army. Behind the Parthian cavalry, the soldiers could see the baggage train and the burdened animals which they already considered as their loot. The Roman rank and file universally pardoned Crassus for his relentless pace and they prepared to defeat the Parthian force as swiftly as possible. The soldiers were also relieved to see that there did not appear to be any of the heavily armed cataphracts, these were the elite Parthian cavalry who fought in virtually impenetrable suits of armour. These heavily armed cavalry were also known by the nickname of *clibanarius* or 'oven man', as the armour was so hot to wear. The Romans had encountered, and defeated cataphracts during Pompey's campaign against the Armenians, although it had been a tough fight. On that occasion the legionaries had attacked the cataphracts from the flank, and the legionaries had followed their orders to strike at the exposed hind legs of the horses. Once the horsemen were unseated from their mounts they were virtually defenceless; as the extreme weight of their armour generally rendered them immobile and they were easy pickings for the legionaries.

The cataphracts were drawn from the Parthian aristocracy, for it cost a lot to equip and arm a cataphract and it was only the nobility who could afford this expense. The Parthian cataphracts wore helmets of bronze or iron, some of which included face and neck guards of scales or mail armour. The helmets were often adorned with plumes of horse hair, which were dyed to indicate the wearer's tribe. The cataphract's torso was protected by a corselet of scale or mail armour, usually made of iron. The arms were covered by laminated armour which was either in a number of pieces, or attached into one long arm-guard which encased the arms from the shoulder to the knuckles. The legs were protected with plate or mail armour which ran all the way to the feet which were covered by mail 'socks' and foot armour. The primary weapon of the cataphracts was a long lance which ended with a sharp sword-like blade at one end, and a butt spike at the other. The cataphracts then sported a secondary weapon of their choice for close combat; this was often a sword, axe or mace. The development of such heavily armoured cavalry had been facilitated by the breeding of weight-carrying chargers from the Nisaean breed of horses in Parthia. These horses were originally closely guarded by the Turanians within the walled oasis city of Er-shih, but other tribes soon sought and acquired them. The Nisaean horses had strong arched necks, powerful shoulders and withers and short thick legs. They did not possess the classic beauty or elegance of the Arab thoroughbreds, but they were far sturdier and could bear the heavily armoured cataphracts with ease.

Unlike the Roman Army, the Parthian force was not a professional body and each man provided his own armour and fought at the behest of his chieftain. This procedure enabled the Parthians to raise a large and loyal force at relatively short notice, without the expense of maintaining a standing army. However, they could not endure a long campaign as the men were needed at their homes to tend their herds and fields. The bulk of any force, therefore, consisted of mounted archers, for the Parthians were descended from nomadic tribes and horses still formed an essential part of their way of life. Horses formed a pivotal part of Parthian society and two centuries later when Justinus described the Parthians he said; 'On horses they go to war, to banquets, to public and private tasks and on them they travel, stay still, do business and chat.' The Parthian horse archers typically wore no armour, and relied on the speed of their mounts to keep them out of danger. The men wore leather or felt jackets and richly decorated trousers tucked into their boots. Trousers were in fact a nomadic invention, which had been developed as the garment most suitable for horseback riding. The horse archers sometimes wore protective leather over-trousers which covered their decorated trousers. They were armed with the Parthian recurved bow, which was carried in the left hand along with three or four arrows for rapid shooting. The main quiver was slung from the waist, along with a secondary weapon such as a dagger or short sword.

With an army formed of both cataphracts and mounted archers the Parthians had developed simple yet expedient military tactics. When faced with a force in closed order the cataphracts would charge, the momentum of this shock attack normally scattered the opponents and the mounted archers would then move in to pick off the disordered soldiers. In other circumstances, when the Parthians were faced with an enemy drawn up in open order, the mounted archers would approach and release a steady stream of arrows until their opponents were forced into a closed order. In a closed order the infantry were able to form a shield wall which would provide greater protection from the deadly arrows, however once in this position the cataphracts could then charge. The simple tactic of the Parthians ensured that any force which opposed them in open battle had to face the constant dilemma of choosing to fight in open or closed order.

The Parthian soldiers also possessed an important technical advantage in the superior design of their bows. Both the Romans and the Parthians used recurved bows; this meant that the bow curved back away from the string at the ends. However, unlike the Roman archers, the Parthian archers used reflexed composite bows which had a much greater range than the bows or javelins of the Romans. Reflexed bows were built around a wooden core with strips of horn on the underside side of the bow and sinews saturated in glue on the topside. The reflexed design enabled the bow to benefit from the different properties of horn and sinew. Horn is a material which stores energy efficiently under pressure, whilst sinew is a material which stores energy well under tension. Thus the composite bow provided a highly efficient weapon, which exploited the different physical properties of its components. Furthermore, the ears of the Parthian bows were slightly extended and reinforced with horn to increase their stability and improve their accuracy by providing a controlled release. The archers often used a horn thumb ring to ensure the smooth release of the bowstring without chafing the skin. The reflexed bows were also shorter than their Roman counterparts, and thus they were better adapted to use on horseback.

As expert and experienced archers, the Parthians made

full use of their superior bows. One tactic was for the Parthian archers to fire high arching volleys as well as more direct straight shots on a flatter trajectory. If their opponents were not in a dense formation it was difficult for a soldier to protect himself from incoming arrows on both trajectories. In addition the Parthian archers used whistling arrows. These were normal arrows to which simple wooden or bone whistles were attached. These devices did not render the arrows less lethal, in fact they somewhat reduced the arrow's accuracy; but the Parthians were fully aware of the disconcerting psychological effect, which the whistling could produce. The Parthian archery tactics also included the notable 'Parthian shot', which subsequently passed into many languages and was corrupted in English to give the expression 'parting shot'. To perform this manoeuvre a mounted archer would turn in the saddle and fire back over the rump of his mount. The Parthian shot allowed the mounted archers to continue attacking whilst they fell back, thus absolving them from the shame of flight. The cavalry frequently feigned a retreat, in order to draw out their opponents and thus provide an ideal opportunity for this manoeuvre.

The Parthian forces were under the command of Surena, a nobleman and relative of the King. Surena was the senior male member of the most powerful of the seven great Parthian clans. Unlike other monarchies, the Parthian crown did not necessarily pass to the son of the previous King, instead the leaders of the seven slans would meet to elect the successor from three possible royal lines. Although a young man, Surena already possessed a fearsome reputation in battle. He was a beautiful man, whose good looks and grace belied the force and strength with which he fought. With his elegance and grace, Surena also stood out amongst the rest of the Parthians who wore their shaggy hair gathered in a mass upon their foreheads after the Scythian style.

When he went into battle Surena habitually applied black kohl to his cheeks to reduce the glare from the sun, which reflected brightly from his polished armour. Kohl is a substance more frequently used by Arab women as eye-liner, and thus Surena was sometimes erroneously reported to have worn make-up in battle. Surena had fought with King Orodes whilst the latter was in exile from the upstart King Mithradates III. When the supporters of Orodes had stormed the great city of Seleucia, it was Surena who was the first man to scale the walls and win the honor of entering the city. As a result of his dedicated and brave support, Surena had earned the honor of placing the crown on Orodes' head at the coronation ceremony.

Surena now led a cavalry force composed of around 9,000 horse archers and 1,000 cataphracts who were drawn from his own clan. This close bond ensured that Surena could rely on the loyalty of his troops, who were anxious to support their leader and bring honor to their clan. The force was intended to probe and assess the Roman strength, whilst delaying their advance into Parthia. King Orodes then planned to bring his full army south from Armenia and unite with Surena to face the Roman Army. Surena wanted to engage the Romans, to test their strength. He knew from Ariamnes, who had betrayed Crassus and gone straight to Surena when he left the Romans, how tired the legionaries were, and Surena knew that if necessary he could retreat safely as the Romans were too exhausted to follow. With this important inside information Surena had decided to attack the Romans even though they outnumbered his force by more than four to one. Surena was an intelligent commander and he had arrayed his forces with care. The fearsome cataphracts were concealed behind the first ranks of horse archers, and they had covered their glittering armour with cloaks and hides. This device had fooled the Romans, who advanced boldly, reassured by the apparent absence of heavy cavalry.

As the Romans approached, Surena gave the signal and immediately the whole plain was filled with a terrible clamour. The unexpected noise rattled the Romans, but they focused on the small size of the force which opposed them and continued their advance. The din came from large kettle-drums with attached bronze bells which the Parthians had positioned all over the battlefield and they were now ringing and beating ceaselessly. The drums produced a disconcerting racket; it disorientated the advancing Romans who only used horns or trumpets during battle. The low timbre of the drums resembled the bellowing of beasts, and the Roman mounts shied and reared in response to the unfamiliar noise. When the Parthians had sufficiently alarmed the Romans with their noise, they threw off the coats and hides which covered their armour and revealed the large body of cataphracts in their midst. There were over 1,000 of these famed fighters in Surena's force and the bright sunlight reflected off their polished armour. The Parthians favored armour made from Margianian steel, a metal which was far superior to that used by the Romans. Consequently, the Parthians really were able to pierce Roman armour whilst remaining largely invulnerable to the Roman weapons, as had been attested by the messengers from the garrisons in Mesopotamia. The Roman Army had yet to see the veracity of these rumors, and they remained blissfully unaware of the situation as they beheld the Parthians arrayed in front of them. The officers attempted to rally the legionaries, and they pointed out to the men that these barbarian tricks had not increased the number of soldiers they faced, and the Romans still greatly outnumbered the Parthians.

When the Parthians had thrown off their cloaks they had also unfurled their banners, and these now floated in the wind above the cavalry as the Parthians advanced. The long banners were made of silk and the lustrous gleam was the first time many of the Roman soldiers had encountered this magical material. Subsequently the lustrous fabric was to become so highly sought in Rome that politicians complained at the exodus of gold which was leaving Rome to pay for this decadent cloth. However, this was the first time that most of the Romans had seen silk, and many of the legionaries stared in wonder at the fabric as they advanced. The Parthian standards were mounted on long poles and designed like Chinese dragons, so as the wind entered the mouth it filled the whole body of the banner and made them dance in a lively fashion. Initially, the Romans were further disconcerted by these apparently animate objects which moved and flew above the Parthian force, whilst glistening and shimmering in the sunlight. The barrage of unfamiliar sights and sounds unnerved the legionaries as they advanced.

Surena was clearly visible amongst the Parthian force; he rode in front of his troops, from whence both his height and magnificent apparel marked him out as their leader. A short cloak of lustrous red silk flicked in the wind behind him as he rode along in front of the Parthian ranks. The bright red color stood out clearly against the gleam of his steel armour, and Surena was the center of attention. He had initially planned to charge the center of the Roman square with his cataphracts, and break their formation so the mounted archers could then approach to attack the dispersed Romans. However, when Surena perceived the depth of the Roman ranks which formed the square he changed his tactics. The entire Parthian force pretended to break order and disperse, and through this ruse they were able to surround three sides of the Roman square before the legionaries were aware of what was happening. Crassus commanded his light infantry to charge the Parthians where they were closest to the Roman square. However, the charge achieved nothing as the Parthian cavalry merely retreated whilst firing such a barrage of arrows that the infantry hastily returned to the relative protection of the square. A tangible sense of unease now passed through the Roman ranks as they perceived the fearful power of the Parthian bows. The reflexed bows fired arrows at a much higher velocity than standard Roman archers, and these arrows pierced every kind of Roman armour including their heavy infantry shields. The Parthian mounted archers now proceeded to attack the square from the front as well as both flanks; they did not even have to take aim as they fired their lethal arrows into the dense Roman ranks. The Romans were not able to engage the Parthians as the latter were out of range of the Roman javelins and archers. Whenever the Roman charged, the Parthians merely withdrew peppering the legionaries with the devastating Parthian shot as they fell back.

It seemed that the Romans were trapped in this vulnerable position, neither able to attack nor withdraw whilst they suffered the depredation of the Parthian archers. The legionaries sought comfort in the fact that the mounted archers would soon run out of arrows and the devastating volleys must then cease. The legionaries would then advance with their short stabbing swords and destroy the Parthians, as they had destroyed so many other barbarian tribes before them. For once the Parthian mounted archers ran out of arrows they would either have to engage the Romans in hand-to-hand combat, or flee and leave the Romans in possession of the field. However, these hopes were shattered as a supply train of 1,000 camels and asses laden with arrows was seen approaching. The Parthians archers began to break off and then return with replenished quivers and the attack showed no sign of abating. Crassus saw no way out of the predicament and he began to lose heart. In response to the fervent pleas from Publius, he consented to let his son lead the Gallic cavalry in a charge which might prevent the Roman square from being totally encircled. The Parthian forces had begun to attack the rear of the square, and threatened to entirely surround the Roman position.

10

Parthia, 53 BC

Publius waited impatiently for the chance to lead his cavalry in an attack against the Parthians. The Gallic cavalry had endured the ceaseless onslaught of the deadly Parthian arrows as they held their position within the square, and they were eager to charge the enemy. The oval cavalry shields which Marcus and his comrades used were designed to protect only the rider, and consequently many of their unprotected mounts had been hit by the Parthian arrows. It took great determination and control for the men to maintain ranks whilst the arrows whistled from above and abruptly picked out the doomed men and mounts from their position. Two of the most conservative officers commented with satisfaction on the rigorous training which had steeled the legionaries to hold their positions even under the deadly barrage of arrows. However, the acrid smell of fear began to tint the air as the infantry men shuffled uneasily and the tension grew almost palpable. The cavalrymen struggled to control their mounts, but the horses could sense that their riders were nervous too, and the whole line quivered and fidgeted uneasily under the continual fall of whistling arrows.

Marcus examined the shield on his left arm, a Parthian arrow was embedded in the shield and the point had passed clean through the re-enforced hide and wood. Fortunately the barb had not struck Marcus's arm where it lay against the shield, and he was now examining the Parthian arrow. It appeared similar in design to the arrows used by the Roman archers and it was of similar length and weight, yet the Roman arrows would normally not penetrate a shield. Marcus deduced that the difference must lie in the Parthian bows, which were somehow able to fire the arrows further and faster than the Roman bows. His engineering interest was piqued and he looked around eagerly for the chance to test his hypothesis. He thought of the long Indian bow which Reuben had shown him in Alexandria, and wondered how the short Parthian bows produced such tension. Marcus's technical interest produced an expression of calm curiosity, which mixed with the unruffled determination on his face. The men in his century were reassured by the cool composure of the officer, and they subconsciously mirrored their centurion.

The Roman archers continued to fire at the Parthians, but their arrows always fell far short of the horse archers. Marcus surveyed the ground in front of the Roman ranks and concluded that the Parthian archers had an effective range of between 45 and 50 metres, whereas the Roman archers could only reach targets 30 metres away. Furthermore the Parthian arrows had a much higher velocity; the eye could barely follow them in flight. This increased velocity accounted for the piercing power of the arrows, for Marcus had now inspected a number of other arrows, and found they were all similar to the Roman design. He had also found one of the whistling arrows on the ground, and he blew into the simple wooden device to demonstrate to his men that the novel weapon was nothing more than a child's toy attached to a normal arrow. At the back of his mind Marcus was determined to examine one of the Parthian bows and establish how they had achieved such a significant technological advancement. Somehow the bows were short enough to be used by mounted archers, yet they shot arrows further and faster than the Roman bows. The simple engineering development combined with rudimentary military tactics had given the Parthians complete supremacy on the battlefield.

Reports continued to reach Crassus that the Parthians were attempting to envelope the rear of the square, so that the Romans would be totally surrounded. Crassus had given his son permission to lead the Gallic cavalry along with a group of support troops, in a charge against the encircling Parthians, and he now waited for the next stage of the battle to develop. Publius had assembled his attack force; it consisted of the Gallic cavalry along with 300 auxiliary cavalry, 500 archers and eight cohorts of heavily armed legionaries on foot. Orders were given for the rear of the square to part, and then the Roman attack force charged out through the opening. The men were eager for action, and after steadfastly enduring the deadly arrows they welcomed the chance to attack the enemy. It had deeply exasperated the Roman Army, that the barbarians had inflicted such heavy casualties whilst remaining entirely invulnerable. This counter-attack would be a chance for the Romans to redress the balance, and the infantry moved with such alacrity that they were not far behind the charging cavalry. Publius and the Gallic cavalry lead the assault at full gallop. A cheer went up from the ranks of the square, as they saw that the Romans were finally going to attack the barbarians and bring a respite from the dreaded Parthian arrows. The assault group rushed towards the barbarian forces, the Romans wanted to cross the open ground as quickly as possible so they could engage with the enemy. Once the Romans reached the barbarian ranks the Parthian archers would also have to stop firing their lethal volleys of arrows as the two forces would be closely intermingled.

The Parthian force, which had been moving to surround

the final side of the Roman square, now faltered. The barbarian ranks hesitated for a moment at the sight of such a determined assault. This indecision bought the Romans precious seconds in which to close the gap between them and the Parthians. It was now impossible for the Parthians to stop the attack with their archers, and they reluctantly relinquished the position as they turned to flee. Publius shouted in triumph as he saw the Parthian ranks waiver and then scatter before his charge. The ardent young cavalryman was leaning forward over his mount with his sword out-stretched in his extended arm, as if he was straining to engage the enemy before his mount had even carried him to the scene. Further along the ranks, Marcus moved with the grace of an adept swordsman, his training and skill clearly showed as he charged. He shifted the sword in his grasp with such familiarity that it appeared to be an extension of his arm instead of a separate weapon. The Romans soldiers in the square let out another cheer as they saw the lethal arrows cease to fall and the dreaded archers scatter before the charge. The Parthian cavalry did not stay to meet the Roman onslaught, and most of them succeeded in fleeing before the Romans were able to engage them in combat. The rapid advance had brought the Roman archers within range of the Parthians, but they were dismayed to see their arrows failed to penetrate the bright steel of the Parthian armour. However, as the cataphracts and horse archers retreated they exposed the unprotected rumps and hind legs of their horses, and the Roman archers fastened on these vulnerable spots with alacrity. Several Parthians were brought down in this manner, and the legionaries rushed to finish off the isolated barbarians. Once they saw their comrades in full flight, the Parthians fell back from the other sides as well.

The Parthians' flight brought an abrupt end to the volleys of arrows and the respite was greatly appreciated by the Roman ranks. Surgeons hurried to dress the wounded. The Army physicians used a purpose-designed tool to extract the barbed arrows. The device resembled a pair of scissors, except that the end was formed by a pair of curved spoons which fitted neatly together over an arrow head. The barbs on an arrow head meant that it was very difficult and painful to extract once it was imbedded in flesh. In some circumstances the military surgeons had even favored driving the arrow right the way through the patient rather than trying to pull it out, such was the damage caused by these barbs. However, the development of these specialised tongs provided an alternative. The physician would insert the tongs into the wound, and then close the spoon shaped ends over the arrow head before withdrawing the whole thing. The smooth tongs prevented the barbs from catching and causing any further damage as the arrow was removed, although the procedure remained extremely painful. The surgeons now set to work and labored hastily to succour the wounded men. The Parthian arrows had frequently passed right through the Roman armour and this made the process of extracting them even more complicated as the damaged armour had to be removed before the arrowhead could be accessed.

Marcus had charged enthusiastically with his century; they were drawn up near the center of the attack force and they struggled to match the pace Publius was setting on his fine stallion. The Parthians withdrew and Marcus saw Publius unhesitatingly pursue them; he dutifully raced after his commander, exhorting his men to maintain their line. As Marcus glanced over his shoulder he noted how far they had come from the main Roman force. The lines of horse archers who were attacking the square had thinned considerably; and as Marcus watched he saw yet more Parthians peel away from the square and scatter. The soldiers from the other sides of the square were relieved by the respite from the lethal arrows and they cheered the distant Roman attack force. However, Marcus felt an unnerving sense of foreboding come over him as he noticed that the scattering mounted archers were uniting into small groups. These groups were all heading after the Roman attack force, and Marcus felt the chill premonition of the threat that the Parthians might encompass them. He spurred his horse forward to warn Publius not to lead them further away from the Roman square, but when Publius saw the bold young centurion waving, he mistook his frantic gestures for enthusiasm. Without checking his pace Publius waved and shouted equally wildly and continued to charge after the fleeing Parthians. Marcus struggled to forestall the impending disaster, but despite his best efforts he was not able to catch up with Publius.

The Roman charge only slowed when they saw their retreating quarry halt and turn to face them. The Gallic cavalry were now some distance in advance of the legionaries which had accompanied them, and the whole attack force was extended in an unprotected line. With a dreadful sinking sensation the hunters now realized that they had fallen for the Parthian ruse, and the roles were reversed as they became the hunted. The Romans hastened to regroup; the cavalry retreated to unite with the archers and auxiliaries whilst the last of the legionaries hurried to join them. The attack force had travelled far during the pursuit and they were now out of sight of the main Roman square. They had crossed a number of gentle sandy ridges and these now hid them entirely from the view of their comrades. Publius and his force prepared for the Parthian attack which they knew must follow, for the arrival of additional horse archers and cataphracts behind the Romans, meant that the barbarians now outnumbered and surrounded the vulnerable Roman contingent.

The Romans formed up in dense body and they prepared to

receive the brunt of the inevitable Parthian assault. However, the next action came as something of a surprise to Publius and his men. The Parthians formed into a circle encompassing the Roman force and with their shields on their left arms, they rode in an anti-clockwise direction around the Romans. The Parthians were at the extreme limit of the range of the Roman archers, and with their shields facing inwards they now circled the legionaries, unaffected by the occasional Roman arrow which reached them. As the Parthians circled around the Romans their mounts stirred up the ground and a great cloud of dust started to rise. The Romans held their position, nonplussed at the unexpected turn which the battle was taking. The dry dust soon irritated them, and as the visibility was reduced they closed ranks yet further into a densely packed body. The dust caught in the men's throats as they breathed it in, and they were soon too hoarse for speech. The cloud of dust had reduced visibility to such an extent that the Romans could no longer see their enemies. However, the continued pounding of horses' hooves and the clank of heavy armour informed them that the Parthians were still close by.

When the first Parthian arrows ploughed into the Roman ranks they went almost unnoticed. The legionaries were too hoarse to cry any warning to their comrades, and the lethal arrows struck silently into the dense body of men. The tightly packed unit of Romans offered an easy target for the Parthian archers, and even with the dust obstructing their view they were able to send a steady stream of arrows into the Roman formation. The merciless arrows continued and Publius watched in dismay as his ranks were thinned time and time again. As the dust began to settle the devastating effect of the arrows became clear. Beside Marcus an injured legionary held up his arm in shock. A Parthian arrow had passed right through his shield and into his arm. The soldier was rendered incapable of dropping the shield or reaching the arrow, he stared in disgust and horror at the shield which had failed so entirely to protect him and now hindered his movements. Marcus leant down in his saddle and with a flick of his sword arm he cut through the arrow. The shield fell to the ground, but the arrow head was still embedded in the legionary's arm and he stumbled off in dazed anguish, gnawing at his wound like an injured wolf. The afflicted soldier was oblivious to the arrows which were still falling around him and he barely flinched as one punched through his neck armour and severed his spine. The legionary was dead before he hit the ground. 'Probably just as well' thought Marcus, as he saw an arrow from the next volley plunge into the man's thigh, and a fourth pass straight through the man's foot and sandal pinning it to the ground.

he tight confines of the Roman formation acted as a restraint on the handful of legionaries who had panicked. After finding themselves once more under the onslaught of those dreaded arrows, several men cracked under the pressure and attempted to flee. Their disordered movements did not last long, those that ran out of the square were soon picked off by the Parthians, whilst within the formation there was not space for them to move. Their stalwart comrades forced them to hold their position, knowing that there was no place of greater safety to which they could flee. The situation looked bleak and Publius conferred hastily with his officers. They agreed that it was impossible to remain in their current position. Messengers were hastily sent to Crassus and the main Army, requesting an urgent relief force, warning of the Parthian shot and the ruse of feigning a retreat, and pointing out the vulnerable rumps and hind legs of the cataphracts' mounts. One messenger was brought down by a Parthian arrow before he had even crossed the first hill. The subsequent riders crouched low over their mounts as they raced to reach the main Roman square.

Meanwhile Publius announced that they were going to charge the surrounding Parthians in an attempt to break out of the trap. Publius knew that he had brought his men too far from the main body; they would probably all be dead before any relief force could reach them. However, it was better to die in a glorious charge rather than suffer the ignominy of being slowly picked off by the horse archers. As their commander, Publius was responsible for the perilous position of his men, and now the only thing he could offer them was a swift and glorious death, rather than the slow agony of waiting to be shot down. Publius rode around the force, urging them on for a further assault on these loathsome barbarians. However, when he called on his men to advance they complained that they could not. Some held up their arms which had been nailed to their shields or armour by the barbed arrows, whilst others gestured helplessly at their feet which had been similarly nailed to the ground by the falling arrows. A look of sheer terror came from the faces of these men, they could neither fight nor fly and they awaited certain death. Some of the doomed men were despondent, others were panicking and thrashing, attempting to withdraw the accursed arrows. Without the surgeon's tongs it was impossible to withdraw the barbed arrows and the afflicted men worsened their injuries as they struggled in vain. Their writhing and twisting merely caused further internal damage and they were maddened by pain. The attack force did not have any surgeons with them, and the wounded struggled to tend their own injuries as best as they could.

In despair Publius lead his Gallic cavalry in a charge against the cataphracts, whilst the rest of the Roman force followed as best as they could. Experience had already taught Publius the futility of charging the nimble mounted archers who withdrew before any attack, so it was against the heavily armed and slower cataphracts that the Gallic cavalry now attacked. Although their spears failed to penetrate the Parthian armour, the Gallic cavalry fought bravely. Despite the futility of their assault Marcus and his men were relieved to engage the enemy and escape from the dreaded volleys of arrows. The Roman cavalry swiftly developed new tactics when they perceived the uselessness of their spears. In the ultimate act of desperation for a cavalryman, many of the Gallic legionaries drove their beloved mounts onto the Parthian lances and then scrambled down to fight on foot. They seized the long lances wielded by the cataphracts and pulled the horsemen to the ground, before diving in to kill them. On foot the legionaries were able to move much quicker than the cataphracts and they hastened to exploit this hard-bought advantage.

The Roman cavalry even resorted to slashing at the Parthian mounts; they stabbed at their exposed bellies and hacked at the withers of the fine horses, doing whatever it took to bring down the riders. Marcus had reluctantly impaled his mount on a Parthian lance, the horse was the same one his father had left him and it had served him well throughout the campaign in Gaul. Now Marcus was determined to make the cataphract pay for the death of his beloved steed, he leapt to the side as he dismounted and slashed at the cataphract's thigh. Marcus's sword clashed with the steel armour but failed to cut through it. The blow rocked the mounted rider and he swayed to the other side under the impact of the determined stroke. As he recovered his balance the cataphract drew his sword. Marcus knew that this was his final chance; he leapt in under the sword's arc and stabbed at the cataphract's face. It was the one area not covered by the impenetrable armour, and Marcus's blow found its mark.

As the injured Parthian fell to the ground his helmet was knocked from his head. Marcus was surprised to see that the man had light brown hair, with long curled locks tumbling over his bloody face. The Parthians came from Eurasian stock and many of them possessed the Aryan features of their ancestors. Marcus's surprise was only momentary and he dispatched the dismounted cataphract with a quick *coup de grace*. Most of the Romans were now fighting on foot, and in the packed melee of battle their greater mobility was proving an advantage. Beside Marcus a mounted Parthian was slashing at a wounded legionary, the Roman was giving ground as he endeavored to parry the powerful downward blows which the Parthian was raining down from his position in the saddle. Marcus turned and with two neat strokes he severed the hamstrings of the Parthian mount. The crippled horse attempted to rear in agony but its rear legs buckled and the rider was thrown to the ground. The legionary and Marcus both rushed to the fallen cataphract, and it took their combined efforts to break through his tough steel armour and finish him off. As the legionary wiped his brow Marcus recognized him as Gnaeus, the man from his century who had fallen sick on the sea voyage from Ostia. Blood trickled from under his helmet and his left arm hung useless by his side with a huge gash opening it from the shoulder down to the elbow. However, Gnaeus continued to fight with dogged determination after curtly thanking Marcus for saving his life a second time.

Both Marcus and Gnaeus threw themselves into the thick of the fray, and as they scrambled over the fallen men and mounts they became aware that the Parthian pressure had lessened. The cataphracts were surprised at the vigour of the Gallic cavalry and their desperate tactic of impaling their own mounts on the Parthian lances. For a horse-loving people this wanton determination was unsettling and the ruthless fury with which the dismounted Romans slashed and hacked at the Parthian horses was equally unnerving. Some of the more nimble Romans scrambled under the bellies of the Parthian horses, and succeeded in stampeding a group of Parthian mounts. The Romans had stabbed the vulnerable bellies of the horses, and as they reared and thrashed in panic the other mounts had become equally uncontrollable. The injured horses flayed out with their hooves, and trampled Parthians and Romans alike in their distress. This small stampede and the retreat of other cataphracts had temporarily eased the pressure on Marcus and his companions.

The Romans held the battlefield temporarily and they swiftly regrouped in the brief respite which the occasion afforded. The dry plain was awash with blood and the screams of dying horses and injured men. Parthian horses stumbled around with great rents opened in their bellies; they neighed and screamed producing a disturbing range of most un-equine noises in their distress. Publius was grievously wounded, and the other officers decided to move to a small hillock nearby where the topography would provide a natural defensive position. The remaining Romans drew themselves up in closed order and the front rank linked shields to form a wall. They tied the few surviving mounts to a picket within the circle on the crest of the hillock. Of the 4,000 Romans who had left the square with Publius less than half now remained alive. The officers endeavored to form a wall around their injured commander, whilst others struggled to succour the wounded. The Parthians had regrouped also, and the mounted archers advanced on the hillock to fire into the Roman ranks. The defensive site which the Romans had chosen proved to be a great hindrance as it further exposed them to the Parthian arrows. For whilst the legionaries were drawn up in ranks on flat land, the front row offered some measure of protection to those behind, however when the legionaries were drawn up on sloping land they were all equally exposed to the Parthian arrows. The Parthians had surrounded the Romans again, and there was no chance for them to select another location, so the

Roman ranks grimly held their position bemoaning the futility of further fighting and the ignominious fate which lay before them.

There were several notable Greeks who had accompanied Publius in the charge, and the survivors now urged Publius to flee with them in the hope of reaching the Greek city of Ichnae which was friendly to the Romans. The Greeks implored Publius to commandeer one of the remaining mounts and save himself. Publius steadfastly refused, and declared that there was no death so terrible or inglorious that it would make him leave his friends and soldiers to die on his account. He told the Greeks to save themselves if they could, and embracing them hastily he sent them on their way with two of the remaining horses. Publius boldly stated he chose death before dishonor and refused to desert the battlefield. Publius's sword-arm was transfixed by a Parthian arrow, and he had lost a great deal of blood. He dolefully recognized that there was no way he could fight or escape and resigned himself to death. Publius struggled to open his armour at one side then he handed his fine sword to his orderly and commanded the terrified man to run him through. Several of the injured Roman officers followed suit.

Marcus had miraculously escaped without injury, and as the only uninjured officer he rallied the remaining legionaries to charge the Parthians again. He refused to commit suicide, clinging with desperate tenacity to his role as commander. As Marcus arrayed the ranks he cast a mournful glance over what remained of his century. Amongst the chaotic lines he picked out a mere dozen of his men, although there could be more elsewhere as the units had become intermingled in the chaos of the battle. The cataphracts saw how few Romans remained on the hillock and they determined to charge the position. The mounted men advanced uphill and engaged the Romans before Marcus had time to organise a second charge. The cataphracts made short work of the legionaries who fell to the long lances before they could even come to blows with the Parthians. Marcus had sustained a few cuts and bruises in the final assault but he still had no serious injuries. Gnaeus now repaid the favor which Marcus had done him, and he watched diligently over his rescuer and centurion. Previously the legionaries had raised the option of surrender, but the memory of Crassus' decimation of his own legions in Italy still haunted the Army. Marcus refused to take his own life, and he was determined to hold out for as long as possible. They would struggle on until there was no hope of a relief force reaching them, and then any remaining legionaries would have to surrender. The Parthian attack broke through the Roman wall with ease and after a few pockets of fierce fighting the final group of legionaries reluctantly surrendered when they were surrounded. This group included the section of the shield wall where Marcus had been fighting; they had held out the longest but it was futile to struggle any further. Marcus now found himself the spokesman and commander of the surviving Romans, and it was only his sense of duty to his comrades which prevented him giving way to the despondency and despair which welled up inside him. Out of the original 4,000 men in the attack force, there were now a total of 500 Romans left alive, including a number of the Gallic cavalry unit. Marcus signaled their surrender, and with great reluctance and a heavy heart he handed over his sword.

The victorious Parthians hacked off Publius's head and hands, before they rode back to the main Roman square. The Roman prisoners were left in charge of a small contingent of horse archers, though as the bulk of the legionaries were injured there was no chance they could escape and the guard was largely superfluous.

Meanwhile Crassus had taken advantage of the respite which

resulted from Publius drawing off the bulk of the Parthian force and he had moved the Roman square to some sloping ground nearby. The legionaries had taken heart from the sight of the Parthians fleeing before the charging Romans, and now they waited for their comrades to return. Only one of the messengers which Publius had sent reached the main Roman square. He gasped out the report which Publius had instructed him to deliver, and added that the remaining Romans were lost unless they received immediate relief. The message dismayed the Roman generals, who believed the battle had finally turned in their favor.

Around Crassus discordant voices rose in a tumult as each man offered different advice. Some advocated sending a relief party who could fall on the Parthians from the rear and exploit the weakness which Publius had highlighted in his message; others insisted that the Romans could not risk splitting their remaining force. A few despondent men even suggested a retreat to the walled city of Carrhae, but they were swiftly shouted down. A Roman Army could never retreat from a barbarian force which was less than a quarter of its size. Crassus was distracted and distraught; he was torn between his military responsibility and his filial duty. He vacillated and issued irrational orders, rescinding and contradicting each decision in his confusion. Eventually the orderlies withdrew in confusion and waited whilst Crassus battled with his personal and professional obligations.

Finally, some of the generals succeeded in calming the situation and with their guidance Crassus reached the decision to take the entire force to his son's rescue. Although this would mean the relief force would make slow progress, it ensured that no other groups of Romans would become stranded or isolated. The orders had just been given for the Army to move when a lone Parthian rider came into sight, galloping over the dunes from the direction in which Publius had lead his men. The rider carried a long lance in one hand although there was no gleam from the point of the weapon. Behind this solitary horseman the rest of the Parthian forces soon appeared, however they were advancing at a slower pace to meet the Romans. All eyes were fixed on the lone horsemen as he sped straight at the Roman square. Archers strained at their bows, hoping he would misjudge the distance and come within their range, then they saw what he was carrying and they released the tension from their bows in shock. The Parthian horseman rode along the front of the Roman wall, brandishing Publius's head impaled on the lance. The lone rider was well within range of the Roman bows but no arrows were sent to test his armour. In accented Latin the man shouted out to the Romans, demanding to know who the beheaded man was. The Parthian declared that such a valiant soldier could never be the son of a blundering fool such as Crassus, and he demanded again who the man was. The Parthians had been greatly impressed with the courage and bravery which Publius had displayed and the rider's comments were both a eulogy to the dead man and a challenge to Crassus. Before returning to join his countrymen, the Parthian hurled Publius's head and hands into the Roman square, where they were reverently collected and carried to Crassus.

The rest of the Parthian Army had now drawn up in position opposite the Romans; they spread out to cover the front of the square and two of the sides. By now the legionaries were no longer disconcerted by the loud bells or deep drums which the Parthians used. The Romans were even growing accustomed to the whistling arrows which accompanied another barrage of Parthian arrows. However, the sight of Publius's decapitated head being paraded before them had a powerful effect on the exhausted men. Their spirits slumped and many men hung their heads in dismay. In other circumstances such a sight would have incited the legionaries to anger and a yearning for revenge. However, this Roman Army now consisted of men who were exhausted, wounded, thirsty, and hungry; they were traumatised by the ordeal of the battle so far. To these dismayed men the gruesome spectacle incited feelings of horror and despair. Crassus had regained his composure and now attempted to rally his men. He strode through the ranks and declared;

'Fellow Romans, this is my own personal loss, and I do grieve for the death of my son. However, the glory of Rome remains intact so long as her Army remains undaunted. If, like me, any of you feel struck to the quick by the loss of our noble countryman let him show it by revenging himself on the barbarians. Show them no mercy, for they have shown none to our comrades. Do not be dismayed, for we still outnumber these barbarians, and Roman endurance and superiority will always prevail. Our illustrious history shows that legionaries are the best soldiers on the face of the Earth. Our ancestors bought the glory of their victories at high prices, and we will do the same here. Those hard-won victories are treasured all the more when their achievement has been so dearly bought. Come now, recharge your spirits, square your shoulders and hold your weapons firmly. As you see the heavy price of our victory has already been paid, all that remains is for us to seize the occasion. Rome did not achieve such greatness by good luck, but through the perseverance and resolution of our forefathers.'

Despite Crassus's impassioned speech the Roman Army remained daunted and dismayed. Crassus saw that his men were not paying attention to his words, and a gloomy air of despondency hung over the Army. When the officers ordered the legionaries to shout for battle, the cry which went up was faint and wavering. In contrast the smaller Parthian Army replied with a bold and resounding shout, and their drums and bells banged loudly. The Parthians approached the Roman force and engaged them in battle once more. They employed the same tactics as before, with the mounted archers riding around and firing into the Roman square, whilst the cataphracts used their long lances to drive the Romans ever closer together, providing a dense and easy target for the archers. Some of the legionaries rushed furiously at the cataphracts, preferring to die attacking the heavily armed Parthians rather than remain at the mercy of the whistling arrows. The Roman infantry who did charge were quickly dispatched by the cataphracts, who wielded their lances to devastating effect. Previously the Gallic cavalry had managed to reach the cataphracts and engage them in combat by impaling their mounts on the Parthian lances, but now the Roman infantry had no way to pass the wall of lances, and they were unable to inflict any serious casualties on the cataphracts.

By now the day was drawing to a close, and the Parthians broke off as the sun dipped below the horizon. The Parthians boasted that they would indulge Crassus with one night to mourn his son and then the following day he could choose between surrender or death. The Parthian force withdrew and camped in the desert where, flushed with their success, they settled down to rest. Meanwhile the Roman camp was a much more disordered and sombre affair, Crassus instructed the army to remain where they were, and the soldiers camped on the battlefield as best as they could. The survivors were too despondent and dismayed to organise a concerted effort to bury their dead or to tend to the wounded, and consequently the night was filled with the groans and cries of the injured legionaries as they lay where they had fallen. The legionaries and officers knew full well that there was no means of escape open to them. If they attempted to retreat across the harsh open desert during the dark they might prolong the inevitable, but there was no way they could escape the Parthians. When the sun rose in a few hours time, the lethal arrows would start to fall again and there was nowhere for the legionaries to shelter from those deadly darts.

The legionaries were all eager to see Crassus, even though he was the cause of the current dilemma. They naively hoped that such a powerful and wealthy leader would find some way to save the Army. It seemed inconceivable that the richest man in Rome could be so utterly helpless in front of this small force of barbarians. However, Crassus remained incapacitated with grief and despair, it fell to his orderlies and officers to issue the necessary orders for the Army to camp and eat. Meanwhile, Crassus wrapped his cloak around him and in a daze he sat rocking back and forth outside his tent. To the ordinary observers it appeared that the bereaved Crassus was a poignant example of the caprices of Fortune, but to the wise observers Crassus was an example of the dangers of ambition. The wealthy man had not been content to be the superior of millions whilst he was inferior to the other two Triumvirs, and his pride and ambition had caused this disaster.

11

Parthia, 53 BC

As Crassus sat keening and rocking in despair, Cassius and Octavius approached him. With the death of Publius, these two men were now the highest ranking officers after Crassus. Cassius and Octavius were totally unable to bestir their grief-stricken commander, who remained incapacitated by his sorrow. The two officers conferred privately and concluded it was necessary for them to temporarily assume command. They hastily summoned the remaining centurions and tribunes, and after a brief discussion decided to order a night-time retreat. There was no defensible position nearby which the Romans could occupy, and it was agreed the Army would not survive another day in the open at the mercy of the Parthians. The surviving Romans were ordered to make for the walled town of Carrhae, travelling through the night to exploit the darkness which temporarily protected them from the Parthian archers. The orders were promptly issued for a swift and covert retreat. Those legionaries who had managed to camp or sleep and those wounded who were still able to walk were hurriedly ordered to rise and pack as quietly as possible. The seriously wounded were to be left where they lay on the battlefield. Speed was of the essence, and the noise of transporting so many badly injured men would certainly alert the Parthians as well as slowing down the Army. Many of the badly injured men were now delirious with pain and dehydration, and their cries would have allowed the Parthians to follow the retreating Romans.

Once the surviving legionaries had left the camp, a strange sense of confusion and despair spread amongst the remaining wounded Romans. Those that were able to, struggled to their feet, and in small groups they endeavored to follow their departing comrades, calling out for them to wait or assist them. In the dark, few of the stragglers succeeded in following the main Army; they wandered deeper into the desert to meet their deaths. However, few of the wounded were able to leave the camp and a sense of despair and terror chilled those that remained more than the cold wind of the desert. The cold night air gnawed the wounded men to the bone as they gradually realized the hopelessness of their situation. Without the comforts of food, fires or friends there were some who gave up their ghosts out of despair before the dawn had even come. All over the battlefield there were scattered pockets of men, and in each situation a different spectacle of humanity could be witnessed. The extreme circumstances had further magnified the individual traits and inclinations of the different men. In one place a group of men had succeeded in lighting a fire, and those that could move were busy collecting combustible material. It was only a few short hours till dawn, but they were determined to spend their last moments of freedom, and potentially of life, with the comfort of a crackling fire to ward off the chill. Elsewhere, a few men slept soundly, their resonating snores revealing a blissful ignorance of their predicament. In another place a man prayed fervently to the silver pendant of Mars, which hung from his neck. He lay on his back with his eyes shut as his lips moved ceaselessly in a trance-like supplication which he repeated to the God of War. Elsewhere, a man stared intently at his unsheathed sword, the point of which rested against his own torso. He had watched his life force sap away from the wounds in his thigh and shoulder, and now he was balefully wondering if he had sufficient strength left to take his own life.

All around the battlefield there were badly wounded men experiencing their deepest revelations as they confronted the terrible prospects of death or enslavement. Before it took their lives, the dark desert night robbed many young men of their naïve and immature faith in their own immortality. The innate faith among young men in their own invulnerability is very hard to shake. If you told 100 new recruits on the eve of a battle, that the next day they would win but only one man would survive, each man would think, 'I'm glad we'll win, but it's a pity so many of my friends will die.' Each man assumed he would be the one out of the hundred that survived, and it was only now in the cold of the night that these men were coming to terms with the real significance of the odds and their likely position within the hundred men.

When the orders for a night-time retreat had been issued, a wizened and experienced Roman officer by the name of Egnatius had acted promptly. He commanded a small contingent of cavalry, and he left immediately with his 300 men in order to avoid the chaos and confusion of a large Army performing a nocturnal retreat. When these men reached Carrhae they did not halt, but called out to the sentries that there had been a great battle with the Parthians, and Crassus was coming that way with his Army. The cavalry then continued on their way to Zeugma, without even stopping to answer the questions which the sentries shouted down to them. This swift flight enabled Egnatius to save himself and his men, though he paid the price of losing his reputation for deserting his comrades in the field. The commander of the Roman garrison in Carrhae was an able man called Coponius, he rightly surmised from the manner in which the message was delivered, that Crassus would be in need of assistance, and he ordered his garrison to rise and arm themselves. Thanks to the forewarning from Egnatius, Coponius was able to march out and meet Crassus as soon as the main Army neared the town. The Roman garrison escorted the exhausted survivors into the town walls, and then returned to their positions guarding the town walls. Throughout the night groups of Roman stragglers who had strayed or got lost during the retreat arrived at the gates. They were all promptly challenged by the guards, and once they had identified themselves they were welcomed into the town.

The availability of water, food and rest soon restored the Romans, and the Army regained their spirits. Out in the desert, the Parthians had noted the Roman's retreat but they did nothing during the night. It was not their custom to fight in the dark, and they knew that they would be unable to use their bows until it was light. Without the significant advantage of their superior archers, the Parthian force was no match for the Roman Army, so they let the Army retreat unopposed. They had already inflicted a humiliating defeat on the Romans, and Surena was careful not to underestimate the strength of the remainder of the Roman Army. The Roman Army still outnumbered the Parthians, and there were undoubtedly firm grounds for the tough reputation which the legionaries had won. As soon as the sun rose, the Parthians fell on the wounded Romans and massacred all the men they found in the Roman camp. Over 4,000 wounded men were slaughtered within a few hours. All of the walking wounded had left the camp, so the only Romans left there were those who were seriously wounded and thus they were not fit enough to be captured and sold as slaves. After this the Parthians and the Arab light cavalry of Ariamnes, who were now fighting with the Parthians, pursued the retreating Romans and succeeded in cutting down a number of the stragglers and various groups who had lost their way during the night.

One Roman contingent of four cohorts had accidentally broken off from the main Army during the night march. In the confusion of the nocturnal retreat, the Roman unit had strayed from the route and when the sun rose they found themselves far from Carrhae. The officer in charge was Varguntinus, and with the first rays of dawn light he was able to correct their course and make for Carrhae. The men had heard the screams of the wounded as the Parthians slaughtered them during the dawn light, and now they marched for Carrhae with a palpable sense of terror. They knew that the Arab scouts would track them and spot them long before they reached the safety of the town's walls, and after that it would be only a matter of time before the Parthians arrived in full force. The officers struggled to prevent their men breaking into a run, as even at full pace they knew they could not reach Carrhae before the Parthians caught up with them, and it was essential to conserve some energy for their final fight. Under the stalwart guidance of Varguntinus the four cohorts continued to make for Carrhae maintaining a fast but steady pace. When the Parthians approached and surrounded the contingent, the Romans drove into the Parthian forces and soldiered on in the direction of Carrhae, attempting to fight their way through the Parthian lines. Many of the legionaries were cut down by the cataphracts, but not before they were in sight of the town. Varguntinus shouted to encourage his men, and then as a last resort he reminded them of the dreaded punishment of decimation which Crassus might employ if they showed signs of abandoning the fight. With this encouragement and the dreadful prospect of decimation raised in their minds, the legionaries fought almost to the last man, inflicting many casualties on the Parthians. In the end, the Parthians were so impressed with the tenacity and bravery of these Roman legionaries, that they parted ranks and permitted the last 20 survivors of Varguntinus's four cohorts to depart in peace, as a tribute to the courage with which they had fought. These bewildered survivors watched in amazement as the horse archers unstrung their bows and fell back to allow the legionaries a clear path towards Carrhae. Varguntinus had been cut down by the Parthian cataphracts in the final charge, but the survivors carried his corpse with them and honored him as an inspirational commander. The Roman garrison came out to meet them, and the 20 astounded survivors were soon recounting their tale to the other Romans when they had given themselves up for doomed just hours before. Within Carrhae, Crassus accorded Varguntinus the full honors of a military cremation in recognition for his stalwart service.

Meanwhile, Marcus remained with the other Roman prisoners under the watchful eyes of Parthian guards. The prisoners had been moved to a temporary camp near the small river, where there was adequate water for the men and their mounts. The Romans had surrendered all their weapons and the legionaries were hastily tied in pairs with their hands behind their backs. The Parthians did not have enough rope with them, so they had used spare bowstrings to tie a number of the Roman, and now the fine strong twine cut into Marcus's wrists. Marcus was tied to Decius, the *tesserarius* whose rank indicated that he was in charge of the sentries. Decius had an arrow buried in his thigh, and a nasty gash from a Parthian lance across his upper arm. Both wounds were still bleeding and Marcus struggled in vain to aid his companion as the pain of his wounds drove him to distraction. The most cursory examination had told Marcus that Decius was fatally wounded, the gash in his arm had opened the subclavian artery and he had lost a lot of blood. Decius was breathing quickly and his pulse raced as he struggled to cope with the injury. Marcus could feel the wounded man's skin become clammy and cold to the touch where their hands were bound together. Marcus shivered in the cold as he struggled to block out the moans of the wounded and get some sleep. As he lay on the hard ground, Marcus shifted and wriggled to settle his armour into place, against his chest he could still feel the tiger brooch which was fastened inside his tunic, safely out of sight. With each breath, he felt the pressure of that familiar brooch against his chest, and Marcus was reassured by its presence.

The discomfort of lying with his hands tied behind his back could not keep Marcus awake and he soon fell into a short deep sleep, shivering as he lay on the hard ground. When Marcus woke in the early pre-dawn morning, the first thing he noticed was the ominous quiet. During the cold night Decius had bled to death along with several of the other wounded Romans. After growing accustomed to the moans and groans of his wounded companion, Marcus was now disturbed by the silence. He attempted to convince himself that Decius was sleeping quietly and that the cold touch of his hands was from the desert wind, but deep down Marcus knew the man had died, and he was now tied to a corpse. Soon after dawn, one of the Parthian guards passed. He paused to examine Decius briefly, then with a flick of his sword he cut his binding. Marcus gasped with relief, feeling suddenly free although he was still a prisoner. It was such a comfort to no longer be tied to Decius's lifeless corpse. Marcus sat up and massaged his wrists as the blood slowly returned to his hands. The guard now indicated that Marcus was to fetch water for the horses, whilst he supervised with an arrow knocked to his bow in case Marcus should have any thoughts of making a break for freedom.

At the main Parthian camp, an erroneous report reached Surena informing him that Crassus had escaped from Carrhae along with his principal officers. The report declared that the only Romans left in the town, were the ones of lowest note and least worth. Surena had no desire to lay siege to a town from which his main target had already fled, and so he set out to verify the details of the report. A messenger was sent from Surena to call in Latin at the town walls for Crassus or Cassius, declaring that the Parthians wanted a conference and Surena wished to speak with the Roman officers. The messenger was accompanied by a few of the Arab horsemen who had arrived with Ariamnes. The Arabs had been in the Roman's camp before their chieftain had departed to join Surena, and they recognized the faces of both Crassus and Cassius when the Roman officers appeared on to the town wall to talk with the messenger. The Parthian envoy declared that Surena would offer the Romans safe convoy out of Parthia if they would make a treaty with the King to withdraw all of their troops from Mesopotamia and restore the Euphrates as the border of Parthia. The envoy further declared that such an agreement was the best for both sides, as neither nation wanted to embroil the region in a long conflict. Crassus eagerly accepted the proposal, and he sent a reply to Surena with his instructions for the conditions and time of their meeting. Surena was greatly relieved to learn that Crassus was still in Carrhae, and the ultimate prize had not escaped him.

The next day, Surena approached Carrhae and his envoys shouted to the Roman sentries, scornfully calling on them to hand over Crassus and Cassius bound if they wanted any mercy from the Parthians. Surena had no intention of offering the Romans a truce, and his ruse the previous day had been designed solely to establish if Crassus and Cassius were still within the town. Coponius had been suspicious of the Parthian proposals the previous day, and now he counselled Crassus to take the earliest opportunity to fly the town. Carrhae was not prepared for a siege, and the provisions they had would not last long with 20,000 extra mouths to feed. Cassius concurred with Coponius and the two men endeavored to sway Crassus. The grieving general was enraged at the duplicity of the Parthian envoy, and the jeering shouts from outside the town walls were adding insult to the deep loss he had already sustained. Crassus retained some deluded hopes of the Armenian forces coming to his relief, but when his officers reminded him that he had snubbed Artavasdes, Crassus reluctantly agreed that help from that quarter was unlikely. Woefully, Crassus finally agreed to fly from Carrhae, though he refused to abandon his Army, and he insisted that the sizeable remnant of his Army accompany him. As there were insufficient provisions for the force to remain in Carrhae this proved a welcome decision from the point of view of Coponius, and he offered Crassus every possible assistance.

The Roman officers then made their plans to leave Carrhae that night. They again planned to take advantage of the Parthians' evident inability and reluctance to engage the legionaries at night. By day break the Romans could reach the Armenian foothills, where the cataphracts would be unable to follow them. The plans for their departure were supposed to be confidential, but Crassus made the mistake of telling a Greek named Andromachus, whom he asked for advice about the best route. Andromachus willingly offered to guide the Roman Army, whilst he sent urgent messages to Surena informing him of the planned departure. The Parthian commander was greatly pleased to have such prompt intelligence of the Roman's decision, and he promised Andromachus a large payment if he carried out Surena's instructions. Within Carrhae, the Romans spent the day resting and recuperating, only a few of the officers knew of the plan to depart as soon as night fell, and they discreetly ensured the necessary preparations were completed.

After the evening meal was finished the officers summoned all the tribunes and centurions to inform them of the night-time departure. They briefly outlined the plan before issuing the necessary orders for a prompt departure. The Army was to split into two equal parts, one part under the command of Crassus and Octavius, whilst the other was to be under the command of Cassius. The two columns left promptly, greatly refreshed by the food and respite which the garrison in Carrhae had provided. The first contingent was led by Andromachus, whilst the second contingent had an Arab guide. In accordance with the instructions he had received from Surena, the treacherous Greek led Crassus and his column on an extremely circuitous route, deliberately choosing the most difficult terrain in order to hamper their progress and ensure they could not travel far during the night. The route which Andromachus chose contained so many twists and turns, that even in the dark and in an alien environment there were some Romans who began to suspect him. In the open countryside the night stars shone brightly, creating a faint luminous glow that was further enhanced by the half moon. The stellar configurations looked different from Parthia than they did from Gaul or Rome, however several of the men still used the stars as reference points and noticed that their route entailed a lot of twisting and turning. Rather than risk being caught in the open when the sun rose, there were a few units who elected to break away from the column and chance their luck either making for the Armenian foothills on their own, or returning to Carrhae. It was a mark of how traumatic the recent experience had been that the legionaries even thought of deserting their commander and disobeying orders despite the risk of decimation.

Initially, Cassius and his column fared no better with their Arab guide. Although the man was not in the pay of Surena, he was still attempting to stall the second Roman contingent and lead them back into the desert where his fellow Arabs could attack the column at will and claim the spoils of war. During the night journey, Cassius had been casting his characteristically restive eyes all around the countryside, flitting from one feature to the next. Consequently he had taken in much of surrounding countryside and he soon began to suspect the Arab guide. After only a few hours of this aimless wandering, Cassius had his suspicions confirmed when they passed the same distinctive mound a second time, acting coolly Cassius summoned the guide. The Arab was riding in front of the Army, and when he received the summons he began to suspect his ruse had been noticed, however he was reluctant to give up the prospect of such a valuable prize, and Cassius seemed calm, so the guide dutifully returned. The man approached and reported to the officers, sweating slightly in the cool night air, he was instantly seized and bound before he was delivered to Cassius. The Arab remained defiant and he refused to reveal who he was working with or the location of his comrades. In response to Cassius's questions he merely jutted out his chin, in the universal Arab gesture of defiance and disrespect. Cassius knew that the precious hours of darkness were ticking away and he coldly ordered the execution of the guide, before he turned the column about and returned to Carrhae.

The Roman sentries were surprised to see Cassius arriving, but they dutifully opened the gates and welcomed him back into the town. After a brief conference with Coponius, Cassius summoned a different Arab guide, whom Coponius vouched would be reliable. However, this man examined the night sky and then advised Cassius to wait until the moon had moved out of Scorpio before they left Carrhae. Cassius reacted with disgust, he pointedly declared that he feared the arrows of Sagittarius more than location of Scorpio, and he was resolved to depart without further delay. With this comment, the exasperated Cassius departed for Syria with 500 cavalry, following the route by which they had entered Parthia. The night was so far advanced by then that it would have been impossible for any infantry to make the journey before dawn; so Cassius only took cavalry, and riding hard throughout the remaining hours of night, they managed to reach safety before sunrise. In this manner Cassius escaped from the disastrous battle of Carrhae; he managed to save his life but at the price of abandoning his General, a stain on his reputation which nothing would ever remove. Cassius later went on to participate in the killing of Julius Caesar, and his subsequent suicide was lamented by Brutus as the death of 'the last of the Romans'.

The nocturnal journey which had begun as an orderly retreat had now degenerated into a confused and disorganised flight. The original two columns had fragmented into a number of different groups, and these groups sometimes joined together or further fragmented as they progressed. One large group of 5,000 men had remained with Octavius, he had secured an honest guide and that contingent reached the safety of the hills before the sun rose. The men scrambled gladly up the scree and loose rocks, content in the knowledge that this terrain afforded them protection from the mounted Parthian forces. Octavius lead his men to the top of the first small hill, and then he ordered them to make camp there, so they could rest and eat before the next stage of their journey back to Roman Syria.

As the sun rose, Octavius was standing on the hilltop inspecting the horizon and searching the other hilltops for signs of other Roman units who had made it to the hills. He was a little disturbed that he had lost contact with Crassus, but he knew that the other Romans could not be far away. As the morning light gradually illuminated the scene below him,

Octavius noticed a Roman column stirring up a trail of dust, they were being pursued by of a large force of Parthians who were rapidly closing the gap between them. The Romans were barely two miles from the safety of the hills, when they unaccountably turned to the right and took up position on a small hillock. Even from his distant vantage point Octavius could see that the hillock was not steep enough to prevent the Parthians attacking. By breaking their flight to occupy such an ineffective defensive position the Roman contingent gave the Parthians sufficient time to surround them. Octavius had shouted to his men to seize their arms as soon as he saw the Romans. As the dust now cleared and the Romans took up position on the hillock, Octavius made out Crassus's standard, and he could even discern the stubborn set of the commander's shoulders as he sat squarely on his horse.

Without a moment's hesitation, Octavius charged down the hill, abandoning his safe position in order to assist his General and comrades. At first Octavius was followed only by his officers, he was a gallant man and had inspired much devotion and respect from his subordinates. However, the other Romans on the steep hill called to each other, and declaring that it shamed them to see their commander fight without them, they all followed him down the hill. Octavius and his men fell on the Parthians from behind as they surrounded Crassus. This unexpected Roman attack from the rear soon routed the Parthian force and they fell back, permitting Octavius and his men to join Crassus on the hillock. Surena knew that his cataphracts and horse archers could attack the hillock, and they had an entire day in front of them with plenty of daylight for shooting. On the hillock, Octavius was content to be reunited with his General. However, he required every ounce of his famed *sang-froid* to restrain his anger when he learnt that Crassus had spied him on the hilltop, but had still decided to occupy the nearer small mound, rather than rush for the safety of the hills. Crassus boldly declared that he knew any Roman officer would return to his aid, and by occupying the mound Crassus had given Octavius a chance to attack the weak Parthian rear. Although this was true, it overlooked the fact that the Parthian force now lay squarely between the Romans and the safety of the hills. There was now an entire day in which the Romans would have to endure the Parthian archers before they could make a break for the hills.

Amongst the Roman ranks there were scenes of a much happier nature. The display of bravery had restored the Romans faith in themselves and their innate superiority. Octavius's force promptly forgot their initial reluctance to follow their commander, and basked in the praise and thanks of the comrades they had rescued. United and reassured by the warm daylight, the Roman ranks now gathered tightly around their commander and boasted that not a single Parthian arrow would reach him, so long as one of his legionaries remained alive to protect him. Octavius had the foresight and self-control to accept the situation, and he encouraged his men and exhorted the Romans to fight bravely, for the safety of the hills was nearby. That day would be their last occasion to revenge themselves on the Parthians, and the legionaries could not leave so many fallen comrades unavenged.

Ocatvius's heroic charge had taken Surena by surprise, he had noticed the Romans on the hilltop but he had never thought they would abandon their position of safety for an indefensible hillock. The Parthian force had been shaken by the assault from behind, and they now began to view the hillock with dismay. The sheer bravery of Octavius's charge had made the hillock seem greater in the eyes of the Parthian cavalry; they refused to believe that anyone would be foolish enough to abandon an unassailable position of safety for anywhere less secure. As the cataphracts and horse archers surrounded and inspected the hillock they began to perceive it as steeper than it really was, so much can the determined actions of one man affect the outcome of a battle. The courageous displays of the Romans, and the manner in which they united confidently to form a defensive ring also dismayed the Parthians. Instead of rejoicing at the chance to catch two Roman contingents, they now began to despair that they had lost both.

Surena was an astute commander and he soon perceived the drop in morale amongst his men. That amorphous and vital entity which is the spirit of an Army, and which can so often control the outcome of an engagement, is a difficult yet crucial thing for a commander to assess. Surena sensed that the current balance had shifted decidedly in favor of the Romans, and he knew that if they held out till night fall the Romans would be able to make good their escape. The Parthian commander realized that he would have to employ more subtle tactics. An envoy was sent to the Romans to request a parley; the Parthians also released a handful of Roman prisoners as a gesture of goodwill. Before releasing the prisoners, Surena had contrived to ensure they had the occasion to overhear some of the Parthian chiefs discussing their plans. The Parthians had carefully explained to each other how the King did not want a war with the Romans, but rather desired to win the good grace of Rome by showing respect and mercy to Crassus as a step towards reconciliation. The released Romans dutifully reported the intelligence which they had overheard.

Shortly after the envoy had been sent to the Romans, Surena rode out with his chieftains. They paused in front of the Roman lines, and then they symbolically unstrung their bows and called out to Crassus to come and meet Surena so they could agree on the terms of a truce. This gesture and the offer of a safe passage out of Parthia were received with much joy and relief by the Roman rank and file. However, Crassus held back from going to meet Surena, he had already been tricked once by the perfidious and wily Parthian, and he had no intention of making the same mistake again. The Roman soldiers were revived from their short rest in Carrhae, and they were less than two miles from the safety of the hills. The tide of battle appeared to have finally turned in favor of Crassus, and the Parthians had shown clear signs of fatigue during their last half-hearted attack on the Roman position. Although the hill was not sufficiently steep to prevent the Parthian cavalry attacking, the elevation did mean the Parthians were within range of the Roman missiles. Whenever the Parthians approached the Roman position, a barrage of arrows, javelins and slingshot swiftly demonstrated this simple piece of geometry. The Romans' elevated position also prevented the Parthian archers from employing the tactic of firing high looping volleys at the same time as direct shots. From their position at the base of the hillock, it was impossible for the Parthian archers to achieve the trajectory necessary for the looping volleys, and consequently the Romans were better able to protect themselves by doubling and over-lapping their shields.

However, at the prospect of an honorable truce the legionaries clamoured for Crassus to meet Surena and accept his terms before the Parthian commander took offence at the delay and chose to withdraw his offer. Neither Crassus nor his officers could perceive any reason for the sudden change in Surena's attitude, and they viewed the current proposal with mistrust and suspicion. Whilst the officers were discussing the situation and assessing their options, the Roman rank and file cried out for Crassus to accept the terms. The traumas and pressures of the campaign had so totally shaken the *status quo* that a commander who had been feared for his ruthless discipline was now being openly cajoled and upbraided by his own men. The legionaries began to mock Crassus, calling him a coward because he was scared to meet Surena. The officers endeavored to calm their men but without success. Crassus made a speech entreating them to hold on until nightfall, at which time they would all be able to make their way to the nearby hills and escape from the Parthians without the indignity of signing a truce, or the danger of a meeting with such treacherous foes. Crassus, once a feared commander, was now reduced to imploring his legionaries to obey him. However, the men showed signs of mutiny and they banged their weapons together in an ominous fashion. The tired legionaries who had so recently vowed to protect their leader with their last breath, were now insisting Crassus go and meet Surena. Crassus was cajoled, threatened, pushed and prodded into going to meet Surena to arrange a truce. The Parthian's masterful and astute reading of the spirit of both his men and the Roman force had paid off, and he had once again wrested back control of the situation.

As Crassus was leaving the Roman position, he turned to his most senior officers and called out to them to observe that he was obliged to go and meet the Parthian, although it was from necessity and not his own volition that he went. Crassus further instructed them, that should Surena prove to be dissembling as he suspected, it was Crassus's final wish that Rome and posterity were to know that he died not through the disobedience of his legionaries but through the base duplicity of his enemies. All of the officers were deeply distressed at the situation, and they were apprehensive about the danger into which their commander was going. Octavius and Petronius refused to remain with the Army, and they accompanied Crassus unarmed as he strode down the hillock to the meeting with the Parthians. The officers and attendants who accompanied Crassus now implored him to send one of them to confirm that the Parthians were coming to the meeting unarmed, and in similar numbers to the Romans. Crassus consented to their request, although he remarked that he had neither any choice nor any control to dictate the terms of the meeting, and he already relied on the honor of the Parthians for his life.

Two Romans were sent in advance of Crassus, they were young brothers by the names of Gnaeus and Gaius Rucius and they were flushed with the honor of the task entrusted to them. However, as soon as they reached the Parthians, they were seized, bound and gagged. The Parthian force was never stationary, and thus it was hard for Crassus to make out what had become of his envoys amongst the swirling mass of cavalry. At the offer of a truce the Parthians had withdrawn from their position surrounding the base of the hillock. They still encompassed the Roman position, but their forces were now stretched more thinly in a larger circle. From a different place amongst the Parthian ranks, a small group of riders now moved towards the Romans. They did not carry the long lances which the Romans had come to know and fear, but from that distance it was impossible to determine if they still had their swords. When they reached the Romans, Crassus noted with foreboding that the Parthians had retained their swords, but Crassus was determined to retain his dignity and make the best of a bad situation. In any case it was impossible for him to flee back to the Roman position; the mounted Parthians would have easily overhauled Crassus and his escort.

Surena rode in advance of his companions as they approached the Romans, and it was obvious by his bearing and apparel that he was their commander. He approached Crassus, and in remarkably clear Latin, he enquired how it had occurred that the Parthian commander came mounted to the meeting, whereas the Roman commander was on foot. Crassus boldly replied that there had been no breach in protocol, as both men came after the custom of their own country. It was the Parthian habit to be mounted, and the Roman habit to be on foot, so their meeting was entirely in accordance with their differing habits. Next, Surena declared in a loud voice, that from that time hence there existed an accord between the Parthians and the Romans, this accord would duly be ratified into a biding treaty for Crassus to sign. Crassus and his Army would be granted safe passage to the Euphrates, where the Roman standards captured in the battle would be returned to them. In specifying this condition Surena revealed his deep understanding of Roman values, for there was no way Rome would accept a treaty which involved the loss of Roman standards. Surena briefly stated the terms of the agreement; the Romans were to recognize his master, Orodes, as King of Parthia. The Euphrates was to be fixed as the border between Parthia and Roman territory, and all the Roman garrisons currently in Parthian territory were to be withdrawn. The agreement was to be signed by Crassus, and then publicly ratified by the Senate upon his return to Rome. Here again Surena displayed his knowledge of Roman politics, for no agreement made in the field was considered binding until it was ratified by the Senate. Surena declared that Crassus must ride with the Parthians who would escort the Roman Army to the Euphrates, there they would sign the agreement and Crassus would be free to leave with his men. Surena bluntly declared that history had taught him to lack confidence in the Romans and their pacts. Indeed, the record of Roman involvement in Parthian affairs was far from laudable and Surena had reason to demand assurance from the Romans. Crassus consented to the conditions, recognising them as considerably fairer than he had expected. He sent for one of his horses to be brought, and he prepared to accompany the Parthians to the Euphrates. Octavius and Petronius were to command the Roman Army in his absence, and they were to depart without delay for the Euphrates. The two erstwhile enemies were to march in parallel, keeping a distance of 500 metres between each force.

Surena called out that there was no need to send for a horse, and he presented Crassus with a fine Parthian stallion with a golden bridle. The steed was a magnificent horse, possessing the fine lines and grace of an Arab mount, along with its flighty temperament. The Parthian commander issued orders for his grooms to assist Crassus immediately. It was clear that the Parthians intended to treat Crassus as an honored guest, whilst he remained, in effect, their hostage. The Parthian grooms rushed to assist Crassus, and they put him into the saddle with bold insistence as they hurried to fulfil their master's instructions. Octavius was alarmed and affronted at the insolent and peremptory manner in which the Parthian grooms were treating Crassus, and he ran up to seize the horse's reins. Petronius and the couple of other officers soon joined him, and they rashly struggled with the grooms who dared not let the Romans prevent them fulfilling the mighty Surena's orders. The Parthian nobles and some of the Roman officers had considered the matter already concluded, and they had turned to return to their respective positions. Consequently they did not immediately notice the scuffle which was breaking out between Octavius and the grooms.

The fracas soon escalated as neither side would back down, from pushing and shoving it quickly developed into the exchange of blows. The Parthian grooms were affronted that the Romans should dare complain about the honorable manner in which they were treating a hostage. The Romans were equally indignant at the sight of their General being manhandled by barbarians. In rash fury, Octavius drew his sword and killed one of the grooms. The noise of this fracas had alerted the rest of the group, and a mounted Parthian immediately struck Octavius dead in retaliation. The Roman officers refused to permit the Parthians to take Crassus with them. Meanwhile, the old General was fully occupied trying to control his flighty mount and he was unable to stop the struggle which now erupted around him. The Parthians were enraged by the conduct of the Roman officers. Petronius was struck next, although he was unarmed he still wore his armour and his breastplate blocked the thrust of the blow, although it still knocked him to the ground. The ordered parley had degenerated into a chaotic and frantic struggle, some of the Romans raced back to warn their comrades on the hillock, whilst those that remained were all killed. As the fracas escalated, Crassus was killed by a Parthian named Pomaxathres, who considered the Roman commander responsible for the outrageous behaviour of his escort.

Surena had come to accept Crassus's word, but instead he departed with his head. The Parthians had beheaded Crassus and cut off his hands, as soon as he fell to the ground. This was standard Parthian practice with any illustrious foe; the head was then publicly displayed as proof of the achievement, and to prevent any impostor subsequently claiming to be the deceased man. There were rumors amongst the Roman ranks of treachery and Parthian plots, but it was generally recognized that the lamentable outcome of the meeting was not that which Surena had intended. The Parthian commander sent a messenger to the Roman Army, declaring that Crassus and his escort had received the punishment they deserved for their insolence. Surena now bade the Romans to descend from the hill without fear and surrender. The Parthians proclaimed that they were sick of this bloodshed and wished for peace. On the hillock, the Roman Army now fell into disarray; with most of the senior officers gone, the legionaries were left leaderless and confused. Some took up the Parthian offer, and laying down their arms they descended from their position and surrendered. Others remained on the hillock and tried to make a break for freedom during the night. The Arab cavalry had arrived at the scene by now, and unlike the Parthians they were willing to fight by night. The Arabs hunted down and slaughtered many of the Romans who attempted to flee but a number did make it to safety in the hills. In all, there were nearly 10,000 Romans taken prisoner, whilst only 10,000 survived the campaign to return to Rome. The Parthians seized the seven legionary standards from the units which had been in Crassus's force; it was the largest number of eagles the Romans ever lost. Over half of Crassus's Army perished, and Crassus earned himself a place in Roman history, as the General responsible for the single most humiliating Roman defeat.

12

Syria, 53 BC.

After the death of Crassus and the capitulation of the remains
of his Army, the Parthians were left with over 10,000 Roman
prisoners. Despite the massive slaughter which had taken place
during and after the battle, the number of captured Romans still
exceeded the size of the original Parthian force. Surena ordered
the prisoners to be split into smaller contingents and placed
under guard, while their fate was decided by the Parthian King.
Surena now waited patiently to know the decision of his master,
for although the victory was Surena's, it was in the name of
his master King Orodes that he had fought. Surena was a wary
man, and he had no intention of marring the outcome of such
a successful engagement by providing the prisoners with an
opportunity to unite and escape. Three centuries earlier, 10,000
Greek mercenaries had performed an impressive and successful
fighting retreat through what now constituted part of the Parthian
empire, and Surena was careful to avoid giving the Romans the
opportunity to attempt something similar. The Greeks' journey
formed the subject of the *Anabasis* by the Greek writer Xenophon,
a famous historical account of the retreat which was well known
to Surena.

Once split into groups, the Roman prisoners were sent to
make temporary camps in the wilderness, under the guard of

mounted Parthians. The groups were carefully dispersed to ensure that each contingent was out of sight of the other groups. Furthermore, these temporary prison camps were all located deep in the desert, so as to discourage any attempts at escape. The Parthians knew from experience how best to employ the vast arid stretches of their homeland; the desert now guarded their prisoners just as it had guarded their frontiers for generations. The prospect of crossing such a dry and perilous region without water, support or supplies was enough to contain the prisoners far more effectively than any man-made fence or wall.

The isolated locations of the camps meant that water had to be fetched from afar, but since the Parthians now found themselves in possession of a large and unoccupied labor force, transporting the water posed no problem. In fact it was an excellent opportunity to keep the prisoners occupied; each day teams of Roman prisoners worked in relays to transport water from the Balissus River, to the scattered camps. The Romans were obliged to work on foot, trudging through the soft sand whilst they were supervised by mounted Parthians. The language barrier had not prevented the Parthian horse archers, from making it abundantly clear that they would shoot down without hesitation anyone who tried to escape. This point had been brutally and tragically demonstrated on the first morning, when a young legionary had wandered to the edge of the camp to relieve himself. The man's modesty had cost him his life, and before the first drops of his urine had even disappeared into the dry sand he was transfixed by three arrows. The Roman had sunk to his knees, unable to stop the flow from his bladder; he remained there on his knees, pissing as he died. The shouts of indignation from his companions had roused the rest of the camp, and in recognition of the practical necessity of some arrangement, a designated toilet area was soon marked out for the prisoners.

The Parthians had not anticipated taking any prisoners at all, and now they had the huge logistical problem of supplying and supervising a force of prisoners who greatly outnumbered the guards. The Parthians had salvaged whatever Roman supplies there remained on the various battlefields, but there was still insufficient food to support the prisoners in the desert for long. The legionaries gradually became lethargic from fatigue and hunger, and to their relief the Parthians were able to relax their guard somewhat. Surena did not know if the King would want the Romans executed, enslaved or escorted back to Roman territory, so he did what he could to sustain them in the meantime. He had already sent for supplies as soon as the battle was over, and when these new convoys of food, tents, fuel and other essentials arrived they were distributed amongst the camps, thus easing the shortages and help restore the prisoners to full health. A small number of prisoners had perished from their wounds, but in general the clean desert environment and the dry air had prevented the wounds from becoming infected, so many of the wounded recovered. With the consent of the Parthian guards, a handful of Roman surgeons had labored steadily to remove arrows and succour the wounded. Often wounds had to be re-opened so that sand and dust could be removed from the cuts, but with the low rate of infection this was a relatively successful, if painful, procedure.

It was rare for the Parthians to take prisoners, and it was largely due to the impressive bravery that the Gallic cavalry had demonstrated when they had continued to attack, that the Parthians had offered terms of surrender to Publius's force when they had been surrounded and Publius had fallen. Subsequently, when the Parthians had pinned Crassus and his force on the hillock, they were already sickened by the scale of the slaughter, and they had gracefully accepted the surrender of the remaining legionaries. Both groups now found themselves in novel positions; the Parthians because they so rarely took prisoners, and never before had they done so on such a large scale; and the Romans because they had never before surrendered. The Romans were generally dispirited as they contemplated a life of slavery in a foreign land. The more optimistic amongst them hoped for a kind master, and the opportunity to earn their freedom. Few of the Romans thought of seeing their homeland again; for even were they to win their freedom, it was questionable that they would want to return to Rome, even if that were physically possible, for they would be inextricably tarred with the shame of their defeat and surrender. The strict social mores of the Romans, which infused the Army as much as its civic society, held that it was unforgivable for a Roman to surrender. Consequently, it was only the most unrealistic and fanciful who could envisage a future in which they could win their freedom and return to Rome. Amongst all the prisoners there was not a single complaint about the social justification or morality of enslavement. It was an accepted part of contemporary society, without which the Roman way of life would cease to be possible. An astute observer once remarked that nobody ever objected to the existence of the social hierarchy, which stretched from lowly slave to haughty patrician, but merely to their own position within the hierarchy.

After their second night of captivity, Marcus found himself becoming the spokesman and translator for the group of 500 prisoners which had surrendered from Publius's column. Several of the Parthians spoke Greek, and this shared language made the ordering of affairs for the prisoners run more smoothly. The Parthian in charge of that group was a burly giant by the name of Tyluxes, who was originally a noble from the Yuezhi tribe. Tyluxes had fought with Surena and the Parthian Army for over a decade now, and it was only the distinctive shape of his head which marked him out as a Yuezhi noble. As part of his tribe's traditions, his head had been bound as an infant. This practice was reserved for the sons of the tribe's higher nobles, and it resulted in the distinctive broad forehead and elongated head which indicated a high Yuezhi nobleman. Some 80 years before, the Yuezhi had conquered the Kingdom of Bactria which lay to the east of Parthia. Bactria had been founded by one of Alexander's generals, and Greek was the common language and predominant cultural influence there. All documents were written in Greek, and Greek plays were performed to entertain the nobles. After the Yuezhi conquered the Kingdom, many of the Yuezhi nobles had learned Greek to communicate with their Bactrian subjects, and this language was still being taught to their descendants years later, as a result of which Tyluxes was fluent in Greek.

Tyluxes's towering frame and broad chest lent a deep resonance to everything he said, such that his voice tended to carry all before him like an ocean wave. Thus when he roared with rage or with laughter, he produced such a volume of noise that it swept over and encompassed all those around him. Initially he had succeeded in issuing instructions to the Roman prisoners using the sheer force of his voice, and when that failed his massive arms explained his instructions in less ambiguous terms. However, Tyluxes was also an intelligent man, and when he heard that one of the prisoners spoke Greek he summoned the man to his tent.

Marcus was led to the commander's tent, and ushered in to meet Tyluxes. He was immediately struck by the physical presence of the burly man, and then by the booming voice which Tyluxes failed to modify even when the person addressed was standing right in front of him. Marcus was unaware of the Yuezhi practice of head-binding, and he was surprised at the strange shape of Tyluxes's forehead, which seemed to stretch and create an unusually large gap between his piercing green eyes and his hairline.

'They tell me you speak Greek, is this true?' thundered Tyluxes.

'I do', responded Marcus tersely, he was unsure what to make of this man, and he was playing for more time in which to assess him. The Parthian was clearly a mountain of a man, but there was also a spark of thought in his deep green eyes.

'Good,' came the next remark from Tyluxes, who was also carefully assessing the clear blue eyes of the Roman.

Concluding swiftly that Marcus was an honest and honorable man, the Parthian issued another thundering blast of speech in accented Greek, in such a manner that it permitted no gainsay.

'Then you shall be interpreter and spokesman for the Romans in this camp, while we await orders from the King. Come, now we shall drink to your co-operation and eat, for I am hungry.'

Food was promptly brought, and Marcus ate calmly, trying to satisfy his hunger as quickly and with as much dignity as possible. The Romans had not eaten since the previous morning, and hunger gnawed at his belly as the food was set before them. It was only after the second helping of dates and mutton that Marcus continued the conversation. Marcus had noticed that Tyluxes had said *this* camp; the man's Greek was too good for that sort of elementary lexical error; that must mean there were other camps of Roman prisoners. Marcus and his comrades had speculated a great deal about the outcome of the battle, the general opinion had been that the entire Roman force had been massacred. This theory had gained support when they had heard the screams of the wounded Romans being slaughtered on the morning after the battle. These screams had been taken as evidence of a successful surprise Parthian attack on the Roman camp. Marcus now felt his spirits buoyed at the prospect of other Roman prisoners being in the desert, and while this revelation was unlikely to improve the position of his men, it was some comfort to know that the rest of the army had not perished. As they talked Tyluxes confirmed that Crassus had been defeated, and that there were other camps of Roman prisoners, but he refused to give any further details. With this new intelligence fresh in his mind, Marcus finished the meal and rose to leave the tent.

'Stop' boomed Tyluxes, as Marcus was leaving.

The roar of his voice brought two guards through the tent flap, before Marcus even had time to turn.

'Show me what you have in your pocket,' demanded the Parthian.

During the course of the meal, Marcus had been eyeing one of the sharp serving knives which had been placed on the low table with the munificent feast. At the same time he was acutely aware that his fellow prisoners were ravenously hungry. In the end he had accepted the impracticality of any escape attempt, and he opted for providing whatever succour he could for his comrades. Consequently he had concealed several handfuls of food in the pocket of his tunic, and left the knife on the table. The rough hands of the Parthian guards abruptly seized him, and his arms were pinioned as his pocket was emptied; bread, dates and a greasy lump of mutton fell onto the carpet which covered the floor of the tent.

'Do you insult my hospitality?' demanded Tyluxes.

'Have I not fed you enough?' continued the host, genuinely offended at Marcus's actions.

'Oh no, I've eaten very well,' replied Marcus, for indeed he had, and his full stomach now pressed against his belt.

'This was for my comrades, they are hungry,' explained the centurion simply.

His honest simplicity immediately convinced Tyluxes, and the Parthian's ire evaporated as quickly as it had flared up. He signaled to the guards to release Marcus, and then leave the tent. As the flap dropped shut behind them, Tyluxes indicated the fallen food and addressed Marcus;

'There appears to be something despoiling my carpet, please remove it and dispose of it as you see fit. Then I wish you to clear this table.'

The last sentence was accompanied by a gesture to indicate the remaining food from their meal. Marcus graciously complied with the instruction, and he left the tent laden with the surplus food, which he promptly distributed to his grateful comrades before the meat had even gone cold.

13

SYRIA, 53 BC.

MEANWHILE, AFTER THE failed parley, Surena and his chieftains had demonstrated that they knew far more about Roman military practices than the Romans knew about those of the Parthians. After the victory, a Roman prisoner had been dressed in women's clothes, and with the unwilling actor pretending to be Crassus, the Parthians created a procession which was a parody of a Roman triumph. The replacement Crassus was escorted by lictors whose fasces were adorned with money-bags, and whose axes were adorned by the heads of dead Roman legionaries. The money-bags were a direct taunt against the deceased Crassus, who was famed even in Parthia for his avarice. One Parthian noble even wished to go further, and he offered to supply gold to be melted and poured into Crassus's mouth. The suggestion was appreciated by all, though it never materialised into action. The triumphal procession was followed by courtesans and dancing girls who jeered and sang ribald songs about the effeminacy of Crassus and his cowardice. In true parody of a Roman triumph, the procession was accompanied by the standards of the defeated Army, including seven of the silver eagles, which were the pride and symbol of the legions.

Following Crassus's death, Surena had despatched Datrius, with the head and hands of Crassus, to announce the victory to King Orodes, and to learn what Orodes wished to do with all the Roman prisoners. Datrius was a trusted officer and close relative of Surena's, who had fought bravely in the battle. Meanwhile, following the brusque dismissal and scant thanks which Artavasdes had received for mobilising his forces in support of the Romans, the Armenian King had withdrawn to his homeland. In Armenia, he had then suffered the onslaught of Orodes, who led the bulk of the Parthian Army on a punitive raid deep into Armenia. Artavasdes had seen no reason to hold out and endure the depravations being inflicted on Armenian farms by the Parthians, and he had accepted the truce offered by Orodes. The Parthian King had proposed an honorable and gracious settlement with Armenia, as he was anxious to take his main Army south to engage the advancing Romans. Orodes wanted to secure his border with Armenia before he took his main force to face the Roman Army led by Crassus. Surena and his cavalry force had been intended merely as a probe to test, and delay the Roman advance, while buying time for Orodes to gather his forces. The Roman legions were the most respected and dreaded fighting force of the time; Orodes intended to face them with every soldier he could muster, but only after he had secured his flank from an Armenian attack.

After the treaty between Orodes and Artavasdes had been confirmed, the two Kings went through the customary Oriental procedures of feasting and entertaining each other. Etiquette demanded that this elaborate process be followed, and despite his impatience to depart, Orodes knew that it was vital to first secure the new alliance with Armenia. Consequently, the two Kings lavished praise and gifts on each other, despite having been enemies merely days before. Each strove to surpass the other in the munificence of their gifts and in the refinement of the entertainment they provided. The influence of Alexander was still evident in much of the East, and while Bactria was the most notable kingdom to retain the Greek language and customs, in both Armenia and Parthia the legacy of the Macedonian conqueror was still strong.

When Datrius arrived at the Palace with the news of the battle, he was told that he could not enter the throne room as Orodes was entertaining Artavasdes there with the performance of a Greek tragedy, and had left explicit instructions that they were not to be disturbed during the play. The two Kings were in the throne room of the Parthian Palace at Nissa; it was an elaborate and impressive example of Parthian architecture which Orodes was eager to display to Artavasdes. The main throne room was a square with sides 20 metres long, the lofty walls were hung with ornate drapes and a vaulted ceiling enclosed the whole. Many of the details from the vaulting and elaborate architecture were covered in gold leaf; this made the room glow with a lustrous light whilst drawing attention to the fine workmanship. The arched roof was supported by four columns; each formed from three circular pillars fused into a single column. The vivid Royal standards and colorful red silken banners hung from the columns. Along each wall there were groups of similar three semi-circular fused columns incorporated into the walls. The design of the columns gave a pleasing stylistic unity to the room, and the bright hangings drew the eye up to admire the impressive grandeur of the vaulted ceiling and huge room. Orodes had chosen to finalise the agreement with Artavasdes in Nissa, rather than in Armenia as he wished to make an ostentatious display of Parthia's might and wealth. The Royal Palace was set inside impregnable fortifications, and there were 43 watch-towers built into the high walls of the city. The location of the proceedings also forced Artavasdes to travel deep into Parthian territory, and even with his large bodyguard, this effectively placed him at the mercy of the Parthians and obliged him to credit their expressed desire for peace.

Datrius had travelled far and fast to bring the news to Orodes, and he was eager to deliver word of the victory to the King as soon as possible. The resourceful envoy now set about to find a way of delivering his news without contravening the orders left by the King. He made a few hurried enquiries and then moved round to the rear of the stage. The play being performed was *The Bacchae* by Euripedes, a Greek drama about divine interference in the lives of mortals. The plot centres on King Pentheus's doubts and disrespectful behaviour towards the God Bacchus; in revenge for the King's hubris, the ladies of Pentheus's court are driven into a Bacchic frenzy during which Pentheus's mother decapitates her own son. One of the actors performing the tragedy that night was a skilled Greek tragedian named Jason of Tralles. Behind the scenes, Jason saw Crassus's decapitated head and realized the unrivalled opportunity for a spectacular *coup de theatre*. Datrius was impressed when Jason explained his plan, and he soon consented to the Greek's suggestion. Datrius delivered the head to Jason and then slipped into the back of the throne room to join the audience and admire the performance. Jason was initially surprised by the weight of the head, but steeled himself to concentrate on the task and exploit the theatrical opportunity of a lifetime.

During the long journey from Carrhae to Nissa, the decapitated head had become dirty and it was encrusted over with dried blood and grime. Jason assiduously washed away the dust and dried blood, and combed the sparse matted locks of Crassus's greying brown hair. Next he applied some of the stage cosmetics to restore a bit of color to Crassus's wan cheeks. The warm water and cleaning process had caused more blood to seep from the head, but Jason was still not satisfied that the head was gruesome enough. His attentions had ensured that the head was easily recognisable to the audience, but he wanted to make the news of Crassus's death as vivid and dramatic as possible. Holding the head tenderly in his hands, he dipped the neck into a dish of pig's blood that was normally used to adorn the dummy head which was employed as a prop in the play. Whilst Jason had been working as a macabre make-up artist, he had also been busy constructing an appropriate soliloquy to fit the unique occasion.

By the time the vital scene came in the play, Jason and his ghastly prop were fully prepared. With an enthusiastic leap the Greek bounded onto the stage with the head cradled in his arms. Crassus's face was turned away from the audience, and Jason opened his soliloquy with the face still concealed. The skilful actor looked up at his audience as he spoke; the stage extended into the throne room and numerous torches burnt brightly around the platform. The clover-shaped fused columns with their ornate banners and profusion of regal standards, made a truly magnificent background for the drama. Around the stage, the two Kings and their attendants sat on couches and cushions in the low light, whilst beautiful slaves plied them with food and drinks. Throughout the play, the company were served wine in elaborate rhyta. The decorated drinking horns had been specifically chosen for that evening, as the bands of ornaments and ornate reliefs around the broad upper end of each one concerned Bacchus, and were thus particularly appropriate to the play being performed. The pointed end of each rhyton was decorated with the sculptured form of a mythical figure, and this provided a counterweight for the vessel and allowing it to stand on a table.

The Royal attendants included the most beautiful women available in all the slave markets. The gracious and subtly-perfumed serving ladies were dressed in diaphanous robes, and Jason knew his performance would have to be outstanding to hold the full attention of his audience. Although Jason was immune to the charms of women, he knew that his audience would certainly be distracted by the seductive curves and coy smiles of the serving women. Initially, Jason did not deviate from the lines in the original play which he delivered in a clear and resounding voice. Then, after a dramatic pause, Jason began what would subsequently be remembered as the pinnacle of his acting career. He announced the tragic revelation which forms the denouement of the original play, and then rather than stopping after the scene was finished, he grasped Crassus's hair in one hand and turned the head to face the audience holding up Crassus's head for all to see and launching into his improvised speech.

There was a loud gasp of amazement from King Artavasdes who rose from his throne appalled at the gruesome sight before him. At the same time a frisson of fear rippled through all the Armenians who immediately recognized the head of their erstwhile ally, and feared for their own safety. Few of the Parthians knew what Crassus looked like, and the man's identity was passed amongst the audience in electric whispers. The beautiful serving women in their tantalisingly translucent gowns were forgotten in an instant. All of the audience believed Crassus was thousands of miles away, yet it appeared that his head had been very recently cut off, for the dripping blood was forming a small puddle on the stage around Jason's feet. In their fear and shock, the Armenians failed to grasp the significant point that the Parthians had not been immediately able to identify Crassus. It had fallen to the Armenians to identify the dead Roman. There was a feeling of desperate tension amongst the Armenians, who feared that a similar fate might now await them; they were deep inside Parthian territory, and entirely at the mercy of King Orodes.

While the fresh blood dripped from the head, and the bright torch light illuminated the Roman General's features, Jason spoke out boldly and clearly. He had adapted the hubristic theme of *The Bacchae* to fit Crassus's actions. Jason now mocked Crassus for the arrogance and pride which led him to assume his vast and ill-gotten wealth permitted him to act so irreverently. In his yearning for military glory, an aged Crassus had presumed to lead his Army against Parthia without a *causus bellum*, and in direct breach of Pompey's earlier treaty. Jason developed the parallels between Pentheus and Crassus with flair and ingenuity; both egotistical men had over-estimated the extent of their transitory power. Despite the clearly unfavorable omens from the Gods, both Crassus and Pentheus had stubbornly persisted in their foolish plans. Both of the mortals paid with their lives for the arrogance and folly they had shown.

In Jason's vigour and excitement he unintentionally signed Surena's death warrant. In addition to clearly crediting Surena with the victory and lauding his personal role in the battle, Jason's parallels between the play and the events compared Surena with the divine Dionysus. Orodes was immediately jealous and he became suspicious of Surena as a potential rival, however the King concealed this and handled the situation with tact. Jason's ingenious improvisation and the good news which it announced earned both him and Datrius large rewards from Orodes after the performance. In the audience, Artavasdes gave thanks that the treaty he had recently signed with Orodes would save him from sharing a similar fate to Crassus. The sight of Crassus's gaping eyes and bleeding head proved too much for Artavasdes to bear and he turned away traumatised. Artavasdes reflected briefly that if Crassus had not snubbed him, the Armenian King would have joined Crassus on his disastrous campaign into Parthia.

'There, but for the grace of Mithras, go I,' muttered Artavasdes under his breath.

The Armenian King had already been impressed by the Palace at Nissa, and the might of the Parthian Army, but now when he saw Crassus's head appear as a prop he was overawed by the power which Orodes exercised. Artavasdes did not realise that Orodes was equally surprised by the sudden appearance of Crassus's head. The Parthian King concealed his shock masterfully, and exploited the opportunity to its full potential. With a nonchalant wave of his bejewelled hand which encompassed the play, Crassus's bleeding head, and the luxuriant surroundings, Orodes declared:

'I hope this humble entertainment pleases you, King Artavasdes.'

King Orodes was delighted at the news of the Parthian victory; he had never expected such stupendous results from Surena and his small cavalry force. Orodes was amazed at the victory which the Surena had achieved, and the sensational method in which the success had been announced. However, he continued to conceal his surprise, and he managed to convey to Artavasdes that the victory was part of his overall military plan, and the announcement was part of the evening's entertainment. After the play, the details of the battle were recounted, and Datrius told the King of the seven captured silver eagle standards and the huge number of Roman prisoners who were being held by Surena whilst the King decided their fate. Orodes was staggered to learn that after the battle, Surena's troops were still outnumbered by the Roman prisoners they had taken. Orodes muttered comments about his plan proving successful and about the fact that the number of Roman prisoners was more than his calculations had allowed. The victory was truly an impressive feat of arms, and the Parthian King was already planning what to do with Surena. Any commander who could defeat forces which outnumbered him by four to one, was a capable and dangerously resourceful man, and Orodes had no intention of allowing a potential rival to gain any more power. Orodes's face showed none of these more foreboding calculations as he now turned his full attention to the question of the Roman prisoners.

The captured legionaries represented a great asset, and the Parthian King was debating the most effective way to exploit this new resource. If he executed them all immediately it would send a powerful message about the fate of anyone who dared invade Parthia, but Orodes knew the Senate would never rest till the Romans had avenged such a brutal affront. He was already aware that retaining and displaying the captured eagles was tantamount to inviting another Roman invasion. However, Orodes was confident that the great barren deserts in the west of Parthia would protect them, as they had done for generations. On the other hand, the north eastern border of Parthia was very much less secure and Orodes now began formulating a plan to settle the captured legionaries in that region and employ them on a number of civil projects. In the north east of Parthia they would be sufficiently far from Roman territory to make any escape attempts or Roman rescue missions impossible. The development of that vulnerable region would increase security for the whole of Parthia by protecting its weakest border.

The nomad tribes, from whom the Parthians were originally descended, still ranged across the steppes to the north east of Parthia. The fierce tribesmen periodically streamed down from their wild homeland to make incursions into Parthia. The nomadic tribes had difficulty surviving without the produce of the sedentary peoples, whereas the sedentary population could live without the nomads. Consequently, it was usually at the instigation of the nomads that any interaction occurred between the two peoples. When the sedentary population were strong, their soldiers powerful and their defences in good order, the nomads came to trade. They bartered their livestock and animal products for the metal tools and weapons that were vastly superior to the traditional bone versions which the nomads could manufacture. However, when the sedentary tribes showed signs of weakness, or when pressure from the east forced the nomads to move west or when the rains failed and they faced starvation, the nomad hordes would sweep down to raid the fertile plains. Their tough steppe ponies could carry them deep into Parthian farmland where they could loot and pillage at will, before withdrawing far into the steppes, safe from any pursuit. Just as the barren desert protected the Parthians from any attack from the west, so the vast expanse of steppe plain protected the nomads from any punitive force that might be sent against them. The nomads could withdraw in the face of any menacing expedition, and wait for the invading force to overstretch its supply lines, or accept the futility of pursuing nomads.

The mobility and invulnerability of the nomad tribes had made it impossible for the Parthians to reach any lasting agreement with them. Ethnically the two peoples shared the same ancestors, but the fiercely independent nomads could not be tied into any form of agreement, and with no fixed settlements, they were immune to any recriminations. Furthermore, within each of the three main hordes the nomads were only loosely united, thus even if one leader could be bribed to agree a truce, it was unlikely that all the men in his horde would recognize the agreement, and it was almost certain that the other hordes would not. Whilst it was true that the fighting style of mounted archers used by the Parthian cavalry was based on the nomad horsemen, and the ranks of the Parthian Army was often swollen with mercenaries from the nomad tribes, it was also evident that the Parthian Army were unable to defeat a force which could retreat for nearly 3,000 miles before it even had to consider engaging the enemy. Furthermore the retreating nomads would not be inconvenienced by the journey, whereas any Army which followed them for that distance would have used all its supplies and resources long before any battle. The nomads chose when they interacted with the Parthians, and they chose the economic and military terms under which any interaction took place. King Orodes was all too painfully aware of this, and with the huge number of Roman prisoners the King believed he had finally found a way to alter the balance of power with the nomads.

It was well-known that when the legionaries were not fighting, they were kept permanently employed on works of civic construction, including building the straight roads and arching aqueducts for which the Romans were famous. Orodes surmised that the Roman prisoners must include competent engineers, builders and surveyors. These experienced and able men would provide a unique and ideal labor force with which to develop the unstable region of north east Parthia. Once the infrastructure was improved the region would be easier to protect. The land in the north east of Parthia was fertile, but what the area needed was irrigation and that required labor to dig the canals. Orodes now decided the Roman prisoners would be set to work constructing extensive irrigation canals and improving the roads. The Roman invasion, which the Parthian King had dreaded so much, would now bring benefits that no one could possibly have foreseen. With the new resources which the legionary prisoners provided, Parthia might finally be able to secure its north eastern border against the nomad incursions and their accompanying depredations. King Orodes seized the opportunity, and ordered the prisoners moved to the north east without further delay, dispatching a group of court officials to deal with the details and to supervise the projects. Then, ostentatiously praising Surena for his impressive victory, he issued Datrius with orders for Surena, instructing him to supervise the transfer of the Romans across Parthia to the city of Merv. When the message reached Surena, the bold commander was content with the praise from his master, and proceeded without hesitation or suspicion to comply with the King's orders.

14

Syria, 53 BC.

THAT SAME EVENING there was a discreet knock at the door of
Orodes's chamber; a knock as discreet and controlled as the man
who performed it. The King dismissed his guards with a curt
wave, and then summoned the visitor to enter. Through the dark
doorway slipped the slim figure of a man, who moved with a
lithe and relaxed self-confidence that belied the taut muscles
of his lean body. The man's name was Tomacles, a Macedonian
Greek by birth; he had been exiled from his homeland at
the age of sixteen, for that was when Tomacles had killed his
first man. One day, the young lad had returned early from his
apprenticeship with his father the local carpenter; Tomacles
had found his tearful mother in the embrace of the lecherous
landowner. The landowner had thrown him a silver coin and told
him to clear off. That night, after much questioning, his mother
had confessed to him that the family was penniless, and it was
only by enduring the sweaty affections of the porcine landowner
that she retained a roof over their heads. The next night Tomacles
had set forth with a bag under his arm, making purposefully
towards the large house where the rapacious landlord lived. The
bag contained his few personal belongings and some borrowed
carpentry tools. Entering through a small window, which he
had prised out of its casement, Tomacles had crept through the

house. He soon located the snoring landlord, and killed him in his sleep. Tomacles had then cut off the man's genitals and nailed them to the front door along with the silver coin, before leaving the village and his homeland forever.

Since that day, twelve years earlier, Tomacles had been a professional assassin and he had lost count of the number of men he had killed. The Greek had soon become an expert in his new profession, and his fees were correspondingly high. The King had summoned Tomacles that evening in order to present him with another of these discreet and deadly missions. Tomacles listened attentively as the King explained that the Greek was to depart the following day, and under the cover of working as a royal official, he was to join Surena and await further orders. Tomacles gave a reserved nod and then spun slowly on his heel and left, clasping the bag of gold which contained his hefty advance. The cold-blooded Greek did not bother to guess, nor did he care in the least, who his target might be, by now he was inured to his work and totally indifferent to everything except the lure of lucre and the pleasures it could buy him. The bulk of the gold would soon find its way into the hands of the local courtesans, for Tomacles had one weakness which was his raging libido.

The convoy which left for Carrhae the following day was now a long and noisy train of officials, clerks, their wives, slaves, and baggage. The Parthian officials did not relish the impending journey to the desert, nor the subsequent trek across Parthia to the north east frontier. The prospect of working in the frontier region, so frequently devastated by the nomad raids, was similarly unappealing, so the officials were determined to take with them as many of their comforts as they could possibly manage. Comfortably hidden among this extensive and cumbersome baggage train, was one man, remarkable only for the manner in which he failed to stand out. His mount was non-descript and his clothes were standard, but it was his very comportment which rendered him so eminently unnoticeable; his subdued glances were fleeting, never making eye contact and he blended so efficiently into any surroundings that few of those travelling with Tomacles even noticed he was amongst their number. This was exactly as the crafty Greek wished it to be. He had spent most of his advance on a wild night of whoring, and now he waited patiently for further instructions from the King.

Many days afterwards, late one evening the column reached Surena's main camp near Carrhae. The large influx of royal officials rendered Surena's orderly camp-ground a chaotic mess of gaggling wives and slaves, struggling to procure whatever comforts they could for the night. Tents were hastily erected, and soon the aroma of hot food was drifting from a number of crackling camp fires. Surena, having received the King's instructions from Datrius, summoned the commanders of each of the contingents of prisoners, and when they were all assembled in his tent, he outlined his plans. All the various groups of Roman prisoners were to be settled in the region of Merv, in the north east extremity of Parthia. The whole body was to convene the following day, and then a general muster would be held to determine the exact number and condition of the prisoners. Where possible the prisoners were to be split into their original units in the interest of providing the most efficient workforce possible. The units were all to set off at staggered intervals, and they were to travel many miles apart to prevent the Romans having an opportunity of uniting. The Roman prisoners had already handed over all their weapons when they surrendered, and shortly after they had been stripped of all their armour. However, Surena was determined to take every precaution to ensure none of his new charges escaped or re-formed into a fighting force.

The Royal officials began work with uncharacteristic zeal, for they were eager to leave the desert behind and move to more pleasant locations. When the muster was held, all the assembled ranks of bedraggled prisoners formed in their original centuries. The Parthian officials reviewed, numbered and assessed all of the prisoners, and then split them into 7 groups of just over 1,400 men each. The divisions were based on the seven legions which had constituted the core of Crassus's Army. However, the Parthians found there was a severe shortage of Roman officers. A disproportionate number of the Roman officers had been killed in the fighting, and those that had not died at the hands of the Parthians had often chosen suicide rather than surrender. This left the difficulty of deciding who would lead the Roman prisoners. The Parthians had noted how efficiently the Romans worked as a unit, both when they had been fighting and when they camped as prisoners, and the captors had no intention of disrupting a system that worked so smoothly. Surena's commanding direction and sheer force of character combined with the meticulous calculations of the Royal clerks ensured that the Parthians soon organised an effective schedule and route for the long journey of the prisoners and their escorts across Parthia.

The Roman prisoners were relieved to find that they were in their familiar units once again, however depleted they were. Marcus and his fellows from the Gallic cavalry found themselves combined with the remnants of the seventh Legion under the command of Tyluxes. When the two groups of Romans met, they eagerly exchanged news, enquiring after comrades and comparing experiences. They were to complete the 1,100 mile journey across Parthia on foot, and the Parthians knew that hungry men marched slowly. None of the Romans had been informed of their final destination, and the prisoners all assumed that they would be marched to the nearest city and then auctioned at a slave market. As the legionaries chatted among themselves, they speculated about the employment to which they might be put by their new Parthian masters. They had seen no large agricultural estates, nor were there any mines or large kilns to be seen nearby, so they were unsure of any form of employment that might call for so large a labor force. The general consensus seemed to be that the prisoners would be scattered across the vast country of Parthia and employed on various small farms and in the towns and cities. The prisoners all hoped to be purchased in groups, so that even in captivity they would remain with some of their fellow countrymen.

The seventh Legion was the first group of prisoners to depart, and Tyluxes was given the command of escorting this convoy. The voice of the giant Parthian was soon heard declaiming his discontent, for he considered guarding prisoners to be lowly employment, and now that the battle had been won, he was eager to return to his wife and family. Surena came quickly to pacify the aggrieved man. They had fought together on many occasions, and Surena was now anxious to ensure that Tyluxes followed the King's order with good grace. From the short time which Surena had spent with the King's ministers, he had learnt a little of the treachery of politics. Surena knew that it was dangerous to rile so openly against the King, and he hastened to pacify Tyluxes when he heard him protesting so vociferously. With difficulty, Surena convinced his companion that the duty required of him was far from demeaning, given the exceptional size of the group of prisoners, and their fearsome fighting reputation. Tyluxes was soon pacified, but only because his mercurial temper cooled as quickly as it rose. He summoned Marcus and gave instructions for their departure the following dawn. As for Surena, he was relieved that Tyluxes had stopped his loud complaining, and he rose to leave and return to his own tent.

Marcus arrived just as Surena was taking leave of Tyluxes,

and when Marcus entered the tent he recognized the Parthian commander who had led his men so bravely and resourcefully against the Romans. Tyluxes switched to Greek and presented Marcus to Surena. The Parthian acknowledged Marcus with a curt but sincere greeting, and turned to leave. Marcus barely had time to assess Surena, but the impact that the visit had made on Tyluxes was still evident after Surena had departed, and from this Marcus was able to form some idea of the man's worth. In the few days which Marcus and Tyluxes had spent collaborating, the Roman had formed a high opinion of him. Thus when Marcus observed how Tyluxes remained influenced by Surena, long after the commander had left the tent, the Roman knew that he had momentarily been in the presence of greatness.

The two men now relaxed in Tyluxes's tent as they sipped cool wine and discussed their imminent departure. Tyluxes mentioned the numerous irrigation projects on which the prisoners might be employed, and Marcus casually referred to his engineering experience. Tyluxes demanded to know more, and Marcus willingly spoke of his early experience in the shipyard at Massalia and his apprenticeship as an engineer with the Legion. Tyluxes pressed him for more details as to the kind of projects on which he had worked, and how far his experience stretched. In the course of the dialogue Marcus took pains to mention how efficient the Romans were when they worked as a team, he referred to their experience as a unit and the obvious necessity of the laborers sharing the same language. Marcus was pleased to hear that the Romans would not all be dispersed across the kingdom, since he was now endeavoring to ensure that he could remain with as many of his comrades from the Gallic cavalry as possible. Captivity would be easier to bear with the company of his comrades, and in any case Marcus had no intention to remain a prisoner for any length of time, if an opportunity arose to escape.

15

Parthia, 53 BC

As the pre-dawn sunshine gave a faint glow to the horizon, Tyluxes gave orders for the breaking of the camp and Marcus and the Parthian officers moved around the camp, waking the men and issuing instructions for their imminent departure. Only Tyluxes knew their destination, which lay 1,100 miles to the north east, but all knew the sooner they started the long journey the better for marching would be much harder once the fierce desert sun began to beat down on them. The prisoners were soon ready to depart, they had few personal belongings left and thus breaking camp was a simple and speedy process. Marcus had remained spokesman and *de facto* leader for the expanded group of prisoners, and Tyluxes had given him detailed instructions for their march. Marcus had exercised all his diplomacy whilst dealing with the giant Parthian, and he had persuaded Tyluxes to allow him some control in the ordering of the prisoners. The Romans were to march in their former units under the constant scrutiny of the horse archers. The powerful Parthian had also accepted Marcus's advice on a few issues for the order of the convoy and the complex problems of arranging adequate supplies for the convoy and those which were to follow. Tyluxes was to lead the first group of prisoners, which included Marcus towards Merv, and at each camp they were to prepare a site for the subsequent groups to use as they followed in turn. The bulk of the royal officials elected to travel in the subsequent train, but a small core was to travel with Tyluxes and organise the logistical details at each stop. The royal officials bore the King's seal which gave them the power to commandeer supplies throughout the kingdom.

When the convoy set off it was composed of an odd assortment of distinct units. At the front rode the royal officials with their luxurious wagons and cumbersome retinues; the ministers had insisted they occupied the best and least dusty position in the convoy. Following the officials there rode the contingent of cataphracts which were under the command of Tyluxes; although they did not ride in their armour, the deadly long lances which the horsemen carried marked them out from the lowly horse archers. The cataphracts were the elite Parthians of Tyluxes unit, and each man was followed by a mounted servant bearing his armour and belongings. The cataphracts were a little annoyed at the presumption of the royal officials who progressed with much noise and disarray at the front of the convoy; however Tyluxes had appeased them by pointing out that he needed the cataphracts to ride near the prisoners so their powerful and ostentatious presence would prevent any escape attempts.

Although Tyluxes had invented this explanation merely to soothe the wounded egos of his cataphracts, there was a degree of truth in his comments. Immediately behind the cataphracts there marched the prisoners, and the sight of the mounted cataphracts with their long-bladed lances certainly dispelled all thoughts of escape. The Roman prisoners marched in their depleted former units; some centuries had sustained such severe casualties that they were reduced to one tenth of their former size. However, as they formed up to depart the legionaries rediscovered some of their former pride, as Marcus had hoped they would. The instincts of their rigorous training and years on campaign were too engrained to be removed by one defeat, and the legionaries appeared less bedraggled once they were arrayed in their units. Around the prisoners their rode a fluid group of horse archers, these guards would also ride between the Roman units, keeping watch with eagle-eyes and arrows already notched on their bowstrings. The Parthian horse archers were unused to ordered military journeys and in this case their fluid movements provided a supremely effective counterpoint to the Romans organised ranks. There was no routine to their inspections and consequently the prisoners felt they were under the constant scrutiny of the omnipresent horse archers. Tyluxes knew that he could not prevent the prisoners from realising how few horse archers there were guarding them, but he hoped through the expedient organising of the convoy, to delay the discovery for as long as possible.

Over the ensuing weeks the convoy was adjusted and altered as they progressed, until it formed a reasonably effective travelling unit. Tyluxes regretted that the royal officials would not be moved from their position at the forefront, nor would they be parted from their cumbersome wagons and wieldy retinues. The exigent officials also demanded that their wagons accompany them at the front of the convoy, rather than follow with the other vehicles at the rear. The officials' wagons often got stuck in loose sand, holding up the whole convoy and forcing Tyluxes to order a group of prisoners to leave their position in the rear and haul the wagons back onto firm ground. This was always a tense time for the Parthian guards, and they supervised the operation with wary vigilance and undisguised scorn for the pampered officials who would not travel without their luxurious baggage. Despite these set-backs the convoy progressed at a steady pace; each day they rose in the pre-dawn light and set off to take advantage of the cooler morning before the heat of the sun forced them to rest in the afternoon. As the convoy travelled further away from Carrhae they moved out of the barren desert and into the low hills which stretched across northern Parthia. The loose stones and rocky roads presented a new type of problem and the convoy was frequently delayed whilst broken axles or snapped wheel-spokes were repaired.

Each morning they marched into the first rays of the rising sun, and as the warm rays dried the dew from his cloak Marcus tried to calculate their position and their ultimate destination. It was hard to gauge how far they had travelled as the Parthians deliberately took a circuitous route to avoid passing too near any towns or cities. On several occasions Marcus observed numerous wisps of smoke rising from the hearths of a large town to form a faint cloud in the clear air, but the Parthians always led the prisoners away from these locations. Marcus attempted to probe Tyluxes for further information about their destination but the large man remained reticent. Although Tyluxes liked and admired Marcus, he also recognized the burning vitality in the Roman's blue eyes, and the determined set of Marcus's shoulders, which indicated that he would not readily succumb to a life of slavery. Indeed it was only to secure the survival and comfort of his men that Marcus had agreed to assist Tyluxes in the ordering of the convoy. Despite the unarticulated tensions which both of them recognized, the two men enjoyed each other's company and a guarded but genuine bond of friendship soon developed out of their mutual respect. After a long day marching Tyluxes would often invite Marcus to his tent for a goblet of wine whilst they discussed any necessary alterations to the order of marching, or any difficulties which had arisen during the day. As Marcus left the tent one evening he hoped once again that he would not have to face Tyluxes when he made his eventual break for freedom.

The powerful Parthian would make a formidable opponent under any circumstances, and with their nascent friendship as a further obstacle Marcus hoped fervently that the situation would never arise when he had to fight Tyluxes.

Marcus was puzzled by the length of their journey, he knew from the Roman maps he had studied that there were sizeable Parthian towns within a few days march of Carrhae. Any of those towns, or indeed any of the larger towns they carefully skirted during their journey, would be big enough to have a slave market and hold an auction to sell the Roman prisoners. Even allowing for the inaccuracy of the Roman maps and for their circuitous route, Marcus was certain that they had travelled a considerable distance from Carrhae and they had already entered the hilly country of central Parthia. Marcus wondered idly if they were being taken to Nissa to be paraded in front of King Orodes. Tyluxes had confirmed that they were to work as slaves, but he had not revealed any further details. With each day's march the prisoners moved deeper into Parthia and further from their homeland, this gradual progress towards the North East relaxed and reassured the Parthian guards. The prisoners slowly accepted the futility of any attempt to escape whilst they were unarmed and totally unprepared to perform the long fighting retreat which any break for freedom would require. Finally, after they had travelled over 200 miles into Parthia, Tyluxes felt sufficiently secure to reveal that the convoy's destination was Merv. The name of Merv meant little to Marcus, and his initial reaction was one of joy that the Romans were to remain as a group and not be auctioned to private owners at a public slave market.

One evening Tyluxes summoned Marcus to his tent. When Marcus arrived he found that the low table over was laden with food. Steam wafted from a large platter of stewed millet which sat in the center, whilst appetising aromas rose from roasted mutton and stuffed desert pigeon, the latter glistened as the sweet juicy fat dribbled off the bird's tender flesh. There were also plates of barbecued spicy sausages, assorted vegetable dishes and a selection of fresh fruit. Marcus's stomach let out an involuntary rumble at the sight of such a feast, after weeks subsisting on their basic diet of soup and thick wheat gruel, Marcus yearned for meat and fresh fruit. His eyes were uncontrollably drawn to the rich buttery sauces and the fatty mutton chops. With a considerable effort of self-control, Marcus looked at Tyluxes and spoke.

'You sent for me.' He stated simply.

'Yes, but first we will eat.' Replied Tyluxes, for whom the customs of the East were considered mandatory.

As they sat down to attack the feast, Marcus reflected on the numerous cultural differences he had observed. In the Roman world, it was customary to address matters of business before dining; for the Romans viewed the meal as a reward for concluding their affairs. Conversely, the Parthians thought it impolite to discuss anything serious on an empty stomach, on the premise that if one's interlocutor was hungry he could not be expected to give serious weight or consideration to any topic. Marcus remained wary as he ate; the feast was considerably superior to Tyluxes's normal fare, and Marcus was the only guest. When they had both eaten their fill they sat back and reclined on the carpets which covered the tent's floor. Marcus was struggling to remain wary, but the rich food, which filled his stomach, was making him sleepy and he relaxed with a contented sigh. A call from Tyluxes brought an attendant with an ornate carafe of fine wine; the servant placed the wine and two cups on the table and then retired. This brief event gave Marcus the occasion for another cultural observation and he continued in his amateur anthropology. The Romans drank whilst they ate;

the chefs employed by the richer Romans went to considerable trouble to match each dish with an appropriate wine or cordial. Conversely, the Parthian habit was to eat without drinking, and then to drink at the end of the meal. Initially, Marcus had some difficulty adapting to this habit, but through imitating his host he soon adjusted. The astute Roman had observed that the Parthians ate slowly but steadily, and each dry dish was balanced by another with a moist and flavoursome sauce. When Marcus ate in the same manner he found that his thirst did not trouble him during the meal and he was able to wait until after the meal before drinking. On this occasion Marcus greatly enjoyed the feast and as they relaxed and sipped the wine he had to force himself to remain alert.

'The meal was excellent, thank you.' He said to Tyluxes.

'Your pleasure is my pleasure,' replied the Parthian, touching his heart as he spoke to indicate the sincerity of his words.

The two exchanged pleasantries and observations for some time as Parthian custom required, before Tyluxes finally came to the point.

'There is something I would like to know,' he boomed, for Tyluxes was still unable to moderate the volume of his voice.

Marcus took a deep breath as he waited for the question; he knew it must be something serious for the Parthian to have gone to such lengths over the meal.

'What is the inscription on the pendant you wear?' inquired Tyluxes with a frown of consternation. He had noticed the pendant when Marcus was helping haul one of the officials' wagons out of some sand some days before when they were still in the desert.

Marcus was surprised at the simplicity of the question, and he gladly explained the Hebrew engraving and how a Jewish merchant had given him the pendant for saving his daughter in Alexandria. As he talked Marcus could not help but wonder if this innocuous information was truly the only thing which Tyluxes wanted in exchange for the sumptuous meal.

'There's another thing,' continued Tyluxes, 'what is the meaning of the tattoo you Romans have on your arm? And why do some of the prisoners not have it?'

Marcus smiled briefly at the Parthian's ignorance, and he explained the acronym of SPQR which all the Romans had tattooed on their right bicep when they joined the legions. Marcus provided the Latin phrase of *Senatus Populusque Romanus,* and then translated into Greek to explain that the words meant 'The Senate and Roman People.' The second questions was equally simple to answer, amongst the prisoners there were a number of auxiliary troops, who did not have the tattoo as they fought at the behest of their chieftain rather than as Roman professional soldiers. As Marcus proceeded he saw the smile of enlightenment creep across Tyluxes's broad face and the frown disappeared from his elongated forehead. The astute Parthian had noticed that Marcus had only provided three words in Latin for the four initials which formed the tattoo. Marcus explained that in Latin the conjunction *que,* meaning 'and' was attached to the second of the two nouns it connected.

The two continued to talk as they finished the wine, Tyluxes asking about Rome, the Romans and Latin, whilst Marcus providing whatever explanations he could. Taking the opportunity offered by a pause in the questions, Marcus asked Tyluxes about the aspects of Parthian society which continued to puzzle him. The Roman was particularly interested to examine a Parthian bow and determine how the weapon achieved its extraordinary range. Tyluxes was a warrior rather than an engineer and his command of Greek did not extend to the technical vocabulary necessary to explain the Parthian recurved composite bow. Frustrated at his inability to provide his interlocutor with an adequate explanation, Tyluxes pulled one of his own bows from its case. With a deft flick of his wrist he cut the bowstring with his dagger before handing the bow to Marcus. The bow had sprung back into a totally different form once the string was cut. With the string cut it was no longer a dangerous weapon and Tyluxes relaxed as Marcus examined the bow. Marcus's knowledge of engineering and woodwork swiftly enabled him to identify the different materials which were used to form the composite bow, and he soon recognized the superiority of a design which made such efficient use of the different properties of the components.

Both men found the conversation deeply satisfying, and the stream of questions and explanation continued unabated. Once the first carafe of wine was finished Tyluxes called for a second, when it arrived, Marcus noticed that the wine was chilled. He had seen no sign of any caves or cellars and he was intrigued as to how the Parthians managed to chill something in that region. Tyluxes spoke briefly to the attendant in Parthian, and when the man returned he was bearing strips of rough hemp fabric. Tyluxes then explained how the strips were soaked in water and then wrapped around a container. The container was then hung from a line, or placed on an elevated ledge where it would catch the wind; as the dry wind blew past the container it evaporated the water and cooled the contents. Using this simple yet expedient process the Parthians were able to enjoy chilled beverages even in hot climates. Marcus was learning a lot and he did not want to leave, but he knew that they would have a long march the following day so he reluctantly rose to depart. As he bade goodnight to Tyluxes his curiosity once again got the better of him, and he asked if the sumptuous feast had really been prepared merely to satisfy Tyluxes's curiosity on such trivial matters.

'Oh no!' exclaimed the Parthian, 'The food comes from my cousin, for we are near his home, and I wished you to partake of it with me, for as you see the kind soul always cooks enough for an entire army.' Marcus chuckled as they took leave of each other, for even with his help the pair had only made minor inroads into the mountain of food.

The next day as Marcus marched along with Titus and the other survivors from the Gallic cavalry, he reflected on the different social customs and values of Parthian and Roman society. The Romans had all observed how easily the Parthians would forgo a meal or ride for an entire day without drinking, and then when they sat to eat or drink they did so with a serious focus and concentrated pleasure in the deed, consuming far more than the Romans thought possible. Several of the Romans had compared their captors to the baggage camels which also accompanied the convoy. The Parthian way of life involved alternating periods of fasting and feasting on a smaller scale, and the Parthians seemed to have adapted to it with ease. Marcus had attempted to imitate his captors, deducing that their method must be the best adapted for the environment in which they lived. However, after the first morning without water he developed a persistent and throbbing headache from the dehydration. He concluded that the Parthian habits could not be acquired overnight, and he continued the journey adapting Roman practices to fit the situation whilst gradually developing an endurance and stamina to match his captors.

It was not until a week later that Tyluxes next summoned Marcus to his tent to resume their evening discussions, and the Roman noted a subdued smile in the Parthian's eyes. With modest pride Tyluxes revealed that the beloved wife he had left pregnant when he followed Surena to fight at Carrhae, had born him a third son and the baby was doing well. The news had reached Tyluxes from his cousin. Marcus had by now guessed that the convoy had orders to avoid all major towns, and Tyluxes confirmed this deduction when Marcus asked about their route. In a further seven weeks they would pass near Nissa, and Tyluxes knew that the royal officials would all scurry off to enjoy the luxuries of the capital whilst his men continued to guard the prisoners and the convoy progressed relentlessly towards their final destination. The journey was an epic affair and as they travelled north east the summer was drawing to a close and the nights were becoming chilly.

As the convoy approached the capital the officials demonstrated an unusual eagerness for travel. They were the first to rise and only reluctantly agreed to make camp after it had fallen dark. Tyluxes chuckled at the transformation which the proximity of their elaborate baths, fine cooks and luxurious residences had wrought on the officials. Formerly they were the slowest and most recalcitrant travellers but now their eagerness knew no bounds. When the convoy finally reached one of the five main roads which radiated out from Nissa like the arms of a starfish, the officials departed en masse, their wagons making much better progress on the tempered road and they would be in Nissa by nightfall. Meanwhile the convoy continued their onward journey as they performed a slow detour to avoid the capital whilst affording the officials a chance to deliver their reports and indulge in their numerous vices. Some three days later the convoy crossed the second of the main roads and made camp early in the afternoon. They were travelling at a leisurely pace and Tyluxes wished to make camp close to the road so he could receive the supplies which were due to be delivered from the Royal stores.

That evening there was a commotion in the camp as an

unusually ornate train was seen approaching. The train was led by a group of twelve powerful guards. As Marcus examined the new arrivals he was struck by the dainty silver lanterns which the burly guards held aloft. The detailed filigree work looked familiar and in another moment Marcus caught the faintest scent of a well-remembered perfume.

'Well that lady does get around,' muttered Marcus with a smile as he watched the courtesan's train arrive in the camp. He wondered briefly who her target could be in the lowly prisoners convoy, before he returned to his task of repairing a broken wagon wheel. Marcus's were not the only eyes which watched in amazement as the curtains were drawn back to reveal Luana reclining on a bed of furs. Unobserved by most of the convoy, Tomacles had accompanied them all the way from Carrhae. His nominal role of attendant to one of the royal officials had justified his presence in the convoy, however he was a master in avoiding attention and few people noticed him. When the officials had departed for Nissa they had only taken their closest attendants, leaving the rest to accompany their baggage whilst the convoy moved slowly around the city. As the Macedonian assassin gazed on Luana, his eyes burned with longing and his whole body filled with lust. She was the most desirable woman he had ever seen and he would pay whatever it cost to possess her just once. Luana was not classically beautiful but somehow her coquettish charms and refined techniques made the courtesan more desired than many more beautiful women. Tomacles was anxious to avoid all forms of emotional contact or commitment, both of which he viewed as potential vulnerabilities; consequently he never slept with the same girl more than once. He satisfied his lust with prostitutes when he could afford to, but he never saw any of them again.

At that moment Tomacles was dizzy with desire, it had been a long time since he had spent his advance from the King on a wild night of whoring in Nissa. During the journey he had subsisted on the rations and meagre pay of a royal clerk. Now, as if by providence, he was in possession of a vast sum of money. Two days before a messenger had arrived from the King, the man had delivered a purse and a sealed letter with one name written on it. The purse contained 400 gold coins, an inordinate amount of money and nearly ten times the fee Tomacles usually received for his services. He had begun to wonder if there had been a mistake, and then he opened the letter. The letter was sealed with an unusual stamp used by the King only when he wanted to issue commands without placing the official seal on them. When Tomacles read the name of his target he understood why the King had used that seal, and why the bag had contained so much money. Tomacles had not even contemplated the implications of the task before he set about arranging an opportunity to complete his assignment. As ever, he was unfazed by the identity, age or gender of his victims. Now Tomacles felt the weight of the purse of gold concealed in his tunic, and as he gazed with lascivious awe on Luana he knew how he would spend the gold he had yet to earn.

After the Romans' departure from Antioch, Luana had also left Syria. She had paid handsomely to be kept informed of the Romans' progress, and she was dismayed to learn of their defeat. The artful harlot found that Marcus remained in her thoughts much more than she wished, and she was partly relieved to hear of the Romans' defeat as it afforded her an opportunity to banish the handsome centurion from her heart. Luana had then decided to head east and hunt in Armenia and Parthia for any eligible and wealthy men. To a woman of her charms and means there was no problem securing safe passage from one city to another, and in each place she was provided with the best of everything. Even those few men who did not succumb to her charms thought it prudent to assist her in every way, for such women had powerful friends and it was always safest to stay on their good side. Luana was sufficiently wealthy to be able to dispense gifts, rewards and bribes at will, so her progress to Nissa had been a spectacular and stately affair. Upon arriving in Nissa, the famed courtesan had set up shop, and displayed glimpses of her highly-coveted wares before the elite Parthian men. It was whilst mixing in these circles that Luana first heard reports about the vast number of Roman prisoners taken after the battle of Carrhae. Her heart instantly resurrected Marcus from the grave to which he had been consigned, and she once again found herself plagued by thoughts of him. Unbeknown to Marucs, it was precisely to determine if he was still alive that Luana had travelled out to meet the convoy of prisoners.

That night Luana's servants set up her fine tent a short way from the main camp. She then issued dinner invitations to the principle Parthian officers and set about completing her toilette and supervising the decoration of the tent. The recipients of these perfumed messages were delighted by the prospect of meeting such a legendary woman, and they all accepted with rapturous glee. Tyluxes also agreed to go, for his curiosity drove him to see the infamous painted woman so artful and coy that men had reputedly paid 100 gold coins for the pleasure of her company. The sum was an unheard of price for a whore, and represented many years' earnings for an official. The guests all attended the sumptuous banquet, where they were suitably charmed and enraptured by the display which Luana provided. However, the hostess concluded the evening rather prematurely as she had received a message during the course of the meal. The note was an anonymous offer, 400 gold coins for one night, and it was accompanied by an advance of 50 gold coins as a token of sincerity. Normally Luana did not operate in that manner, she preferred to select her customers and then allow them to shower her with gifts rather than accept cash payments. The experienced courtesan had found that rich men were more willing to part with expensive presents than cash, for they preferred to think of the financial arrangement as them buying gifts for a girl friend rather than paying for her services. Either way it amounted to the same thing, and Luana profited greatly from her encounters. However, her lavish lifestyle also used up her funds quickly and she had not found any suitable targets in Nissa so her cash was running low. Now there was an offer of 400 gold coins for one night, the sum was so large she would scarcely have credited the offer were it not for the valuable 'token' sum which accompanied the note. Luana was curious to know who in the convoy could have such a sum of money, she had invited all the senior officers to dinner and none of them had struck her as suitable targets.

With masterful art and discreet instructions to her attendants the courtesan had ensured that the meal drew to a close promptly, and without the guests noticing her haste she had dispatched them all into the cold night in under an hour. Her initial enquiries about the Roman prisoners had proved fruitless, and she was anxious to conceal her interest. Shortly after her last guest had departed a second message arrived. It was accompanied by a further 50 gold coins, and instructed her to dismiss her attendants. The courtesan complied and waited with curiosity for her mysterious and wealthy client. The tent flap was drawn aside and Tomacles entered. The man was so unremarkable and plain that Luana initially took him for the page of her wealthy client. When she realized her mistake the accomplished harlot swiftly concealed her surprise and focused the full force of her attentive charms on Tomacles.

In the early light of the following pre-dawn Luana's tent

flap lifted slightly and Tomacles passed back into his role of innocuous royal clerk. As he walked quietly back to his tent he concluded that the night he had just spent with Luana would probably remain the high point of his life. She had surpassed his expectations in every way, and he had no regrets for the huge sum of money he had paid her. It had not even crossed his mind to kill the woman and keep the money; he was so satisfied with the night he had enjoyed. Tomacles concluded that his fee had been well spent, and his only regret was that under the courtesan's wily charms he had let slip an obscure reference to the nature of his profession. Luana had remarked that the vast sum of gold was sufficient to ransom the most powerful chieftain, to which Tomacles had remarked that it was also enough to pay for his death. The Macedonian consoled himself with the thought that Luana had probably not understood the significance of his comment and in any case she would never meet his target. Furthermore if word did get out it would be unlikely to make his task any more challenging than it already was.

As Luana lay in bed she reflected on what she had just learned. She was aware that the knowledge also placed her in a position of danger and she instructed her bodyguards to remain alert and watch over her with extra vigilance. From her bitter experience of royal courts she knew that she might pay with her life if she made the wrong move in the world of political plots and power struggles. However, Luana refused to leave the camp until she had established whether Marcus was amongst the prisoners. During the evening Luana had failed to garner any information about the Roman prisoners beyond the fact that there were over 10,000 of them and they had been split into seven convoys to make the journey to Merv.

After a light breakfast Luana went straight to see Tyluxes. Over dinner she had found the Parthian amiable and interesting, once she had adjusted to the man's thundering voice. Tyluxes had been the first of the officers to relax in her presence, and she had recognized the calm confidence which showed his marital fidelity. There was no way the giant warrior would seek to enter Luana's bed, and consequently he was almost immediately at his ease with the famed seductress. 'Just as well', Luana thought to herself, and she was not in the least offended, for his huge frame and weighty muscles would probably have crushed the bed and her along with it. When Luana crossed the campground she felt a chill run down her spine, it was as if some malignant force was watching her, but when she scanned the campground she saw nothing unusual. The vague sense of unease disappeared as soon as Luana entered Tyluxes tent; she saw Marcus seated on the carpet. He was more tanned than when she had seen him in Antioch, and the desert sun had bleached his blond hair even lighter, but she recognized him instantly. He smiled at her and rose to leave, assuming she had come to see Tyluxes. She stayed him with a deft touch of her hand and smiling to Tyluxes she settled gracefully on the carpet. The hulking Parthian had summoned Marcus to review some proposed adaptations for the convoy's wagons, now that they were travelling through rocky hills Marcus had suggested some ways in which the harnesses and loads could be adjusted to suit the different terrain.

Marcus was surprised at her action, but he was glad to remain, for Luana had lost none of her magnetism, and during the cold desert nights his thoughts had often returned to her famed charms which he had declined to enjoy. Since his capture Marcus had given up all hopes of seeing Rebecca again, and he had now accepted the possibility of finding fulfilment and happiness with another woman. Whilst Tyluxes and Luana greeted each other, Marcus inhaled the distinctive and seductive fragrance which gently enveloped the courtesan and those around her. Tyluxes was surprised to observe that Luana and Marcus knew each other, and he chuckled heartily when Luana hinted that she wished to be left alone with Marcus. With vocal excuses and a large grin on his face, Tyluxes had departed to perform some 'essential duties' about the camp. The large man's poor acting and attempts at subtlety had caused both Luana and Marcus to blush with embarrassment. There was a brief pause of indecision after Tyluxes had left but it only lasted a moment. The young couple leapt on each other, their frantic urgency apparent as they made love on the carpeted floor. Seizing the moment before circumstances tore them apart again.

As they lay in post-coital daze Luana reached over to touch the tiger brooch which Marcus still wore concealed inside his tunic. She had smiled to herself earlier when she had noticed it as she pulled his tunic over her head. This time Marcus unclasped the pin and showed her how the blue light could be made to sparkle from the polished stone. Luana lay in childish bliss as she nestled against Marcus's muscled chest. She was glad that he had not been injured in the battle, for an ugly scar would look out of place on a young body as beautiful and taut as his. Briefly Marcus recounted what had happened at Carrhae and the capitulation of the surviving cavalry after Publius had been killed. In a few words he described the long journey they made since then, and his vague understanding of their final fate. Next Luana told him what she knew; she lay propped on one elbow, running her other hand through the golden curls on Marcus's hairy chest. From her powerful acquaintances in Nissa, Luana knew much about the plans for the Roman prisoners in Merv. She was already planning how to arrange to pay for Marcus's freedom, something she could easily afford with the large sum of ready cash which was now in her possession. At this thought a frown darkened her face and she remembered the fearful new intelligence she had so recently learned.

Marcus noticed the change immediately and asked her about it. Luana paused to reflect that she had really taught the Roman a lot; few men were astute enough to read her body language, for her self-control and composure were formidable. She concluded that this man was special and then she sank into his arms and unburdened herself. Marcus was one of the most perceptive and observant men she had ever met, a skill which she knew she had helped to hone in the long night they spent talking whilst in Antioch. Marcus stored away this new intelligence and devoted his attention to the beautiful creature in his arms. As he stroked her silken hair which fell languidly over her round breasts, Marcus felt a brief chill pass over them both. His first response was to smile as the cool air caused Luana's nipples to harden. They stood erect like dark berries against the creamy white of her skin and he went to lean forward and kiss them when Luana's whole body stiffened in his arms. Looking up in surprise he just had time to see a hand withdraw from a hole which had been cut in the tent's fabric. A small dagger protruded from Luana's thigh; it had been thrown from a few metres away and despite the razor sharp point the light weapon had only driven a few centimetres into Luana's smooth leg. Marcus was too stunned to speak, and Luana's hand was covering his mouth before he could call out. As he gazed into her dark eyes they seemed deeper and more tragically beautiful to him at that moment than they ever had before. With firm determination she pushed him back onto the carpet and she extracted the dagger herself. Her body blocked his view and Marcus caressed the soft contours of her back as he lay in puzzlement.

Luana withdrew the dagger and inspected the blade before she even looked at the wound. As she feared, both sides of the blade contained indented ridges filled with a viscous black liquid.

It was an assassin's dagger, and even the slightest scratch from the poisoned blade was fatal. With tears in her eyes she lifted the carpet and buried the dagger safely in the sand underneath. Next, Luana cleaned the surface of the wound and deftly tied a scarf in a tourniquet around her thigh. She paused to wipe the tears from her eyes before she turned back to Marcus. Next she closed her eyes as she kissed him passionately, determined to conceal the truth for as long as possible. Her warms lips stifled his questions before they could be articulated, and when she did speak it was in a low throaty voice, she whispered in his ear, commanding, instructing and begging him to make love to her again. There was a new note of deep sensuality and vitality in her words which Marcus noted and was to reflect on subsequently. At that time his entire attention was focused on Luana and their love-making. They moved together with a slower and more deliberate process, building up a crescendo of passion. Instinctively each knew exactly where the other wished to be touched, caressed or kissed. They lost all track of time and the outside world, as their passion secluded them in a private space. Luana opened her heart to the young Roman as she had never done with any other man, and Marcus accepted her precious gift with tender consideration as their bodies united. When it seemed as if their pleasure and passion could not get any more intense they both climaxed. As Marcus clasped Luana in his powerful arms he felt her warm tears trickle down his back. Marcus continued to hold her as her body shook with sobs of joy, fear and love.

When she finally regained her composure, Luana told him about the assassin's blade. She had no doubt that it had come from Tomacles. The Macedonian had decided it was too risky to leave even a potential clue to his mission and shortly after leaving her tent he had decided to kill Luana. He had watched from the shadows of a wagon as she had crossed the camp and entered Tyluxes's tent. The entrance to the tent was well guarded and it had taken Tomacles some time to work his way around to the back of the tent without being observed. He had then cut the fabric of the tent and thrown his deadly missile at Luana, knowing that the blade's dark poison would complete his task even from the merest scratch. Luana was certain that Tomacles would have left the camp immediately after his fatal delivery, racing to reach Surena before any warning could alert the noble Parthian that the King had sent an assassin to murder him. It was as futile to pursue Tomacles as it was to fight against the poison which was coursing through her bloodstream. However, Luana knew that she could not remain in Tyluxes's tent with Marcus. Although an experienced soldier, the naïf centurion was totally unfamiliar with the dangerous world of political intrigue, and she did not want him or Tyluxes involved in the potentially devastating recriminations which would follow her death. With a supreme effort she dragged herself to her feet and returned to her tent, supported by her attendants. After she had explained the situation Marcus was beside himself with grief, he had never encountered such an enemy and he was stunned at the enormity of Luana's revelation. He had attempted to follow her and Luana had been obliged to order her bodyguards to seize him and leave him bound and gagged in Tyluxes tent. The guards promptly obeyed their mistress, remaining totally oblivious to the nefarious assassin who had avoided their vigilance.

An hour later the whole camp turned to watch the ostentatious departure of the famed courtesan and her luxurious train. None of the spectators were able to see that behind the diaphanous curtain of the ornate sedan chair, Luana's body lay lifeless against the rich furs. When Tyluxes returned to his tent his affable grin dissolved instantly at the sight of Marcus bound and gagged on the floor. He quickly released the Roman and demanded an explanation. When Marcus delivered his account of the incredible events Tyluxes sank to the floor in dismay. He realized immediately that Luana's actions had saved both of them, and he silently admired her fortitude. However, the Parthian's greatest concern was about the news that the King had sent an assassin to kill Surena. Tyluxes knew that he would be unable to save Surena, for even if he warned him in time there was nowhere that was safe from the expert assassin. Tyluxes mourned for the loss of his comrade and bitter hatred filled his heart as he reflected on the treachery of King Orodes. However, his cold logic and experience told him that no man is an island entire unto himself, and Tyluxes had responsibilities towards his recently expanded family. Reluctantly, Tyluxes forced himself to abandon all thoughts of revenge and he gave the order to break camp.

For some time Marcus remained in shock, traumatised by the intensity of the morning's events. His mind was just beginning to grasp that Luana had come to Parthia looking for him, and that once she knew she was dying her final desire had been to make love with him. Their passion had increased her pulse and quickened the speed with which the poison was pumped around her body. The tears which Marcus could still feel on his back now seemed all the more poignant and significant. Tyluxes now knelt beside him and tried to explain the situation to the distraught Roman. His first words went unheeded and Tyluxes had to slap Marcus before he could force him to focus on the situation. Meanwhile the camp was bustling with the preparations to leave. Tyluxes summoned a trusted attendant and ordered him to remove the side of the tent with great caution, and then to burn it once the convoy had departed. The Parthian knew how lethal the assassins' poison was, and he did not intend to take any chances. The man was also instructed to bury the dagger under two metres of sand to ensure its lethal poison did not harm any others. Marcus marched all that day in a daze. Titus and his companions endeavored to support him and lift his spirits but Marcus was struggling through a difficult transition. Whilst training and fighting with the legions Marcus had grown from a boy into a man, but it was only in that morning that he passed through a baptism of fire when he encountered the extreme range of evil and sacrifice of which people were capable. It took Marcus three whole days to recover his spirits and it was a worldly, experienced and much chastened man who arrived in Merv some five weeks later.

16

Merv, Parthia, 53 BC

By the time the first convoy arrived at the city of Merv, the autumn was well advanced and the nights were bitterly cold. Titus and a number of the other prisoners had developed deep racking coughs from sleeping in the open. Marcus and Tyluxes were anxious that the coughs could develop into consumption, and they lost no time in organising the materials and construction of simple huts to hold the prisoners at night. Once they had completed their camp, the healthy prisoners started work on six other camps for the remaining convoys which were due to arrive shortly. During the day the sun warmed the sick prisoners and they soon showed signs of recovery, but each night the camp still shook with their reverberating coughs. Gradually the benefits of having a roof to sleep under combined with the rest from incessant travelling, ensured that all the prisoners recovered and the camp escaped the threat of consumption. Marcus had learned about the disease from a fellow officer whilst serving in Gaul, and each day he had warily examined the sputum which the men coughed up for the tell-tale rust-colored splotches which showed the onset of the disease. An outbreak of consumption would have sounded the death knell for many of the prisoners; there were no medical resources available and the infection would have spread quickly. Fortunately the dreaded disease did not appear in the camp.

Titus was amongst the first to recover, and Marcus was delighted to have his comrade and companion restored to good health. The effort of combating the infection had quickened the greying of Titus's hair, and by the time the legionary was back on his feet there was not a trace of black left in his unruly hair. During the long journey, Marcus had spent much time in conversation with the old legionary and the two had unburdened their respective concerns to each other. Titus was the only person that Marcus had told about Rebecca, and the worldly-wise legionary had been Marcus's natural confidant whilst he reflected on the enormity of the sacrifice which Luana had made for him. Marcus enjoyed talking to Titus, for the man was by far the most experienced legionary in his century. Marcus had often wondered why Titus had failed to gain any form of promotion or advancement during the 19 years in which he had followed the eagle. Titus always fobbed off such inquiries by joking that he dared not leave the inexperienced kids who formed the rest of the century, for fear they might get into a fight. The danger of professional soldiers getting into a fight tickled his dry sense of humour, and he chuckled to himself each time he repeated the phrase.

However, some weeks into the long journey Titus had revealed the real reason to Marcus. One day during his first campaign, Titus had been given command of a foraging detachment, after successfully collecting their supplies the group had started to return to the main camp. On the way back, Titus had led his men through a small copse barely a mile from the camp. In the dark wood they had been ambushed, and all twelve of the men under his command had been killed. When a support column arrived from the main camp, summoned by the noise of fighting, they had found Titus fighting single-handedly with his back to the supply wagon. The barbarians had fled into the forest and a distraught Titus had accompanied the supply wagon bearing the twelve bodies back to the camp. He blamed himself for their deaths, the farmers had offered no resistance when the legionaries came foraging, and in retrospect the ease with which they had given up their hard-earned harvest showed that an ambush had been planned. Titus believed the ghosts of the twelve dead legionaries still haunted him, and since then he had carefully avoided any position which placed him in charge of others. Occasionally, on a cold dark night when the winds whistled fiercely between the mountains, Titus had spoken to Marcus of the twelve ghosts who called to him.

The seasoned legionary had survived five different campaigns, and he had been confidently looking forward to his discharge and retirement on the plot of land which veterans were awarded at the end their service. Marcus had learnt all this information as he marched along in conversation with the old legionary. Initially these discussions had to be carried out in furtive whispers as the wary guards forbade all conversation, but once they had travelled deeper into Parthia the guards relaxed, and they permitted the prisoners to chat as they plodded along. The prisoners were very tough men; they were all experienced veterans. The long journey on foot did not tax the legionaries who were trained to march 20 miles in a day whilst carrying a large load, and then build a fortified camp each night. The Parthians were surprised and impressed by the Roman's ability to go on marching, and Tyluxes made several remarks on the subject to Marcus.

Tyluxes remained deeply grateful to Marcus for the intelligence from Luana which the he had passed on. With an immense effort of self-control Tyluxes had been able to control himself when a royal messenger had arrived in the camp two days after they left the outskirts of Nissa; the messenger reported that Surena had rebelled against the King and had been promptly executed by soldiers loyal to the King. As this message was delivered the messenger had watched Tyluxes closely, for it was well known that he had been close to Surena and the messenger had a sealed order for Tyluxes's execution in his pocket; the order was only to be used if Tyluxes showed any signs of questioning Surena's abrupt demise. Tyluxes had been able to sufficiently restrain his grief and anger at the news, and the messenger had departed with the death warrant unused. The booming Parthian had expected the news of Surena's death, but to standby whilst he heard his commander, comrade and relative, falsely accused of treason had been a difficult task. Indeed the subsequent conversation and the renewal of his oath of loyalty was one of the few occasions when Tyluxes spoke in a quiet voice rather than with his characteristic boom. Tyluxes knew that he owed his survival to the forewarning from the Roman prisoner, and whilst concentrating on keeping a low-profile he did not forget his obligation to Marcus.

Upon their arrival in Merv, the pressing need to ensure that his men were adequately housed, and the sick were tended, meant for the first few days that Marcus did not have time to examine their new surroundings. When he did look up from the simple but sturdy camp, he observed that they were quartered to the west of a large roughly square city with impressive high walls. Marcus later learnt that the city walls measured several miles in length, and the inside of the city was equally impressive in magnitude and design. Unlike many other major settlements at that time the city had not been built on the site of a previous settlement but it was sited next to the previous city. The new settlement was a planned city and the consideration which had gone into its construction was evident in the grid pattern of streets and the orderly manner in which buildings had been constructed.

A large irrigation canal ran parallel to the western wall of the city, and this was the direction in which Marcus and the prisoners approached. The canal was similar in design to many of those which the convoy had passed during the last weeks of their journey, but this canal was much larger than any of the others which they had seen. Marcus appreciated the opportunity to observe the Parthians' engineering techniques and he immediately spotted some improvements which could be made. The Parthians used iron wedges to split large rocks; first a hammer and chisel were used to score a line where the desired split was intended, and then a series of progressively widening wedges were laboriously driven into the rock to split it. Marcus knew that the Roman method was far more efficient, but he intended to save this knowledge until such time as it would be beneficial to reveal it. Marcus had never given up his hope of escape, but he knew that any attempt from Merv would require serious organisation and orchestration, for the Romans were surrounded by miles of hostile territory in every direction. Marcus knew that he would have to secure supplies and information from local sources, and one of the few tools he had at his disposal was his engineering knowledge.

The north east of Parthia contained many miles of irrigation canals; for whilst there was an abundant supply of water from the snow-melt in the mountains, it naturally flowed rapidly down the various rivers without irrigating the surrounding countryside. In order to rectify this, the Parthians had created long irrigation channels which took water from a higher point up the river to the various fields and orchards. These channels were clearly visible against the bare brown background as each one was marked by the green foliage which grew wherever water was available. Many different farmers shared the same water supply, and a complex social system had developed to ensure that maintenance work was carried out promptly, and that each farmer did not draw off more than his allotted share of the water. The need to regulate this communal resource and settle any disputes which arose, had contributed to the development of a tightly connected and structured society.

Marcus could tell at a glance that the construction and maintenance of these extensive channels required a great deal of labor, and he accurately concluded that many of the prisoners would be employed on these irrigation projects. Marcus was also interested to note that the sole visible means of crossing the River Murghab was a precarious wooden bridge which wobbled visibly as each wagon passed over it. The bridge's design was extremely basic and only wide enough for one wagon; consequently during the more busy times of the day there was always a queue of wagons waiting to cross the river and enter the city. Many of the trade routes which traversed the region converged on Merv to use the bridge, despite the bottlenecks, for the appearance of the River belied the strong currents which made fording it a dangerous option. The convergence of so many merchants and routes in Merv meant that the city had soon developed a flourishing market along with all the other amenities which merchants sought along a trade route. For the business side of life there were large caravanserais where the trains of camels, mules or horses could be stabled, customs houses where the appropriate duties or bribes were paid, and warehouses where goods could be stored. The city also boasted facilities for the personal side of life, and there were baths, taverns, gardens and brothels galore. And if any of the Jewish or Zoroastrian merchants felt the desire for spiritual solace, Merv also contained the only synagogue and Zoroastrian temple for miles around.

The city officials knew that the lucrative flow of trade

depended chiefly on the bridge, yet no one group had been willing to provide the capital to enlarge the bridge despite the evident benefits which it would bring to the whole city. Now, the arrival of such a large labor force meant that the widening of the bridge could finally be implemented, for the major cost of the scheme was the labor, and this would now be supplied by the prisoners. The project would also keep the prisoners outside the city walls, for many of the officials were apprehensive about welcoming 10,000 Roman veterans into their city, even as prisoners. Such was the fighting reputation of the legionaries that even as unarmed prisoners they were viewed with some awe and fear. Whilst the convoys had been completing the final stages of their epic journey, the city Governor and his advisers had met to organise the dispersal of the prisoners in accordance with the Royal instructions. The advance party of royal officials had delivered the King's orders, and then promptly dispersed to sample the luxuries which the city had to offer, whilst the Governor saw to the considerable logistical details.

In conversation with Tyluxes, Marcus had learned that Merv was famous throughout Parthia for its ironworks. The best steel weapons and impregnable armour of the Parthian cataphracts were made there, and the blacksmiths were famed all over Parthia. The armourers were constantly looking to buy slaves for the gruelling tasks of working the bellows and stoking the fiery furnaces. The demanding work and ruthless foremen meant that few slaves survived for more than a few years in the ironworks. Marcus hoped fervently that none of his unit would be selected for such an unpleasant fate, and he took some comfort from Tyluxes's information that many slaves were to be employed on public engineering projects. However, Marcus knew it was useless to worry about an issue over which he had no control, and he concentrated instead on ensuring the smooth running of the camp. Marcus's services as a translator were frequently in demand. In all their labors the Romans were still watched over by the horse archers, though the guards were more relaxed now; for both captors and captives knew that over 1000 miles of hostile territory separated the prisoners from the nearest Roman garrison.

Once the remaining convoys had arrived, the prisoners were all reviewed. In total only 34 of the Romans had died during the long journey, and there were still 190 members of the Gallic cavalry contingent which had left Massalia with Marcus. The Governor lost no time in organising the auction of the prisoners; the Parthians were unused to their new role as captors and they were eager to disperse the Romans as soon as possible. Half of the prisoners were to be auctioned as private slaves, whilst the remainder would work on public projects around the city. Notices were sent to all the ironworks and foundries in the region, and when the day of the auction came, there was a large concentration of buyers assembled at the auction ground. Thanks to Tyluxes's influence, Marcus and his unit were not amongst the prisoners offered for auction. As the bidding ground filled with the foremen from the ironworks and foundries, Tyluxes looked over their hard-eyes and blistered faces and he concluded that he had repaid his debt to Marcus. The cold calculating faces of the foremen showed that they had come there to buy new tools for their trade, and like tools the slaves would be worked ceaselessly until they broke and then they would be discarded.

The auction proceeded with the organised chaos of any large civic event, and the different lots were soon dispatched to their new owners. The Governor had elected to sell the Romans in lots, and these groupings were generally based on the depleted centuries. He hoped in this way, to off-load a number of the weaker and sick prisoners in addition to the healthy ones, as well as speed up the auction process. When the auction was finished, the Governor was able to focus his full attention on the civic projects which would occupy the remaining prisoners. The sale of so many fit male slaves had generated an enormous amount of money, and whilst the Governor was permitted to keep some funds for their engineering projects, the bulk of the money was sent to King Orodes. The prisoners who had been auctioned as slaves were immediately dispatched to their new masters, and the half-empty camps seemed eerie. Marcus had a fairly good idea of the possible engineering projects in the region which could employ such a large labor force, but he had not shared his thoughts with any of the men except Titus. From Marcus's original companions in Gaul there remained his fellow centurion Gaius, the wily old Titus, Gnaeus who had recovered fully during the journey to Merv, Quintus, Appius, Servius and the feisty red-haired Caius, along with a handful of others from his century. The Gallic cavalry had been at the forefront of Publius's final charge, and they had suffered devastating losses.

Tyluxes had taken considerable pains to maintain a low-profile after his arrival in Merv, he suspected that he was under observation and he dared not endanger his family or himself by any hint of sedition. He was waiting for the first opportune moment, and then he intended to return quietly to his family and stay out of political matters. When one of the royal officials asked the hulking commander to supervise a contingent of the prisoners, he concealed his reluctance and agreed. Tyluxes had been looking forward to returning to his wife and family, but when this new task was foisted onto him he was obliged to postpone his departure. Tyluxes had hoped his contingent of prisoners would include Marcus and the other Gallic cavalry, but when this proved not to be the case there was little he could do about it. The Governor and the other officials controlled the various projects and the resources for their completion, and Tyluxes had no intention of entering into the world of bribery and coercion in which they lived and worked. Two days later, Tyluxes bade a curt but sincere farewell to Marcus, his brief booming words conveying the respect that the two men had developed for each other whilst they travelled together.

When the orders came, Marcus found that he was in a contingent of 300 prisoners which included all of the surviving Gallic cavalry. They were placed under the command of a Parthian called Melchior, and their task was to construct an extension to one of the irrigation canals. The extension would require a channel to be cut through a sheer mass of rock, which blocked one side of a valley, and prevented a stretch of potentially fertile land being irrigated or farmed. The contingent were to work far from the city, so they would set up a new camp near the worksite and remain there for the duration of the project. The new commander of Marcus's contingent was a short man, and Marcus was instantly on his guard when he first met him. Melchior had swaggered into the Roman's camp with a desire for confrontation clearly evident in the pugnacious set of his jaws and the aggressive glare in his eyes. Marcus immediately recognized Melchior as one of the universal stock types which Luana had warned him about. With her astute perception and humour Luana had described how some short men developed inferiority complexes and then suffered from 'short-man-syndrome'. During their long nocturnal conversation in Antioch, the courtesan had expanded her theories to Marcus. Luana's theories were all based on her own observations, but her wealth of experience in dealing with men ensured that her conclusions included many poignant and universal truths. Marcus had laughed when Luana had first mentioned 'short-man-syndrome', but as he listened to her expand her theory he was struck by its accuracy. Luana had described the stereotype of a short man who felt obliged to compensate for his diminutive stature by overly aggressive behaviour. Such men often moved with excessive vigour and speed, stretching out their limbs in an attempt to occupy more space. Even within his own century Marcus had been able to identify one or two men who displayed some of the traits she described. There was one fiery Gaul whose pugnacious temper had often been attributed to his red hair, but after all that he had learned from Luana, Marcus now recognized the aggressive fashion in which the man strove to compensate for his perceived inadequacy.

Melchior displayed all of the traits which Luana had identified, and Marcus warily observed his arrival at the camp. Melchior was evidently looking for an occasion to make his presence felt and to exercise his authority over the prisoners. As he dismounted he summoned a legionary in Greek to hold his horse, the Roman did not understand the instruction and it took a moment for him to make the logical deduction that he was being ordered to take the official's mount. This delay provided Melchior with the pretext he was looking for, and he immediately ordered his guards to bind and beat the prisoner. The rest of the prisoners watched in amazement as the helpless legionary was roughly seized and bound. His tunic was ripped from his back and at a signal from Melchior, the guard commenced beating the legionary. Melchior halted the beating after a brief moment and took the cane from the guard; he then personally continued to beat the prisoner. As he thrashed at the man's exposed back, the stubby commander felt in control; he was exercising his power and the other prisoners would soon fear and respect him. The savage vigour with which Melchior completed his task splashed blood over his own tunic and as the blows rained down on the helpless legionary there was a palpable sympathetic stiffening throughout the camp as the other prisoners watched the unjust punishment. During that brief and brutal example, Marcus and the other prisoners in his unit learnt that their new commander was a cruel and stupid man.

Marcus felt his muscles contract with apprehension and rage as he witnessed the undeserved and brutal punishment. He knew that the new commander would have to be treated with extreme caution. However the courageous centurion was in no way daunted by the ferocious display which Melchior had orchestrated. Marcus despised the new commander. As Marcus continued with his duties, he reflected on the recent turn of events and mused to himself. The new commander had revealed himself immediately, and for a while the advantage was temporarily with Marcus. Melchior clearly did not realise that most of the prisoners could not speak Greek, and in his ignorance he had earned the scorn and hatred of all the men he commanded. From the pre-emptory haste with which Melchior had issued all his orders Marcus deduced that the diminutive Parthian had no experience of leadership. His haste to conceal this fact, coupled with his general feeling of inadequacy would make Melchior a prickly man to deal with.

Marcus had made another important observation during the beating; one of Melchior's retinue had turned away his face in undisguised disgust at the cruel display, the compassionate man had then walked off to inspect a nearby wagon wheel. The man in question was grey-haired but still in good physical condition, as evidenced by the manner in which he carried himself. From his position within the train it seemed that he was merely a lowly official, yet he acted with the presumption and confidence of a more powerful man. The wagon wheel was one which Marcus had mended, and the elderly attendant knelt to examine it more closely. Both the Romans and the Parthians constructed their wagon wheels from wooden sections, the sole difference being that the Romans placed an iron band around the outside of the wheel. This iron rim held the various wooden pieces together and prevented the wood from being worn out and splintered by the rocky roads. The rim was formed from a single ring of iron which was placed over the wooden wheel when it was red hot. The wheel and rim were then immediately plunged into cold water. As the iron cooled rapidly, it contracted to form a tight fit around the outside of the wheel, and this held the different wooden pieces firmly in place.

Marcus recognized the appraising eye of a fellow engineer, and he was about to approach and engage the man in conversation when he was arrested by a shout from Melchior. The belligerent little man had snapped the cane over the legionary's back and he was now calling vociferously for a replacement. When no other canes were found to be at hand, Melchior decided to abandon the beating. Whilst engaged in the brutal spectacle he had felt assertive and masterful, but now with the stump of the bloody cane in his hand, and all eyes on him, he disliked the attention and felt a prickly sweat break out under his tunic. He lacked the courage to stand inactive whilst he remained the center of attention, and he had marched directly into the tent which had been erected in anticipation of his visit. In a voice which was surprisingly shrill for his stocky frame, Melchior had ordered some of the other prisoners to remove the wounded legionary. Marcus had been one of the few to understand the Greek command, and he moved forward with alacrity to aid the stricken legionary. Titus was at his side in an instant, and they swiftly carried the injured man back to his hut. Marcus had been reluctant to reveal that he alone understood Greek, but the unnatural squeakiness of Melchior's voice had shown just how tense and nervous the man was, and Marcus knew worse would follow if the squat commander thought he was being disobeyed. Once the purport of the instructions was clear, several other legionaries had started forward to aid their comrade, so the speed of Marcus's response was only noted by the attendant who had been examining the wagon wheel.

After Marcus and Titus had got the injured legionary into a hut they dressed his shredded back as best as they could. The pain of moving him had caused the man to pass out, so Marcus was able to bath the wounds in salty water without causing him anymore pain. The stream of obscenities which Titus had been muttering about Melchior, had grown progressively more colorful and audible as they had moved away with the legionary. Now as they knelt over the bloody mess which Melchior had created, Titus cursed the man with all the vitriol he could muster.

'I couldn't agree more, the man is an utter shit.' added a voice in passable Latin, and as the two Romans looked up they saw the figure of the elderly attendant blocking the doorway of the hut.

'But you should pity him, not hate him,' continued the new arrival in a calm and peaceful voice.

'I'll pity him once I've ripped his back to shreds like this,' muttered Titus, his angry indignation still burning strong.

'So you speak Latin,' observed Marcus.

'And you speak Greek,' rejoined the observant Parthian.

'If you know he is a shit, and you pity him, then why do you still serve him?' enquired Marcus cautiously.

'I don't serve him,' came the reply, 'I work for the Governor, and at present my task is to accompany this contingent of prisoners. Melchior is in charge of the contingent but I do not serve him.'

Marcus wanted to ask how their visitor dared to behave so boldly in front of Melchior, but his curiosity was cut off by the man pushing them aside and kneeling by the stricken legionary who was slowly regaining consciousness. The elderly man immediately took control of the situation, and withdrawing a number of phials from his tunic, he sent Titus to fetch fresh water, as he completed bathing the wounds. From the confidence and skill with which he worked, Marcus could see that the man was experienced, and he moved back to let the Parthian dress the wounds. When Titus returned with fresh water, the man shook in the contents of two phials, and stirred them together.

'Bathe his back with this solution every hour through the night, and there will be no infection.' The last words were uttered with such a sense of conviction that Marcus almost imagined the old man was banishing any infection from the wounds, rather than describing his medication.

The man rose to leave, and turned to address Marcus.

'My name is Olthar,' he stated simply, 'What is yours?'

'Marcus,' came the succinct reply.

With an all-encompassing wave of his wrist, which took in the medication, his appearance in the hut and his earlier bold display of disgust, Olthar explained, 'My cousin is the King's concubine.'

Marcus had been wondering how Olthar had dared to behave so boldly before, and now that the explanation had arrived unbidden, next Marcus found himself wondering how the elderly man had read his thoughts. Once again the reply came before he had even articulated the question.

'You have learnt to read people, but your thoughts remain written on your face for all to see,' added Olthar with a wry smile. 'It is like an infant mouthing the words and following the text as he learns to read, now you must learn to read without revealing it.' With this mysterious injunction Olthar departed, and left Marcus and Titus to tend the legionary.

Melchior took up residence in the camp that night, and the

following morning he issued instructions for his contingent of prisoners to depart to their work site far from the city. After the brutal display which the new commander had made on the first day, the Romans had been anxious to guess and obey his instructions, even when they did not understand the language in which he addressed them. This practice had proved successful for such simple tasks as holding horses and unloading baggage, but the reality that none of the prisoners appeared to understand Greek soon became apparent to Melchior. At this revelation he was troubled by momentary guilt at the needless beating of the first legionary, but on reflection he decided it was safest to conceal his ignorance and pretend that it had been an intentional and exemplary lesson for the prisoners. Amongst Melchior's staff, Olthar was the only one with a reasonable command of Latin and the wise man was soon acting as intermediary between the petulant commander and the prisoners. Melchior disliked the old man, and he was determined not to rely on Olthar to relay all of his instructions. He had no desire to converse with the prisoners, and once work began he resolutely believed he would soon teach them to understand his basic commands.

Once the contingent of prisoners had moved to their work site, they were instructed to construct a camp nearby. The camp was to be their base throughout the winter and Melchior reluctantly accepted that it was necessary to spend some time on its construction. Melchior had split the prisoners into two groups, the first of which he supervised and the second of which was supervised by Olthar. Melchior was convinced that with harsh punishments and simple gestures he would be able to instruct the prisoners as well as Olthar could in Latin. However, at the end of each day the competent old man and his group had always achieved more than the other group. Melchior was immediately on the defensive, and rather than being pleased with the progress of their task, he viewed Olthar's success as a direct challenge to his authority and decisions. The stubby commander drove his group with ever more exacting determination, and the severity of his punishments increased accordingly. Marcus had been fortunate to fall under the command of Olthar, and when the two realized what was occurring they discretely agreed to slow their rate of progress.

At last, Melchior was able to achieve more work in a day than the Olthar's team, and he gloated about it with evident satisfaction. However, the diminutive commander's new satisfaction did nothing to alleviate the severity of the beatings he ordered on a daily basis. On one occasion, Melchior even instructed the same man to be beaten twice in one day. The resultant wounds crippled the unfortunate prisoner and he was no longer able to work. When the Governor found out about this, he demanded that Melchior pay the city for the damaged slave. The news had greatly annoyed Melchior, for a fit male slave was an expensive commodity. However, the experience did oblige him to consider his use of force more judiciously, and the beatings were less severe subsequently. Once the camp was complete the prisoners began work on the extension to the irrigation canal. They continued to work in two groups, and Olthar did his best to manage the speed of progress such that Melchior did not feel threatened. This was no easy task, for the stubby little man viewed each set-back or delay as a personal attack on his ability as a commander. Melchior was so sensitive to the prospect of criticism that he became distraught if a large rock obstructed the progress of the channel, or one of the frequent landslides blocked the canal. As the weeks passed and the work advanced, the prisoners learnt how to manage their irascible commander.

One day, Olthar summoned Marcus to the front of the work site. Olthar was examining a large number of boulders which blocked the proposed route of the canal. The giant stones were too large to be pulled out of the way and Olthar had reluctantly concluded that they would have to be split into more manageable sizes before they could be moved. This would require hours of back-breaking labor, as the prisoners chiselled and hacked the boulders into smaller pieces. Olthar knew that Melchior had examined the whole projected route before they started work, and it was no co-incidence that he had allocated this difficult section to Olthar and his group. Marcus decided that the time had come to demonstrate one of the superior Roman engineering techniques. He pulled a spar of wood from one of the supply wagons and wedged it into a natural fissure in one of the boulders. Then he took a water-skin from the supply wagon and loosened the stopper, he laid the water-skin so that a slow dribble of water ran onto the wooden spar. Marcus then returned to his work, leaving Olthar bemused beside the boulder. The next morning when Olthar returned to the scene he saw that the spar had split the rock in two. He marveled at the ingenious technique which meant wood and water could split stone and he picked up the spar with wonder. The spar was wet and heavy, for it had swollen with the water it had absorbed.

Using this Roman technique, Olthar's group of prisoners was able to clear the boulders from their section of the route with relative ease. Meanwhile, Melchior continued to supervise a different section of the new watercourse. The obstinate commander refused to learn Latin, and he continued to issue all his instructions in Greek with imperious disdain, relying on the threat of further beatings to clarify his meaning. In one part, the channel had to pass across a particularly steep slope of loose rock. Melchior had instructed the prisoners to build the necessary supports, but as this part of his orders had not been followed by any pushing, shoving or beating the Romans had not understood the instruction given in Greek. Having issued the order, Melchior promptly forgot all about the safety supports and he continued directing work on the channel in his usual despotic manner. The men were too terrified to raise any comment about the danger of working without the safety supports, and it was only when a quick shower prompted a terrible landslide that Melchior realized the supports had never been installed. The landslide trapped most of Melchior's workforce in the falling rocks.

As soon as word of the disaster reached him, Olthar brought his group of prisoners to help with the rescue efforts. During the afternoon the rain started again and it fell continuously as the soaking Romans struggled to drag their battered, crushed and maimed comrades from underneath the rock-fall. The rain made the rocks slippery, and the prisoners worked under the constant spectre of another landslide. It was three days before the landslide was completely cleared, and the casualties were 35 prisoners killed, 3 paralysed and 18 injured. During the rescue operation Melchior has remained in his tent, he had taken the landslide as such a direct attack on his efficiency and capability as a leader that he could not even muster the courage to leave his tent. When the stubby commander was eventually summoned by the Governor he left the sanctuary of his tent in a panic. He strode quickly to his mount, and felt his skin burning with inferiority every step of the way. His hands shook as he fumbled for the reins, and mounting swiftly he rode towards the city. Melchior believed the landslide would be seen as incontrovertible proof of his own inadequacy and failure, he was ashamed not by the needless deaths he had caused but by what the landslide had revealed to one and all; he was not a leader of men, and never would be. The Governor found his explanation unsatisfactory and Melchior was dismissed from his post immediately. The city was unable to recoup the full cost of the dead and injured slaves, for the sum was far beyond Melchior's means and he was thrown into the debtors' dungeon.

17

MERV, 53-48 BC

AFTER MELCHIOR WAS dismissed as commander, Olthar was given control of the remaining prisoners and instructed to complete the irrigation canal as best he could. The wise old man worked with Marcus as his deputy, and the team managed to complete the canal ahead of schedule, despite the losses they had sustained. Under the guidance and control of Olthar, the work had progressed rapidly. The Parthian was always willing to hear any suggestions or feedback from the Romans, and consequently the group worked using the best engineering techniques from Parthia and Rome. The benefits of improved communication between the two polyglot supervisors and the men also aided the rapid progress of the work. The Governor and his officials were particularly impressed by Olthar's achievement; they planned to assemble all the prisoners over the winter so they could work on widening the main bridge at the entrance to the city.. During the cold winter months the River Murghab was at its lowest and it would be easiest to work on the bridge at that time. However, the short days and inclement weather meant that they would need all the manpower they could muster, in order to complete the work before the spring melted the snows and the River level rose.

The Governor summoned Olthar to his official residence and

asked him to explain how he had completed the project at a faster rate with fewer men. Olthar had outlined his different approach to the task and he had spoken of the role Marcus has played as his deputy and technical adviser on various engineering aspects. He also spoke of the Roman advances in engineering and how these had permitted the project to proceed more rapidly. The hoary engineer became quite animated at the opportunity to expound on the Roman innovations he had observed and adopted. Olthar had even rushed out of the lavish meeting hall to fetch one of the iron-rimmed wheels which he was attempting to describe. He ordered a group of guards to lift his wagon onto some blocks whilst he removed a wheel as an example, then as an afterthought he had the guards remove a normal wheel from a nearby wagon. With the two different wheels in his possession Olthar had hastily returned to the Governor and his advisers. His robes were now besmeared with mud and grease and he made a bizarre sight as he marched with eager determination into the ornate hall with a large wagon wheel under each arm. Fortunately the man's sheer force of enthusiasm carried all with him, and those present eagerly examined the proffered wheels. The only problem arose when Olthar left the hall; an irate and portly housewife stormed up the steps as fast as her rotund frame would permit, she then proceeded to belabor and harangue him for sabotaging her wagon and delaying her shopping. It took a pair of determined guards to return the woman to her wagon, which by that time had its wheel replaced and she was sent on her way.

The Governor expressed an earnest desire to meet the Roman who had introduced these technical developments, and they granted Olthar special permission to bring Marcus into the city. The Roman prisoners had now spent nearly a year working around Merv, but the ban preventing them from entering the city remained in place. Marcus was delighted when he heard the news, for he had long yearned to see the inside of the huge city, and to inspect the graceful monuments and temples which Olthar had described to him. Unlike Roman towns, the city walls of Merv contained the entire city, rather than just the military and administrative center, consequently Marcus and the other prisoners had seen nothing of the city which sheltered elusively behind its tall walls. As Marcus and Olthar rode through the west gate they passed the large caravanserais which fringed the city. These had been purposefully located just outside the city walls to avoid the difficulties of leading the laden baggage trains through the crowded city streets. Each caravanserai was based around an internal courtyard which was often ornately decorated and comfortably appointed. However, Marcus had to rely on Olthar's descriptions as he could not see past the stables and storerooms which formed the outside of each caravanserai.

Marcus and Olthar first passed through one of the craftsmen's quarters, where innumerable little workshops opened directly onto the street. In one section the air was filled with the delicious clean scent of wood shavings and sawdust, and the smell was accompanied by the soft tapping of chisels and the grating of saws. The smells and sounds transported Marcus back to his father's shipyard in Massalia, and he reflected nostalgically on those happy times as they passed the carpenters. Another part of the city contained the storerooms and shops of the perfumers and incense shops, the air was redolent with the heady smell of expensive oils, which were laboriously extracted from masses of flowers. Behind the perfume shops Marcus saw the piles of wilted petals, stacked like discarded packaging now that they had been robbed of their precious fragrance. Next, Marcus heard the main market, the clamour of which reached them long before they saw the stalls. There was a constant cacophony of sound from the myriad small shops as the vendors vociferously advertised their wares. Amongst the din Marcus was pleased to identify many of their calls, for during the time he had spent in Parthia he had learnt many words of the language, and now he could make out the names of most of the wares and foodstuffs being offered for sale.

After the calm and solitude of their isolated camps and life in the open, it was a shock for Marcus to be back in a city. Since their capture at Carrhae, he had spent nearly 16 months as a prisoner, travelling, living and working in the open countryside, now the din of all the workshops and the shouts, smells and sight of so many people surprised him. However, he soon re-adjusted to the onslaught on the senses. Marcus was also re-adjusting to the familiar sensation of riding a horse; Olthar had lent him his spare mount to make the journey into the city. This was a great honor and a mark of confidence, for the Parthians guarded their horses more jealously than the any other possession. It was in part to accommodate their treasured equine herds that the Parthians had built such large city walls; in the event of an attack it was vital for the Parthians to protect their mounts. At the approach of any enemies the horses would be moved within the city walls, for without their mounts the Parthians felt paralysed. This dependency was, in part, due to the vast distances between settlements in that region, but the Parthians were descended from nomadic stock, and the cultural legacy had never totally disappeared. Without their horses the Parthians felt vulnerable, isolated and weak; Marcus had remarked with interest during the journey from Carrhae, that the Parthians had guarded their mounts more heavily than their weapons. The Parthians knew that the distances in their country were so large that no prisoners could escape without horses, however many arms they managed to procure.

Marcus was constantly turning in his saddle as his inquisitive gaze took in all of the sights he passed. The streets were laid out on a grid pattern, making it easy to find their way, and the junctions also offered brief insights far down the alleys and streets they passed. As they neared the center of the city, Marcus observed that the houses grew progressively grander; these were evidently the dwellings of the military elite who ran the city. The noise of the market and the craftsmen was left far behind them, for the elite did not live near the clamour of the markets or workshops. Each of the large houses they passed was built around an interior courtyard, and as they rode past Marcus caught brief glimpses of shaded gardens and ornate rooms adorned with vivid frescoes and rich carpets. The two riders were now approaching the city center, and Marcus was impressed by the large temple which opened onto the main square. In the center of the square was an elevated tomb, which Olthar explained housed the bones of the Seleucid General who had founded the city. The circular temple to the right was Zoroastrian, and behind the main structure there were the other buildings associated with that religion. Olthar pointed out the ossuaries of the Zoroastrians and the tombs of the Jews. There was also a large synagogue which opened onto the square on their left; the city had a Jewish population who monopolised the lucrative mercantile trades. As in many cities, the wealth of the Jewish community gave them influence far beyond their numbers, and the synagogue was a grand affair even though each Sabbath it was only half full.

As they passed the synagogue, Marcus discretely checked to see that the pendant from Reuben was still hanging inside his tunic. He found it reassuring to know that if the occasion arose, he might claim some aid from such a powerful group. During the ride from the camp Marcus had given further reflection to the position in which he found himself. Whilst in the saddle his yearning for freedom returned ever more strongly, and he once again turned his mind to thoughts of escape. He was however conscious of the trust which Olthar had placed in him by lending him his horse, and Marcus banished all thoughts of making a break for freedom on that occasion. He never intended to remain a slave in Parthia for the rest of his days, but he knew that any escape attempt would be a demanding and dangerous affair. He and any companions who joined him would only have one chance, for any prisoners caught trying to escape were executed immediately.

During the months they had spent working on the irrigation canal, Marcus had managed to acquire some general information about the surrounding countryside. He had stored these precious pieces of information away for any future escape attempt. There was no doubt that they would require horses, and this presented another serious consideration, for the Parthians continued to guard their beloved mounts with vigilance. As the two riders entered the city, Marcus became caught up in the vivacious flow of humanity. Olthar now indicated the large house on the far side of the square.

'That's where we're going,' he stated as they directed their mounts through the throng of people who filled the square.

'It's the Governor's mansion, though I don't envy him the location,' remarked Olthar. Over the whole square there hung a faint but distinct stench of death and decay. The smell came from the platforms behind the temples, where the bodies of the deceased were exposed for dogs and vultures to eat the flesh.

The Zoroastrian faith held that neither earth nor fire could be polluted by the flesh of the dead; they believed that when the soul departed from the body at death, all the impurities were left in the flesh. This polluted flesh could not be burnt or buried, so the Zoroastrians exposed the bodies of their dead to carnivorous animals, and then the bones were collected and stored in the ossuaries which Olthar had pointed out to Marcus. The dogs and vultures which performed this service were treated with reverence and accorded the same level of respect as the deceased people they consumed. Marcus was deeply shocked at the explanation which Olthar provided, but he endeavored not to be judgemental as he focused on learning about the Parthians and their culture. Both the Jewish and the Zoroastrian ossuaries faced East, for the religions shared the belief that the dead would be resurrected at dawn. Unfortunately, the supply of cadavers kept even the greediest dogs satiated, and many of the corpses began to decay before they were fully consumed. The resultant stench hung over the main square, and although the Governor's mansion was in the most prestigious position, the honor came at a price.

When Marcus and Olthar dismounted, the Roman noted the strong smell of incense which was burnt continuously in the Governor's house. A page ran to take their horses, and then the two men climbed the short flight of broad stairs which brought them into the main reception hall. Olthar nodded good-naturedly at the guards who had recently delivered him from the onslaught of the irate housewife whose wagon wheel he had borrowed in the course of his last visit. The men waved back with warm smiles, for they liked Olthar and they also liked the generosity with which he tipped. After a brief wait Marcus and Olthar were shown into the Governor's presence. The Governor's ample figure was seated on silken cushions, with a semi-circular table in front of him on which he wrote and sealed his orders. Marcus's attention was focused on the silken material which possessed a lustre unlike any other he had seen. It was even more brilliant than the fine veil which Luana had worn, or the bolts of cloth he had seen in Reuben's storehouse or the Parthian silken banners at Carrhae. Olthar acted as interpreter for the brief conversation which followed, but even with his most diplomatic efforts there was no way he could transform Marcus's simple and blunt replies into the elaborate and flattering responses to which the Governor was habituated.

The interview was not a success, for the Governor was accustomed to the grovelling sycophancy, and he was annoyed by the clear pride and independence which Marcus unconsciously displayed. For although the Roman had performed the requisite bows and greetings, there remained a defiant spark of pride in his eyes. Even as Marcus bowed to the recumbent Governor, the broad set of his shoulders showed him as a man unaccustomed to a life of slavery or servitude. In providing only the information that he was asked for, and delivering his replies in the most succinct fashion, Marcus was acting with traditional Roman reticence. He was ignorant of the Parthian customs when dealing with powerful men, and despite the artful gloss which Olthar strove to add in translation, his abruptness offended the Governor. Olthar was quick to pick up on the Governor's unfavorable reaction, and he brought the interview to an end as swiftly as possible.

During the course of the conversation with Olthar, the Governor confirmed that the prisoners were to be assembled in the next few days with a view to commencing work on the bridge leading up to the city's gates. Marcus was pleased that he managed to follow the gist of this exchange in Parthian, although he was careful to keep his face a mask of blank ignorance. After meeting one of the Roman prisoners at such close quarters the Governor found himself disquieted by the burning ardour in the man's blue eyes, and he reflected that whilst the city would benefit from the Romans' labor, there was a definite risk in keeping such a large force of trained soldiers so close by. After Marcus and

Olthar had departed, the Governor's minions continued with their habitual praising. The Governor settled back into his soft cushions and took consolation from the fact that he was obliged to obey the King's orders, and there was nothing further he could do in the matter. With this thought, the old man called for food, and while he ate he listened to the familiar stream of praise which came ceaselessly from his retinue, and the words reassured his confidence.

As Marcus and Olthar rode back to the camp they were both deep in thought. Marcus had realized that the interview had not gone well, and in his mind he was trying to determine how he had misjudged the situation. He knew that Olthar would explain if he asked him, but his independence pushed him to solve the problem on his own rather than ask for the answer. From what he had observed of Parthian society, Marcus knew that the world of politics was as vicious and corrupt as in Rome. However, there was another crucial difference which Marcus had noticed; the Parthian attendants, including Olthar, were unashamedly sycophantic in the presence of their superiors. In Roman circles such exaggerated praise was only offered ironically, for attributing a man with deeds or virtues which he did not possess was seen as a way of highlighting his short-comings. As he reflected further on the matter, Marcus concluded that he had failed to make allowance for the cultural differences between Rome and Parthia, and consequently he had inadvertently offended the Governor. Marcus's conclusion was largely accurate, and he was a little peeved at the wasted opportunity which the interview had presented, but he had still enjoyed the opportunity to see the inside of the city, and to ride a horse again. Marcus chuckled to himself as they rode on, given that he was already a prisoner and a slave, it was impossible for him to fall any lower in the social hierarchy, so the unsuccessful interview had hardly worsened his lot. With this thought his innate optimism buoyed to the surface again, and he whistled as they trotted back to the camp, enjoying the ride in the sunshine of the autumnal afternoon.

Two days later, the different contingents of prisoners were united in their original campsite outside the city walls. They were to commence work on the bridge the following day, but that day they were free to repair the damage to their huts and settle into their old quarters. The Romans chatted eagerly as they were re-united with their comrades. They exchanged news of the projects they had been working on, the nature of their supervisors and their general observations of the region. The cold north wind was blowing hard that evening, and none of the men were looking forward to the prospect of working on the River over the winter. Marcus had gone to bed and was huddled under his cloak when he heard delirious shouts coming from outside. There was something familiar about the voice, and he hastily wrapped the cloak around his shoulders, and pulling on his boots he ventured out into the cold night to investigate. It did not take him long to find the source of the noise, for Titus was standing in front of a roaring fire, screaming away oblivious to everything. In each hand he had a bottle of wine, and he took large gulps from them between his outbursts. Marcus saw at once that Titus was roaring drunk, but what puzzled him was the torrent of incoherent speech which he kept shouting. Marcus was also intrigued to learn how the seasoned legionary had acquired the wine.

As Marcus approached, he made out a number of words in Titus's slurred shouts, there were names and various references to a forest. Marcus was anxious to get Titus into a hut, where he could sober up out of sight. His noisy performance had already drawn a small audience, and the Parthian guards would soon come to investigate. The scarred veteran's display had woken many other prisoners and they were now shouting for him to be quiet. Marcus broke into a run, discarding his cloak as he rushed to tackle Titus. He had just wrestled him to the ground when the first guards rode up. The guards ordered all the prisoners back into their huts, and they even shot a few arrows after the slower Romans. The captain of the guard then dismounted and approached Marcus and Titus, they were still on the ground and Marcus was scrambling to conceal the wine bottles. At a signal from the captain, four guards rushed forward to seize the two prisoners. Titus struggled with the men, and as he flayed around he caught one guard with a lucky blow to the nose. The man's face erupted in a fountain of blood, and his companions lost no time in knocking Titus to the floor.

The captain briefly permitted the guards to beat Titus as he lay on the ground, then he ordered them to stop.

'How did you get drunk?' he demanded of Titus in accented Latin, but the veteran merely continued to rave incoherently about ghosts.

'You,' demanded the captain, pointing at Marcus, 'how did this man get drunk?' One wine bottle had rolled away from the fire and Marcus was carefully cradling the other under his tunic, but he still managed to stand up straight as he answered the question.

'I don't know,' answered Marcus, simply.

'Lies,' thundered the captain, 'tell me where he got the wine or I will beat both of you tomorrow.'

'I can't tell you what I don't know,' replied Marcus with a nonchalant shrug of his broad shoulders. The tough physical labor had built up Marcus's muscles, and they now rippled with restrained power as he faced the captain.

Marcus knew that he was antagonising the captain, but his pride was swelling up in him. The brief taste of freedom which

Marcus had experienced whilst riding into the city made him yearn for more. All his resentment at the long months of servitude had now risen up in Marcus, he was desperate to assert his will. His fighting spirit could not be quelled and despite the cold voice of reason in his head, he felt his nostrils flare slightly as he took a deep breath, squared his shoulders, and stared the captain in the eyes. It was a stupid reason to instigate a confrontation, but Marcus continued regardless. Even in the flickering firelight, the Parthian was unable to hold the fierce gaze of Marcus's intense blue eyes, and he turned away. The captain barked out the next orders as he struggled to retain his self-control.

'Both of you will be beaten at dawn, now go to your huts,' he shouted imperiously.

'Anyone who leaves their hut before dawn will be shot,' he added with more determination than he felt.

In the flickering firelight, the brief confrontation had not been witnessed by any of the others, but Marcus knew he had won, and that was enough for him.

Marcus quickly hauled Titus to his feet and helped him to their hut. The blows which Titus had received had sobered him up, and he accompanied Marcus with remorse, repeating his regret that his own actions meant Marcus would also be beaten. Marcus did not bother trying to explain the staring contest, for he was too modest to gloat about his trivial victory. Once they were back in their hut, Titus did his best to explain his actions. The whistling north wind had brought back his twelve ghosts, and the only way in which he could escape their torment was in wine. He had sneaked into the guards' tent and stolen a bottle of wine. He had finished the bottle within minutes and returned for two more. Marcus was astonished that Titus had managed to repeat his clandestine mission without getting caught, and he gave thanks that nothing worse than a beating would come from the whole affair. If the guards had seen a prisoner sneaking around their tent they would not have hesitated to fill him with arrows. The ease with which Titus had managed this feat gave Marcus something to think about, but that night he had a more pressing matter for his attention. The second wine bottle was still concealed under his tunic, and he now extracted it with a flourish.

'As I'm getting the punishment anyway, I might as well enjoy the crime,' he chortled, as he drew the cork from the bottle with his teeth.

'Deftly done, young man,' complemented Titus, 'I was wondering where that one got to.'

The two comrades then finished off the wine, savouring each swallow all the more as they knew they would pay dearly for it at dawn. After a few mouthfuls, Titus observed that he had already drunk more than enough wine for the night, so he insisted Marcus finish what was left. Thanks to the soothing effects of the alcohol, Marcus fell asleep soon after he had imbibed the last drop. He slept soundly even when Titus muttered about ghosts in his sleep, and both men slumbered through the night untroubled by thoughts of the beating they were going to receive. When the guards woke him, Marcus walked with a light heart to receive his punishment. Under normal circumstances he would never have accepted a beating in exchange for a bottle of wine, but he had been a prisoner for nearly a year and a half, and his circumstances were far from normal. His mouth tasted of stale wine, but neither that nor the imminent beating could dislodge his smile. The experience had made Marcus feel alive once more; his foolish arrogance had been an assertion of his free will and no price was too great for that. The captain did not look Marcus in the eye as he supervised the beating. Both men knew that Marcus had won a minor victory the previous night, and although the incident was extremely trivial, it had restored Marcus's quavering resolve.

When the first blows fell across his back, Marcus started. The pain woke him from his reverie but he clenched his jaw and refused to utter a sound. With grim determination, Marcus forced himself to focus on other thoughts. In his mind's eye he recalled images of his family in Gaul, first he pictured his father working in the shipyard, and then the day they launched the Albatross and his trip to Rome. Next, he recollected his mother and brother, he could still feel the pressure of the tiger brooch against his chest and that knowledge renewed his courage and fortitude. Then Marcus allowed his thoughts to pass via his time in Gaul with the legions, until he was picturing the wonders of Alexandria and Rebecca. From there his mind passed onto Antioch and the first time he met Luana, then he remembered the terrible slaughter at Carrhae and the defeat of the legions. Finally he recalled in vivid detail the last time he had seen Luana, and the tragic sacrifice she had made for him. As the beating drew to an end, Marcus was reflecting that he had seen and experienced a great deal for a man who was still only in his twenty sixth year.

Work commenced on widening the bridge that day, and despite their bruised backs both Marcus and Titus took an active part in it. The existing bridge consisted of heavy wooden beams spanning the gaps between the six columns which stood in the River. The design was basic but adequate, and none of the Parthians saw the need to experiment with any alternatives. The initial plan was simple to build up each of the six columns until they were wide enough to support a second set of beams parallel to the existing ones. This plan would widen the deck and make the bridge broad enough for two wagons to pass, and thus relieve the bottlenecks at each end of the bridge. The prisoners were divided into new working groups; the vast majority of the men were employed in quarrying and transporting the rocks and ballast which were to form the bases for widening the columns. A smaller contingent of prisoners was sent under heavy guard to the nearest forests from whence they had instructions to procure and transport sufficient trunks to form the widened bridge deck. Marcus and the other prisoners from the Gallic cavalry were in the first group, and each day they trudged through the chill morning to the nearby quarry.

Despite the vast labor pool, the work progressed very slowly. A steady supply of rocks and ballast came from the quarry each day, but when it was tipped from the bridge the River washed it away. The upstream side of each column effectively blocked the force of the current, but when the supervisors tipped more rocks in front of the column, the concentrated force of the current washed them away. In vain the Parthians spent weeks tipping load after load of material into the River, without any sign of a firm foundation appearing. The work on the bridge was contributing to further delays for the merchant trains trying to cross, and tempers were soon becoming frayed at the worksite. Some weeks later Marcus and Quintus were taking delivery of rocks to the bridge when they observed a heated exchange of words between a merchant and the captain of the guards. The merchant was annoyed that there were a number of wagons full of rocks in front of his baggage train. The captain had instructed him to wait, whilst each wagon was brought onto the bridge and the rocks were emptied into the River. Marcus was engrossed in his attempts to follow the argument in Parthian, but his concentration was soon broken by a howl of laughter from Quintus.

The cheerful legionary was pointing in amazement whilst his whole frame shook with mirth so much that he could not speak. Marcus followed the direction of his gaze just in time to witness the Parthians tip another load of rocks over the upstream side of the column. The dismayed face of the supervisor presented a particularly comic sight, as the man watched the River take away another load of rocks. Both Marcus and Quintus now understood why they had been kept working the quarry for so long, and the bridge showed no signs of being widened. It was over three months since work had commenced, but there was still little sign of any progress. The logging group had transported the required timbers to the site of the bridge, and the great beams were now laid out on the bank, but there were no columns on which to place them. Marcus and Titus now laughed aloud as they realized the fruits of their back-breaking labor were being wasted by the ignorant supervisor. When Marcus had seen the bridge that they were to work on, he had realized immediately that an arching Roman bridge would be far more effective. However, given his current low state of favor in the eyes of the commanders he had not even attempted to suggest an alternative design. Olthar had returned to the city, and Marcus had not developed any form of rapport with the current commander.

The argument between the merchant and the captain had been temporarily halted by the violent outburst of laughter from Quintus. Both men now approached the wagon and in menacing tones they demanded to know what was so funny. Quintus was still chortling to himself, so Marcus found himself explaining the source of their amusement. His command of Parthian was now adequate for the task, and he soon conveyed his meaning. All four men turned to the bridge, and as they watched, the supervisor tipped the final load of ballast into the River. The lively waters accepted the latest offering and quickly dispersed the stones downstream. All four men now chuckled at the supervisor's frustrated expression, which was accompanied by him kicking a nearby stone into the River and then hobbling back to his task with an injured toe. The captain was the same man who had ordered the beating, but the Marcus bore him no resentment. Marcus now exploited the temporary bond which their mirth had created to explain that the new material had to be tipped into the downstream side of the column before any form of foundation could be constructed. The captain listened, and Marcus briefly outlined how the first column would shelter the new rocks from the full force of the current, and permit a stable column to be constructed.

The merchant and captain both recognized the logic in Marcus's explanation and as the captain strode onto the bridge to issue the appropriate orders, the merchant chatted affably with Marcus. As they spoke Marcus noticed the Star of David on the merchant's ring, he decided to take a risk and he managed to extract the pendant which hung from his neck. Marcus only had a few moments before the captain would return, and he was anxious not to risk losing his treasured souvenir from Rebecca. However the merchant was beside Marcus, and his entire attention was focused on the bridge. Marcus attempted in vain to draw the merchant's gaze to the inscription on the pendant with abrupt nods and movements of his hand. There were precious few moments left before the captain returned, and Marcus would have to conceal the silver souvenir beneath his tunic. The merchant shifted his feet and was about to face Marcus, when a shout from his baggage train distracted him. One of the heavily laden mules was attempting to eat the leaves from a nearby shrub, and in the process its load had become dislodged. With a curt farewell to Marcus, the merchant hurried off to see that the precious load was more securely attached, and the animals were ready to move as soon as the bridge was clear. Marcus gave a frustrated sigh at the wasted opportunity, and he worked with a peculiar restlessness for the remainder of the day.

After the essential engineering tip which Marcus had provided, the work on the bridge advanced steadily, and the prisoners from the quarry soon found they could witness the columns which were slowly rising from the River. The Romans took satisfaction from observing the fruits of their labor, and despite the winter chill there was a general glow of pride throughout the camp as they watched the completion of their task. By the time the spring thaw brought the snow-melt flowing down the River the work was nearly finished. The beams had been laid and all that remained was to fit a side rail to the new deck. As soon as the widened bridge was opened to traffic, the extra lane removed the previous bottlenecks. Marcus's solution to the engineering problem at the bridge led to his advice being sought by the Parthian commander on future projects. Marcus continued to work with the same unit of 300 prisoners, and hiding his ambitions to escape, he soon became the leader of the entire unit. Through his active co-operation in solving the various engineering problems which arose, Marcus became a trusted deputy to the Parthian commander. After the passage of some time the Governor awarded Marcus special permission to enter the city without an escort during daylight hours. This came about because the Parthian commander wished his deputy to have access to the City's markets in order to purchase the necessary supplies for the camp and their engineering projects.

During the first days that the new bridge was open, one enterprising young man from the Parthian guards had even succeeded in charging a toll from the passing merchants. His plan had worked for over a week, and he had spent all the takings each night in a riot of feasting and drinking, for he knew that once he was caught the commander would confiscate any moneys that remained. The commander had promptly discovered the abuse, but he was so amused and impressed at the man's initiative that he had promoted him, after the necessary beating had been administered.

Throughout the following years the prisoners were moved around the region in different contingents as they were employed on public works. Often Marcus managed to construct a satisfactory rapport with the Parthian in charge, but the chief constantly changed which man commanded which contingent. The regular movements from one work site to another also made it difficult for Marcus to formulate any plan of escape. However, Marcus used the opportunity to build up a detailed mental map of the surrounding region. He noted every watercourse, along with the places where it could be crossed, and he eagerly stored away all the information he could garner. As the months and years passed Marcus found his command of the language improved steadily and he was soon able to chat with any of the locals they encountered during their labors. Many of the shepherds and villagers had never seen red-haired men before, and during the warmer months the children often came from miles around to watch the Gauls at work. Marcus chatted with the children whenever he could, and he acquired a lot of useful information about the region from their off-hand comments. All the children cheered with delight whenever Caius took off his shirt and revealed the magical curly red hairs which covered his chest and stood out clearly against his white skin. Despite these lighter moments in the routine, Marcus often found his gaze drawn to the horizon and the distant hills. He had been a prisoner for too long and he yearned for his freedom.

18

Merv, 49 BC

The Romans had settled with minimal difficulty into the routine of their new lives as prisoners, in many ways their duties were no more demanding than their former lives as legionaries. One day Marcus observed the familiarity with which his comrades set to their tasks and he realized that any escape attempt would have to be made soon. The legionaries were growing accustomed to their servitude; the habit of a regular routine had soon inured the men to a life of slavery. The Romans had been prisoners for over five years by then, and the conditions in which they worked had gradually improved. Marcus was confident that the remnants of his own century would follow him anywhere, but he was unsure about the remaining Gallic cavalry. At Marcus's request, Titus and Quintus undertook to sound out their comrades whilst their centurion was out of sight. There was still a certain diffidence accorded to the officers by the legionaries, even though the Parthians treated all the Romans without regard to their rank. Titus and Quintus soon developed a neat double act; they would argue about the possibility of escape, with Titus vehemently supporting the idea and Quintus opposing it. In this manner they soon assessed the general view of the prisoners, and then reported to Marcus.

Marcus was relieved to learn that the vast majority of the

legionaries were still in favor of an attempt to escape, though there was some dispute as to where they should make for once they left Parthia. With the shame of defeat still hanging over them, some of the prisoners preferred to head north or east looking for a new life in a foreign land, rather than attempt any return to Rome. The advocates for this scheme also pointed out that if they returned to Rome they risked decimation for their surrender at Carrhae, even if they did survive the arduous epic journey across hostile territory which such a plan would require. Marcus had given a considerable amount of thought to the different routes they could take to escape the Parthians. He had immediately accepted the impossibility of procuring sufficient weapons, horses and supplies to permit a fighting retreat through Parthia. Therefore, their first priority was to get out of Parthian territory, and the quickest way to do that was to head north east. To this end Marcus had gathered all the information he could about the inhabitants of that region.

The land to the north east of Parthia was controlled by the Xiongnu, they were a loosely connected group of nomadic tribes who roamed the steppe plains with their herds of livestock. They lived in dark, domed tents which were constructed on wooden wagons; these wagons were then towed from site to site by teams of oxen each time the tribe moved. The Xiongnu controlled a great swathe of territory, but they were comparatively few in number. The tribes travelled with their flocks as they constantly moved in search of fresh pastures. The nomad flocks consisted of several different types of herbivore; the ratio of these different animals was carefully controlled by the herders to extract the maximum benefit from the available pasture. There were some plants which only certain animals could eat or reach. By maintaining mixed flocks, the nomads were able to exploit the different strengths of each species, and make the fullest use of the scant pasturage without their animals having to compete with each other. Between the different animals there would be no visible vegetation left after the nomads had passed with their flocks; it was this total consummation of all fodder which obliged the nomads to take their flocks and move on, for the closely-cropped pasture took months to recover.

Marcus knew that the only way for the Romans to escape would be to venture into the territory of the Xiongnu, and he had eagerly listened to all the tales which the Parthians told about the nomads. The settled Parthians viewed their nomadic cousins with a mixture of fear, disdain and respect. The Parthians admired the endurance and toughness which the harsh lifestyle gave to both the nomads and their ponies; they freely admitted that a nomad on his steppe pony could ride much further than any Parthian on a fine horse. Yet the Parthians also disdained the nomads for their lack of development and foresight. Whenever Marcus heard the Parthians speak of the Xiongnu he was aware of the inherent awe which the Parthians felt for their neighbours, however much they mocked them as filthy savages. Amongst their other habits, the Xiongnu placed strips of raw meat under their saddles as they rode; the pummelling tenderised the meat, though it also accounted for the distinctive miasma which surrounded the nomads and their mounts. The nomads viewed water as too precious for washing, and consequently there was a genuine basis for the claims that the nomads stank. Marcus initially hoped that he would not encounter the fierce nomads when he led his men through Xiongnu territory, but the more he heard about the nomads the more intrigued he became.

The most divisive issue amongst the prisoners was what they should do once they had escaped. A minority of the men favored taking a large looping route towards the North West which would eventually bring them back to Roman territory.

However, the majority did not want to risk another epic journey through hostile territory, and they hoped instead to sell their services as mercenaries. The Romans had learnt that there was a near constant state of warfare between various chiefs and tribes in the region, and with their experience and superior training the Roman veterans would make ideal mercenaries. After some questioning Marcus established that neither group was likely to acquiesce to the plan proposed by the other. However, that was a problem which Marcus would deal with when the time came, their first priority was to organise an escape, and both groups concurred that they would have to head north, and that they would need supplies and horses. Marcus assumed control of the operation, and although there were three other centurions involved, all the major decisions were referred to him.

Throughout that autumn and winter the Roman prisoners were again united in the camp outside Merv. The Parthian Governor had decided to keep all the prisoners employed on repairing the city walls, for it was in the lean winter months that the nomad tribes most often streamed down from the steppe in their ferocious raids on the Parthian countryside. With so many prisoners engaged on repairing the walls and watchtowers, the work progressed quickly. Over the years the Romans had grown accustomed to working with their new Parthian masters, and they readily adapted their engineering skills to each task. In light of the practical necessities which arose from working on the city walls, the chief had altered his original decree which forbade any of the prisoners from entering the city. Any Romans who entered the city required an escort, but as so many prisoners passed during the course of their work on the wall, the guards became lax in the enforcement of this rule. As time passed, the Parthians had grown accustomed to the presence of the Romans, and the guards were becoming correspondingly slack. Marcus had noted this fact, and the Romans had used the occasion to acquire a number of weapons. These were then smuggled back to the main camp, where they were concealed in readiness for the escape.

During the winter months Marcus had drawn up the list of men he would take with him. With the help of Titus and Gnaeus, he had reviewed each of the men to ensure that they were reliable and tough enough, both physically and mentally, for the rigorous demands of the escape. All of the legionaries were seasoned veterans so there were few worries on that count. However, Marcus was concerned that not all of the legionaries would make good horsemen. The remnants of the Gallic cavalry could obviously be relied upon, but many of the other legionaries had very little experience in the saddle. Marcus knew that the escape would demand several days of tough riding, and the group would not be able to slow down their pace. The less-experienced horsemen would have to learn fast, or risk being caught by the Parthians. Marcus had no doubt that the Parthians would pursue them, and there was an uncomfortable prickle along his back when he thought of the lethal bows which their pursuers would be carrying. However, Marcus forced himself to think of how to overcome the immediate problems, rather than envisage potential obstacles. Marcus remembered his father telling him that if you look for obstacles then that is what you will find, just as surely as if you look for solutions then that is what you will find.

The Romans would need horses and supplies of food. Although both of these were abundant in the city, they were the impossible to acquire stealthily over time, as they could not be easily stored. Finally, Marcus decided that the horses and supplies would have to be stolen on the night of the escape. As the prisoners worked on the city walls they were careful to observe what was delivered to the various warehouses near the city gates. With this intelligence, Marcus selected an appropriate warehouse which was used to store dried foods. The building adjoined the city wall, and it would be possible for the Romans to lift some tiles from the roof and remove their supplies, without disturbing the watchman who slept by the door. There was scaffolding on the watchtower, so the supplies could be passed over the wall without having to smuggle them past the guards at the gate. It was perfect. The next logistical problem was how the prisoners could acquire the horses. Marcus had toyed with the idea of trying to scatter the remaining horses to delay the pursuit, but on reflection he decided that the noise of the stampeding horses would alert the Parthians. Marcus concluded that they would have to rely on their head-start and outride their pursuers.

Marcus and Titus calculated that at certain times of the year when the major caravans came through the area, they could steal enough mounts from the merchants camped around the city to make their escape. This would avoid the risk of entering the city and hopefully mean their escape would not be noticed till the morning. Meanwhile, the prisoners continued to work on repairing the city walls and watch towers. As the preparations progressed, Marcus fixed a date a week hence for their escape. It would be just before the full moon, and there would be enough light for the Romans to ride by night when necessary. On the night they made their break they would need to put as much distance between themselves and Merv as possible, the moonlight would allow them to maintain a steady pace even at night. The group would consist of 248 men, and Marcus had ascertained that there would be sufficient mounts for them all in the surrounding caravanserais. The merchants were all within the city walls, and their goods were stored in warehouses, so they left only a minimal guard on their mounts and beasts of burden which were left to graze outside the city. Three days before the allotted date a piercing whistle was heard, immediately afterwards the large warning bells suspended above each watch tower began their resounding peels. Marcus and his men were on the scaffolding and the booming sound immediately filled their ears, as they looked down they saw the city erupt in a frenzy of activity. Inside the city, merchants hurried to close their shops and secure their goods, while screaming mothers called for their errant children to return home at once. Outside the city, drovers and herdsmen struggled with the merchants as they all tried to drive their flocks, mounts and beasts inside the safety of the city walls.

From the speed of the response it was obvious that all of the inhabitants were familiar with this procedure. Marcus quickly learnt from one of the guards that the warning bell signaled the approach of the Xiongnu nomads, and as it was during the late lean winter months, there was no way that the nomads had come to trade. At that moment Marcus felt the scaffolding structure on which he was standing start to shudder, he looked down to see one of the guards hacking at the main timbers with an axe, whilst another was calling all the Romans to descend. With each blow the whole frame shook. Marcus had never mastered his fear of heights and he lost no time in leading his comrades down the ladder and off the scaffolding. The guard had decided it was too risky to leave such a structure standing against the city walls, and he was destroying it as quickly as possible. Marcus watched in dismay as the scaffolding came crashing down, and the merchants' horses were all brought within the city wall. For Marcus and his comrades, the bell signaled more than the approach of the nomads, it was also the death knell for their escape plan. There was no way they could escape without horses and supplies, and the proximity of the nomads made any attempt to leave the safety of the city walls tantamount to suicide.

With dismay and dejection Marcus was forced to abandon his escape plans. The prisoners were set to work, aiding the merchants move their belongings within the city walls. Although the labor was light, Marcus worked with a heavy heart and each load seemed to tax him more than the last. After all his careful preparations the escape plan had to be abandoned; having come so close to escaping, Marcus and his comrades resented their captivity all the more. They worked in silence and there was a sullen glow of resentment in their eyes. Fortunately, the Parthians were too busy securing the city to notice the uncharacteristically morose demeanor of Marcus and his comrades. The city was soon secure, with all the livestock and horses safely within the city walls. With no work for the prisoners, the Romans were given a temporary holiday until new tasks could be found for them. Marcus and Titus climbed up onto the city walls, and from their vantage point they watched the distant figures of the Xiongnu appear. The dark shapes of mounted men sped across the distant plains on their sturdy steppe ponies as they raced towards the outlying villages. Columns of smoke soon marked the dwellings which the nomads had raided, and despite the distance Marcus fancied he heard the screams of the villagers and the squeals of their slaughtered livestock.

Marcus and Titus stayed on the wall long after the sun had set, the guards had invited them to sit around their brazier and they shared their wine good-naturedly. For the Parthian guards it was a happy occasion, all but the furthest farmers and villagers had reached the safety of the city walls, and the nomads would leave in a few days time. Marcus was able to understand their conversation as they sat around the brazier and compared stories of past atrocities committed by the Xiongnu. However, Titus and Marcus spoke Latin between themselves and the guards were unable to follow their conversation. Both of the legionaries had developed the habit of flavouring their speech with a variety of Gallic terms and soldiers' slang to ensure that even if any of the Parthians knew Latin they would be unable to follow the conversation. Titus was disappointed by the failed opportunity as well, but he knew how much of a figurehead Marcus had become for the rest of the men, and as such it was important that he continue to display his former determination and optimism. If the rest of the men saw their leader in this crest-fallen state then they would become equally disheartened. Titus, was trying to cheer up Marcus before they returned to their quarters.

'We might have missed a good opportunity this time, but don't worry there will be other chances,' consoled the grizzled legionary.

'I'm tired of waiting; I don't want to work for another's gain anymore. I am a Roman citizen and an officer, yet I have wasted 5 years laboring like a common slave. It's abominable!'

Marcus's comment brought a guffaw of laughter from Titus.

'What's so funny?' demanded the centurion, peeved at his comrade's laughter. 'I can't see anything funny about this situation, yet you're laughing. What's so funny?'

With a grin, Titus leaned forward to warm his hands as he explained, 'We are not laboring *like* slaves, we *are* slaves!'

'And that amuses you does it?' demanded an outraged Marcus.

'No, being a slave certainly isn't funny. These blisters aren't funny, and I can see nothing funny about building another bloody canal. What amuses me is that you still think of yourself as a Roman citizen and an officer. The rest of us have accepted that we are now slaves, but you still think you're an officer. That's why I know you'll lead us out of this place.'

Marcus was struck by Titus's observation. He had never ceased to view his enslavement as a temporary state, and he had never ceased to view himself as a Roman citizen and an officer. It was this innate confidence which had made him such a figurehead and leader for the other prisoners. Marcus was reflecting on the duties and responsibilities which came with the burden of leadership when his thoughts were interrupted by another burst of laughter from Titus. In response to the Marcus's quizzical look Titus explained;

'If I wasn't a slave I wouldn't even be a legionary anymore. I'm retired! If you're still an officer, then I am still a legionary, only I've served my time by now and I'm retired! Now move up and let an old man warm himself by the fire.'

Now Marcus joined Titus as they chuckled at the thought of his retirement. Marcus translated the joke for the Parthians, and the guards joined in with good spirits. More wine was brought, and they all made a show of caring for the old pensioner. Titus entered into the part and was soon wrapped in a blanket and holding forth to the rest of the company. He had picked up enough Parthian to play the part, and in the flickering firelight he became the stereotypical grandfather who transcends all cultural barriers. As the guards plied him with more wine, and the company respectfully gave him their attention, Titus launched into the generic grumbles of old men the world over. He began by bemoaning the disrespectful and obstreperous youths who had barely left their wet nurses before they saw fit to boss around their elders. At this point Titus, with staged subtlety indicated Marcus, and the whole group burst into laughter. Then Titus continued with his list of woes, he bemoaned the rises of prices and the decline in quality of everything in the market. By the end of that speech Titus had even attempted to convince his audience that modern water was not as good as the water from his youth. They had all chuckled at this, and offered him more wine 'to save him from drinking the bad modern water.' Titus accepted the wine readily, whilst concurring with his hosts that it was only on account of the poor quality of modern water that he drank wine.

'But, that's not the worst of it!' exclaimed Titus, whose ruddy cheeks now fitted the role he had assumed.

'It gets worse! When I was a young lad that warehouse was a lovely garden where children could play.' Whilst working on one watch-tower Titus had learnt that the warehouse he was indicating used to be a garden. The Parthians were most impressed with his accuracy, and with the flickering light and circling wine bottle they began to see vestiges of their own grandfathers in the red-cheeked old man who sat by the fire declaiming to the crowd.

Titus continued to play it up; his dry sense of humour came to the fore as he reeled off a list of the recent developments in the city, and the buildings or shops which had changed location or function.

'But that's not the worst of it,' exclaimed Titus again, using his recently developed catch phrase; he waited for the tension to build up before he continued, 'No, that's not the worst of it by far. I don't mind them moving the bath house, building a warehouse on that beautiful garden, or even closing my favorite tavern. What I really mind, what really confuses me now, what really annoys me about this city is that when I was young it was called Massalia and situated 4000 miles west of here by the sea! Now imagine that, some snotty-nosed young upstart has gone and moved my hometown from the coast of Gaul to the middle of the Orient. Now that's disrespecting your elders!'

The whole group roared with laughter as Titus feigned confusion. Marcus's sides were aching by the time they had finished; he dragged his drunken deputy to his feet and they staggered back to their temporary quarters. As they descended the stairs one of the guards called after them;

'Look after that old fellow, he's retired you know!'

'But that's not the worst of it…' replied Marcus, 'He's drunk too!'

19

MERV, 49-47 BC

AFTER THE NOMADS had left the area of Merv, Marcus and the other Roman prisoners were moved from their temporary quarters back to their camp outside the city. They spent the early spring months completing the work on the city walls and watch-towers. All of the legionaries were disappointed that their escape plan had to be abandoned when they were so close to making their break for freedom. Marcus attempted to retain his determined focus and it was only with Titus that he discussed his doubts about another likely opportunity arising. Titus was already an elderly man, but now the cold winter and continued labor were taking their toll on him, and he was weakening with age. Marcus did his best to ensure that his old deputy was allocated the less arduous tasks on the work site, and Titus pretended not to notice these favors. Before the last winter he would have been too proud to accept any such special treatment, but now his joints were getting stiff and he was quite content to take things more easily. The more sedate pace of life of Titus's new life lent him an additional air of gravitas, and many of the legionaries now regularly came to ask his advice.

The Governor of Merv had pronounced himself well-satisfied with the Romans' work on the city walls, and he had sent a flock of sheep to the camp for the prisoners to slaughter and roast. As the men feasted on the hot meat they discussed the improvements which had occurred in their working conditions. Marcus had to admit that they were now treated with a degree of respect and consideration; their swift completion of the various projects had earned them the admiration of the Parthian commanders. There was less and less talk of any attempt to escape, and the veteran legionaries began to settle into their new roles as skilled slaves. On several occasions Marcus found himself arguing vainly about the inherent need to be free, rather than work as indentured slaves, but soon his reasoning failed even to convince himself. Marcus had nothing to go back to in Massalia; his mother was almost certainly dead, and Marcus was sure that after all these years he would find even less common ground with Flavius. The family shipyard belonged entirely to his brother, and Flavius's profligate ways had probably ruined it by now. As a disgraced soldier there would be relatively few options open to Marcus or his men.

Marcus had reluctantly conceded that he could not hope for any kind of future with Rebecca in Alexandria, for despite the high opinion that Reuben might hold of him, there was no way her would permit his daughter to marry a Gentile, and Marcus refused to convert to a faith in which he did not believe. There were no attractive options open to Marcus if he did make it back to the Mediterranean. The Roman prisoners' current status and lifestyle were certainly satisfactory in many respects; the only thing they lacked was their freedom. Marcus forced himself to question how much he valued his freedom. Was it worth risking his life, and those of his men? Even if they did win their freedom, there was no way of knowing what life they could hope for in the alien lands to the east, it could be much worse than their current situation. The answer to Marcus's deliberations varied on a daily basis; when his spirits were buoyant and the wind brought the fragrances of distant plains, he yearned for his freedom and determined to escape. However, when he was weary or down-spirited after a long day's work, Marcus wanted nothing more than the comfortable familiarity of his hut.

The months passed and Marcus once again settled into his routine as a skilled slave. The man in charge of Marcus's unit was called Vardanes, he was a portly and jovial fellow, whose red cheeks bore testament to his fondness for wine. Vardanes had told Marcus that their next project would be constructing a bridge across an irrigation canal to the east of the city. Marcus acted as Vardanes's deputy on the project, and the group of 300 prisoners were soon preparing the requisite materials and supplies for their departure from the main camp by the city. As they left Merv, the spring was advancing and the city had started to prepare for the merchants' caravans which they confidently expected. During the winter months snow blocked the high mountain passes, so the merchants stopped travelling and waited for the spring to thaw the snowdrifts and open the roads again. As Marcus and his men worked on the bridge, they regularly saw merchants approach from the east with their heavily laden baggage trains. The merchant leading each caravan would normally stop to share a flask of wine with Vardanes and exchange news. Each caravan delivered an update on the condition of the route they had just taken, and they enquired about the route ahead. The Parthian commander readily passed on the detailed information he picked up concerning the trade routes, despite the fact that he had never even seen the places he talked about so authoritatively.

Each time a caravan stopped, Marcus looked around with curiosity. He would cast a quick glance over the bundles, sacks and barrels which the beasts carried, but his chief interest was reserved for the horses. Marcus retained his cavalryman's interest in horses, and from a distance he inspected all the mounts with a critical eye. Years before, Reuben had told Marcus about the blood-sweating horses of the Ferghana valley, and Marcus remained intrigued by the tales of these animals. Tyluxes had confirmed the existence of the horses, but Marcus had still never seen one, and with the approach of each caravan he hoped he might finally have the chance to see a blood-sweating horse. According to the legend, which Tyluxes had confirmed, the horses bred in the Ferghana valley were of abnormally fiery stock and of such high mettle that they actually sweated blood. The tribes in the region guarded these prized mounts with great jealousy, and there were precious few to be found outside the Ferghana valley, although their reputation stretched far and wide. Tyluxes had told Marcus that these blood-sweating horses were prized by the Yuezhi, Xiongnu and Parthians above all other mounts, as their endurance, intelligence and loyalty was unsurpassed. A Yuezhi noble had once exchanged two of his young wives for one of the blood-sweating horses, prompting the observation that horse was certainly more loyal than the man who rode upon its back.

Although there were certain staple goods which most caravans carried, the merchants were an enterprising bunch, so they often brought strange and wondrous objects as experimental cargoes. It was through these trade routes and the resourceful merchants who travelled them, that many advances and innovations were transmitted between countries and cultures. Marcus remembered the elaborate tales he had heard Reuben and his merchant friends in Alexandria tell about Parthia. From his personal experience Marcus was now able to distinguish between the facts and the myths, he concluded that whilst the merchants did exaggerate, there was normally a genuine basis to their tales. The wonders of the Orient were already so manifold, that it was unnecessary to fabricate any more.

As Vardanes's deputy, Marcus was often able to leave his

work and chat with the merchants when a convoy stopped. From a Cypriot Jew who was travelling east, Marcus got an update of the news from the Roman world; although it was months out of date by that time, Marcus greatly valued the information. Marcus had heard rumors about Caesar's continued success, and the civil war which had erupted when he had crossed the Rubicon and entered Rome in defiance of the Senate. After meeting the great man once in Portus Namnetus, Marcus had always felt an affinity with Julius Caesar, and he rejoiced at the news of his victories. The Cypriot Jew then told Marcus about the outcome of the civil war; Marcus felt a rush of elation when he learnt of Caesar's victory, next Marcus empathised with Caesar when he heard how the great leader had wept at the news of Pompey's treacherous murder in Alexandria. The Jew was in full flow now, and he tumbled out news mixed with salacious gossip about the events in the Roman world. In Alexandria, Caesar had been bewitched by an Egyptian princess, her name was Cleopatra and thanks to Caesar's assistance she was now Queen of Egypt. Marcus was intrigued at this bit of information; he remembered the lean, fierce commander he had met in Gaul with the eyes of an eagle, and he found it hard to imagine him bewitched by anyone, let alone a teenage girl. But as Marcus reflected on the matter he calculated that the svelte girl he had seen in Alexandria would now be an attractive young woman, and if she had fulfilled her early potential then the Egyptian Queen would be a beautiful and skillful leader. Marcus remembered the dignity and precision with which the young Cleopatra had diffused the dreadful tension in the Palace following Publius's *faux pas*, and he concluded that in Cleopatra, Egypt had an extremely capable ruler.

Like all the legionaries in Gaul, Marcus had heard the stories about Caesar's amorous conquests, most of the men were genuinely proud that their commander was such a notorious old *roué*. It was rumored that the elderly Senators were so eager to send Caesar on campaign merely to protect the chastity of their wives and daughters. As Marcus cast back his mind to Gaul, he remembered the personal magnetism which he had noticed upon meeting Caesar. After that encounter Marcus had easily credited the stories about Caesar's powers of seduction, such was the impact of meeting the great man. Marcus had been lost in a brief reverie of reflection when his attention was sharply brought back to the news he was being told. In a flurry of excitement the Jew recounted how Caesar had declared himself Emperor, and returned the province of Cyprus to Egyptian control. The Jew delivered both these pieces of information as if they were of equal importance; Marcus could not care less about who nominally controlled Cyprus, but he was flabbergasted to learn that the man who previously embodied the ideals of the Roman Republic had now declared himself Emperor. Marcus hastened to direct the Cypriot away from the discussing the status of his homeland, and back to the events in Rome.

The caravan was soon ready to move on, and the Cypriot Jew promptly hurried off to catch up with his comrades, leaving Marcus to digest all the news. Marcus returned to his work whilst wondering what the current situation in Rome would portend. Marcus had not even bothered to show the Jew his silver pendant with 'Chaver' inscribed on the reverse, he was no longer pre-occupied with trying to escape. A few weeks later, another caravan was seen approaching. This one came from the East, and Marcus was slightly disappointed that he would not be able to procure any further news on the situation in Rome. However, there was a chance that the merchant might have procured one of the blood sweating horses, and Marcus surveyed the approaching convoy with interest. As the burly figure of the chief merchant rode towards them, Marcus had an undeniable sense of *déjà vu*. There was something strangely familiar about the figure, and as he watched the merchant halted, whilst still a long way distant, withdrew something from his bag, held it to his face, and then galloped towards the Marcus with a shout of recognition. As the figure of the excited merchant approached, Marcus was able to distinguish the features of Reuben bar Ezra. The large man was not wearing his traditional gabardine, but his long dark ringlets and beard remained the same. Without a word of explanation Reuben rushed passed a bemused Vardanes and went straight to Marcus.

The Parthian commander and the rest of the prisoners watched in amazement as the two men embraced as old friends. Reuben had tears streaming down his face as he gave thanks for Marcus's preservation. Reuben hastily presented himself to Vardanes, and then delegated his deputy to entertain the Parthian and ply him with wine whilst Marcus and Reuben caught up.

'I thought you were dead,' began Reuben, 'Rebecca mourned you for 4 weeks when we heard what happened at Carrhae. Was it really that bad? We heard the Romans were massacred.'

The questions tumbled out of Reuben's mouth before Marcus could answer any of them. Meanwhile, he was desperate to hear about Rebecca and Rome.

'How is she? Did all her injuries recover? Is she married? How long are you here? Is Caesar really Emperor now?'

As the two men chatted Reuben's convoy drew up to the new bridge. Marcus broke off to stare in awe at a wooden cage which sat on top of a wagon. The cage contained a huge tiger, and the animal was prowling languidly back and forth within the confines of its cage. It was the largest and most beautiful animal that Marcus had ever seen, and as the tiger nonchalantly yawned, it displayed a fearful set of fangs with regal indifference.

Reuben saw at once that Marcus was fascinated by the tiger, and he readily provided an explanation.

'That's for Caesar's Games. That beautiful beast will be the first tiger to be seen in Rome. I travelled far into the north east lands of the Xiongnu nomads to get that beast, it's one of the finest tigers I've ever seen and it's by far the most valuable item in my cargo! But somehow I don't think anyone will steal it!' added Reuben with a chuckle. He then explained how Caesar had ordered the most magnificent games ever to celebrate his coronation as Emperor of Rome, and there were huge prices being offered at the arenas for the most spectacular animals. The two were only able to converse for a short time before Marcus was called back to his labors, and Reuben had to depart with his caravan, but they arranged to meet the following day outside the synagogue.

The next day was the Sabbath, and Reuben had specifically timed his journey so that he would be in Merv, in order to worship at the synagogue in the city. Vardanes had delegated to Marcus the task of arranging supplies and provisions for the prisoners whilst they worked on the bridge. There were a number of materials which they required, and it was also time to collect the prisoners' weekly rations from the Governor, so Marcus had little difficulty in arranging to go to Merv the following day. The rest of the working day passed in a blur, as Marcus re-examined the snippets of information he had learnt from Reuben. In their excitement both men had talked simultaneously, and Marcus was now trying to disentangle their comments and news.

The providential meeting with Reuben had re-awakened Marcus's desire for freedom and he was already wondering how he could persuade Reuben to assist him. Marcus knew that the wealthy merchant would happily buy Marcus's freedom from the Governor, but Marcus was unwilling to leave the comrades he had spent so long leading, and there was no way Reuben could afford to purchase an entire contingent of slaves. After these swift calculations Marcus deduced that a mass escape would be the only way to give his men back their freedom. As the sun set and Marcus's mind returned to Alexandria he thought of Rebecca, with a momentary blush he hoped he had not been too indiscreet in asking if she was married. Reuben had not answered that question, and now Marcus steeled himself to feign indifference on the matter.

'Of course she's married,' he told himself. 'A beautiful girl like that does not stay single for long, and she's a young lady now,' Marcus told himself, for it was seven years since they had last seen each other in Alexandria.

'Reuben recognized me instantly!' thought Marcus, 'I can't have changed that much; I wonder if she has changed?'

With that thought, Marcus started thinking about when Reuben had seen him. The large man had taken something from his bag, raised it to his face, and then rushed towards Marcus with a cry of recognition, long before Marcus had been able to positively identify him. Marcus was confident his eyesight was still excellent, yet somehow Reuben had identified him before he was close enough to see him properly. Marcus made a mental note to ask Reuben about that when they met the next day; then Marcus stared into the flames of the fire and let his imagination run wild. As the logs burnt down into glowing embers, Marcus envisaged a life of freedom suddenly being open to him. He even allowed himself to dream of seeing Rebecca again, and with that Marcus's imagination went into overdrive. He found himself constructing ever more outlandish circumstances under which Reuben would accept him as a son-in-law, and he could marry Rebecca. Marcus saw himself working with Reuben and accompanying him on epic journeys to exotic destinations, before he would return home to Rebecca laden with riches.

The orange glow of the embers then made Marcus think of the magnificent tiger. He had been entranced by the beast, and he found it somehow significant that the first live tiger he saw was in Reuben's caravan. Ever since his early fascination with the blue broach his mother wore, Marcus had felt certain that one day a tiger would feature in his life. The animal was his talisman, despite the fact that he had never seen one before that day. Marcus still wore the lapis broach inside his tunic, and the silver pendant from Reuben and Rebecca still hung from his neck, both ornaments bore the image of a tiger and Marcus treasured them for the links they provided with his past. The other prisoners had also seen the tiger, and Marcus now listened to their chatter with interest. They were discussing the spectacle which the tiger would make in Rome, and wondering what animals it would be matched against. Now it occurred to Marcus that the magnificent tiger was on the way to a gruesome death on the sand of an arena. He was strangely saddened by the thought of the graceful animal being torn apart by a pack of hounds, and he fervently hoped it would be matched against a worthy opponent. This thought also prompted a revelation for Marcus, he could no longer remain inert in his situation, he would have to play an active role if he wanted to get Reuben's help and organise an escape. 'Nothing comes of nothing,' muttered Marcus to himself as he retired to his hut and began to plan the escape. The saying had been one of Lucius's favorite dictums, and Marcus reflected that he owed much of his ambition and motivation to the excellent example set by his father.

20

Merv, 47-46 BC.

IT WAS THE SABBATH and Marcus could make out the distinctive skullcaps worn by the city's Jews as they made their way towards the synagogue. Marcus had arranged to meet Reuben for lunch after the service, this left the morning free for Marcus to collect the supplies and materials which were needed at the camp. He was driving the first of the three wagons which would transport their supplies, in the back sat Gnaeus, Caius and a number of other Romans. The Romans were accompanied by two mounted Parthian guards who rode along beside the lead wagon. Marcus and Vardanes had long since learnt that it was wisest to take their own men to collect the supplies, the porters in the warehouses and stockyards were notorious thieves who supplemented their meagre income with whatever they could pilfer. On previous occasions Marcus had tried to watch diligently over the supplies from the moment they were checked out of the storerooms until they were safely stacked in the wagons, but the porters were masters at their art, and they took Marcus's supervisions as a challenge to steal even more. After returning with several diminished deliveries, Marcus had reluctantly conceded that the only way to avoid this was to take his own men to act as porters.

This week they required a large consignment of wooden beams to re-enforce the deck of the bridge, along with the fortnight's food supplies they normally collected for the group of 300 prisoners; consequently Marcus had brought 16 men with him to load all of the supplies. The Romans chatted happily in the back of the wagons; such an outing into town was a coveted perk as it meant the men were spared a day's labor. The legionaries often managed a quick visit to the tavern too, after they had loaded the wagons, consequently there was a definite atmosphere of joviality as the wagons bumped along with the men joking and chatting in the back. Marcus's mind was on his meeting with Reuben; during the night he had thought of many more questions to ask the merchant, but his top priority remained organising an escape. Marcus wondered if Reuben would help him escape with all his men; the only way to find out would be to ask. They had passed Reuben's caravan outside the city gates at one of the large caravanserais; from a distance Marcus had seen a number of Parthians taunting the tiger through the bars of its cage. They were poking the animal with sticks and dangling bits of meat beyond its reach. On observing the spectacle, Marcus could not help feeling that the majestic tiger behaved far more admirably than the men; the beautiful animal was clearly annoyed by the taunts, but it retained a regal air of disdain for its tormenters as it skulked around the confines of the cage

When the wagons drew up at the warehouse they were received with unfriendly scowls by the porters; the presence of the additional Romans clearly meant that the porters' services would not be required. There was a distinctly hostile atmosphere in the yard as Marcus arranged the drawing of the supplies with the warehouse supervisor and their subsequent loading by his men. Marcus had given his men strict instructions to avoid any conflict, but the porters were spoiling for a fight, in their opinion the Romans were robbing them of their wages. It was common knowledge that the porters did not earn enough from the warehouse owner to live on, and it was only by pilfering from their deliveries that they managed to survive. Marcus was aware of this fact, but he had no intention of subsidising the porters' wages, if their employer did not pay them enough they could find a different job. When food was stolen from his supplies it meant some of his men would go hungry, and he was loath to let that happen. With evident strain the legionaries did not rise to the bait, and they shrugged off the taunts and insults from the porters as they loaded all the supplies into the first wagon. Marcus supervised the process, checking off each item from his inventory. When that was complete the Romans clambered back into the other two wagons and they proceeded to the stockyard to collect the timbers. The large beams would take longer to load and secure, but Marcus was not worried about anyone trying to steal them at the stockyard. There was a slight chance that the supervisor would try to off-load a damaged beam on the Romans, but the legionaries all knew their trade well enough by now to spot any serious flaws in the timbers.

Marcus was able to leave Gnaeus supervising the loading of the timbers whilst he went to meet Reuben. The legionaries had strict instructions not to leave the wagons unattended, and Marcus had told the men to meet him outside a popular tavern once the timbers had been loaded. The choice of meeting point was greatly appreciated by the men, they knew it would not take all 16 men to guard the wagons, and those who didn't draw the short straws would have time for a drink. When Marcus reached the synagogue, the *shacharit* or 'morning prayer' was not yet finished. Whilst waiting outside, Marcus grew curious about what was going on within the synagogue. The intricacies of the Jewish faith were a mystery to Marcus, and he was intrigued by the unfamiliar rituals and customs. When the service was over and the congregation emerged, Marcus was surprised to observe all the women exiting form one side of the door whilst the men exited from the other. Marcus looked into the synagogue and saw the *mechitzah* curtain which separated the two sexes during prayers, and which accounted for the men and women exiting in distinct groups. Many of the worshippers removed their skullcaps as they left the synagogue, but between the flurry of arms and caps Marcus was still able to distinguish Reuben.

'Marcus, my dear friend, I still can't believe you are alive,' called Reuben as he embraced him in a bear hug.

'Come, let us go and eat whilst we talk,' suggested Marcus as he led the stout merchant to a nearby Jewish tavern. The owner assured Marcus and Reuben that all the food was kosher, and the two men ordered a feast to celebrate their reunion.

Over their hearty meal the two men spoke rapidly. A torrent of questions, answers, explanations and exclamations flowed back and forth between them. Reuben was evidently distressed to see that Marcus was a slave, and he immediately offered to buy his freedom from the Governor. Marcus was touched by the offer; the Governor's price for one of the Roman slaves would certainly be high, but there was no way Marcus could accept. Marcus leant closer to Reuben, and in a discrete voice he outlined the position. He was determined not to remain a slave any longer, but there was he refused to leave his comrades. They had lived, fought, suffered and labored together and now Marcus refused to desert them to secure his own release. Reuben whistled in amazement.

'I'm afraid you have over-estimated my wealth, if you think I could afford to buy you and 300 of your comrades,' declared Reuben.

Marcus interrupted him before he could continue.

'Don't try and buy us from the Governor, help us escape.'

This time Reuben's whistle of amazement was even louder.

'Escape? Here? You must be mad, you're over 1000 miles from

the nearest Roman province, and there is no way 300 escaped slaves could make it that far across Parthian territory, however much help you had.'

Marcus cut him off again, and he briefly told Reuben about their thwarted escape plan and how close they had come. He explained that rather than attempt to cross Parthia, they were going to head north east into the lands of the Xiongnu.

Marcus then outlined his idea. Reuben was impressed with the thought which had evidently gone into the plan. Marcus had gathered a lot of useful information during his years of captivity, and he had foreseen many of the different contingencies and eventualities. Marcus told Reuben exactly what weapons and supplies they would need; he had kept the plan as simple as possible. The guards were to be given wine, and then the Romans would escape during the night. Under the cover of darkness they would sneak up on the merchant convoys in the caravanserais, steal sufficient horses and supplies, and then ride for the border. Rather than try to arrange most of the supplies beforehand, Marcus reasoned that most of the merchants would already have adequate supplies for their journey, and the Romans could steal these, thus avoiding the need to enter the city. Although Marcus did not have a guide, he hoped the head-start would give them enough time to make it out of Parthian territory before the inevitable pursuers were able to catch them.

'I can't help you,' blurted out Reuben before Marcus had finished explaining his plan. 'I'm sorry, but I can't help you all escape, maybe if it was just you it would be different, but I can't help you all escape. Your plan is good, but it will be obvious that you've had help, and I cannot flee from the Parthians with my entire caravan. I have to go west not east, so I will be in Parthia for another 3 months at least. Besides, I pass through Parthia every year; if they suspected me I would risk my life every time

I entered Parthia. I have responsibilities too; I can't risk the lives of my men on something rash like this.'

Although he saw the truth in what Reuben said, Marcus was dismayed by Reuben's short speech. However, the escape required outside assistance and there was no way Marcus could manage without help. After a tense silence the two men reverted to discussing other matters. Reuben told Marcus all the news from the Roman world, he confirmed that Caesar was to be invested with dictatorial powers indefinitely, and that the days of the Republic seemed over. Marcus was interested in hearing all the news, although learning that Rebecca was engaged to a young Jewish merchant sent a bolt of pain through his heart. Immediately afterwards Marcus felt guilty for his jealousy, there was no way he could return and marry Rebecca, and if he really cared for her then he should rejoice in her happiness. Although this worked in theory, Marcus still found it difficult to imagine her in the arms of another man, but he forced her to the back of his mind and focused on other matters. Despite the tension which had arisen after Reuben's refusal to help, the two men still got on well, and the discussion continued amicably for the rest of the meal. Reuben made one attempt to persuade Marcus to let him buy his freedom from the Governor, but Marcus was steadfast in declining the offer. Similarly, Marcus attempted one more time to convince Reuben to assist them escape, but the practical merchant only reiterated his refusal.

Reuben and Marcus were still deep in conversation as the two men walked back to the tavern where the wagons were waiting. Reuben had collected his horse, and then rode along next to Marcus, chatting as they left the city. From the determined set of Marcus's jaw, Reuben had surmised that Marcus still intended to make the escape attempt. The large merchant reached into his bag, withdrew a long leather container and handed it to Marcus.

Initially the Roman thought it was a sword, for the package was the same length as the short stabbing sword favored by the legionaries. However, it was much too light to be a sword and Marcus opened the package with curiosity. Inside he found a long hollow plant stem. Marcus was totally nonplussed at what to make of the gift, the stem was far too light to make an effective club, and there were no markings on it to suggest it had any significance as a caduceus or symbolic baton or staff, yet it was evident from the elaborate protective case that the stick was valuable. Then Marcus remembered his initial sighting of Reuben, the merchant had raised something to his eye and recognized Marcus from a great distance. Marcus now raised the stem to his eye, and closed the other. He was startled to discover that through the stem everything appeared further away and diminished in size. At this point Reuben chuckled and told him to turn it around. When Marcus looked through the other end he was amazed to see a magnified but blurry vision of the road ahead. He compared the magnified view with what he could discern without the device, and he was greatly impressed with the superior vision which the device offered.

Reuben stated that the device was a gift, and Marcus spent several rapturous minutes examining the road ahead. Reuben explained that the device was called a dioptra, and inside the hollow stem of a giant fennel there were two glass lenses. The nearest was fixed, but Reuben showed Marcus how the further lens could be adjusted to alter the point of the focus. Following Reuben's instructions Marcus was able to achieve a much clearer image and he was even more amazed at the new device. With a tacit wink Reuben said he hoped Marcus would find the gift useful. Reuben then pointedly mentioned that he was in the habit of posting double guards on his mounts and supplies whenever the caravan stopped. Marcus chuckled ruefully; he had no intention of stealing from Reuben in any case. Marcus thanked Reuben sincerely for the dioptra and commented on the superfluous, yet wise measure of guarding his horses. Marcus had forgotten to ask Reuben how he had recognized him from afar, but now he understood and he was quick to see the advantage of the dioptra in any escape attempt.

The wagons had passed through the city gates, and they were approaching the caravanserai when Reuben looked up in alarm as they heard the uproar which was coming from his camp. Marcus stood up in the wagon seat, and from his elevated position he scanned the chaotic caravanserai with the dioptra. There were people running in every direction, and the panic was spreading to the baggage animals. The mules were bucking and rearing, struggling with their tethers and attempting to break free. As Marcus watched, one large camel wrenched the pole to which he was tethered from the ground and fled into the countryside pulling the pole behind him. The pole snagged around the leg of a brazier and knocked it over, the coals swiftly ignited one of the woollen tents and dark smoke soon rose into the clear air.

Marcus continued scanning the melee of people and animals as he tried to ascertain the course of the panic. At that point an agonising and protracted scream came clearly above the general noise of the crowd. In one corner of the caravanserai Marcus saw the tiger; it had broken out of its cage and seized one of the young men who were tormenting it. The tiger had floored the man with one blow and it was now biting into the man's neck. The scream was cut off abruptly as the tiger's teeth severed the man's windpipe. Blood spurted over the tiger's head and Marcus watched in horrified amazement as the man gave a final twitch before the life drained out of him. The tiger made an oddly beautiful sight, resplendent in its savage mastery with the bright red of the aortal blood showing vividly against its vibrant black-striped orange fur.

Meanwhile, Reuben and the others had stopped one of the fleeing men and demanded to know what had happened. The terrified mule-driver recounted how a group of drunken men had been taunting the tiger and poking it with sticks. Spurred on by their comrades the men had then dared each other to grab the tiger's tail. One man had succeeded in grasping the tail, and he held on with determination as the others cheered. Finally driven into a rage, the tiger had spun round and broken the bars of its cage, despite the metal which reinforced the wooden bars. The drunken man had tried to run but the tiger had overtaken him within a few bounds and leapt on him. The horrifying spectacle of the tiger toying with its erstwhile tormentor had prompted the chaos and panic amongst the rest of the camp. The baggage animals and horses had caught the scent of the tiger and the smell of fresh blood, and the animals panicked as they struggled to escape their tethers and flee the fearsome predator. Reuben was distraught at the news, and he cursed the fools who had taunted the tiger with a burst of profanities that belied his devout habits. Reuben quietly explained that the tiger was by far the most valuable item in his convoy. It had been extremely difficult to capture the fierce animal, and now it looked like it would escape only to be hunted down by the Parthians.

Thinking quickly, Marcus leapt from his wagon and called his men to follow him. The tight bond of comradeship and the rigorous discipline of the legionaries meant that they did not hesitate to accompany Marcus as he battled his way against the fleeing crowd and made straight for the corner where he had seen the tiger. The legionaries had followed their officers into dangerous conflicts many times before, and it was only when the unit caught sight of the tiger that they realized they were completely unarmed. Marcus was determined to capture the beast alive, but he knew it would be a difficult task. The two Parthian guards were greatly surprised and shocked by the Romans' actions; with Marcus and his men making directly towards the tiger, the guards were obliged to follow their prisoners. The urgency of the situation stirred the two guards from their sullen reverie, and whilst they would have preferred to flee with the crowd, they now determined to make the best of the grim situation and shoot the tiger with their powerful bows. As the Romans and guards watched, the tiger ripped a large bite from the dead man's thigh and pawed at the corpse as he set about devouring it. By now the caravanserai was deserted, with the only movement coming from the few panic-stricken beasts which were unable to escape from their tethers. Marcus quickly calculated that he could not spare the men to secure the baggage animals; he would need every one of his 16 men to recapture the tiger alive. News of the animal's escape had soon reached the guards at the city gate, and the more adventurous Parthians were now riding out towards the caravanserai, to hunt down the tiger. Marcus and his men would have only a few minutes to recapture the tiger, before the Parthians shot it down.

The legionaries seized whatever materials they could from around the caravanserai; tent ropes, rolls of cloth, barrels and baggage harnesses were quickly pressed into service, as the Romans sought to arm themselves for a new type of combat. The tiger was still in the corner of the caravanserai, and Marcus ordered his men to construct a barrier to prevent the animal escaping. Whilst the tiger was busy devouring its former tormentor, the Romans worked to pen the animal into a corner of the caravanserai. On two sides the high tiled walls of the caravanserai already prevented the tiger from escaping, but the other two sides were open. The Romans worked quickly, anxious to avoid attracting the attention of the ferocious beast which was only yards away from them. Compared to the normal din of the caravanserai, and the chaos which the tiger's escape had prompted, an eerie hush had now fallen over the scene. The silence was only disturbed by the crunching of the feeding tiger, the grunts of the laboring Romans, and the occasional bellow from the remaining baggage animals. The tiger seemed unconcerned by the activity of the Romans, who were laboring with controlled haste. The legionaries quickly erected a makeshift barrier of wagons, sacks and barrels. The barrier was soon large enough to present a significant obstacle, even if it was unlikely to withstand a determined onslaught by the tiger.

Meanwhile Reuben was struggling to restrain the two guards who were searching for a safe position from which they could shoot at the tiger. Reuben was fraught with tension as he glanced up to measure the progress of the other guards who were riding from the city. When they arrived, it would all be over, for the Parthian guardsmen would hunt down the tiger without hesitation; it was a clear and present danger to their countrymen, and had already killed one man. However, Reuben had expended a huge amount of effort and money in trapping the tiger, and he was reluctant to see his investment slaughtered by Parthian arrows. Caesar's vast celebratory games were in seven months, and Reuben did not have time to go back across Bactria to the forests of the north east to trap a replacement tiger from the lands of the Xiongnu.

The two Parthian guards ignored Reuben's entreaties and abruptly pushed past him as they climbed onto the caravanserai's walls. Below them, Marcus and his men were wheeling a wagon full of timbers into the final gap in the barrier. The Romans quickly stacked some of the timbers to block the gap between the wagon's wheels, and then looked at Marcus, ready for their next instructions. Gnaeus and Caius had located a couple of nets which the merchants used to secure their cargoes during sandstorms. There were also a number of unfurled rolls of cloth which the legionaries eagerly seized. Armed with ropes, nets, poles and lengths of cloth the Romans climbed over the barrier and began to move slowly towards the tiger. It would be impossible for any single man to withstand an attack from the tiger, and they all relied on their comrades to rush to their aid and entangle or overwhelm the beast. Meanwhile, the Parthian guards had notched arrows to their bows and were preparing to shoot at the tiger, heedless of the advancing Romans. The first guard's arrow struck home, and the tiger roared with rage as the arrow drove into its thigh. The tiger's roar saved it from the second arrow, for the noise so disturbed the second guardsman that his shot went wide, it hit the hard dusty floor and skidded along. Robbed of its lethal velocity the second arrow looked oddly harmless as it lay inert on the dusty floor.

With pain shooting up from its thigh, the tiger looked up and beheld the advancing Romans. The animal immediately associated the newcomers with the pain, and it charged at the nearest legionaries. Marcus called for all his men to rush on the beast and save their comrades. Meanwhile, Reuben was desperately shouting at the Parthians to stop shooting. The guardsmen saw the tiger charge the Romans and without hesitation they shot another two arrows at the charging beast. This time neither arrow found its intended mark; one arrow caught a Roman in the back, whilst the other thudded inertly into the ground just beside Gnaeus's foot. The tiger's charge, and the thrashing of the dieing Roman stirred up a lot of dust and in the melee it was hard to discern what was going on. The remaining legionaries rushed to aid their comrades. Caius was one of the unfortunate pair which the tiger had charged, he had been bowled over by a fierce blow and he lay stunned and immobile as the struggle continued over and around him. The tiger's movements worked the arrow deeper into its thigh and the beast was enraged by the shooting pains. One legionary tried to stall the tiger by jabbing at its eyes with a stave, whilst his comrade attempted to lasso the tiger's head. However, the tiger struck the stave from the first man's grasp and leapt on him before any of the ropes or nets could restrain it. With one savage bite the tiger ended the legionary's life and blood erupted over the scene. Next the tiger swiped at the nearest Roman, a swarthy Gaul named Servius whose face was pockmarked with acne scars. The tiger's swift blow caught Servius on his thigh and it shattered his femur causing him to collapse with a scream of agony.

Meanwhile, Reuben had climbed onto the caravanserai walls, and he now rushed unheeded towards the guardsmen with arms flailing and loud shouts of alarm. The melee of enraged tiger and struggling Romans was far too dense to risk a shot, and Reuben thought nothing of charging into both of the guards, and knocking them off the wall. The guards were taken back by the unexpected attack, and the fall from the high wall knocked the wind out of them. Within the caravanserai the Romans had managed to entangle the tiger's rear legs with a couple of ropes, they hurried to pull the ropes tight and secure them to prevent any further charges by the tiger. The tiger reared and thrashed with its front paws as the legionaries struggled to lasso further ropes onto the enraged beast. Marcus saw that Caius was still within range of the tiger, and he darted in to retrieve his unconscious comrade. Gnaeus threw a large piece of cloth over the tiger, and with the help of the others they struggled to pin the tiger down. As Marcus was bent double pulling Caius out of danger, the cloth ripped. One powerful paw shot out from the rent and swiped through the air, the tigers claws struck Marcus's thigh and gauged out five parallel wounds. Marcus fell to the side, pulling Caius the last few feet out of danger before the shock and adrenalin gave way, and all he could feel was the pain of his wound.

More nets and cloths were swiftly thrown over the tiger as it thrashed on the ground, and soon the Romans had the beast securely trussed up. By that time Reuben and the Parthians had approached, the guardsmen surveyed the scene of destruction around them and muttered ominously. Reuben did not pay them the slightest bit of attention; first he ran to check on Marcus, and after satisfying himself that the injury was not fatal, he turned to the remaining Romans. They heaved the struggling tiger into its cage, and hastily re-enforced the broken bars. Once the tiger was in its cage, Reuben supervised as the Romans tied it securely to the frame. Next the Romans left Reuben to tend to the tiger as they looked to their own wounded. Two legionaries lay dead, one from the Parthian's arrow and the other from the tiger's mauling. The Romans were furious with the Parthian guards, especially as the two archers were now claiming credit for the tiger's capture. The guards vociferously claimed that it was their arrows which had injured and slowed the beast, and without their intervention the tiger would have run amok and killed them all.

By now a crowd was forming as the merchants and staff returned to the caravanserai. There were wails of distress and cries of thanksgiving as various merchants returned and found their stocks either damaged or unharmed. The caravanserai physician had dressed Marcus's and Caius's wounds, and set Servius's broken leg in a splint; Marcus's were not considered life-threatening but Caius was still unconscious from the blow, and his condition was critical. Servius would probably be crippled, but there was some hope that the limb would not have to be amputated. The remaining Romans then withdrew from the scene. They loaded Caius and the bodies of their slain comrades onto their wagons and rode off to their camp. As the wagons jolted over the bumpy track Marcus winced with pain, the five deep scores across his thigh were bleeding freely despite the tight bandage the physician had applied. The wounds had been washed, but Marcus knew that they would have to be sterilised with vinegar at the camp. The prospect was not something he was looking forward to, but at least the sting of the vinegar would be better than the lingering lethal pain of an infection. As the wagons pulled into the camp a joyful shout came from the wagon which carried the comatose Caius, he had stirred and was regaining consciousness. Marcus was glad to be distracted from the pain of his wound, and he called out for more news about Caius.

Once the men arrived in the camp, Titus and Vardanes quickly organised the care of the wounded men, and the burial of the two dead Romans. They could not wait on ceremony and the two men were interred swiftly with minimal ceremony. Most of the legionaries who had been involved in recapturing the tiger had sustained some form of minor injury, for the powerful beast had thrashed around a lot, and the Romans were bruised, scratched and battered. The other legionaries listened with interest as the 14 survivors recounted their versions of the events over some wine. Marcus drank deeply from the circulating wine bottle, for he knew his wounds still required sterilisation. Once the wine had taken the edge off his pain, he motioned to Titus and pulled out the vinegar. In the last of the afternoon sunshine, Marcus bit hard on his belt, and Titus poured vinegar over the wounds, opening, probing and washing each cut to ensure no dirt or material remained inside. There were several threads from Marcus's tunic which had been caught by the tiger's claws, and Titus carefully removed each of these, before closing the five wounds with five rows of neat stitches. Marcus went to bed early, leaving the others to talk into the night about the day's events, and the possible ramifications it would have on the group of Romans. Although they toasted and mourned their dead comrades, the Romans were professional soldiers and the violent death of a comrade was nothing new to them.

21

Merv, 46 BC.

MARCUS SLEPT DEEPLY despite the pain in his leg. His dreams were filled with images of wrestling a tiger. In his visions the tiger metamorphosed into human form, and then offered Marcus his hand to shake, but each time Marcus went to grasp the proffered limb the man reverted to the form of a tiger and painfully clawed at Marcus's thigh. Then the whole procedure would recommence with the same outcome, finally Marcus imagined that their wrestling caused the very Earth to tremble. At that point he awoke to find Titus shaking his arm in an attempt to rouse him. Marcus had been muttering in his sleep, and Titus was concerned that he might be delirious. Marcus's movements had re-opened his wounds, and the pain from his thigh which he had felt in his dreams was real. Titus removed the bloodied bandages and checked carefully for any signs of infection; despite the fresh bleeding the wounds were healing and no puss oozed from the cuts when Titus probed them. Titus brought Marcus some breakfast and broke the bad news that Caius had died during the night.

Caius had recovered consciousness but remained drowsy, he had complained of pains and mounting pressure in his skull. A physician had been summoned from Merv, but it took several hours for the man to arrive. Meanwhile, Caius displayed signs of confusion and extreme drowsiness. The headaches had worsened during the night and between lucid intervals he had slipped back into unconsciousness. Before the physician arrived, Caius's condition worsened; his right side became paralysed much to the surprise of his companions, for the blow was clearly on the left side of his skull where a large amount of blood was clotted into his fiery red hair. When the physician arrived, he examined the injured man and muttered ominously. Caius's breathing had become irregular, and his left pupil had dilated, although his right pupil remained unaltered. The physician declared that the situation was almost hopeless, but announced that he would do his best and he drilled a hole in Caius's skull to relieve the pressure. However, the trepan was too late and Caius died before dawn.

Whilst Titus broke the news to Marcus, the rest of the Romans were already laboring to fit the new timbers to the deck of the bridge. The work on the bridge and road was scheduled to be completed within a fortnight. Titus had been left at the camp to tend the wounded men; after Caius's death, Servius and Marcus were the only serious cases but both showed promising signs of recovery. The physician at the caravanserai had made a good job of cleaning and setting Servius's leg, and there was no sign of infection. The group of 300 prisoners who were working on the bridge and the stretch of road on either side of the bridge contained all of the surviving members from the Gallic cavalry, along with legionaries recruited in Gaul and the province of Nearer Spain. Now Titus, Marcus and Servius spent many hours in conversation as they waited for Nature to take its course and the wounds to heal. They spoke about their memories of Gaul and their lives before they joined the legions. As his wounds recovered Marcus spoke of his frustrated escape plans and his yearning for freedom. One afternoon, a few days after the episode with the tiger, Reuben rode into the camp. He was glad to see that Marcus was recovering, and he reiterated his gratitude for the Romans' courageous intervention at the caravanserai. Reuben then told Marcus that the Parthian Governor was charging him for the damage caused by the tiger. In addition to paying blood-money to the family of the deceased Parthian, Reuben was required to compensate the Governor for the loss of the three dead Romans, and pay for some of the damage at the caravanserai. Reuben was furious, as the whole incident arose from the stupidity of the Parthian who pulled the tiger's tail, and now Reuben was obliged to compensate the man's family. Furthermore Reuben was being charged, and grossly overcharged at that, for the three dead Romans, even though one of the legionaries had actually been killed by an arrow from the Parthian guard.

Several of the merchants and other traders had also presented claims for damages, both real and spurious, resulting from the episode. However, the Governor had dismissed the claims immediately, not from any concern about their legitimacy, but to ensure that Reuben would have sufficient funds to meet the claims the Governor was making. Reuben was furious at the injustice of his treatment. The tiger would not have escaped if the drunken Parthians had not tormented it, and now Reuben had to pay for their folly. Reuben was confident that the Romans would have recaptured the tiger without loss of life if it had not been for the interference of the two guards, yet now Reuben was being charged for the three dead Romans and for the injuries to Marcus and Servius. Reuben had not revealed the true value of the tiger, for he was sure that the Governor would have confiscated the beast or increased the fines, if he knew the tiger's potential value. When Reuben learnt he had to pay compensation for the whole episode despite it being instigated and then aggravated by the Parthians, he seethed with anger and resentment.

The Governor, however, knew that with certain Parthians calling for Reuben's arrest and trial, the Jew was in no position to argue, and the Governor grasped the opportunity to squeeze all he could out of the wealthy merchant. The huge sum being demanded of Reuben forced him to sell all of the cargo from his caravan in Merv, leaving him with just his personal belongings and the tiger. There was no market for a tiger in Merv, especially one that had killed a Parthian, so Reuben managed to retain the beast whilst making it appear to be from necessity rather than choice. In the city everyone knew of his dire predicament and initially the merchants made him ridiculously low offers for his cargo and beasts. Fortunately, the Jewish community rallied behind one of their own, and between them they purchased Reuben's entire stock at a fair price. Reuben was also obliged to lay off most of the men he had employed with his caravan, but he first commended them to the main Jewish merchants and many were promptly re-employed. After all the negotiations and arrangements Reuben was left with the tiger, which had recovered from the wound to its leg and was kept sedated in a stronger cage. Nothing else remained of Reuben's cargo, but with the tiger and the handful of men who had elected to remain with him, Reuben could still turn a reasonable profit if he got the animal to Rome in time for Caesar's Games. Before Reuben had left Alexandria, a contact in Rome had informed him that Caesar's insistence on surpassing all others, meant the next Games that he organised would provide an unrivalled market for fierce exotic animals.

After the Governor's intervention Reuben was no longer encumbered with a bulky caravan or a large number of men; furthermore Reuben was determined to take a different route in future, and avoid passing through that part of Parthia. He also had a distinct grudge against the inhabitants of Merv. The

Governor had inadvertently removed every reason Reuben had cited for not helping the Romans escape. Reuben had now come to inform Marcus of his whole-hearted support for the plan, and to organise the details of the escape. Marcus empathised with Reuben for the losses he had sustained, and he was delighted to learn that Reuben was now willing to help them escape. Reuben also suggested a refinement to Marcus's original plan. In order to sedate the tiger, Reuben had acquired a large quantity of haoma, and he suggested using some to drug the Parthian guards. Haoma was a substance used by the Zoroastrian priests in their ceremonies; it was a powerful sedative with hallucinogenic properties which the priests claimed facilitated divine communication. The origins of the drug and the recipe for its production were shrouded in secrecy and religious mystery, but the ingredients included ephedrine, opium and cannabis, all of which had to be combined in a large copper cauldron. Although the Zoroastrian priests drank haoma in a liquid form during their ceremonies, Reuben had been able to purchase a fair quantity of the dried powder, which was the purest form of the drug. The whole city had been shaken by the tiger's escape, and the priests had been only too happy to sell Reuben some haoma to keep the tiger sedated.

Reuben was confident that the tiger would not need to be kept so heavily sedated once they were on the road, and he had earmarked a sizeable quantity of the haoma to drug the guards at the camp. Reuben also informed Marcus that the Xiongnu guide, who had led the caravan across Sogdia and into Parthia, would lead the Romans into Sogdia as he returned. The man's name was Cheli, and Reuben described him as a barrel-chested man with brown hair and a luxuriant beard which glistened from the regular coats of oil which Cheli assiduously applied. Reuben also described the guide's distinctive high bridging nose, green eyes and the white stallion he rode. Marcus carefully stored away all this information, for he would have to meet and identify Cheli in the pitch dark on the night of the escape.

'Are there any other particular features or traits you can remember?' asked Marcus, for he was anxious to positively identify the guide.

'Of course, how stupid of me to forget!' exclaimed Reuben, 'His face is slashed on both cheeks and his forehead, he's still in mourning for his younger brother, and it's the custom amongst their tribe to slash their faces in mourning. The brother only died a month ago, so the scars are still easy to see. I'd become so use to it, I nearly forgot to mention them.'

Marcus was a little surprised to learn of the strange custom, but it certainly provided a useful way to identify the man; any impostor would have had to slash his face weeks ago to get the appropriate scars. Marcus then asked why Cheli was still in Merv if he had already been paid and dismissed for his services guiding the caravan. With a deep chuckle, Reuben explained that it would take even the most debauched man many days and nights to spend all that money on wine and women in the city's taverns. After many weeks of tough travelling through the steppes, the guides always welcomed the chance to enjoy the comforts of a city and blow the wages they had accumulated during the journey. Consequently, it had not been difficult for Reuben to track down Cheli even after he had paid and dismissed him. In return for an additional payment, Cheli had agreed to meet the Romans on the night of the escape and lead them to the Xiongnu chief in Sogdia. Reuben now handed Marcus a purse containing the additional sum which he had agreed upon with Cheli. The services of an experienced guide would ensure that they took the quickest route out of Parthia, and time would certainly be of the essence once the Parthians discovered their escape. The Romans would have to cross the Amu-Darya River to leave Parthia. Crossing the huge River presented another significant challenge, for the Amu-Darya was a vast watercourse which drained the Pamir Mountains into the Aral Sea. In normal times the River was about a mile wide, but when the River burst its banks during the spring it could fill the flood plain which stretched for many miles on both sides of the main watercourse. The spring floods had subsided, but there was still no way that the Romans could hope to ford or swim the River, and they would have to procure passage from the local inhabitants before the Parthians caught up with them. The guide knew where and how this could be best arranged, and Reuben had emphasized their need for speed.

Once the Romans crossed the River they would be safe from Parthian pursuit, but a whole new range of dangers would then face them. The Xiongnu nomads who controlled the plains of Sogdia were notoriously ferocious, as Marcus and the Romans had witnessed from the walls of Merv. Reuben had spent the harsh winter months in Sogdia, living with the Xiongnu and working out how to trap his tiger. As Reuben and Marcus discussed their plan, Reuben passed on some information about the Xiongnu. Many generations ago the rapacious Xiongnu had invaded Sogdia. The sedentary and peaceful Sogdians were no match for the fierce nomads, so they had reached a compromise. The Xiongnu were a Turkic people and like most nomads their society was illiterate; they relied on the traditions of epic ballads sung by bards to pass on their history. The Sogdians had been involved in trade for many generations, and now they acted as the administrators and clerks for the illiterate Xiongnu. As the area under the control of the nomads expanded, Sogdian became the *lingua franca* for many of the trading routes which formed the Silk Road.

The Xiongnu nomads were pastoralists who measured

their wealth in cattle, and power in the number of men a chief commanded. A census was held each autumn to count the number of men and cattle in each tribe, this census formed the basis for the levy which a chief sent out when he went to war on a grand scale. The rest of the time, the different tribes were free to raid and squabble amongst themselves. This internecine feuding was actively encouraged by the chief as it kept the men in fighting form. The nomads were a fierce and warlike people, who respected military prowess above all else; and Reuben was confident that the Xiongnu chief would employ the Romans as mercenaries. Cheli would present the Romans to the tribe's chief, along with Reuben's personal commendation of their fighting and engineering abilities. Along with the gold to pay Cheli, Reuben had left letters to several Xiongnu chieftains, although the chieftains were all illiterate they had Sogdian scribes.

The Romans would need a considerable number of horses on which to make good their escape. Fortunately Marcus's group of prisoners consisted largely of former cavalrymen, so the Romans should be capable of the long tough riding which the plan required. Whilst transacting his business and selling his cargo, Reuben had visited most of the caravanserais round the city, and he had discreetly surveyed the number and quality of the horses in each camp. Marcus listened eagerly as Reuben passed on his observations. The injured Roman was already sitting up alert in his bed, but when Reuben mentioned that a caravan had arrived recently with one of the blood-sweating horses from Ferghana, Marcus jumped to his feet with excitement. The caravan belonged to a Syrian merchant who had spitefully lodged an inflated plea for compensation against Reuben, and the Jew mentioned this fact in case Marcus required any further motivation to steal the prized horse. Marcus now hopped around the hut, finalising the details of the plan whilst wishing his leg would heal more quickly.

'We need weapons,' declared Marcus.

'I kept the weapons from my guards when I dismissed them yesterday, you can have those,' said Reuben. 'There won't be enough for all of your men, but it's better than nothing.'

'How many men will you take?' asked Reuben.

'Well, there were 312 prisoners working on the bridge and this section of road, 3 have now died so that leaves 309, assuming both Servius and I will have recovered in time. Now from what you said earlier, we should be able to get enough mounts from the two large caravanserais to the north of the city, including that blood-sweating horse you mentioned,' replied Marcus. His eyes were aglow with excitement at the prospect of riding one of the famed steeds.

'I'm sure my good Syrian friend would also be delighted to furnish you with some supplies,' added Reuben in a sarcastic tone. The Syrian had attempted to exploit Reuben when he was in dire straits, and now the portly Jew savoured the opportunity for revenge.

'Yes, we'll help ourselves to everything we need for the journey,' agreed Marcus, although his mind was still clearly focused on the blood-sweating horse.

'It's a dun mare,' added Reuben, who could easily see what Marcus was thinking about.

The snippet of information came as a surprise to Marcus; he had imagined that the famed blood-sweating horse would be a magnificent stallion with a jet black or pure white hide. Then Marcus remembered what Tyluxes had first told him about the famous horses; their value lay in their endurance, loyalty and intelligence rather than their appearance. It was readily admitted that Arab thoroughbreds with their graceful lines, long legs and wide nostrils, were more beautiful, but none of them could match the Ferghana horses for stamina. The fine elegant legs of the Arab horses certainly made the thoroughbreds a magnificent sight to behold, but the same graceful legs were not sturdy enough to tackle rough terrain at a fast pace; nor did the svelte muscles of the Arab horses provide enough power to ride continuously for days on end.

Reuben, Marcus and Titus continued finalising the details of their plan whilst Servius kept watch for the approach of the guards or the return of Vardanes. Reuben had not forgotten about the bibulous commander and his fondness for wine; along with the haoma Reuben had procured two bottles of excellent wine, one of which he intended to share with Vardanes that evening. This would ensure that when Reuben sent a drugged bottle of the same wine a week later, they could be confident that Vardanes would not wait long before opening it. Reuben also arranged to send an entire crate of drugged wine to thank the two guards who had participated in the recapture of the tiger. The wine would be accompanied with an explanation commending their bravery, and requesting their pardon for any confusion during the episode. There was little doubt that the guards would take the bait, and then obligingly share the wine with their comrades; this would take care of all the Parthians at the camp. Marcus was so caught up in the excitement of planning the escape that it was some time before he thought of Reuben.

'What about you? Where will you go once we've fled?' asked Marcus with concern for it would be evident that the prisoners had used haoma to drug the guards, and any investigation would soon lead to Reuben.

'I'll be long gone by then,' explained Reuben with a chuckle. 'I'm building up for a big row with the caravanserai manager in a few days time, and then I'll storm off in a rage. Once I'm safely out of sight I'll change course and make for Armenia where I have a number of influential contacts and I will be safe. My Jewish friends within Merv will kindly spread a little misinformation about my route and plans; anyway, most of the guards will be chasing you lot. Besides, now that I have lost my caravan it is only the tiger I need to transport, so I can move faster.'

Marcus was relieved to hear that Reuben would be out of danger, and he admired the refinements which Reuben had made to the original plan. Both men chortled at the idea of sending wine to thank the Parthian guards whose ignorance and haste had resulted in so many problems whilst recapturing the tiger. Marcus was confident the guards would accept the explanation; Titus had reported that the two men had not stopped bragging about their part in the episode, to the extent that the guards had almost come to believe their own stories. At that point, they were interrupted by a low whistle from Servius; this was the signal that Vardanes was approaching the camp. Reuben and Marcus only had a few moments of privacy before the Parthian arrived. They ran through the plan one final time, and fixed the date for eight days hence. The interval would give Reuben sufficient time to instigate an argument with the caravanserai owner and storm off in a rage after arranging to deliver the drugged wine to Vardanes and the guards on the day scheduled for the escape. It was hoped that it would also be sufficient time for Marcus and Servius to recover enough to ride again. They dared not risk delaying the escape any longer, as the work on the bridge and road sections was nearly complete, and once the Romans were transferred back to the camp outside the city, or put in charge of different guards, a new plan would be required.

A second whistle from Servius announced that Vardanes had entered the camp. Reuben went to meet him with open arms and the wine bottle protruding visibly from his pocket. Vardanes readily accepted the Jew's invitation to share the wine, and as he opened the bottle Reuben explained that he had come to thank the guards and the prisoners for their help in recapturing the tiger. Reuben sipped the wine, and with masterful self-control he specifically mentioned the brave conduct of the two guards and their timely intervention.

'Perhaps I could send your guards a reward, after all it was their actions which saved the day,' commented Reuben. 'Maybe they would like some of this wine,' he wondered aloud.

'Oh no, this is far too good to waste on mere soldiers, such fine wine would not be appreciated by the likes of them. It is only refined men such as you and I who can savour the complex flavours of fine wine,' insisted Vardanes.

'Is this stuff any good?' asked Reuben innocently.

'Good? It's excellent! The best I've tasted in months,' added Vardanes, 'and I pride myself on my knowledge of wine.'

'I had no idea it was anything special,' said Reuben nonchalantly, 'I'm afraid I am no connoisseur.'

This last comment elicited a shrug of feigned modesty from Vardanes.

'I'll send your guards some cheap bottles then,' added Reuben, 'and if you really like this stuff I'm sure I've got another one somewhere, it's wasted on a man such as myself, but as you clearly appreciate it I'll send it to you. It'd be a shame for decent wine to be drunk by someone who doesn't appreciate it.'

Vardanes fell for the bait and there was a faint trace of dipsomania in the readiness with which he accepted Reuben's offer. Once Reuben had departed Vardanes sank back into a chair and opened another bottle of wine with a deep sigh. He knew that the new bottle would not taste as good as the last, but he would drink it anyway, like he had drunk so many others, searching for the elusive taste of the perfect wine and its soothing effects. When he had tasted the wine Reuben had brought, Vardanes thought he had finally captured the Bacchanalian bliss which he sought in every bottle. The wine had a pure taste, full-bodied, rounded and perfectly balanced; for the precious hour that the bottle had lasted Vardanes relaxed. Now, Vardanes sighed with resignation as he drank his own inferior wine, his only consolation lay in the prospect of Reuben sending him `another bottle of the exquisite wine they had shared. As the second bottle of wine took effect on him, Vardanes passed through the four stages of drunkenness. Reuben's wine had soothed and cheered him until he was jocose, after that was gone his inferior wine had made him first lachrymose, then briefly bellicose, before he finally slid to the floor of his tent comatose. Later, Vardanes' personal slave slipped quietly into the tent, and following a familiar pattern he manoeuvred his master on to the bed and removed the empty wine bottles.

22

MERV, 46 BC

WITH SOME TREPIDATION, Titus cautiously lifted the flap of the guards' tent to allow Gnaeus and two other legionaries to slip inside. Their care proved unnecessary for inside the tent all of the twenty guards were sprawled out in a drugged state on the floor. The few Parthians who were not asleep were mumbling incoherently about the myriad hallucinations they were experiencing. The four legionaries worked quickly, they tied up all of the guards securely, and then gagged them. Gnaeus wanted to leave out their gags in case any of the drugged men choked on their own vomit, but Titus overruled him; the prisoners could not afford to take any risks during their escape for it was already extremely dangerous. If the guards were left un-gagged their cries might well be heard by someone using the nearby bridge, and the Romans needed as much of a head-start as possible before their escape was discovered. The legionaries then left, taking the guards' weapons with them. At the other end of the campground, a junior centurion named Gaius had led another group of Romans as they burst into Vardanes's tent. The first legionary to enter the tent had tripped over the sleeping form of Vardanes's personal slave. The old Greek had scrambled to his feet with a cry of alarm, but Gaius quickly punched him with a hard uppercut. The blow caught the old man's chin and as his head snapped back he was knocked out cold. The cry had not disturbed Vardanes at all, the Parthian officer remained stretched out in his sleeping cubicle. He had eagerly consumed the entire bottle of drugged fine wine which Reuben had sent him, and the combined effects of the alcohol and haoma ensured he would not stir for hours. Nonetheless, Gaius and his comrades quickly bound and gagged both the slave and master and then left taking all of Vardanes's fine weapons with them.

The crate of drugged wine had arrived that afternoon, along with a coded note from Reuben to confirm his departure from Merv the day before. The ingenious merchant had also sent Marcus a sack full of caltrops along with instructions on how best to employ the vicious devices. The small sack was extremely heavy; it was made of doubled camel leather as that was the only material which was tough enough to contain the sharp devices. In Alexandria, Reuben had told Marcus about caltrops but none of the Romans had ever seen them. Each device was made up of four sharp spikes, arranged in such a fashion that however the caltrop fell, one spike would be pointing upwards. Reuben had learnt about the cruel devices during his travels, and now he had secured a sack full of caltrops for Marcus.

During the day most of the guards were busy supervising the work on the bridge and road sections, so Marcus and Titus had no difficulty concealing the weapons which Reuben had also supplied. Reuben had sent them a bundle containing twenty swords and a dozen daggers, it was not much but it would be adequate to arm the raiding parties which were going to steal the horses and supplies from the two large caravanserais. Marcus hoped there would also be an occasion to acquire more weapons from the caravanserais that night, in addition to those taken from the guards at the camp; but above all else Marcus had his heart fixed on stealing the 'blood-sweating' horse. When Vardanes and the guards returned to the camp that evening, they were delighted to find the wine which Reuben had sent them. When Reuben had mixed up the drugged wine he had added a little salt in each bottle; it was not enough to mar the flavour, but it did ensure that the guards drank more deeply as the salt increased their thirst. In any case, the guards were not in the habit of questioning the flavour or vintage of any wine they were offered for free and they drank the lot without hesitation. Vardanes had noticed that the second bottle of Reuben's fine wine did not have the same superlative flavour as the previous one, but that did not stop him finishing the entire bottle in under an hour.

Once Gaius and Titus confirmed that all of the Parthians at the camp had been taken care of, the two raiding parties set off into the night for the caravanserais which they had chosen as targets. The men were dressed in dark clothes and they had blackened their faces with ash and soot from the fireplaces. The swords, daggers and clubs which they were to use had also been blackened with a mixture of grease and ash to ensure no tell-tale gleam of steel gave away their presence in the dark. The two groups were to raid the different caravanserais simultaneously; Marcus was in charge of one group whilst Gaius led the other. Marcus's injury had healed well, although it was still a slight impediment to his mobility. From the useful intelligence which Reuben had been able to supply, both of the raiding parties knew the approximate layout of their targets. They had a rough idea of what the caravanserais could be expected to contain, and most importantly they knew where to find the horses. Both raiding parties rode towards their targets on the mounts they had stolen from the Parthian guards; there were two Romans on each horse, but even riding double-mounted was much quicker than covering the distance to the caravanserais on foot.

'Good hunting.' Marcus whispered to Gaius, as the two

groups separated in the darkness and headed for their different targets. As soon as they could make out the glow of the campfires and the murmur of distant chatter, Marcus slowed his mount and his men followed suit immediately. They dismounted and left the horses with a legionary named Appius. The legionary was a stocky young man, short in both height and conversation. He hailed from the province of Nearer Spain, although Appius rarely spoke to his fellow legionaries he had earned Marcus's admiration by the masterful way in which he could handle horses. His dark eyes, unimposing stature and unshakeable calm seemed to reassure horses, and none of the experienced cavalrymen could match Appius's ability at calming a spooked horse or controlling a fiery stallion. The taciturn Iberian appeared to actually communicate with the horses as he stroked each mount and murmured to them in the native dialect of his village. Marcus was confident that during the night Appius's soothing words and attentive care would prevent any of the horses from revealing their presence with an untimely neigh or whinny.

'We'll be back as soon as possible. The signal for all clear is two low whistles, if there's a problem it's three whistles,' confirmed Marcus as he departed. 'If we don't come back in an hour, take the horses you have back to the camp, and go without us. We must escape tonight; it's too late to turn back now.'

With a curt nod Appius indicated that he had understood his instructions. Marcus had gone over all the details of the plan several times and all of the men knew exactly what part they had to play. Appius did not see any reason to indulge in unnecessary conversation; hence he saved his precious words for the horses. Marcus and the other legionaries advanced slowly and stealthily. There was only a solitary pair of disgruntled guards watching over the mounts and the baggage animals corralled in the part of the caravanserai which Reuben had indicated. The two guards were standing around a small fire grumbling at their task and complaining about the futility of guarding horses, mules and camels when the valuable cargoes were all locked up inside the caravanserai storerooms. One of the guards had found a frog in the darkness, and they were now amusing themselves by flicking the frog into the fire's embers and watching it jump out in agony. The two men were so engrossed in their puerile amusement that they did not even notice the approaching Romans until it was too late. One guard was knocked out with a blow to the head, whilst the other decided against crying out when he felt the cold edge of Marcus's dagger against his throat. The guards were bound and gagged, and whilst they lay in the darkness the injured frog hopped back to the soothing waters of the nearby irrigation ditch. Four of the legionaries left to lead all of the mounts to the meeting point where Appius was waiting. The baggage animals were left in their pens, as they would be needed to transport the supplies which the legionaries now intended to steal. Despite the danger of their immediate situation, Marcus's thoughts were entirely focused on stealing the 'blood-sweating' horse. With an effort he forced himself to focus on the raid as a whole, and not just his personal fascination with the legendary mount he hoped to steal.

Reuben and Cheli had confirmed that it would take at least three long days of tough riding for the Romans to reach the Amu-Darya River, and a further day for the prisoners to cross the River. There were few large boats on the River, and it would take many hours for the whole group to be ferried across in small fishing boats. Then once they had entered Sogdia, it could at least a week before they reached a permanent Xiongnu settlement and could be certain of acquiring further supplies. Consequently, the Romans needed to steal sufficient supplies to last for at least two weeks in open country. Spring was well-advanced by then, but they would still need blankets as the nights were still bitterly cold. As Marcus cautiously surveyed the caravanserai, he gave silent thanks to Reuben for the intelligence he had supplied. The caravanserai formed a square, with a solid storeroom forming the side closest to them, whilst a collection of tents and huts formed the other three sides. The storeroom was heavily guarded, as one would expect for it contained the spices, silk, gems and money which formed the most valuable part of the merchants' cargoes. Fortunately, none of the supplies which the Romans planned to steal were kept in the storeroom, so the legionaries would not have to tackle the guards.

A dozen dark shadows followed Marcus as he crouched low and gave the storeroom a wide berth. They skirted the caravanserai before approaching from the opposite side. The Romans were now close enough to hear the conversation of the few merchants and camp attendants who were not asleep. There were a handful of men grouped around the campfire as they chatted and drank, but most were sleeping in their tents, wrapped in their blankets. The Romans crawled closer until they were in position, hidden behind two of the tents adjacent to the kitchen area. They slit open the rear sides of the kitchen store tent and hastened to remove the blankets and stores of food they had found inside. Marcus watched over the caravanserai, ready to give a warning if their presence was noticed in anyway. He had one of the powerful Parthian bows beside him, but in the moon light he could not be sure of his aim with the unfamiliar weapon, and if pressed he would prefer to use the cold hard steel of a dagger. There were a lot of people in the caravanserai, and although most of them were asleep, there was no way the Romans could risk leaving someone bound and gagged in such a location. The raiding party knew that all of their lives depended on stealing the horses and supplies, and then leaving unnoticed.

Their orders were to avoid contact with the Parthians wherever possible, but if it proved necessary the legionaries had been told to kill swiftly and silently.

Marcus now turned his attention to the 'blood-sweating' mare. It was corralled separately from the other horses, in a special pen behind the merchant's quarters. There were three men guarding it, and it was clear that they took their duties more seriously than the two men in charge of the other horses. The mare had provoked a great deal of interest amongst the horse-mad Parthians, and numerous horse-traders had already tried to buy the mare. The Syrian merchant was taking no chances with his prized possession; he had set his best men to guard the mare, and he had already beaten one guard for a perceived lack of vigilance. The remaining guards were careful to appear attentive as they watched over their charge. Although Marcus had never seen the Syrian merchant who owned the caravan, it was not difficult to pick him out by his distinctive long white beard which Reuben had described. Even without the description, Marcus would have identified the man from the proprietary glances he kept directing at the mare. The other few men around the campfire deferred to the bearded Syrian with the hasty and uneasy manner which showed he was feared rather than respected as a leader.

Marcus had already turned his attention to stealing the mare, when one of the legionaries informed him that they had removed and loaded enough supplies for their journey. Marcus sent eight of the men back with the supplies, whilst he discussed with the remaining four how they could steal the mare. The small group were soon caught up by Marcus's enthusiasm and excitement, and in low whispers they debated the different options. Whilst the others had been removing the supplies, Marcus had seen a pair of curious Parthians come to inspect the legendary horse.

Despite the late hour, the guards had permitted them to approach the pen without undue trouble; since the horse had arrived at the caravanserai there had been a steady stream of curious Parthians and horse-enthusiasts who came to see the mare. Most went away disappointed, for the dun mare was nothing special to behold, and the guards were regularly called upon to confirm that they had seen the animal return with a visible sheen of fresh blood on its coat after being ridden hard. Marcus was confident that he could openly approach the pen without any problem; it would merely require the boldness to walk up and inspect the horse and to say a few words in Parthian, and whilst Marcus still spoke with a strong accent, his level of Parthian was sufficient for that purpose . Once they were that close, the Romans could overpower the guards and steal the mare, but the Syrian would soon notice that the pen was empty and his guards had disappeared.

'We could leave another horse in the pen instead,' suggested one bright legionary.

'Brilliant idea!' said Marcus, 'it's too dark to see the mare clearly, and by the time it's light we'll be far away.'

'What about the guards?' added another man, 'he'll notice that they're gone.'

'We'll have to pretend to be the guards whilst the horses are swapped, and then we can put their cloaks over something to give the right shape at least. It'll be too dark for anyone to tell,' added Marcus with more confidence then he felt.

It was an extremely audacious plan, but it was the best they could manage with such short notice. Marcus sent one of the legionaries back to Appius with instructions to bring the quiet Iberian and a substitute horse back to the mare's pen. Marcus was unsure of the 'blood-sweating' mare's temperament and he decided Appius's expertise might be useful to implement their plan with as little noise as possible. Whilst Appius and the replacement horse were being fetched, Marcus and the other two remaining legionaries worked their way round the caravanserai. They planned to approach from the side nearest the city gate, as if they were a group of Parthians who had come to see the 'blood-sweating' horse. As they skirted the camp, Marcus lifted up the side of one tent and stole two bottles of wine and some bread. Once they had reached the appropriate side of the caravanserai, the Romans strode along the track and made nonchalantly towards the mare's pen. They swigged cheerfully from the bottles, and shared the bread as they crossed the campground. With mouths full of food, and affected drunken slurs, none of the guards or the handful of men by the campfire realized that their accents had a suspiciously foreign edge, or that beneath their hoods the men's faces were all artificially blackened.

Marcus had liberally splashed wine over his cloak, so that when he approached the first guard the smell of wine was the first thing which the Parthian noticed. It was also the last thing that the man noticed, for in the midst of an apparently drunken stagger Marcus stopped abruptly, stepped forward and violently head-butted the man. The guard was stunned by the effect of Marcus's forehead crashing down onto the bridge of his nose, and Marcus caught him before he fell to the ground. Marcus had opted for a head-butt because it did not require an obvious swing, and the other guards did not immediately realise what had occurred. The precious seconds of surprise gave the other two legionaries time to move in and tackle them. The legionary to the left stabbed one guard through the throat, cutting off any cry before it could escape. The third guard gave a brief grunt as he was stabbed in the chest, and collapsed with a look of surprise fixed to his face. The Romans hastily dragged the guards into the shadows behind the pen; Marcus's guard showed signs of stirring, so Marcus slit his throat.

The whole assault had taken place in a matter of moments, and by the time the Syrian merchant next looked up he saw the familiar forms and cloaks of his three guards in front of the pen. Although Marcus and the other two men shivered, they were not cold in the slightest; the adrenalin still coursing through their veins kept them alert and wired. The Romans stamped their feet and pretended to blow on their hands as if they were cold and bored after hours on guard duty. The actions came easily to the legionaries, for they had spent many a cold evening on sentry duty and they knew the universal gestures and mannerisms of bored and cold guards. Marcus occasionally turned to inspect the mare he already viewed as his, the horse had been slightly disturbed by the fracas, but now it had returned to munching quietly on some oats. After a tense few minutes of guard duty, a low whistle from the darkness behind the pen informed Marcus that Appius and the other legionary had returned along with the substitute horse. Marcus lifted his tunic as he moved into the darkness and urinated noisily against one of the bushes. After the bright flames of the campfire his eyes took a moment to readjust to the darkness, he noticed with a chuckle that he had narrowly avoided pissing on the legionary who was crouching in the bushes. In whispers Marcus gave the man the guard's cloak and sent him back to the front of the pen.

Appius and Marcus then worked with their daggers to prize away the top bars at the rear of the pen. The wood was weakened with dry rot, and it did not take long for them to remove the bars. As they worked Appius murmured to both of the horses; in the soft tones of his maternal tongue he explained to the horses what he was doing and reassured them. Once the bars were removed, Appius slipped inside and found the halter of the prized mare. The mare was tied tightly, and in the end Appius had to cut the halter cord with his dagger; the Syrian was taking no chances with his precious horse escaping. Conversely, Appius did not even bother holding the mare's halter; he was so assured of his ability to control the animal. Crouching low, Marcus led the substitute horse into the pen, before Appius removed the prized mare. The other legionaries were strolling back and forth in front of the pen, trying to shield what was going on from the view of the caravanserai. However, at that critical moment a branch covered with dried leaves burst into flames on the camp fire and briefly illuminated the scene. The Syrian looked up and called out a joke.

'Hey guards, this wine must be good, I thought I saw two mares in my pen instead of one.'

'In your dreams,' replied one of the legionaries in gruff Parthian.

Appius and Marcus had frozen when the light had flared up, but now that the flames had died down the two men completed the exchanging of horses. The substitution plan had worked wonderfully, had the Syrian seen an empty pen he would certainly have investigated, but at the sight of two mares he merely assumed the wine was affecting his vision. Marcus quietly refitted the bars of the pen, and moved everything back into place as best as he could. Meanwhile, Appius was leading the mare away from the caravanserai and into the darkness where he remained waiting for the others to join him. Marcus and the other three legionaries then worked to construct dummy guards; they used a nearby water barrel and some branches from the bushes to build three frames over which they draped the guards' cloaks. The frames were then padded out with hay from the pen to give them more body and a less angular appearance. The dummies were deliberately positioned in dark corners, but their silhouettes were clearly visible from the main camp fires.

The devices were crude, but it was hoped they would provide the Romans with a valuable head-start.

Marcus also knew that the theft of the 'blood-sweating' mare could be attributed to any number of envious locals, and it would not be immediately linked to the Romans whose camp was some miles east of the caravanserai. The stolen supplies and the other stolen horses might be attributed to a nocturnal raid from the Xiongnu nomads, and the tracks would lead towards Sogdia and the River Amu-Darya. Moreover, it was well known that the nomads did not value the cloth or spices which the merchants guarded so closely, but they placed great importance on the goods and supplies which their nomadic lifestyle made difficult to acquire. It would only be when the Romans' disappearance was discovered that the various events would be connected, and Marcus was gambling that even the Governor's fastest guards would not be able to catch them by then. Meanwhile, Appius was waiting with the prized mare in the darkness. All five of the Romans then moved with quiet jubilation through the darkness as they went to join their comrades with the other horses. Gaius reached the meeting point before Marcus returned; his raid had been equally successful, though neither of the groups had been able to secure many additional weapons.

The Romans now had over 300 horses in addition to two dozen mules loaded with supplies. The horses were harnessed together in long lines, and the legionaries had no trouble leading the mounts out towards the camp. The other Romans had been waiting impatiently and they called out in hushed excitement as Marcus and Gaius approached with the train of horses. Titus had mustered all of the men, and they quickly mounted and fell into formation. For most of the Romans it was the first time they had been on a horse for several years. However, the former cavalrymen soon re-adjusted as their dormant instincts returned and the other legionaries managed as best they could. With evident relief, Titus handed Marcus the purse of gold which Reuben had left for the Romans. Marcus had entrusted it to Titus when he left for the raid, along with the instructions to take as many men as possible and escape if Marcus did not return by dawn. The clouds now parted and the moonlight illuminated the scene as the Roman prisoners bid farewell to their camp and rode off into the freedom of the night on their new mounts.

23

MERV - SOGDIA, 46-45 BC

MARCUS WAS IMMEDIATELY impressed by the blood-sweating mare he rode; even in the darkness the horse was sure-footed and confident, and he soon decided to let the mare pick the way through the undergrowth and stones. The Romans were cutting across open country as they headed north east away from the camp, and there was no path for the riders to follow. In the darkness, the rough terrain meant the men were starting to spread out, and Marcus was glad when they reached a track and were able to regroup. He had the dioptra in its case by his side, but as yet there was insufficient light to use it, nonetheless Marcus was reassured to feel the rub of the cylindrical case by his side, and the weight of the purse of gold inside his tunic. Marcus appreciated the thrill of riding such an excellent horse it gave him a buzz of elation and increased his confidence that their escape would succeed. First the Romans had to meet their guide, and then get across the mighty Amu-Darya River. Reuben had instructed Cheli to meet them beneath the lee of a small hill a few miles from the Roman camp, which he had described carefully and pointed out to Marcus. There were few hills on the Parthian plains to the north of Merv, and this one was particularly distinctive due to the giant, cracked boulder which sat on top of it. Marcus had no difficulty in recognising the silhouette of the boulder against the night skyline. As they approached the hill, the moonlight was even sufficient to show the crack running down the center of the rock.

When the column of Romans drew near to the hill, Marcus sent a few scouts in advance to check for any signs of an ambush, whilst the rest of the column rode slowly towards the hill. There was a considerable sum of money in the purse which Marcus carried to pay Cheli; by aiding the Romans, the guide was risking his life and livelihood. After the escape, Cheli would never be able to work in that part of Parthia again, and Marcus was also aware that Cheli would certainly receive a large reward if he revealed the Romans' escape plan to the Governor of Merv. However, they needed a guide to lead them into Sogdia and present them to the Xiongnu chieftain, so Marcus had no choice but to trust in Reuben's judgement. Nonetheless, Marcus had distributed all the available weapons amongst the men at the front of the column. The armed legionaries at the front rode with their swords drawn, this was a necessity as well as a precaution; the scabbards had been given to other men in an attempt to make it appear in the darkness that most of the column was armed. Marcus had taken every precaution he could think of, and when there was no warning from the scouts, he took a deep breath and led the column towards the dark lee of the hill. The hill blocked some of the light from the moon and stars, creating an even darker shadow in its lee. Subconsciously, Marcus noted that his mare had slowed down, but the horse still proceeded with sure-footed confidence in the darkness.

The Romans rode bunched together in a tight, long column as they rounded the first spur of the hill. The formation ensured each man had his front, rear and one flank protected by a comrade, whilst the column could still rapidly break order and charge or retreat, if required. Although the horse-shoe shaped lee of the hill made a well-concealed meeting place, the projecting spurs of the hill also made it ideal territory for an ambush. Marcus was at the head of the column, and he now signaled for the front four pairs of cavalrymen to follow him, whilst the others waited at the opening to the gulley. Marcus had no intention of leading all of his men into a trap, and he left Titus in charge of the main body of Romans whilst he advanced with the escort. Although the precautions were necessary, they were also time-consuming, and Marcus was anxious to continue riding and put as many miles as possible between themselves and the Parthians before their escape was discovered and the dreaded horse-archers sent in pursuit.

In the darkness ahead, Marcus saw something move. He halted and called out quietly. There was no response; it was only a light patch of rock, visible against the darker hillside. As he advanced, Marcus made towards the white patch of rock. On the still night air Marcus caught the scent of fresh wood-smoke, but he could not see the glow of any flames or embers. All of the Romans were anxiously scanning the darkness ahead of them for any sign of movement but it was too dark for their eyes to distinguish much. The advancing men were all acutely aware that they were silhouetted against the moonlight behind them, so they could be seen clearly by anyone in the gulley; yet it was difficult for the Romans to see into the dark gulley. As Marcus advanced towards the light patch of rock he felt a quiver of excitement run through the mare, but the horse was clearly not frightened, and it proceeded into the darkness without hesitation. Marcus trusted the animal's instincts and rode on slowly. Ahead of them, the white rock appeared to move again and Marcus realized that it was a horse and not a rock at all. Reuben had told Marcus that Cheli rode a white stallion. 'That explains the mare's quiver of excitement,' thought Marcus with a chuckle, and he advanced deeper into the gulley with less trepidation. Moments later, Marcus saw the glow of a fire. A carefully constructed bank of rocks screened the fire from the view of anyone further down the gulley.

'Marcus?' called out a gruff voice from the darkness.

'Cheli?' replied Marcus.

'That's me,' confirmed the gruff voice, as a shadow advanced from the side of the gulley.

Marcus dismounted and approached the fire. The two men shook hands as they appraised each other in the flickering light of the flames. Marcus had no difficulty in distinguishing the scars of mourning which marked Cheli's face, and the man's shiny beard was exactly as Reuben had described. As Cheli sized up the Roman, a chuckle started to build up inside him. The noise started deep in the guide's barrel of a chest, and gradually it moved up until it burst out in full and sincere laughter.

'Marcus, my friend,' declared Cheli, 'you could have asked any of your scouts to check it was me, before you rode up here yourself. I would not have been offended. As it is, I've been immensely amused by their inept attempts at stalking.' Cheli now roared with laughter, as he pointed out the exact locations from where the concealed Roman scouts were watching.

Marcus called out for the scouts to come and join them. The men advanced, thankful that the darkness concealed their embarrassment, even if it had not concealed their presence. Marcus was impressed with the sangfroid which the good-natured guide displayed, and his instincts told him that Cheli was trustworthy. Marcus now brought Cheli up to date on their situation. He explained the urgency for the Romans to cross the Amu-Darya River and escape from Parthia, and he also delivered Cheli a frank account of the supplies and weapons they had, and the current condition of the men. As he listened to Marcus, the guide kicked sand over the fire and quickly packed up his few personal belongings.

The two men exchanged a few brief comments and observations as they finalised the plan and the order of the column. They did not have time for lengthy discussions, so Marcus bowed to Cheli's superior experience and local knowledge, and allowed the guide to dictate the marching order. Cheli rode at the front of the column, where the bright white of the guide's stallion made a clear marker for the Romans to follow. Next in line came half of the armed men with Titus in charge, though now their scabbards had been restored to them, so the men were able to sheath their swords rather than carry the weapons in their hands. The bulk of the Romans made up the next part of the column, followed by the baggage mules, and then Marcus led the small armed rearguard. Even in the darkness Cheli set a demanding pace, and the Romans had to struggle to keep up. Fortunately they were now following a rough track, and the horses had no trouble finding their footing. After a few hours of hard riding the pre-dawn light lent a deep glow to the skyline before the first rays of the morning sun were visible on the horizon.

Marcus turned to look over his shoulder, the distinctive hill where they had met Cheli was still clearly visible, but they had covered a lot of ground during the hard hours of riding. Beyond the hill, it was possible to make out the distant pillars of smoke rising from the early morning fires in Merv. Despite the progress they had made during the night, the Romans had a long way to go before they were out of danger. The theft of the blood-sweating mare and the other horses would be immediately noticed once it was light. And once it was discovered that the Romans had escaped, parties of horse-archers would certainly be sent in pursuit. Marcus looked back to the column of Romans in front of him. It was clear from their postures that a number of the men were already saddle sore, and the going would only get tougher. Marcus was pleased to find that the mare showed no sign of fatigue at all, and although the cuts on his thigh were oozing a little blood, he was able to ride with minimal discomfort. Despite the agony from his recovering limb, Servius was keeping pace with the column. Marcus could see that the man was suffering, but there was nothing they could do to alleviate his pain, and the column dared not slow down. After two more hours of hard riding, Cheli called a halt by a small stream. Following Cheli's advice, Marcus ordered the Romans to water the horses, whilst a hasty breakfast was distributed to be eaten on the hoof.

The bright morning sun illuminated the scene, and Marcus realized that he was still blackened from the nocturnal raid. He splashed cold fresh water onto his face and washed himself quickly whilst the horses drank. Then Marcus turned to inspect the mare. It was the first time he had the occasion to inspect his mount properly, and he was pleased by the sturdy shape of the horse's limbs and the robust bulk of muscle which bunched and contracted as he led the mare back and forth after it had finished drinking. Although there was a sheen of gleaming sweat on the mare's dun coat, Marcus could see no traces of blood. The ride so far had evidently not taxed the horse, and Marcus wondered if he would see the mare actually sweat blood. The column soon moved off, and Marcus fell into position at the rear. Cheli continued leading the Romans at a relentless pace as they raced to get away from Merv. The sun crept up the sky and then passed its zenith, but still Cheli showed no signs of slowing the pace. He had called two further breaks but both had only lasted as long as it took to water the horses.

The column had soon left the arable, irrigated land which surrounded Merv, and now they were riding through open pasture. The countryside was dry but far from barren, there was evidently still sufficient water to support the coarse grass and shrubs which covered the plain. At one point they startled a half-wild shepherd boy, with his flock of goats and sheep. The lad was one of the illegitimate children who were sent out at an early age to tend the flocks in the wilderness. Bereft of human contact for months on end, the shepherd boys became feral and often deranged. The only interaction they had was with their animals, and the shepherd boys looked to their flocks for all their food, clothing and sexual needs. The boy had fled from the approaching riders, calling with strange guttural yelps for his flock to follow him. However, Cheli was unwilling to take the risk of leaving a witness, even a half-wild one, who could report their whereabouts to the pursuers, and he had ridden down the shepherd and killed him. Any hint of the initial light-hearted atmosphere in the column had soon disappeared when this brutal point made it clear just how serious and perilous their situation was. Cheli's white stallion was flecked with blood when he rejoined the group, but nobody commented. Marcus rode up to consult with Cheli, as the guide assiduously watered and walked his stallion. Cheli explained that on the open plains it was vital to keep the horses moving when they were that sweaty and tired, otherwise they risked getting cramps.

Cheli's beard was covered with dust from the journey, and it had now lost its shiny gleam.

'The next bit is particularly dangerous,' stated Cheli, 'we have to cross a dry basin and there is a high chance that the Parthians will see the dust cloud from our horses.'

'Is there no other route?' asked Marcus, anxious to avoid revealing their position to the Parthian pursuers.

'There is, but it would take too long to go round the basin,' explained Cheli.

'What if we split up into smaller groups?' asked Marcus,

'Would that reduce the dust cloud?'

'No, that would just make it clear that a large group of horsemen are passing. Our best option is to bunch up close, and hope that the Parthians think the cloud is coming from a merchant caravan.'

The flat Parthian plain gave the Romans the advantage that there were precious few vantage points from which the pursuers could scan the region, but it also meant that any dust cloud or the smoke from a fire would be visible for miles around. The air was totally still, without even the hint of a breeze to disperse the dust which the horses would raise. However, the Romans could not afford to wait for a favorable wind, so Cheli called all the men to mount up and move into as tight a bunch as possible. They would ride four abreast, in the hope that the Parthians would mistake the dust cloud for that of a heavily-laden Sogdian caravan. There were numerous groans and grimaces as the Roman remounted, it was clear that many of the men were now saddle-sore and blistered from the tough riding. During their years of slavery, the cavalrymen had all lost the toughened skin which comes from many days spent in the saddle, and now many of the Romans had legs chafed raw from the demanding ride. Marcus noticed the discomfort and pain of many of his men, but there was nothing he could do to alleviate their suffering, and they dared not slacken the pace. Fortunately, stoicism was a deeply engrained virtue in the legions, and there were no grumbles or complaints as the Romans mounted up again to continue the ride.

The dry basin formed part of the ancient flood plain of the Amu-Darya, when it had followed an earlier course bringing it much nearer the city of Merv. The basin contained a natural salt deposit, so even though it had received the fertile alluvial sediment from the River, it was too saline for any plants to grow.

The clear division between the saline soil and the surrounding countryside was evident from the absence of vegetation within the basin. There were a number of salt-licks in the shallow depression where herds of wild gazelle and other wild animals came in search of the vital mineral. Doves and other birds also flocked to the depression to bathe in the fine dry dust. As the column passed from the wild pastoral land into the basin, Marcus tied a kerchief across his face. Cheli had warned the Romans that a lot of dust would rise from the basin, and the column would not be able to stop until they had reached the other side. Many of the legionaries also followed Marcus's example and tied kerchiefs or rags over their faces before they left the pastoral land.

At the back of the column, Marcus and his rearguard got the worst of the dust. The fine powder rose up all around them and covered men and mounts in a homogenous white coat. As the column trotted on, at the same unrelenting pace, the dust began to work itself into everything. At the back of the column the dust was so thick it obscured the view, and the rear guard had to rely on their mounts to follow the other horses. Frustrated by the lack of visibility, Marcus ground his teeth and found that some dust had even got past the kerchief which covered his face, and his teeth crunched over the salty dry particles. The dust cloud would be clearly visible to the pursuing Parthians, and Marcus was anxious to find some high ground from which he could use the dioptra to scan the horizon. It took over an hour to cross the basin, and when the column finally reached the scattered vegetation on the far side, they were all completely covered in the fine white dust. The group had crossed the basin in tense silence, the dust and kerchiefs had obstructed any conversation. Having left the dry basin their spirits quickly revived and there was a visible improvement in the atmosphere of the group and the general mood of the men. Marcus was constantly observing the men, for it took a lot of attention to gauge the mood of a group of troops. At times the mood of the legionaries could make the crucial difference between the success or failure of a plan, and Marcus now concentrated on picking up the faint signals which indicated how the men were coping.

As they moved slowly away from the basin and made towards a verdant line which indicated a water source, Marcus rode up to the front of the column to join Cheli. The Romans now rode at a much slower pace, and both the horses and the men were appreciating the clear air after the dust of the basin. As he passed the other horses, Marcus noticed that many of the other mounts were showing signs of fatigue. Several of the horses were foaming at the bit, and one mount also had the uneven gait which Marcus feared might indicate a damaged fetlock. However, the mare which Marcus was riding was still in fine fettle and showed no signs of fatigue despite the long tough ride.

'There's a kurgan over on the right there,' indicated Cheli with a jerk of his hand, 'It's the ancient burial mound of a Scythian noble, and will provide a good vantage point. I'm going to check if there's any sign of pursuit yet. Keep leading the column towards those shrubs. There's a small stream there. We'll rest for an hour whilst the horses are watered and fed. The stream is only a trickle, so the men will have to spread along its course to find enough water for all of the horses. Make sure the men know we have to regroup and leave in an hour.' Cheli's instructions were terse but not rude. Both men were weary from the hard riding, and this was not the occasion for idle conversation.

When Marcus responded he was equally abrupt, 'Titus can lead the column, I'm coming with you.'

Titus duly led the column on towards the small stream, whilst Marcus and Cheli made for the vantage point of the slight mound. When the two men reached the kurgan they left their horses at the base and scrambled through the thorny bushes to the top. The mound was covered with tough thorny plants which could resist the dry conditions, and both Marcus and Cheli received a number of scratches. They knew that on such a flat landscape the silhouette of two men would show clearly against the skyline, and they did not want to give the Parthians any further signs of their whereabouts, so they crawled up to the skyline and peered over with caution. The sun was descending towards its nadir, so Marcus and Cheli found they were looking directly into its bright rays as they scanned the horizon. Whilst the sun's rays made their task more difficult, it provided ideal illumination for the pursuers. The dust cloud which the column had stirred up was still suspended in the still dry air above the basin, and the setting sun shone directly onto the basin.

With reverent care, Marcus extracted the dioptra. Cheli had previously seen Reuben use the device, although the guide was too superstitious to hold such a powerful magical object to his own eye. Cheli knew that Reuben considered the dioptra and his tiger the most important items in his caravan, and it was obviously a mark of great esteem that Reuben had given the dioptra to Marcus. With their naked eyes neither Marcus nor Cheli had been able to detect any sign of the pursuers, especially as they were obliged to look into the setting sun. Now, Marcus used the dioptra to meticulously scan each part of the horizon. In the distance he saw something move. He adjusted the lens to focus on the area, and when the picture cleared he saw a pair of crows had just landed on the shepherd's body. The first crow was pecking at the corpse's eyes, and Marcus swiftly moved the dioptra to scan the rest of the horizon as he felt the gorge rise in his throat.

Cheli tapped Marcus on the shoulder, and indicated a dark spot which appeared to move across the green plain. Marcus aimed the dioptra to investigate, and as the area moved into his field of vision both men caught the ominous gleam of sunlight on steel. When Marcus focused the dioptra's lens he made out a group of Parthian horse-archers, riding across the plain. As Marcus watched, the leader of the group pointed towards the dust cloud still hanging over the basin, and the group altered course to make towards it. The Parthians were now bearing directly towards the Romans, and once they crossed their trail, they would have no difficulty in following them. Marcus turned to communicate this information to Cheli, but the guide was already scrambling down the side of the mound heedless of the thorn bushes which snatched at his cloak. Cheli had accurately surmised that the Parthians would ride to investigate the dust cloud, and he now rushed to gather the men and assemble the column. The Romans had to keep riding. If they could avoid the Parthians till nightfall, then there was some chance of giving them the slip and making it to the River. Whilst the sun was still illuminating their tracks, the Parthians could follow them with ease. The setting sun made the perfect conditions for tracking, as the angle of the light cast shadows from each hoof print and made them more visible. The group of Romans was too large to make any attempt to conceal their tracks and their only option was to flee.

Marcus carefully slid the dioptra back into its case, and then hurriedly descended and ran to join Cheli. The two men hastily assembled the scattered Romans and the group rode off at a brisk trot. All of the men were fatigued and weary from the tough journey, but the urgency of Marcus's instructions had provoked an adrenalin rush as the men rushed to mount and keep riding. Marcus had seen that many of the pursuers were leading spare mounts, so the Parthians would be able to ride at a faster pace and not worry about tiring their horses. The column of Romans maintained a swift trot, which was the best pace the weary horses could manage. Despite their progress, it was not long before the Romans could see the dust cloud stirred up by the Parthians as they crossed the dry basin in pursuit. The sun seemed to take an interminable length of time to descend. The column rode on, desperately waiting for darkness to provide some cover and the opportunity to throw off the chase.

There was a slight rise in the ground to the left, and Marcus left the column and rode towards that. The Parthians had found the clear trail left by the column, so Marcus made no attempt to conceal his silhouette against the skyline. Seated on his horse, the slight rise provided enough of a vantage point for Marcus to make out the Parthians through the dioptra. The group of pursuers was smaller than when first sighted, and as Marcus looked back along their trail he saw that two men had been left to follow with the tired mounts. The main group of Parthians were leaning forward over their horses, as they raced to catch the Romans before the darkness hid them. The Parthians let out a yell when they saw Marcus's, and they raced towards the Romans. Marcus calculated that the pursuers would overhaul them within an hour, long before the sun set.

The blood-sweating mare was still not showing any signs of fatigue, and Marcus was amazed at the horse's endurance. Although he was alarmed at the proximity of the pursuers, Marcus knew the Parthians had not yet passed through the narrow channel where he had deployed the caltrops. Previously, the column had passed through an area where two groups of thorn bushes grew close together with only one channel between them. The Roman column had funnelled through the gap, and Marcus was confident the Parthians would do the same as they followed the trail. He decided that the site would be an ideal location to deploy the caltrops, so Marcus and several legionaries had carefully placed the caltrops where they would not be noticed until it was too late. The wicked devices were soon scattered and then covered with dust. Then Marcus and the legionaries rode off to rejoin the column, with Marcus inwardly wincing at the suffering which he knew they would cause the Parthian horses. As the Parthians caught sight of Marcus and the legionaries riding after the column they let out further shouts and lashed their horses even faster in pursuit. The shouts and hunting cries soon gave way to cries of distress from men and mounts alike as the Parthians rode over the caltrops.

Marcus galloped after the Romans, trying to block his ears to drown out the agonising cries of distress from the disabled horses behind him. As he rode Marcus noticed some red liquid spread across the mare's sweaty withers. Initially he thought one of the caltrops had scratched the mare, but when he lent forward and wiped the area with his hand there was no sign of a cut. However, his fingers came away red, and Marcus stared in amazement. The mare showed no signs of discomfort so Marcus did not slow the pace. Marcus stared in disbelief at the red liquid drying on his hand. He licked one finger but could not tell if the salty taste was due to sweat or blood. The red liquid certainly looked like blood, but there was no visible scratch or cut from which it could have come. It was only now that the mare was galloping and straining hard that it sweated this mysterious red liquid. Marcus clearly saw why the nomads claimed the horses sweated blood, but he was at a loss for any logical explanation.

At the front of the column Marcus slowed to consult Cheli.

'Those cruel caltrops of yours have bought us some time, but once the spare horses arrive, they'll continue the chase. There's a rocky area a few miles in front of us, if we can make it there before night fall, we've got a chance,' stated the guide simply.

'What's your plan?' asked Marcus.

'We'll split into small groups, and then ride back and forth. The rocks should help disguise the trail, and the Parthians will not be able to follow us in the darkness. They'll have to wait for sunrise to distinguish the tracks, and by then we should be at the River.'

'And how can we cross the River?' asked Marcus anxiously. The crossing would certainly take hours, even if they did find enough fishing boats, and on the open river bank the waiting Romans would present an easy target for the Parthian archers.

'We'll manage,' stated Cheli bluntly, 'I think you'll find all of your men become eager swimmers when the Parthian arrows start flying.'

The last hours of daylight finally drew to an end, and the fearsome horse-archers were still many miles away from the Romans. The column reached the stony area Cheli had spoken of without mishap. Under cover of darkness, the Romans split into small groups and followed Cheli's instructions to ride back and forth to confuse the trail. The Romans and their mounts were now reaching the limits of their endurance, but fortunately the cover of darkness meant they could proceed at a slower pace. Once the trail was sufficiently disturbed, Cheli led the column off at a tangent to strike the River nearby. Even at walking pace it only took a few hours to reach the River. Two of the mounts had been seriously injured on the rocky ground, and they abandoned the horses in the night. Their riders were now walking along with the baggage mules, for the other horses were too tired to risk mounting two riders on one horse. The Romans were relieved to reach the River, and they collapsed by its banks to rest and eat. Cheli left Marcus to supervise the Romans, whilst he followed the River upstream to find a fishing village. Cheli had arranged to return at dawn with as many boats as he could procure, and he had instructed Marcus to have the men awake and ready before dawn. They would only have an hour or so to embark, before the Parthians found them in their exposed position.

At first light, Cheli arrived in the first of a dozen fishing boats. The boatmen insisted on being paid in advance, and Marcus counted out the extortionate sum of three gold coins to each man. There were not enough boats to take all of the men, so Marcus and Cheli swiftly supervised the first load. The boatmen had also brought inflated animal skins, ropes and wooden barrels with which to construct rafts. All the supplies and the weakest horses and men were quickly packed into the boats and the first group pushed off to row across the River that marked the Parthian border. The morning light showed the Romans just how wide the Amu-Darya was. Marcus remained on the riverbank, whilst Gaius and Titus lead the first group across. The remaining group worked to construct rafts from the materials the boatmen had delivered. The men had only slept for a few hours since the escape two nights ago, but now they worked with haste and zeal born of urgency.

A whistle from the lookout warned Marcus that the Parthians were in sight. Marcus ran to climb the bank and quickly concluded that there would not be time to wait for the boats to return. They would have to make do with the rafts, and hope the boats could meet them mid-way across the River. The weary Romans dragged the rafts into the water, and then tied the halters of all of the horses to the rafts. There was room on the rafts for most of the men, but the remaining 50 men would have to swim. The swimmers could choose whether they preferred to hold onto their horse, or the rafts for buoyancy. Marcus thought the rafts were already overladen, so he elected to swim with his mare. Despite Marcus's exhortations, the Romans were reluctant to push the rafts away from the shelter of the bank, and begin the crossing. Some of the horses also shied away from entering the

River, and this mass hesitation delayed the departure. It was only when the first Parthian archers came into sight, and the arrows started to fall around them that the Romans pushed off the rafts and paddled out into the wide River. Cheli's prediction had proved accurate, and the storm of arrows made eager swimmers of the Romans. The Parthians lined up along the shore and released a steady stream of arrows after the departing Romans. The lethal arrows fell on the horses as well as the men, and the Romans rushed to cut loose any injured animals before their thrashing dragged down any of the other horses or overturned the precarious rafts.

The current soon bore the Romans downstream, but the Parthians merely rode along the riverbank to keep the Romans within range of their arrows. Gradually the rafts and swimmers moved out into the River, and away from the Parthians. Their progress was agonisingly slow, and each minute added to the tally of men and horses injured and killed. Most of the swimmers had moved into the lee of their horses, and thus they presented a much smaller target to the Parthians, whereas the densely packed Romans on the rafts made an easy target for the archers. On the far bank, Titus and Gaius had unloaded all the boats, and they were now working frantically to return and meet Marcus's group in the middle of the River. Finally, the Romans were out of range of the Parthian bows, but they had paid a high price for their hesitation in launching the rafts. A score of Roman bodies were tipped off the rafts, and those swimmers that became fatigued were able to climb onto the rafts. However, the rafts were not out of danger yet, they still had to contend with the currents of the mighty River.

The current had taken them far downstream, and the Romans on the far bank were no longer able to see the rafts. Titus and Gaius each stood on the prow of a boat as they directed the fishermen out to meet the rafts. The two groups finally converged, and the weary swimmers were dragged onto the boats, along with some of the men from the rafts. When they made it to the far bank, the Romans collapsed on the earth with relief and exhaustion. The other group had landed much further upstream, but they soon joined their exhausted comrades, and fires were kindled from driftwood to cook a hot meal, the first since they had escaped. The Romans were jovial and content, despite the losses which they had sustained in the crossing, 27 men had been killed, and a further 6 were seriously injured. Servius was amongst those killed in the crossing, in some ways his death was a merciful release from the enduring agony of riding with his broken leg. The arrows and the River's current had also claimed 25 horses dead and injured, but the rest of the mounts were fine. Marcus and his mare had both survived unscathed, and Marcus was busy rubbing down the horse when Cheli came to talk to him. The rest of the journey would be comparatively easy going, so the two men agreed that the column could spend the rest of the day recovering and recuperating by the River. The location was ideal, with a ready supply of water, driftwood for fires and fresh grass for the horses.

Once they landed, Cheli had commandeered all of the oars from the fishing boats to ensure that the fishermen did not try and further exploit the situation by returning to row the Parthians over the River. Cheli's precautionary move had provoked shouts and angry curses from the fishermen, but when faced with several hundred armed and desperate Romans the fishermen had little choice but to comply. The Romans burnt or broke most of the oars, leaving just a handful so the fishermen could return to their village. After the extortionate payment which the fishermen had demanded, neither Cheli nor Marcus felt any compunction about the harsh nature of their actions. The next day the column formed up and rode away from the River and into Sogdia. They had lost more men than horses, so there were enough mounts for all of the Romans. Two of the injured men had died during the night, but the other four were able to ride with the column. Cheli lead them at an easy pace, for the horses needed time to recover, and the Romans were in no hurry now. There was ample grazing besides the river, but fearing a raid most of the local shepherds drove their flocks away in a hurry as soon as they saw the Romans approach. After a few hours of riding, the Romans met a nomad family from whom they bought all the milk, cheese and meat which the family could spare. Cheli spent several hours chatting with the head of the family, and exchanging news. The fresh supplies replenished their stocks, and with the addition of the occasional hare or gazelle brought down by Cheli's expert archery, the Romans were able to subsist on their supplies till the reached a small Sogdian trading town.

The local chieftain was surprised to learn that a column of men were approaching, and he was even more surprised when he saw the group of 289 Gallic Romans ride into his town. The Sogdians were all stunned at the sight of so many fair-haired, blue-eyed men, and the few remaining red-haired Gauls provoked even greater amazement. Cheli approached the chieftain and explained that the column was on the way to visit Zhi-Zhi, the great Shanyu who was the Xiongnu ruler and thus master of Sogdia. 'Shanyu' means 'leader on horseback' and the word showed the great importance which the Xiongnu placed on horses. At this point the chieftain also noticed that Marcus was riding one of the blood-sweating horses from Ferghana. The chieftain was greatly impressed by these illustrious and exotic arrivals, and he was only too happy to provide food and shelter to any guests who were going to meet the great Zhi-Zhi.

24

SOGDIA, 45-38 BC

THE COLUMN OF ROMANS enjoyed an uneventful ride through Sogdia on their way to meet the great Xiongnu leader Zhi-Zhi, they were now free men and the journey provided an interesting voyage of discovery. At each town or camp they were welcomed with respect and warm hospitality, for all of the Sogdians and Xiongnu were eager to ingratiate themselves with anyone who was en route to see the Zhi-Zhi. The Romans' tunics were little better than rags by this time, and the various tribes provided them with whatever clothing they could spare. Soon, the Romans were all dressed in trousers; the nomads were the first to develop trousers as the most suitable garment for riding. Although there was no danger of pursuit, Marcus and Cheli still led the men at a steady, tough pace. Marcus had decided that the journey would be an excellent opportunity for the men to re-adjust to life in the saddle, and he wanted all the Romans to be fighting fit by the time they met Zhi-Zhi. The nomad chief did not stay in one camp but constantly moved around his vast territory, so it took several weeks of riding for the Romans to locate him. The time had been well spent, and the Romans no longer displayed any signs of the blisters and saddle-sores which would have disgraced them in the eyes of the nomads. The rigours of the journey combined with the elation of freedom ensured that when Cheli led the column into Zhi-Zhi's camp, the Romans presented an impressive sight.

Marcus had learnt a lot about the Xiongnu from Cheli during the journey, and he knew that the Romans would never make as good horsemen as the Xiongnu. The Xiongnu's nomadic way of life meant that many of the children could ride before they could walk, with the youngest infants being tied into their saddles. The Xiongnu boys became expert horsemen and archers from a very early age as these skills were vital for survival in their nomadic way of life. No allowances were made when the tribe moved on, and if the children were not able to keep up then they were left behind.

That night Marcus noted the gleam of joy in Cheli's eye when he recited a Xiongnu ballad enumerating the joys of a young nomad man. The list began with a fast horse, a fine bow and a successful raid against another tribe's herds. Wealth for the Xiongnu was measured by the number of head of cattle which a man possessed, so the herds were important to the nomads for status as well as a source of milk and meat. However, the men left the care of the animals to the boys and women. The Xiongnu considered caring for the flocks only marginally less demeaning than tilling the soil. The only fitting occupations for the men were raiding, hunting or fighting; when the men were not engaged in these noble pursuits they ate, drank, sang and slept. The custom of raiding was a time-honored practice, and it was considered entirely different to fighting, although it did utilise and develop many of the same skills. With the frequent raids and counter-raids, it was not unusual for the same animals to change hands a number of times. During a raid the purpose was to steal as many cattle as possible, and although this was a violent affair the nomads tended to avoid unnecessary bloodshed as it then entangled the tribe in a blood feud. Two tribes which had spent months raiding each other, might happily unite to go to war against a common enemy. When the nomads went to war, their purpose was to destroy the enemy, and they spared neither children, nor women; the tradition of blood feuds was so embedded that the nomads knew better than to leave any survivors who might grow up and seek revenge.

Marcus had been intrigued to learn how far the Xiongnu carried their respect for strength and vigour; the nomads always gave the best cuts of meat to the strong young men. The nomads' diet relied heavily on meat and dairy products from their herds, for the thin steppe soil produced few cereals, fruits or vegetables. This high-protein diet contributed to the nomads' strength and ferocity, and they grew taller and stronger than the sedentary peoples. The aged and weak nomads got the leftovers once the warriors had eaten their fill; when there was a shortage of food these vulnerable members of society went hungry. The tribe placed such an overwhelming focus on power and potency, that when times were hard they preferred the weak to starve in order to ensure the warriors remained well-fed and strong. The Xiongnu lived on the windswept steppe which formed the bulk of their territory, and they raided or extracted tribute from the sedentary peoples who lived around the steppe. The Xiongnu preferred to leave the arduous task of tilling the soil and reaping the harvest to others; they considered such work unmanly and they were much happier to raid or receive payments in tribute rather than farm the land themselves.

The steppe where the nomads roamed could be a harsh and unforgiving place; during the winter the temperature could sink to minus 30 degrees centigrade, and freezing winds swept snow across the steppe and the nomads shivered inside their felt tents, known as yurts. Then came a brief and verdant spring, the pastures were suddenly filled with abundant fodder and the flocks bred and multiplied. Next came the burning heat of the summer, and the winds which swept the steppe were now dry and searing. They sucked the moisture from every living thing, including the very earth which became parched and cracked in places. During the summer the nomads moved to any reliable water source in their territory, or to higher grazing grounds. The summer heat finally gave way to autumn, and the nomads would ride out to take their part of the harvest from the sedentary tribes, either by arrangement or by force. As Marcus learned about the nomads he came to understand that their society reflected the conditions in which they lived. Just as the inhabitants of Massalia were reputed to be mercurial like the Mistral wind which blew through the region, so the Xiongnu seemed to share the same merciless toughness, strength and harsh beauty of the land they inhabited.

When the Romans entered the nomad camp, Marcus rode at the front of the column. He had galloped around the group before they reached the camp, and his mare was covered with a gleaming coat of blood. Marcus had not been able to identify what the red liquid was, but it certainly drew attention from the Xiongnu nomads as he rode into their camp. They knew and revered the blood-sweating horses of the Ferghana valley, and they automatically accorded Marcus an elevated status due to his impressive mount. Marcus dismounted, and leaving his horse with Titus, he walked into Zhi-Zhi's yurt accompanied by Cheli. During the previous weeks Marcus had grown accustomed to the overpowering stench of the nomad yurts, and he was no longer disconcerted by the obnoxious miasma when he entered the circular felt tent. Zhi-Zhi rose to his feet and came to greet Marcus, with Cheli acting as interpreter. The first thing that Marcus noticed was Zhi-Zhi's large stature. Thanks to his Gallic origins, Marcus had grown accustomed to being taller than the

Italian Romans or Parthians he met, yet Zhi-Zhi was as tall as Marcus and equally broad-shouldered.

At thirty-four years of age Marcus was still in peak condition and a good two decades younger than Zhi-Zhi, yet Marcus could sense the vitality and strength which radiated from the Shanyu. Zhi-Zhi's fierce black eyes bored into Marcus's gaze with the intensity of a predator. When Zhi-zhi finished assessing the new arrival he returned to drinking his *kimiz* from a richly decorated bowl. Marcus later learnt that this bowl was fashioned from the skull of a Yuezhi chieftain who Zhi-Zhi had recently defeated. The drink inside the bowl, was equally unusual to Marcus, *kimiz* was made from mare's milk which was fermented to produce a sour, gaseous liquid. When he relaxed, the Shanyu's eagle-eyes appeared to become hooded in a more gentle fashion. Zhi-Zhi had a glorious flowing black beard, which glistened lustrously from its latest oil coating. Despite the grey hairs which flecked Zhi-Zhi's beard and hair, the Shanyu had risen with the suppleness and agility of a man half his age. He moved with a certain feline grace which Marcus had observed in many of the Xiongnu. Compared to the Romans, the nomads exhibited the same calm control and agility of a powerful cat, and in their proud independence there was also the distinct impression that they could strike at any moment. After greeting and assessing Marcus, Zhi-Zhi had returned to his cushion, and he now sat there fondling the ears of one of his favorite dogs as he listened to Cheli translate Marcus's introduction.

All of the nomad tribes kept large dogs, which ran beside the mounted men and travelled with the tribe. The dogs were used for hunting, protecting the flocks, guarding the camp and they were even used in battle to attack and harass enemy mounts. The nomad dogs were large and powerful animals with thick coats that could withstand the cold winds. The dogs were bold and tough, characteristics which had been developed from their lifestyle constantly moving with their tribes, and defending the flocks. Marcus's glance took in the presence of the imposing pair of dogs, nonetheless threatening even though they were stretched out on the carpet. Zhi-Zhi listened to Marcus, and then he directed a Sogdian scribe to break the seals and read the letters from Reuben.

When the scribe had almost finished reading, Zhi-Zhi let out a brief high whistle. Immediately, the recumbent dogs leapt to their feet and faced Marcus with savage fury. As the dogs snarled they bared impressive sets of teeth, and the quivering muscles of their haunches indicated that they were tensed for the signal to attack. Marcus was startled by the sudden change in circumstances. His hand went immediately for his sword, but he had left the weapon outside the tent, in accordance with custom. Marcus had crouched a little, but he had not retreated an inch, and he kept his eyes fixed on the fierce dogs as he calculated how best to tackle them. Cheli was equally alarmed at the unexpected turn of events, and was desperately racking his memory to see what inadvertent *faux pas* had caused such a reaction from Zhi-Zhi. Marcus calculated that the large bitch on the left would attack first, and he slightly altered his stance accordingly. Zhi-Zhi watched the whole spectacle with calm interest and relaxed detachment. Then after a few brief but tense moments, Zhi-Zhi reached out and stroked both of the dogs, muttering to them softly. The aggression vanished from the animals, and their hackles quickly settled as they turned to lick their master's hands and lie down by his side.

'He says you are hired,' translated Cheli, when Zhi-Zhi uttered a brief statement and dismissed the visitors.

'So that was just a test,' said Marcus, as he left the tent still tingling with adrenalin.

'Yes, you didn't back away, so you have evidently passed,' confirmed Cheli.

From that day the Romans joined Zhi-Zhi's tribe, living and travelling with the nomads. Zhi-Zhi undertook to provide clothes and weapons for the Romans, and in return they were to form his personal bodyguard whenever the Shanyu summoned the tribes to ride to war. Meanwhile, the Romans were accorded the status of warriors within Zhi-Zhi's tribe, and they were to live, hunt and raid with the other nomads. The legionaries had to adjust to a completely different way of life, and the nomads were much amused each time the Romans constructed a fixed camp, only to abandon it when the tribe moved on. As warriors, the legionaries were treated deferentially by all the members of the tribe, and the Romans soon flourished on the excellent carnivorous diet which was so different to the grain rations they had received as legionaries and prisoners. The Romans were expected to take part in all the affairs of the tribe, and this meant sharing the responsibilities and duties which came with their status. Thus the legionaries soon found themselves joining the other nomads in their incessant raids, fights and horse races. On his blood-sweating mare, Marcus won many races and the begrudging respect of the nomads. The legionaries took a while to adjust to the different style of combat, and during that period they suffered a number of casualties and losses. The nomads fought in a much move fluid and mobile manner than the Romans. As soon as the tribesmen thought an engagement was turning against them, they would turn their horses around and gallop away across the plain. As they fled the nomads would turn in the saddle and loose off Parthian shots at any pursuers. This style of combat led to very short and intense conflicts, and the casualties were often minimal. The Romans did not have the same habit of retreating, and they were furious when their comrades apparently deserted them at such crucial moments. However, after several years with the tribe, the Romans soon became accustomed to the different style of combat and their cohesion as a group and obedience to the commanding officer often gave them an advantage over the unruly nomads.

Two years before the Romans arrived at Zhi-Zhi's camp, the great Shanyu had sent a deputation to the Han Chinese Emperor in the East. The Emperor possessed such vast resources of man power and materials, that Zhi-Zhi had realized the Chinese were almost impossible to defeat. No matter how many armies of Han soldiers the nomads slaughtered, there was a seemingly endless supply of replacements waiting to fill their place. The Chinese had constructed a number of fortified walls to keep out the nomads, and these walls were now stretching further and further as different stretches were joined up, keeping the nomads out of the fertile Chinese lands. A wall was by far the most effective weapon against the mounted nomads, for it countered the mobility which was their essential advantage. Despite the massive amount of labor which building the different walls demanded, the Chinese soon learnt that the investment paid off. The nomads had neither the technology, nor the time, nor the inclination to engage in a siege and break through a fortified wall. When they found their route blocked in one direction, the nomads rode off in another direction, to bypass the obstacle or find an easier target.

Zhi-Zhi had sent his son Otyuru as an envoy to the Emperor, the Shanyu hoped to establish cordial relations with the Emperor. Zhi-Zhi proposed that the Xiongnu would cease to raid the Chinese lands in return for the Emperor recognising Zhi-Zhi as master of all the lands north and west of the Great Wall and the extensions the Chinese were building. The Chinese had the resources to raise and equip vast mounted forces, which they sent on punitive missions deep into the Xiongnu homeland. These punitive raids, salted the nomad wells, burnt all the vegetation and slaughtered every living thing they encountered. These harsh measures caused whole tribes of nomads to starve even if they managed to retreat faster than the advancing Chinese. The tribes could not live without their herds, and the herds could not live without the pastures. Zhi-Zhi hoped that his pact of mutual recognition would bring an end to these punitive missions, and protect his eastern flank whilst he concentrated on raiding to the west. When Otyuru entered China he saw the size of the Chinese armies which were being amassed. He had never seen such a vast force in all his days, and he did not even realise that so many people existed in the world. The latest Chinese Army was intended to drive so deep into the Xiongnu heartland that they would bring the Xiongnu to their knees, and permanently remove the nomads as a threat to China. Otyuru swiftly exceeded the mandate of his mission, and announced that he had come on behalf of the Xiongnu to confirm their submission to the Chinese Emperor.

The Emperor accepted the submission, but he ordered part of the punitive forces to remain in full readiness whilst the terms of the submission were agreed. A Chinese official by the name of Guji was sent to meet Zhi-Zhi and conclude the agreement whilst Otyuru remained with the Emperor. The following year Guji arrived at Zhi-Zhi's camp. Guji was a military officer and an arrogant man who was overly-inflated with the importance of his task. Zhi-Zhi had been warned in a secret communication from his son, that it was absolutely vital to conclude an agreement of submission with the Chinese, or the Xiongnu faced certain annihilation. However, Guji approached Zhi-Zhi with such disdain and disrespect that the proud leader became infuriated and promptly set his ferocious dogs on the Chinese envoy. Zhi-

Zhi and the other Xiongnu watched calmly as the fierce hunting dogs ripped Guji apart. The envoy's death was a prolonged and grisly affair; his instincts for self-preservation proved stronger than his shock, and he had raised his arms to defend himself as the two dogs leapt at him. The dogs had bitten and ripped at the man's arms in savage determination. The powerful canine jaws had soon crunched through to Guji's bones, and immobilised his arms. The terrified envoy was then powerless to fend off the dogs as they proceeded to devour him alive. Zhi-Zhi had then ordered the rest of the Chinese delegation to be killed to conceal his actions. The next day the nomads broke camp and rode away across the steppe, leaving the stripped Chinese corpses to be picked bare by the vultures and crows. Zhi-Zhi knew that his actions had been foolish and rash, but he was a proud and impetuous man. As it was impossible to bring Guji back to life, Zhi-Zhi decided to deny that the envoy had ever reached him.

When he was not troubled with political matters, Zhi-Zhi regularly joined the men of his tribe in their raids, however when he did so it was without the golden insignia of the Shanyu, for he was riding as a member of his tribe, rather than the leader of the Xiongnu. Zhi-Zhi only exercised the power of the Shanyu when it was necessary to unite the tribes against a common enemy which threatened them all. Under Marcus's guidance, the legionaries had learnt to work with the nomads' style of fighting, and their raids became ever more successful. One day, during a raid against another nomad tribe to the north, one of Zhi-Zhi's cousins named Chi-Yu was hurled to the ground when his horse was brought down by an arrow in mid-gallop. His cry of alarm caused Marcus to turn round as they were riding away with a herd of stolen cattle. Chi-Yu was on his feet, but his horse lay thrashing on the ground where it had fallen. The warriors from the other tribe were bearing down on Chi-Yu, and he had no support. Marcus turned his horse back towards the lone man and he lashed the mare's hindquarters as he strove to get every bit of speed out of his magnificent steed.

Although Chi-Yu had noticed the approaching warriors, he had not seen that Marcus was coming to assist him. Thus, Chi-Yu had resolutely pulled his bow and weapons from the side of his crippled horse and bravely prepared to meet his death. Marcus shouted at the young man as he raced towards him, but the wind caught Marcus's call and carried it away before Chi-Yu could hear him. The group of enraged tribesmen were thundering towards Chi-Yu from one side as Marcus raced towards him from the other, although Marcus was far away he relied on the superiority of his horse to buy him the precious seconds it would take to rescue Chi-Yu. Marcus continued shouting to the resolute young man as he galloped towards him, and when there was only a hundred metres between them Chi-Yu finally heard him. He dropped his weapons and ran towards Marcus, seized the proffered arm and swung himself onto the mare behind Marcus. There was a bright red coat of blood on the mare's flanks as Marcus now turned and raced away from the approaching tribesmen.

Ahead of them, Gaius had noticed Marcus's actions and the Romans were now riding to his support, although none of the other nomads turned round. However, there was still a lot of distance to cover, and with two riders even the blood-sweating mare could not outpace the other tribesmen. Arrows began to whistle around Marcus as he lent forward over the mare. Moments later there came a thud and a groan from Chi-Yu, his arms locked around Marcus's chest in a suffocating iron grip as two more thuds brought fresh groans from Chi-Yu. Ahead of them the Romans were approaching at full pace, the group split in the center so that Marcus could pass through their lines with the injured Chi-Yu. Some of the Romans galloped after the tribesmen, who had turned and fled when they saw the Roman contingent coming in support. Titus and the other Romans gathered around Marcus, and they quickly dismounted and helped Chi-Yu to the ground. They laid his face down on the ground, for there were three arrows embedded in his back.

Marcus and Titus knelt down to examine Chi-Yu. They cut away the leather outer jerkin which all of the nomads wore, and then they cut through the felt shirt underneath. Fortunately, Chi-Yu had been wearing one of the silk undergarments which the nomads prized so highly. The loose silk garments were worn against the skin, and even when an arrow pierced the leather jerkin it was often stopped by the silk, for the finely woven fabric resisted cuts. Despite the silk shirt, all three arrows were deeply embedded in Chi-Yu's back. Marcus and Titus now eased the arrows and silk out of each wound in turn. The silk had been driven into Chi-Yu's back with all three arrows, but fortunately it had only torn in one case. Thus the Romans were able to draw out two arrows without the barbs catching in Chi-Yu's flesh. Although the young nomad grunted with pain, he lay still and let the Romans tend his wounds. 'In fact, he's too still,' thought Marcus as he noticed that when Chi-Yu did squirm or flinch, it was only his upper body that moved. Soon after that Chi-Yu passed out from the pain, and he was placed over a horse and lead back to the camp.

When the Chi-Yu recovered consciousness, it was as Marcus had feared. One of the arrows had severed his spinal column, and he was paralysed form the waist down. Zhi-Zhi had personally come to thank Marcus, and to congratulate him on his good fortune. This last part confused Marcus, although they had spent several years with the nomads, and Marcus had learnt a reasonable amount of their language, at times he was still totally thrown by the nomads' totally different way of thinking. Zhi-Zhi saw the puzzled look on Marcus's face and explained;

'You brought Chi-Yu's body back from the battlefield, therefore everything he owned is now yours.'

'But he's still alive, why are you talking as if he's dead?' asked Marcus incredulously.

'Because he's as good as dead,' explained Zhi-Zhi.

'No he isn't!' insisted Marcus, 'providing there's no infection he'll recover fine. He'll be paralysed, but he won't die.'

'Tonight he rides into the sun,' stated Zhi-Zhi simply, as if that was sufficient explanation, and then he turned on his heel and padded away.

Marcus was deeply puzzled by all this so he went to seek further explanation from the other Xiongnu. The other nomads explained that as Chi-Yu was not able to ride, he was as good as dead. The tribe could not and would not support useless members, so that evening Chi-Yu would be strapped onto his horse to ride towards the setting sun. He would continue riding into the wilderness, and there he would perish. The nomads considered this one of the most desirable ways to die, and there was no trace of pity for the injured warrior. The nomads worshipped the vast open sky which stretched above them as the steppe stretched out beneath them. In combination they also worshipped the sun and moon, as the manifestation of the sky's power by day and by night. Therefore, Chi-Yu was to be envied as he would meet his end in the peace of the open steppe, alone with the mighty sky, dieing from wounds sustained in the noble pursuit of raiding.

Xiongnu custom held that if a man recovered the body of a fallen comrade from any conflict, then the man inherited all of his deceased comrade's wealth and possessions. Marcus had been unaware of this custom, but all of the other nomads had assumed that the only reason Marcus had returned to rescue Chi-

Yu was to claim his property. It was for this reason that neither Zhi-Zhi nor his fellows had returned to help Marcus, if they had done so then a share of the booty would be theirs by right, and they assumed Marcus did not wish to divide the prize. Marcus was already finding it hard to accept that the nomads were all talking about Chi-Yu as if he was already dead, and it took some time for him to realise that he was now a comparatively wealthy man. Chi-Yu was the cousin of the great Zhi-Zhi, and his herds included several hundred head of cattle, along with the herdsmen and boys to attend them. That evening Marcus and the other Romans were shaken to see Chi-Yu dauntlessly ride into the sunset, with his useless legs hanging loosely down the side of the horse. Then came another shock, Marcus remembered that Chi-Yu had recently got married, thus Marcus's heroic act meant that he had unwittingly acquired a young wife!

The girl in question would spend the next three days in mourning, and then she would come to share Marcus's tent and cook his meals. A kindly old warrior explained the finer points of nomad etiquette to the nonplussed Marcus who intended to release the girl from the obligation. The old man swiftly brushed aside Marcus's protestations and explained that if he rejected the girl then she would be disgraced, and consequently abandoned to die alone on the steppe. Chi-Yu's wife was called Liu and after three days of mourning she collected her few personal possessions and moved into Marcus's tent. The first time Marcus saw Liu he nearly recoiled in shock, for she had slashed her face in mourning, as was the Xiongnu custom. The young woman's soft cheeks were covered with plentiful, though superficial cuts from which oozed fresh blood. When Liu saw Marcus's surprise she smiled, however this only provoked fresh bleeding from her cuts, and concern showed quickly in Marcus's blue eyes as he moved to help her. After a few sympathetic smiles and concerned looks, Marcus tenderly bathed and dressed her cuts. As Liu felt the gentle touch of his toughened hands, she accepted him as her new husband.

The first time they made love, Liu was surprised by Marcus's consummate skill and deftness; the next day there was no need for Liu to tell her women friends what an accomplished lover the Roman was; the whole camp had heard her cries of delight during the night. After Marcus's masterful performance, many of the other nomad women showed a sudden interest in the Roman men. A number of informal alliances were quickly contracted, and temporary matches proliferated between the Xiongnu women and the legionaries. Though the women soon found that by and large the Romans shared the same skills and shortfalls as the Xiongnu men, and none were as accomplished in the amorous arts as Marcus. Marcus found his nubile new wife deeply intriguing. Even after Marcus had mastered the language he often found himself staring blankly with incomprehension at his beautiful bride.

Liu had long dark brown hair and after the cuts healed Marcus saw that when she smiled there were dimples on her cheeks. Marcus was fascinated by the things he learnt from and about his Xiongnu wife. Liu had come to share his tent and his bed at the end of the spring, and she was soft and curvaceous as a result of the season's plenty. Then as the sweltering summer arrived, Marcus noticed that the weight slowly disappeared from Liu's waist and bust. Her body became taut and lean to cope with the heat. During the mellow autumnal abundance, Marcus noticed that Liu put on weight in preparation for the bitter winter. Like all the nomads, Liu built up a soft layer of subcutaneous fat, her buttocks grew plump and round and she wiggled coyly as she moved around the tent. The long cold winter nights no longer seemed so daunting to Marcus, now that he would be sharing them with Liu. As the time passed, Marcus realized that Liu's body altered to match the seasons much more than he was able to. However much Marcus ate during the autumn the thin layer of fat he built up did not block out the winter cold. Similarly, although he exercised and hunted vigorously during the spring, he still sweltered far more than Liu in the summer heat. The nomads had adapted both their lifestyle and their bodies to suit their environment.

Despite the intimacy of living and sleeping together, Marcus soon discovered that there was a determined and independent streak in Liu which was too strong for their affection to develop into love. After one particularly passionate bout of love-making, Marcus held her face in his hands and stared deep into her sparkling brown eyes. At moments like this he regretted that Liu would never open her soul to him. Marcus was enticed by the light in her eyes which flared with pride, passion, or anger as the mood took her. Liu had loved Chi-Yu, and after he had ridden into the sun she refused to leave herself open to such pain a second time. She did not blame Marcus for Chi-Yu's death, nor did she resent the fact that the Roman's bravery meant she had become his wife and he had taken her former husband's wealth. Liu genuinely liked Marcus; he was a kind, caring and attractive man. She enjoyed his company and she cared for him with an honest affection. At times she had to force herself not to fall in love with him, but the pain of losing a loved partner would never leave her, and she resolutely refused to let herself love Marcus.

25

SOGDIA, 38-36 BC

Sometime after the Romans had joined the nomads, Zhi-Zhi announced that he intended to build a fortified base which would become the Xiongnu capital. During the previous 100 years the Xiongnu had been so successful in their raids that Zhi-Zhi now had many wagons laden with heavy treasure. The great Shanyu had more than enough ready money to pay and equip 300 mercenaries, and the idea of having his own guard appealed to him. In 166BC the Xiongnu tribes had united to invade China, and they had come within sight of the Chinese capital before they withdrew taking vast amounts of gold, silver and jade with them. Since that time the Chinese had been engaged in a constant struggle against the Xiongnu, and now Zhi-Zhi decided that a secure capital was necessary to defend his treasure trove. Traditionally, the nomads tactically retreated and dispersed in the face of any superior force, yet their vast amount of treasure now slowed their pace and impaired their mobility.

In the back of his mind, Zhi-Zhi knew that the Chinese would send an army to avenge the murder of their envoy. However, he showed no fear in front of the other Xiongnu, and when Chinese officials came to enquire about the fate of Guji, Zhi-Zhi denied that the envoy had ever reached him. Despite his brash confidence, Zhi-Zhi knew that a major conflict with the

Chinese was almost inevitable, and he wanted his capital to be appropriately defended. Whilst they were so heavily-laden, the nomads had the worst of both worlds, for they could neither move fast enough to avoid their enemies nor did they have a defensible base to protect them from attacks. Zhi-Zhi had spent several evenings consulting with Marcus, and the two men had discussed the first Xiongnu capital in considerable detail. The Romans continued to erect fortified camps wherever they slept, and Zhi-Zhi was impressed with the skill and efficiency with which the legionaries worked under Marcus's supervision; thus at the age of forty one, Marcus was given the greatest commission of his engineering career. Zhi-Zhi put Marcus in charge of building an entire city from scratch.

Since the humiliating summer of 166BC, in addition to joining up various earlier walls and increasing their fortifications to form the Great Wall, the Chinese had engaged in a series of massive campaigns to crush the Xiongnu. The Han Emperors repeatedly sent vast armies as large as 100,000 men on punitive campaigns deep into the Xiongnu territory. Each army was supported by a huge supply column, for the Chinese knew that the nomads would withdraw across the steppe without leaving any possible supplies for the invaders. The Chinese losses were always high, and for any lesser Empire it would have proved ruinously expensive to fight a war of attrition using such costly columns. However, the Han had sufficient manpower and resources to continue equipping and dispatching these columns, and eventually the Xiongnu were permanently driven back from the Chinese border and forced to retreat deep into the harsh Gobi desert and the steppes of Central Asia. Once the Chinese had established control over the central Asian approaches to China, the Great Wall was extended to incorporate the Kansu corridor, and the newly enclosed area was strengthened and colonised by

700,000 Han Chinese. In the middle of the first century BC, work was still continuing on these extended stretches of the Great Wall. Regular new convoys of Han immigrants arrived to work on the Wall, either willingly or as convict labor.

The Chinese had long had an obsession with the 'blood-sweating' horses of the Ferghana Valley, and in addition to driving back the nomads, the Chinese armies had instructions to procure breeding stock of these superior horses. The Chinese cavalry rode the small Mongolian steppe ponies, and for many years they had been attempting to secure better horses, and improve the equine stock in China. Although the Chinese regularly managed to acquire the excellent nomad horses, they were unable to propagate the breed, and thus the demand for these horses in China remained insatiable. In response to the perennial problem of securing good horses, Chinese convoys and trading missions were to continue making their way to the Ferghana Valley right up until the Qing Dynasty (1622-1911). Unbeknown to the Chinese, the pasturage in China contained different levels of minerals to that in the Ferghana Valley, and thus when the Chinese did secure breeding stock the difference in diet prevented the breeding of the fine Ferghana horses in China.

Over the previous years, the Han columns had advanced deep into the Xiongnu territory, and a number of nomad chieftains had now accepted Han dominance, and switched their allegiance to the Emperor, permitting the Chinese to incorporate part of the Xiongnu territory into their Empire. Subsequently, with the support of their new nomad allies, the Chinese columns were able to press even deeper into the Xiongnu territory. Zhi-Zhi knew that it was a distinct possibility that one day his capital would have to withstand an attack by a Chinese army. However, Zhi-Zhi also knew that any Chinese force which arrived at his capital would have skirted a treacherous desert and travelled hundreds of miles across the steppe, so the Chinese soldiers would be tired and weary. The long journey would also stretch the Chinese supply lines, and make it impractical for them to enter into a lengthy siege. The mountain passes leading into Xiongnu territory were protected by groups of fierce nomads, and any Chinese army would sustain heavy losses before it could enter the nomads' territory.

Whilst there were already fixed settlements in the Xiongnu territory, these were mainly trading towns operated by Sogdians, and the nomads did not consider the towns to be Xiongnu centres. The only constructions which the nomads created were the burial *kurgans* whose small mounds pockmarked the entire swathe of territory inhabited by the nomads. The nomads followed an annual cycle which was designed to bring them and their herds to various pastures and water sources at the optimum time. The new city would be the first Xiongnu capital, and it would be a significant cultural change for the Xiongnu tribes. The city would bear Zhi-Zhi's name as he was its founder. The Shanyu had several potential sites in mind for the city, and Marcus accompanied him as he rode out to inspect the different locations. Eventually, they selected a site beside the Talas River where the water supply meant there were fields which could be cultivated and woods to provide timber. The River would provide a reliable water supply as well as protecting one flank of the capital, for even in the dry season the Talas River was fed by the snow-melt from the Tien Shan Mountains, and the River would provide an additional obstacle to any attacking force. Marcus had also stressed to Zhi-Zhi the importance of a reliable water supply and effective sewers to prevent the spread of disease within the city. The Xiongnu were unfamiliar with many of the risks of contamination and disease. Their nomadic lifestyle precluded regular bathing as they were always on the move, and rarely near a plentiful water source. The nomads never stayed in one place long enough for the site to become contaminated. Thus the only problems they had to deal with were the fleas, lice and bugs which lived and bred in their tents, carpets, clothes and hair. Initially the Romans had suffered much more than the Xiongnu from the various biting insects, but over the years the legionaries had adapted and learnt to tolerate these unwelcome travelling companions.

Zhi-Zhi assembled the nomad chieftains and shamans on the proposed site for his new city, and they performed sacrifices to their Gods of the Sky, the Steppe, the Sun and the Moon. Like the Zoroastrians, the Xiongnu worshipped fire, and once the animals had been sacrificed, the choice cuts were dedicated as a burnt offering to the Gods. Blood from the sacrificial animals was then sprinkled over the designated site, and the next day work began. Marcus had already sent a large group of men upriver under the command of Titus to fell trees and float the logs downstream, for a great deal of timber would be required. Before work began, the two centurions had marked out the different parts of the city with pegs and string as they would for a legionary camp. One group now set to work sinking the wells which would provide the city's water whilst they waited for the timber to arrive. The site was close to the River, so the men did not have to dig far before they hit the water-table and were able to draw fresh water from the wells. Zhi-Zhi had emphasized that speed was of the essence; it would be difficult to persuade the nomads to endure any prolonged physical labor if they did not see rapid results rising from their toils. These limiting factors meant that Marcus had reluctantly agreed to build the city almost entirely from wood, despite the risk of fire.

The legionaries had readily re-adjusted to the demanding

labor of building the city; however the Xiongnu response was far more mercurial. When the nomads deemed that a task was manly or worthy work for warriors, they would work with bursts of energy and intense focus, yet when they considered a task demeaning they would shirk it and progress was very slow. Thus the city developed in fits and starts, with Marcus constantly having to supervise the recalcitrant members of the workforce. When the timbers arrived, work began in earnest on the city walls. The city was encompassed by two city walls; the outer wall was a palisade of wooden stakes whilst the inner wall was made from compacted earth, and a ditch separated the two. The walls also enclosed enough ground for the nomads to bring their herds and horses inside the protective barrier when danger threatened. Most of the buildings within the city were simple huts; however, there were also a few larger constructions. Zhi-Zhi's palace and treasure stores were made from stout birch trunks and they were built to last.

Marcus had spent many fruitless hours discussing the city defences with Zhi-Zhi and the other chieftains. The nomads intended to use the city as a secure base in which to store their treasure, whilst the rest of the men rode out to raid and fight the enemy in the open plains. Zhi-Zhi reasoned that this approach would give them the best of both styles of fighting; the Xiongnu cavalry would be even more mobile as they would not have to worry about defending their families, herds or treasure, and the archers on the walls could defend the city. The other chieftains all agreed with Zhi-Zhi, and it was in vain that Marcus tried to explain the weaknesses of a fortified city which could also be surrounded, besieged and stormed. The Xiongnu failed to understand how their mobile cavalry could be surrounded; they maintained that even if the Chinese encircled the city, the nomads could break through and then harry the Chinese from two sides at once. Marcus grew increasingly exasperated at trying to explain the situation to Zhi-Zhi, and in the end he gave up, and built the city as Zhi-Zhi instructed.

However, Marcus was still in command of the Roman soldiers, and he recognized that any attack could potentially pin the entire Xiongnu cavalry force inside the city walls, rendering them virtually useless in the defence of the city. Thus, Marcus arranged to equip and arm his men as Roman legionaries who could fight as heavy infantry. In the event of any attack on the city, the contained area meant a force of heavy infantry would be much more effective than cavalry. The city of Zhi-Zhi had workshops and smithies manned by Sogdian craftsmen who had moved there as soon as they heard about the construction of the new city. After some trials and modifications, these men were able to satisfactorily produce weapons and armour to Marcus's specifications. The legionaries were once again equipped with Roman style weapons, and Marcus formed the men into two large centuries. Nearly a dozen Romans had died during the seven years they had spent living and raiding with the nomads, and now there was a total of 278 legionaries. Marcus knew how important it was for the men to be led by an experienced officer, and as Titus still resolutely refused to accept promotion, Gnaeus was the only other Roman in the contingent with sufficient experience to command part of the legionaries. Thus, Marcus had decided to form the men into two over-sized centuries, one commanded by Gnaeus and the other under his command. When they were not working on the city, Marcus and Gnaeus drilled their centuries in traditional Roman tactics.

Marcus also found that dividing the Romans into two groups proved advantageous for the construction work on the city. When they came to tackle each new task, he would allocate an equal portion of the work to each century, and then challenge them to race each other to complete the task. When he was not working with the men, Marcus inspected the progress, stopping to offer encouragement and praise as he passed amongst the legionaries. The natural spirit of competition meant that each century struggled to work faster than their rival. At the completion of each task, the winners were rewarded with a red silk banner, which they proudly displayed beside their worksite. Then a new task would be set, and the losing century would have an opportunity to reclaim the honor of displaying the silk banner by completing the new task faster. In addition to speeding up the construction of the city, the challenging competitions fostered the bonds of solidarity within each century as the men toiled together. The cohesion of a century was vital for Roman military tactics, for if a shield wall or testudo gave way at one point, it exposed the other legionaries' vulnerable flanks. A developed sense of unity was also necessary for the legionaries to move as a body during combat without breaking their defensive formation. Marcus was pleased to note that the arduous construction work meant the Romans soon returned to optimum physical condition.

A year after work had begun on the city, an important despatch arrived for Zhi-Zhi. The messenger informed Zhi-Zhi that Tumo, a disaffected noble, had defected to the Chinese and was preparing to guide a Chinese Army into Xiongnu territory. Apparently Tumo had boasted that he would lead the Chinese Army to the site of the new Xiongnu capital in return for half of the captured treasure. The despatch informed Zhi-Zhi that the Chinese were amassing an Army of over 40, 000 men under the command of General Gan Yan Shou and his deputy Chen Tang. Both of these names were respected and feared by the Xiongnu, for General Gan and his able deputy had earned fearsome reputations for the savagery with which they operated against the nomads. Work on the city had progressed well by the time this news arrived. However, once the basic defensive walls were in place, Zhi-Zhi had directed the labor force to focus on constructing and decorating his palace. Now that an attack on the city was certain, Marcus convinced Zhi-Zhi that all of the labor should be concentrated on improving the defences.

As a centurion in Gaul, Marcus had taken part in the siege and storming of many fortified cities, much larger and stronger than Zhi-Zhi's capital, and he was acutely aware of how vulnerable the Xiongnu city was. The wooden walls and buildings could be easily ignited, and once burning the very structures which had protected the inhabitants would become dangers to them. All of the Romans had seen the same thing happen in other wooden cities, once the attackers managed to start a fire the defenders were forced into an ever decreasing part of the city as they retreated from the flames. Eventually, the smoke and flames would force the defenders to attempt to break out and charge the enemy. Each charge would be cut down with volleys of arrows and javelins from the waiting attackers, and the city would be left a smouldering ruin or at best a pyre to the slain defenders.

Marcus knew that the nomads did not have the discipline or habit of fighting in units, and they would not respond well to a siege. The nomad style of combat required the space of the open steppe which permitted each mounted man to charge and withdraw on his own initiative. This technique of simultaneously engaging the enemy at numerous points produced a fluid fight which never provided the enemy with a fixed target or focus to concentrate on. However, within the confined space of a city these tactics were not possible. Centuries of Roman experience had shown that disciplined and heavily-armed infantry were the most effective troops with which to defend or attack a city. Marcus knew that despite their bravery and strength the nomad warriors would be ineffective at defending their city, so he concentrated on improving the city walls and training his legionaries. The Romans deepened and widened the trench around the city walls and then they fixed angled stakes to obstruct any advancing attackers. Meanwhile alarming reports continued to arrive of the amassing Chinese force. However, the mood remained buoyant within the city, and the Xiongnu prepared their new capital for its baptism of fire. Zhi-Zhi and the other nomads were confident that any Chinese force which reached the gates of their city, would already be so exhausted and weary that the nomads would be able to overcome them with ease. There was already a large contingent of Xiongnu warriors holding the mountain passes, and even if the Chinese did get past them, it was a long and circuitous journey to reach the city of Zhi-Zhi.

Within the city, the Romans had settled into their own quarters. Marcus had designed and built a home for himself and Liu. The building consisted of a large central room and a smaller room at the back. Marcus and Liu slept in the small room, whilst at night sleeping mats were laid out in the hall for the slaves and attendants. Marcus and his new wife had settled into their new abode happily. The last cold winter had not proved as dull as the previous ones, and Liu was now pregnant with their first child. She had consulted the shaman and after examining the stars and sacrificing a foal, Liu confidently informed Marcus that she would give birth to a boy in the autumn.

The Romans had returned to a settled life with contentment, and they soon began to organise some traditional Roman amusements for their free time. The Xiongnu readily participated in, and supported the bouts of wrestling and boxing which the Romans organised, but the nomads remained impervious to the appeal of dice or jacks. The Xiongnu greatly enjoyed playing a variant of polo using spears and a goat's head. The dangerous sport was played on horseback, and it required the players to be highly skilled riders. When the spring came, and the breeding season meant the bulls were on heat, the Romans introduced the nomads to a Gallic form of bull-fighting where two bulls fought each other. The two bulls were securely tethered in an enclosed pen, and then a young fecund cow was lead back and forth between the bulls causing the two hormonal males to bellow and pant with excitement. The cow was then led away, and when the two pent-up bulls were released they charged at each other. The bulls butted, charged and bellowed at each other in a spectacular display. However, it was rare for either of the bulls to be seriously injured, and the contest ended when one animal conceded the fight and walked away with heaving puffs and sweat-soaked flanks. The Gallic tradition fitted neatly with the Xiongnu's inherent respect for the prowess of their bulls, and the sturdy steppe animals possessed the stamina and strength for lengthy and thrilling bouts. All of the inhabitants of the city were soon passionate supporters of their favorite bull, and they eagerly discussed the form, tactics and merit of each bull between bouts.

26

SOGDIA AND CHINA, 38-37 BC

THE XIONGNU NOBLE who rode up to the Great Wall was a wiry and lean man named Tumo. His dark eyes were shifty, and he fidgeted constantly. Tumo had grounds to be uneasy, for he was riding to betray his tribe to their age-old and embittered enemies. Although he was of average height, Tumo's restlessness made him appear lanky and awkward. He was not comfortable in himself, and consequently few people found themselves comfortable in his presence. Tumo believed that he had been denied his rightful position in Xiongnu society, and he blamed the Shanyu Zhi-Zhi entirely for this fact. Two months previously, Tumo had collected his belonging and set out across the steppe, riding away from his tribe and towards their traditional enemies. Tumo had taken a circuitous route on the way to the Chinese garrison. He wanted to avoid the other nomads and he did not want any of his countrymen to realise where he was going. During the journey Tumo ruminated on the injustices and slights he had withstood, his bitterness sustained him when he was tired, and he consoled himself with thoughts of the rich reward he could expect from the Chinese Emperor.

Despite his fidgeting, Tumo presented an imposing figure when he rode up to the Chinese garrison; he had stopped while out of sight of the Chinese to don his best attire and ensure he would make a striking impression. Tumo was alone, mounted on his finest stallion, with the pelt of a snow leopard ostentatiously draped over his shoulders. The fur had a beautiful sheen, and even those Chinese who did not know that the pelt indicated nobility, were impressed by the luxuriant fur, and the haughty manner of the wild man who had ridden in from the steppe. The stallion was a particularly fiery steed, but Tumo had calmed him some years before using a simple but effective procedure employed by the nomads; a wooden mallet had been tied to the stallion's mane, and when he reared or bucked too violently the mallet would swing round and knock against the stallion. After several months of this treatment, the stallion had learnt to control its temper, and now it carried Tumo gracefully and regally into the Chinese fort. Tumo had approached at a controlled trot, and then slowed to a walk before he entered the gate. Amongst the nomads it was considered rude to approach at a canter or gallop, as only messengers bearing bad news arrived in haste. Thus the Chinese border guards had plenty of time to observe the lone horseman coming across the steppe, and the commander had been duly summoned. Despite his fidgeting hands, Tumo was a Xiongnu nomad and after a lifetime in the saddle he rode with a confidence and poise which impressed the Chinese. The commander of the garrison ordered his troops to escort Tumo into the fort, in the guise of a guard of honor, but with their crossbows loaded. Fortunately for Tumo, his elaborate clothing and the impressive stallion that he was riding meant that few of the Chinese noted his mendacious demeanor or restless and uneasy eyes.

Tumo met the commander of the Chinese garrison, and convinced him that he was an influential figure in Xiongnu society, second only to the Shanyu in importance. The garrison commander had duly provided an escort to take Tumo to the

Han capital of Chang'An. The journey was fast and uneventful, Tumo and his escort travelled along the Chinese roads at a brisk pace. The Chinese had an advanced system of major roads, which extended across the vast territory controlled by the Han Emperor. Along with the road network, there was also a system of canals which crossed the vast provinces and ensured that goods and soldiers could easily be transported around the Han Empire. The road surface was made of compacted rubble and gravel which provided an even surface, without the jarring rigidity of the paved Roman roads. Consequently the Chinese roads withstood the weather better, and were more pleasant to travel along. Trees were planted along the sides of the road to provide shade, and there were rest houses, watch towers and staging posts where horses could be changed, at regular intervals along these roads.

Tumo was surprised at the major cultural differences he observed whilst travelling through the land of the Han Chinese. Unlike the nomads, the Han Chinese venerated the elderly. Tumo considered it foolish to venerate men who were too old to fight or ride, but he kept his opinions to himself as he rode towards the capital. When the group stopped to eat, Tumo found the food very different. The Chinese subsisted on rice and other cereals, with meat being added in small amounts as a luxury. Tumo was accustomed to dining largely on meat, and he found the Chinese meals to be stodgy and unsatisfactory. The Han Chinese did not use milk in their cuisine; indeed many of the adults had developed a lactose intolerance. After several days without milk, Tumo finally went in search of the drink he considered a fundamental part of his diet.

After the Han Chinese had subdued the Kansu corridor through which Tumo was riding, over 700,000 Han Chinese had been sent to colonise the region. The original inhabitants of the regions were a branch of the Xiongnu tribe who had submitted to Chinese rule. The settled Xiongnu were easily distinguishable from the Han Chinese, for they were taller, darker and stockier than their new overlords. Like their independent brethren, the settled Xiongnu still used a great deal of milk and meat in their cuisine. The Han Chinese regarded all of the Xiongnu inhabitants as inferior and backward, and they were widely persecuted. Tumo was relieved to find a more familiar society, and he greatly appreciated the hospitality of the settled Xiongnu who offered him milk and meat and refused any payment. However, Tumo had noticed the evident scorn with which his escort viewed the subjugated Xiongnu, and after that one meal he decided not risk to compromising his position by associating with the other Xiongnu. After that first occasion, Tumo adapted his diet to match the Han Chinese who were escorting him.

Late one evening Tumo observed an official courier arrive at the rest-house where they had stopped. The sun had set, and there were no rooms for the courier, however a lowly merchant was soon roused from his sleep and evicted from his bed. The official courier carried the instructions of the Emperor, and thus he received priority at all the government rest-houses. The following morning Tumo watched with curiosity as the courier produced his bundle of bamboo tubes containing the official messages. Each message was written on a long bamboo strip, and then stored and sealed in a bamboo tube for delivery. The clerk at the rest-house examined the seals of each tube and then recorded that the messages and courier had reached that location. Unlike the Roman roads, the Chinese post roads followed the easiest course across the terrain. So whilst the overall distance between two towns might be greater, the journey was often quicker as it avoided the need for steep ascents or descents. Tumo made no attempt to converse with his guard, he affected disdain for their company or conversation to conceal the fact that he lacked the confidence or fluency to converse in Chinese.

When Tumo reached Chang'An, his escort showed him to the official guest quarters, and left him in the hands of the Palace officials. A message had already arrived from the garrison commander, stating that an important Xiongnu chieftain had come to submit to the Emperor. Tumo was staggered at the sight of the city. It was the largest settlement he had ever seen, and the greatest number of people he had seen in one place in his entire life. He had no idea that the world contained so many people; there were even more people than head of cattle he had seen in the very largest herds. After the quiet consistency of the open steppe, the city seemed to provide Tumo with an overdose of sensual information. His every sense was bombarded. He heard a cacophony of new sounds; smelt a bewildering array of unknown aromas and saw so many new sights that it bewildered and disorientated him. He realized that the ruler of such a country must have immense power. However, Tumo had long since passed the point of no return, and he resolved to stick to his decision and make the most of the precarious gamble he had taken. Palace officials duly arrived, and Tumo was instructed in the procedure to follow when he was presented to the Emperor. The officials were so adamant and deadly serious in their instructions that Tumo obeyed them without question; he had been overawed by the sight of the city.

Three days after he arrived at Chang'An, a palace official came to escort Tumo to his audience with the Emperor. Before entering the reception hall, Tumo was checked for weapons. Then he was instructed to leave his shoes and approach the Emperor keeping his head bowed. This last part proved a particular boon for Tumo, as it meant that nobody would notice his furtive eyes. For several years the Chinese Emperor had been anxious to learn the fate of his envoy Guji, and so Tumo was accorded the honor of being presented by himself, rather than in a group. Tumo entered the long hall with his head bowed, he was dimly aware that the Emperor was seated at the other end of the hall on a raised dais. Tumo took one step into the hall, and then performed the kowtow as he had been instructed; the procedure involved kneeling and then prostrating himself before the Emperor. Tumo was careful to ensure his forehead touched the ground, before he rose to his feet and advanced further into the hall.

One of the officials had explained to Tumo the enormous significance of the procedure. It implied that Tumo, as a noble and thus representative of the Xiongnu, had come to submit to the Emperor, and this implied that his entire Xiongnu tribe were submitting to the Emperor. Tumo advanced four steps into the hall, and then repeated the procedure two times. Although his head remained bowed, Tumo's furtive eyes were glancing all around him and he got some idea of his surroundings. On either side of the door there stood armed guards. Along both sides of the hall there were groups of mandarins and lesser visitors who had already been presented to the Emperor that morning, but were not deemed worthy of conversation. Tumo knew that the closer he was permitted to approach to the throne, the greater the honor which was being bestowed on him. If he got over half-way down the hall, then that was a sure sign that the Emperor wanted to talk with him. Tumo duly continued his ritualised approach. At the third stop he kowtowed three times. When he had risen the Emperor summoned him to approach. Tumo promptly moved towards the throne, keeping his head bowed, although his eyes scanned anxiously from side to side.

The Emperor demanded to know the fate of his envoy Guji who had been sent to contact the Shanyu some years previously. With some discomfort, Tumo recounted how Zhi-Zhi had set his ferocious dogs on the Chinese envoy, and had watched whilst they ripped him apart and ate him alive. Tumo had not actually witnessed the event, but he did not let that technicality prevent him from providing a colorful and gory account of the event. The crafty nomad embroidered the episode artfully, stressing the barbarity and cruelty of Zhi-Zhi's action. Tumo claimed that it was the unprovoked and unpardonable murder of the Chinese envoy which had finally caused him to leave Zhi-Zhi, and submit to the Chinese. The Emperor accepted Tumo's submission, and instructed his mandarins to provide Tumo with suitable treasures and gifts as a token of esteem. The interview progressed successfully, and Tumo told the Chinese how Zhi-Zhi had started to construct a city in which he was storing all his treasure, including the many valuables stolen from China over the previous decades.

Tumo explained that the new city was hidden deep within the Xiongnu territory, where Zhi-Zhi arrogantly presumed he could hide from Chinese justice. Tumo then took the initiative of offering to guide a Chinese force to the site of the city. The Emperor longed to send a punitive force against the Xiongnu, but he was all too painfully aware how the nomads retreated and dispersed in the face of superior forces. However, with a city to defend, Zhi-Zhi would not be able to retreat on this occasion. The Emperor seized the opportunity and promptly gave the instructions for a punitive expedition, with Tumo to act as the guide. Before leaving, Tumo swore an oath of allegiance to the Emperor, then he left the reception hall, walking backwards as he had been instructed, so as to avoid turning his back on the Emperor. The next day Tumo left the capital. The journey back to the Great Wall was quick and uneventful. Tumo and his escort rode into the garrison late one afternoon, with a cold wind from the steppe blowing into their faces. The wind came straight from the cold northern plains, and the icy dry air bit at the riders sucking away moisture and chapping any exposed skin. The wind blew from the steppe, and after the chaos of the city, Tumo was glad to embrace the harsh simplicity of the steppe wind which blew from his homeland.

27

CHINA AND SOGDIA, 36 BC

AFTER TUMO'S REVELATION, the Chinese Emperor ordered one of his leading generals named Gan Yan Shou to lead an army against the Xiongnu, and destroy the new city of Zhi-Zhi. General Gan Yan Shou and his deputy Chen Tang duly assembled the Han army, and they were joined by the forces of the Western territories allied with the Han. The Chinese force and their allies numbered more than 40,000 men and they were divided into six divisions. General Gan split his Army into two for the first part of the long journey, with his deputy Chan Tang commanding one section, whilst he led the other. Dividing the force meant that the Chinese would be able to move quicker as the delays at bridges and other narrow points would be reduced. It would also be easier to secure sufficient water and supplies for the men and their mounts during the journey if the Army travelled in two sections.

Chen Tang led his force along the southern route around the Taklamakan Desert, whilst General Gan led the other half of the Chinese Army around the north of the Desert. The name of the desert means 'Go-in-and-you-won't-come-out', and the journey across its dry plains was tough. Around the major oases, there were several sizeable towns which serviced the merchants who travelled along the overland routes with their caravans. After circling the desert, the two forces united before they crossed the high Torugart pass and entered the Xiongnu lands beyond. After descending from the formidable Tien Shan Mountains, they arrived at the Western shore of a vast lake named Issyk-Kul. The lake was famous because it never froze, despite being at an altitude of 1700 metres, and surrounded by numerous snow-capped peaks. This bizarre trait had led to the name Issyk-Kul which means 'warm lake'. Issyk-Kul measures 180kms long and 50kms wide; there are over 50 streams and rivers which drain into the Lake, but none that flow out from it; over the centuries this has led to an increase in the mineral content of the Lake's water, which became slightly saline. In addition to the mineral content, extreme depth, and continued thermal activity ensure that the Lake never freezes.

Throughout the journey Tumo acted as a guide to the Chinese force, although he complained regularly to General Gan at the slow speed of their progress. Ignoring Tumo, General Gan ordered the Army to camp some 60 li (30kms) away from the Xiongnu capital, whilst he gathered fresh intelligence and assessed the situation. The Chinese scouts captured a Xiongnu nobleman named Kaimiu, son of Beishe, who was hunting in the area. The Chinese tortured Kaimiu for some hours until they learnt about the current state of affairs amongst the Xiongnu and within the city of Zhi-Zhi. The next day the Han force advanced another 30 li and made camp. Zhi-Zhi had been informed of the approaching Chinese Army and he sent a messenger to ask why the Han had come there. In his heart of hearts, Zhi-Zhi knew that the Chinese Army had come to avenge the murder of the envoy Guji, and when he learnt that Tumo had defected and was guiding the Chinese, he knew that he would no longer be able to deny murdering Guji. However, Zhi-Zhi and General Gan still went through the ritual motions of political exchanges and greetings; both powerful men were playing for time in which to assess their opponents and identify any weaknesses.

The Chinese General explained that the Xiongnu had sent an envoy to the Chinese Emperor saying that they found it hard to live in the open plain, and they wished to become subjects of the Chinese Emperor. The General explained that the Emperor felt pity for Zhi-Zhi leaving his great open plains, and the Emperor had sent General Gan and his Army to act as an escort for Zhi-Zhi and his family on their journey to China. To prevent disturbing the countryside and surroundings of the Xiongnu capital, the Chinese General had respectfully remained some distance from the city. Several messages were exchanged between the Zhi-Zhi and General Gan, before the latter complained;

'Our army has come a long way to the land of the Xiongnu, but so far there has not been a single representative of noble rank who has come to make a formal visit and welcome the General and his deputy. How could the Xiongnu overlook this important breach in protocol? Our armies have travelled a long way over arduous terrain, and we are very tired. We have exhausted our supplies, and will need to replenish out stocks before we can travel back. We hope that the Shanyu and his ministers make some appropriate plans.'

The next day the Chinese army came closer to the Xiongnu city. Although the city had only been erected in the last few years, it showed little evidence of its recent construction; the roads were already well-trampled, there were piles of refuse outside the city walls, and the surrounding area had been stripped of all potential firewood. The Chinese set up camp within sight of the city walls, and they deployed in battle formation; they could see the flags and banners defiantly displayed on the fortified walls by the assembled nomads. Hundreds of Xiongnu soldiers, wearing armour, were standing on the city walls, and there were two groups of armed foot soldiers deployed outside the city gates. The different sections of both armies were drawn up in their units in preparation for battle; the diplomatic gestures had been completed, and now blows would decide whether the Xiongnu were to be subject to the Chinese or independent.

When Zhi-Zhi first heard word of the approaching Han armies, he planned to flee and withdraw deep into the plains, dispersing his forces over the vast steppe. However, he was worried that a number of the disaffected Xiongnu nobles might collaborate with the enemy and aid the Chinese to pursue him. Zhi-Zhi knew that some of the other nomad tribes such as the Wusun, had sent soldiers to join the Chinese. Thus Zhi-Zhi decided that he had no choice but to fight the Chinese. He reasoned that the Chinese soldiers had travelled far, and they would be weary from their journey and low on supplies, this meant that the siege could not last for long. General Gan had confirmed that the Chinese Army was tired and low on provisions, so Zhi-Zhi took courage, strapped on his armour impetuously and climbed into one of the watch towers.

The Xiongnu soldiers waved their banners and called to the Chinese to come and fight. Hundreds of Xiongnu foot soldiers and cavalry rushed at the Chinese camp, however, the Chinese soldiers protecting the camp were waiting with their crossbows. The Chinese crossbows were even more powerful than the re-curved composite bows of the nomads, and whilst the crossbows took longer to re-load, they had a much greater killing range. Now the Chinese had the same advantage over the Xiongnu which the nomads had exploited so devastatingly against the Romans at the battle of Carrhae; the Chinese were able to shoot the Xiongnu whilst still out of range of the Xiongnu archers. The Chinese had also developed the tactic of firing volleys from their powerful crossbows; these volleys had a much greater psychological impact than individual shots. The Chinese archers were formed up in ranks, with the archers in the front row kneeling so that those behind could shoot over their heads. The first rank fired a volley, and then reloaded whilst their comrades behind fired. This meant the Chinese were able to fire their devastating volleys in quick succession, providing a lethal and traumatising bombardment. The Xiongnu charge quickly stopped when they realized this, and they retreated out of range of the formidable Chinese crossbows.

After the Xiongnu charge had withdrawn, General Gan sent forward a group of archers to shoot at the cavalry and foot-soldiers who were deployed outside the city gates. When the Chinese approached the city they saw a group of soldiers deployed in an unusual formation. The Chinese had never seen this strange formation before and in their reports and records they were at a loss how to describe it. The Chinese accounts describe a contingent of soldiers fighting in 'fish-scale' formation, with over-lapping shields around the sides and over the top of the unit to form a defensive shell for the infantry. Once they had settled in the city, the Romans had made shields for themselves, and they now used the tactics and formations, which they had used in the legions. Marcus and Gaius were each in command of an enlarged century, and these two units had formed up in the classic Roman *testudo* outside the city gates.

Under fire from the Chinese cross-bows, the Xiongnu cavalry withdrew inside the city walls. Generals Gan and Chen ordered the drums to beat, and the Chinese soldiers to march up to the city walls. The Chinese surrounded the city and sealed the Xiongnu inside. The Chinese dug trenches, guarded their positions and blocked all of the city gates. General Gan did not have sufficient resources to besiege the city for any length of time, but he was determined to prevent Zhi-Zhi from escaping across the steppe and summoning the full might of the dispersed nomad warriors.

Once the city had been surrounded and all possible escape routes had been blocked, the Chinese attacked. The foot-soldiers marched forward under the cover of large shields, the soldiers at the front carried halberds and dagger-axes, whilst those behind them were armed with crossbows. The Chinese archers shot up at the defenders on the city walls and towers, under the heavy bombardment many of the Xiongnu withdrew from the exposed positions. There were two wooden walls surrounding the city, and the defenders now retreated behind the wall as they continued to shoot at the Chinese. The Chinese units were in a much more exposed position, and many of their soldiers were killed or wounded by the Xiongnu archers. In order to attack the city walls, the Chinese had been obliged to come within range of the Xiongnu archers.

The initial Chinese advance had forced Marcus and the Romans to withdraw inside the city walls. The *testudo* formation had protected the Romans from the Chinese arrows, but the defenders within the city were eager to bar the gate and barricade the entrances to the city, and Marcus could not risk the Romans being cut off from the other defenders and surrounded by the Chinese. The Xiongnu cavalry had withdrawn inside the city walls as soon as they had come under sustained fire from the Chinese archers. Marcus reluctantly withdrew the Romans into the city, although he saw that such actions would inevitably permit the Chinese to advance and attack the city walls, he did not have the authority to direct the defence of the city. Marcus was exasperated at how ineptly the nomads were defending their new city; they had never fought in this manner before and their inexperience showed clearly. However, the Romans had been hired as a bodyguard for the Shanyu, and Marcus had to constantly remind himself that his duty was to protect the Shanyu, and not the city. Marcus knew that Liu was in the city, sheltering with their young son, and he was painfully aware of the dangers to which the pair would be exposed if the Chinese stormed the city.

Zhi-Zhi engaged the Chinese in battle with the same rashness and ferocity with which he undertook any project. Although Zhi-Zhi never reflected for long on his decisions, once he had chosen a course of action he always committed himself with determination and drive. His wives and scores of soldiers were shooting down arrows at the Han, but the Chinese archers were protected by large shields. One arrow from the Chinese archers flew so close to Zhi-Zhi that the arrowhead nicked his nose, and drew blood. Inside the tower, several of Zhi-Zhi's wives were killed whilst they were shooting arrows at the Chinese. Zhi-Zhi realized that the nomads would be unable to stop the enormous Chinese Army in this manner and he descended the tower, mounted his horse and rode to his palace. As night fell, the Chinese succeeded in setting fire to the outer wall.

Under cover of darkness, several hundred Xiongnu cavalrymen tried to break out of the city. They were shot head on by the Chinese archers, and the charge was stopped instantly. Each volley from the Chinese archers brought down another rank of the Xiongnu cavalry. Armed with their powerful cross-bows, the Chinese archers were able to slaughter the Xiongnu before the fierce horsemen even had a chance to engage the Chinese. The whole episode lasted a matter of minutes, but it had a profound and shocking effect on the nomads who had seen the flower of their famed cavalry shot down before they were even able to engage the enemy. After they had felled the Xiongnu horsemen, the lowly Chinese archers advanced to finish off any wounded Xiongnu nobles. The Chinese picked through the tangled bodies of horses and men, stopping briefly to bludgeon or stab any surviving nomads. A little after midnight, the wooden city wall was breached; it had become impossible for the Xiongnu to defend the wall once it was set alight. The defenders retreated into the center of the city and yelled battle cries to encourage their comrades. At the same time, 10,000 Xiongnu cavalry were divided into a dozen columns. They rode around inside the city, assisting the defenders and repelling any Chinese who tried to enter the city. However, the Chinese blockade meant that the cavalry could not leave the city, and the horsemen did not have enough room to operate effectively within the confines of the city. Several times during the night, the Xiongnu cavalry attempted to break out of the city, and attack the Chinese, but each time the cavalrymen were met with a fierce barrage of arrows from the Chinese cross-bows, and they were forced to withdraw inside the city walls after suffering heavy losses.

Marcus had moved the Romans into the city center where they had taken up defensive position beside the Royal Palace with the aim of protecting Zhi-Zhi from any Chinese infantry that managed to get past the Xiongnu cavalry. Both Marcus and Gaius were all too painfully aware that the Royal Palace was built from wood, as was most of the city. Once the fires from the city wall spread to the other buildings, or the advancing Chinese started new fires, the structures which currently defended the nomads would hinder and endanger them. Consequently, Marcus and Gaius had formed up their centuries in the large courtyard to one side of the Palace. There was a well in the center of the courtyard, and there was also sufficient space for the legionaries to form up in two *testudos*. All around the city, the Romans could hear the screams of agony and anguish from the nomad women and children. Marcus struggled hard to steel himself, and focus on his role in the battle. Previously he had never had any difficulty in concentrating on following his orders without worrying about what was going on elsewhere in the battle, but this was the first time his child and partner were at risk. Throughout the night the Romans struggled to douse the fires around the Royal Palace. Zhi-Zhi was disturbed and traumatised by his first experience of a long battle, previously the nomads had always been in a position to break off any engagement, but now they could not flee. The battle had gone on all night, and the nomads were not accustomed to such drawn-out fights; initially they had fought with their characteristic zeal and fervour, but the defenders were now running low on energy and arrows. The fighting began to take on a desperate and determined air, there were no more jaunts or cheers as the soldiers battled on, relentlessly fighting and slaying.

At dawn, fires broke out all around the city. The Chinese were encouraged by this advantage, and the officers spurred on their soldiers to capture the city. The Chinese beat their battle drums and bells so hard it felt like the earth was shaking and the air vibrated with the noise. Many of the horses and animals within the city panicked and one group of horses which included Marcus's beloved mare, kicked down the wall of their stables. The stampeding horses charged through the encircling Han and escaped into the steppe. Within the city, the Xiongnu gradually fell back from their positions and the Chinese pressed home the advantage. The Chinese used their large shields for cover, and they managed to break through the inner city walls. Zhi-Zhi and his surviving entourage retreated to the Palace. The Chinese officers pursued Zhi-Zhi and then set fire to the Palace. Marcus ordered half of the Romans to maintain a shield-wall, whilst he led the other half in an attempt to fight the fires which were threatening to engulf the Palace. In his fervour, Zhi-Zhi rushed from one place to another. Marcus had unsuccessfully tried to convince Zhi-Zhi that he would be safer outside in the open, away from the wooden Palace, however Zhi-Zhi refused to leave his Palace where his treasures were stored. Marcus attempted in vain to explain that the Roman bodyguard could not protect Zhi-Zhi if he remained inside and continued to move around so rapidly. Zhi-Zhi's eyes were wide with panic and distrust, he remembered that the Romans were only bound to protect him as mercenaries and he decided he would not trust them any longer. In these dire straits Zhi-Zhi wanted to be surrounded by his most trusted relatives, for they had as much at stake as he did, and if Zhi-Zhi fell then all his closest family would also be killed. In a lucid yet squeaky voice, Zhi-Zhi ordered Marcus to remain outside the Palace with the Romans. Marcus recognized the intractability and the panic in Zhi-Zhi's voice, and he returned to the courtyard where the Romans had taken up position. Before he left, Marcus told Zhi-Zhi exactly where the Romans were drawn up, and he implored the Shanyu to seek refuge there when the fires caught and spread in the Palace.

When Marcus rejoined his comrades he saw that despite the best attempts of the legionaries, the Palace had caught fire and would soon burn down. Dark smoke was engulfing the courtyard and obscuring the city. Screams and cries issued from the smoke-filled buildings around the courtyard. Marcus and his men resolutely held their position, as he had promised Zhi-Zhi. Unbeknown to the Romans, a group of bold Chinese officers had used the smoke-screen to break into the Palace and attack the remaining defenders. The Chinese soldiers made short work of Zhi-Zhi's panic-stricken entourage, and a junior officer by the name of Du Xun cut off the Shanyu's head. Marcus and the Romans continued to hold their ground hoping that Zhi-Zhi would emerge from the smoke and seek sanctuary with his bodyguard. A gust of wind blew through the city, and as the smoke cleared the Romans beheld a figure emerging from the Palace. The man was tall and powerfully built, and Marcus hoped that it was Zhi-Zhi who had come to his senses. As the figure approached through the smoke, the Romans beheld Zhi-Zhi's face, however it was being brandished triumphantly by Du Xun. The Chinese officer held the Shanyu's bloody head high in the air, so that all the Xiongnu could see that their leader was dead.

The Romans stopped fighting once they saw that Zhi-Zhi was dead. They had vowed to fight for him as his bodyguard, but now that he was dead they had no cause to continue fighting against the Chinese. The remaining Xiongnu fought on, even though the situation had become hopeless, fires were engulfing most of the town and forcing the survivors into smaller and smaller pockets. The Chinese showed no quarter, and they killed all of the Xiongnu defenders that did not perish in the flames. Marcus was worried about Liu and his son. Now that Zhi-Zhi had been killed, Marcus was released from his oath. He hurriedly placed Gaius in command of the remaining Romans, and turned to leave the relative safety of the courtyard and search for Liu. Marcus only got two steps before he was felled by a blow to the head. He collapsed unconscious, dimly wondering what had struck him. Behind Marcus, Titus stood over his fallen figure. He had heard Marcus's intentions and decided to intervene rather than let Marcus risk his life so rashly. Titus had used the rounded pommel of his sword hilt to knock out Marcus with a blow to the back of the head. Gaius and Titus then dragged Marcus into the center of the courtyard, and ordered the Romans to form one large *testudo* around the well.

As various figures approached through the smoke, the legionaries held their ground. Some of the panicking nomads attacked the Romans, forgetting who they were and recognising only the otherness of the strange light-skinned legionaries. None of the nomads chose to remain with the Romans; in the urgency and extreme danger they preferred to be with people of their own race. Thus the Romans were left isolated by the Xiongnu defenders whilst the fierce endgame of the battle was fought in various pockets around the burning city. The legionaries had suffered heavy casualties throughout the long battle, and nearly half of the Romans had fallen before they ceased to fight. As the battle progressed, the Chinese advanced and beheld the Romans. The invaders were momentarily nonplussed by the sight of these tall, blond soldiers, formed into one large *testudo*. The Chinese saw that there were no Xiongnu amongst the ranks of the Romans, so they decided to leave the mysterious soldiers alone whilst they dealt with the Xiongnu defenders. Inside the burning Palace, the Chinese had found the credential staffs and silk memoranda of the envoy Guji, who had been killed by Zhi-Zhi some years before. All envoys of the Chinese Emperor bore a staff with a yak tail fixed to it as a symbol of their authority, and Zhi-Zhi had foolishly kept Guji's staff as a trophy. Now, the Chinese officers ordered all of the Xiongnu defenders to be slaughtered in retaliation.

The Chinese officers also found the great hoard of treasure which Zhi-Zhi had accumulated during his lifetime of raiding and looting. As the officers were emerging from the ruined Palace, flushed with the elation of their valuable discovery, and confident in their victory, Gaius approached. He held out his sword, hilt first to General Gan and signaled the surrender of the remaining Romans. The General was greatly intrigued by the mysterious soldiers, with their blond hair, light eyes and unusual military formations. He accepted the proffered sword, and gave orders for the surviving Romans to be spared until he could learn more about them. After the battle, General Gan rewarded all of the Chinese Army, including the 15 kings and chieftains from the Western regions who had joined the Chinese as allies, with booty from Zhi-Zhi's great treasure trove. The Romans were spared, as they had stopped fighting when Zhi-Zhi died, but all of the other Xiongnu defenders were slaughtered. There were 145 Romans left alive at the end of the battle, although Marcus was out cold for the rest of the day. The Chinese killed all the Xiongnu women and children without compunction; Liu and her son died whilst Marcus was unconscious.

28

SOGDIA AND CHINA, 36BC

AFTER GENERAL GAN had accepted the surrender of the Romans, he ordered the new prisoners to be marched out of the burning city, and kept under guard in the nearby Chinese camp. General Gan had far more pressing matters to attend to, and he decided to deal with the strange prisoners later. The General was anxious to supervise the collection and distribution of the captured treasure before any problems arose. In the smouldering aftermath of the battle, tempers were running high and Gan wanted to prevent any disputes erupting into bloody fights. Gan knew that the job of commanding his men was far from over; a successful general needed to exercise control over his men after a battle, as well as direct them during the actual fighting. General Gan always attempted to empathise with his soldiers in order to understand their motivation and capabilities; so Gan knew that after the intense and fierce fighting, the soldiers would still be battle-crazed. It would take several hours for an army to settle down after an engagement, and these hours could be more dangerous than the battle itself. It was all too easy for one group of men to believe that they were being cheated of their share of the loot; then, with their bloody weapons still in hand seek revenge for their perceived injustice. Internal fights were a major risk under any circumstance, but Gan was acutely aware that the dangers were increased by the presence of the various allies who had joined the Chinese Army. General Gan was commanding a disparate force, and many of the allied chieftains had fought with the Chinese solely in the hope of getting a share of Zhi-Zhi's famous treasure.

The Romans surrendered all of their weapons to the Chinese officer, who General Gan had delegated to guard them; then they marched out of the smoking remains of the city and into the Chinese camp. The Roman prisoners were down-hearted and despondent; they had fought all night, initially against the Chinese attackers, and then against the spreading fires, and many of them were injured. Over a hundred Romans had been killed whilst fighting to defend the city and the Shanyu, and the surviving legionaries were now shocked to see how depleted their ranks had become. Unlike the Chinese, the Romans did not have the elation of victory to sustain them, and they were all exhausted. As they trudged out of the city the Romans saw the piles of Xiongnu corpses amongst the smouldering ruins. The Chinese had slaughtered all of the Xiongnu without mercy, and the Romans beheld the pitiful result of their barbarity. The women, children and elderly had all been massacred along with the defenders; their contorted bodies had been left where they died, grotesquely frozen by death in the preternatural positions in which they had fallen. Amongst the dead, Gaius was upset to catch sight of Liu and her son. Gaius knew that he would have to break the news to Marcus when he came round, but he was too tired to give the matter much thought. All around the city, the air was thick with the acrid smell of burning flesh as the burning buildings provided a funeral pyre for the dead defenders. Gaius and Titus struggled along in bleak silence as they carried the still unconscious Marcus between them. Marcus's head hung limply and it swayed from side to side with each pace and a trickle of saliva ran from the side of his mouth. Titus had struck him with all the power his aging limbs could muster, and it was a mark of the residual strength in Titus's old arms, that even the jolts and jerks of being carried out of the burning city did not wake Marcus. In fact Marcus remained so silent that Titus began to wonder if he had struck him too hard.

When they arrived at the Chinese camp, Gaius anxiously checked Marcus's inanimate form. Marcus was still breathing, and after they splashed some water on his face he stirred a little. Gaius and Titus were relieved, and they laid Marcus down to rest whilst he slowly regained consciousness. Meanwhile, the Romans were being guarded by a small contingent of Chinese infantry. The Chinese guards watched warily as the Romans crowded around Marcus; when he revived and the Romans cheered with relief, the guards all lowered their weapons and tensed with alarm. However, there were no further signs of action and the Chinese cautiously relaxed their guard. Gaius attempted to bring Marcus up to date with the latest developments, but Marcus's head was throbbing so fiercely that he had difficulty in following what Gaius was telling him. Marcus was worried for Liu and his son. When Marcus had fully revived and was able to concentrate, Gaius told him the sad news about the fate of Liu and her son. Although Marcus was saddened to learn of their deaths, his relationship with Liu had never developed beyond that of companionable affection. Whereas, after all that the legionaries had been through together, the other Romans were the only real family Marcus had.

Marcus gingerly felt the large lump on the back of his head, as he listened to Gaius and endeavored to focus on their present situation. With a start, Marcus reached inside his breast-plate. He sighed with relief when his fingers fastened on the tiger broach and silver pendant which were still securely concealed beneath his tunic. Although Marcus maintained that he was not superstitious, he felt a surge of hope knowing that his precious talismans had survived. After twenty years with the legion Marcus had spent over half his life with these men, and they had become his real family. His eyes now scanned the familiar faces of the Romans, checking to see who had survived. Along with Titus and Gaius, Marcus saw Appius, as taciturn in defeat as he had always been after their victories in Gaul. Each familiar face that he saw brought a wave of relief to Marcus; however, he was specifically looking for the man who had intervened to save him. Titus was lurking sheepishly in the background; he was doing his best to hide from Marcus's gaze, but all of the Romans had been herded into a small area, and Marcus soon spotted him. A nod and a grin were all it took for Marcus to indicate that he had forgiven his comrade. Relieved at his reprieve, Titus came to join the two centurions as they discussed their options, and reviewed their situation. The Romans knew very little about their new captors, and they found it hard to predict what the Chinese would do with them. Whilst the three men discussed their options, the exhausted legionaries around them had stretched out on the ground to sleep in the morning sunshine. The surviving legionaries willingly left the decision-making responsibility to their officers, whilst they settled down for some much needed rest. Marcus, Gaius and Titus had some time to discuss their options before they also relaxed and went to sleep. During the day General Gan was occupied securing, guarding and distributing the captured treasure trove, so he put off dealing with the Romans until the following day.

The next afternoon, General Gan summoned the leader of the Romans to his tent. Marcus duly went to meet the Chinese commander, although he still had a pounding headache from the blow Titus had given him. Tumo acted as interpreter for the interview that followed.

'Who are you? And where do you come from?' demanded General Gan, who had never seen anyone like these tall blond big-nosed foreigners, and was totally mystified by their presence in the lands of the Xiongnu. Standing just under six feet tall, Marcus towered above the Chinese guards who flanked him.

'We are Roman soldiers, from Gaul', replied Marcus.

However, Tumo was unable to translate either 'Roman' or 'Gaul' as he did not know the equivalent terms in Chinese. The Xiongnu nomads had a much looser notion of nationality and nationhood, so Tumo was not even able to use the Xiongnu terms. In fact, no words existed in Chinese for 'Gaul' or 'Rome'! The two greatest contemporary empires and societies were at either ends of the world, and before this occasion there had been almost no interaction between them. After the complex chain of events which had brought the Romans from Gaul to Sogdia, Marcus and his men were the first Romans to encounter the Chinese. To the north, the vast steppe plains and the fierce nomads which inhabited them had acted as an effective barrier between the Chinese and the Romans for many centuries. To the south, the powerful empires of the Parthians and the Yue-zhi had also ensured that no direct contact had been made between the Romans and the Chinese. General Gan was intrigued by these tall fair men, and the organised manner in which they had fought as a unit. Marcus's initial answer had not satisfied his curiosity, and the General now began a long process of questioning.

'How did you come to be here in the lands of the Xiongnu?' asked Gan, his curiosity had now got a grip of him, and his tone of questioning was becoming softer.

'We were prisoners of war, captured by the Parthians, and when we escaped from Parthia we came into the lands of the Xiongnu. Then Zhi-Zhi employed us as his bodyguard,' replied

Marcus.

'So you are Parthians?' said Gan.

'No, we are Roman legionaries,' replied Marcus, 'We were captured by the Parthians at the Battle of Carrhae.'

'These names, 'Roman', 'Carrhae' and 'Gaul', they don't mean anything to me. Where does your homeland lie? Are your people subject to the Parthians or to the Xiongnu?'

General Gan was quick to note the flash of pride in Marcus's eye, and the faint stiffening of his back when Tumo translated his comments.

'The Romans are subject to nobody,' answered Marcus defiantly, 'Our armies have conquered vast lands, and the Mediterranean Ocean is now called 'our sea' for we possess or control all of the countries around its shore.'

This comment brought a reaction of considerable surprise from General Gan; who was prompted to enquire further about the location of Rome and the extent of the Roman territories. When Marcus mentioned that Egypt was effectively a vassal state of Rome, General Gan let out a cry of recognition. The Chinese had heard of the marvellous city of Alexandria and the Pharos, its famed lighthouse. Unbeknown to Marcus or Gan, several crucial details were lost in translation, and Tumo erroneously conveyed the impression that Rome and Alexandria were one and the same. General Gan was delighted to find at least a partial solution to the mystery, and he readily accepted that the Roman Empire was controlled from Alexandria. It seemed highly plausible that a civilisation which had built the unsurpassed gigantic lighthouse should be in control of the entire Mediterranean. The interview continued, with General Gan now referring to the Romans in Chinese as 'Alexandrians' and their homeland as 'Alexandria'. Now that Gan believed he had established where this group of mysterious prisoners had come from, he was eager to know how they had ended up fighting with the Xiongnu, so far from their homeland. Marcus was able to answer these questions with greater ease, and Tumo had little difficulty in translating the brief overview which Marcus provided.

General Gan felt his admiration growing for the Romans, when he learnt that they had set off to conquer Parthia. But when Gan heard how the Romans had been massacred at Carrhae, he was unsure if these strange blond soldiers were exceptionally foolish and rash, or if they had just been ill-prepared and poorly commanded. Gan then reflected on the role the Romans had played in the defence of the city of Zhi-Zhi. Gan remembered the strange 'fish-scale' formation which the legionaries had used, and the controlled and ordered manner in which they had moved and fought as a unit. The Romans had been the last troops to withdraw behind the city walls; it was only once all the defenders had withdrawn, that Gan had been able to advance his infantry and attack the walls. From what he had seen General Gan concluded that the Romans were experienced and capable soldiers. The Romans had certainly employed tactics and formations which were far more advanced than those of the headstrong Xiongnu nomads. General Gan now resumed his questioning.

'What is your name?' he asked.

'Marcus,' came the reply.

'Ma, sit down, I want you to tell me about the military techniques and formations which you use. I have never seen anything like them, and I am curious,' said Gan bluntly.

Gan's frank tone and direct approach reassured Marcus, who noted without the translation that his name had been shortened to 'Ma'. Marcus was not to know that the Chinese were accustomed to much shorter names, thus Gan had heard 'Ma-Cus' as a two part name, and chosen to use only the first part. In a similar fashion, the Chinese name for Alexandria was based on the single character 'Li'. The Chinese disliked words beginning in vowels, so their name for the Egyptian metropolis was based on a corrupted version of the first phoneme in Alexandria once the initial 'A' had been dropped.

Marcus relaxed a little, and sat down on the carpet as he had been directed. Over the next couple of hours 'Ma' did his best to answer all of the questions which General Gan put to him. Marcus was aware that the longer he managed to engage Gan in conversation, the more of a rapport he could develop with his captor, and the greater would be the chance of reaching some compromise. As Marcus told General Gan about the tactics, weapons, formations and training of the legionaries, he also made some discreet enquiries about China and the state of the Chinese Empire. When General Gan made a passing reference to the Great Wall which was being extended along the Northern border of China, Marcus was quick to note this potentially important piece of information. During the ensuing dialogue he took pains to emphasise the engineering and building experience which the Romans had acquired. He explained to Gan that throughout the Roman Empire, when the legionaries were not engaged in fighting, they were employed building roads or forts. Gan had noticed the unusual design of the palisade which had surrounded the city of Zhi-Zhi, and he was impressed when Marcus affirmed that the Romans had been responsible not only for the construction of the palisade, but of the entire city.

As Marcus continued with his account of the Romans' engineering experience, he shifted his position on the carpet, as he did so his tunic moved a little and revealed the five parallel scars on his thigh from the tiger. General Gan noticed the scars immediately and he asked Marcus where they had come from. Marcus explained that they were from a tiger, but Tumo did not know the Chinese name for the animal, and he was at a loss to translate the reply. Tumo had only spent a few months with the Chinese, and his knowledge of their language was still basic. Fortunatley, Marcus quickly understood the problem, and guessing the reason for the confusion, he reaching inside his tunic and withdrew the tiger brooch which his mother had given him when he sailed from Massalia. General Gan took the brooch with clear approbation. When he understood that Marcus bore the mark of this revered animal General Gan treated Marcus with a newfound respect; he called for a stool for Marcus, and insisted the Roman take some refreshment. Marcus was unaware of the significance of being honored with a stool whilst in audience with the General, but he noted the deferential manner in which the attendants now treated him, and he realized that the abrupt alteration had been brought about either from the brooch, or the association with the tiger.

Marcus had no way of knowing that General Gan had been born in the year of the Tiger, and the animal had thus become a particularly potent symbol for him. It was at the age of 24, in the year of the Tiger, that Gan had won his first major victory against the nomads. A number of other triumphs and victories had followed, but it was another twelve years before Gan reached the position of General. The fact that these momentous events had occurred during the year of his animal spirit was not lost on General Gan, and he revered the Tiger accordingly as his talisman. Before he had left for his latest campaign, General Gan had consulted the foremost astrologers and palmists; they had informed him that his mission would be a success, as the spirit of the Tiger would watch over his endeavors. Meanwhile, Marcus had been thinking furiously of how he could exploit the sudden change in his situation. An idea had already been slowly forming in Marcus's aching brain, and he decided now was the best time to make his proposal. Before he spoke, Marcus scratched his chin and deftly extracted the silver pendant which hung around his neck. He was unsure if it was the brilliant blue of the lapis lazuli brooch, or if it was the tiger, which had brought about the abrupt improvement in his situation, but Marcus decided to take the gamble and reveal his pendant anyway. Although Marcus did not want to risk losing his treasured talismans, he now decided to take the risk and show both the pendant and brooch. The lives of all the Romans were at stake, and Marcus reflected briefly that neither of his treasures would be of any use to him if he was executed beside the smouldering remains of the Xiongnu city.

Marcus took a deep breath, and then looking directly into General Gan's dark narrow eyes he proposed that the Romans return to China to work as engineers and builders for the Chinese. General Gan maintained eye contact with Marcus as he waited for Tumo to translate. This was exactly what Marcus had intended, and he now lent forward so that the silver pendant would hang loose and swing from his neck. As the pendant turned it gleamed and drew Gan's eye. The General glanced down briefly at the pendant, when he beheld the tiger engraved on it he was taken aback. At first General Gan had been surprised to see the sign of his animal spirit on one of these tall big-nosed, smelly foreigners, but now the combination of the broach, scar and pendant struck him as undeniably significant.

Once he had satisfied his curiosity about their provenance and military tactics, General Gan had intended to execute all of the Romans. The Emperor had sent General Gan to lead a punitive expedition, and there were many Chinese officials who believed the length of peace achieved with any of the barbaric nomads was in direct proportion to the cruelty of the slaughter inflicted upon them. General Gan and his deputy had achieved their prominence and position through the merciless manner in which they dealt with the Xiongnu, and now General Gan was not eager to risk his position or his reputation. Gan had been in two minds when he saw the brooch and the scar, there was no denying that both were clear symbols of the Tiger, but the Romans had fought with the Xiongnu against the Chinese Army. The Emperor had sent Gan on a punitive expedition with strict instructions to ruthlessly impress on the nomads the full strength of the Chinese Empire, and revenge the murder of the Chinese envoy Guji. However, all of the General's doubts were dismissed when he beheld the tiger on Marcus's silver pendant. The three clear symbols showed Gan that the Tiger spirit protected Marcus. By the time Tumo had translated Marcus's suggestion, General Gan was already searching for a way to spare the Romans.

Marcus's proposal was a perfect solution to the predicament, and General Gan readily acquiesced to it. With that, the audience drew to a close, and Marcus was dismissed to return to the other Romans. General Gan had much to think about as he sat quietly eating his midday meal. With this latest victory, the sphere of Chinese control would extend beyond the current protective wall, making it necessary to extend the Great Wall to include the recently pacified Kansu corridor. Such a large engineering project would require all the man-power available, and General Gan recognized the potential usefulness of a group of experienced engineers and builders. The only problem was that once Tumo had confirmed the murder of the Chinese envoy, General Gan had been ordered to slaughter all of the Xiongnu he encountered. However, Gan reasoned that his ruthless orders did not apply to the Romans, as they were clearly not from the same race as the nomads, and they had not even arrived when Guji was killed.

After the long interview with General Gan was over, Marcus returned to the other prisoners. He sat down and recounted what had happened, then Marcus realized how exhausted he was. The strain of the recent events caught up with him, and Marcus curled up and slept, snoring soundly. The burden of responsibility for the surviving legionaries had passed from Marcus's shoulders, and he slept easily whilst General Gan ruminated on the details of his plan. Marcus was woken by a summons to return to General Gan's tent, he rubbed the sleep from his eyes and stretched his arms as he followed the attendant back to the General's tent. When Marcus entered, he saw that there was a stool waiting for him. Marcus sat in front of General Gan and listened to what the Chinese commander had decided to do with the Roman prisoners. The 145 Roman prisoners were to make the long journey back to China with the Chinese Army. Once in the Kansu corridor, the Romans would labor on the construction of a designated section to the extension to the Great Wall. The Romans would be provided with food and shelter whilst they worked on the Wall; then, when their work was finished, the Romans would be given their freedom, and be provided with an area of land to farm and permission to settle.

Two days later, the Chinese Army set off on the long march back to their homeland. Once again the Romans found themselves journeying east, into the rising sun. As prisoners, the Romans were the lowest ranking members of the column, and they had to march at its rear in the dust stirred up by the Chinese Army. As each day's march drew to a close, Marcus felt the sun on his back and saw his shadow stretch across the trampled way in front of him, where the Chinese Army had already passed. The ground was broken and the dust had been stirred up by the passing soldiers, but the legionaries were not troubled by the rigours of the journey. The surviving Romans were very tough men who had already travelled over 6,000 miles from their homeland in Gaul. Before they even began their journey eastward, the Romans had survived Caesar's fiercely intense and highly mobile campaigns in Gaul. Then the cavalry had sailed across the Mediterranean to Alexandria, linked up with Crassus's main force in Syria and invaded Parthia. Those legionaries who now marched into China had survived the brutal slaughter at Carrhae, and then endured years of servitude in Merv before they escaped and joined the Xiongnu nomads. Marcus and the other prisoners had passed through the deserts of Parthia and the snow-capped peaks of the Tien Shan Mountains; they had sailed across the Mediterranean, and journeyed across the ocean-like expanse of the Central Asian steppe. The 145 Romans who arrived in the Kansu corridor of China had travelled beyond the boundaries of the world as known by the Romans.

When the large convoy reached China, General Gan dismissed the allies who had joined his Army. The Romans were now at least 5000 miles from the nearest Roman outpost, though they had no way of knowing or calculating the distance. During the long journey from Zhi-Zhi, General Gan had taken a personal interest in the Roman prisoners, and now he dispatched an experienced officer to organise their settlement. The Romans were soon established in a small village near the site where they would work on the extension to the Great Wall allocated to them. The new village was named 'Li-qian', meaning 'Village of the Alexandrians', for General Gan persisted in referring to the legionaries as 'Alexandrians'. Marcus, or 'Ma' as his Sinicized name became, remained the unofficial leader of the Romans, although a Chinese mandarin was appointed to run the village. The elderly mandarin brought his entire family with him when he came to take up the post. For six years the Romans labored on the extension to the Great Wall under the supervision of Marcus and the mandarin. When the work was finished the mandarin decided to remain with the Romans when they began building their own village. The legionaries had spent most of their military careers as builders, and the village of Li-qian was well-planned and expertly constructed. Over the years a number of local Chinese families also moved into the new village, and a small but thriving mixed community was soon established. Within the village, the Romans retained a number of their customs and traditions, and Liqian prospered as it combined the best elements of the Gallic-Roman and Han-Chinese societies. Marcus took a leading role in this cultural fusion, he learnt Chinese and married the mandarin's daughter. When an exuberant Marcus carried his new bride across the threshold of their home, he realized that his life's travels were finally over. Placing his wife gently on their bed, Marcus slipped the tiger pendant and brooch from around his neck and hung them above the doorway. He would travel no further. Marcus had learnt that not all roads lead to Rome.

List of place names

Alexandria – The main port of Egypt and the capital city of Ptolemaic Egypt; at the time of our story the city was the largest port in the Mediterranean and the chief city trading with the East. The Egyptians called the city Rhokotis which in Egyptian means 'Building site' as the city was the creation of the Ptolemies who spent many years in its construction.

Antioch – The capital of the Roman province of Syria, and a major city at the time.

Amu Darya River – Now known as the Oxus River, it was the north-eastern border of Parthia. The Oxus is now a much smaller river than at the time of our story due to the greater desiccation of the region over the last two millennia.

Bari – Port town in the heel of Italy from where Crassus and his forces crossed the Adriatic en route to Antioch.

Carrhae – A small Roman garrison town, now located in Turkey near the border with Iran.

Li-qian – The town built by the Roman prisoners when they settled in China. The site is some 12kms south west of the modern town of Yongchang, a county capital located in the Kansu province of China. The Roman remains are still visible beside the village of Zhelaizhai.

Lucca – A town now in northern Italy, but at the time it was in the province of Cisalpine Gaul.

Massalia – Originally a Greek colony, it was the chief town of that area of Transalpine Gaul, called by the Romans 'The Province'. Today the city is called Marseilles and the region is now known as Provence.

Merv – At the time of our story the city was known as Antiochus Margiana but is better known historically as Merv, which is the name we have decided to use. The city rose to prominence in Parthian times but was rebuilt twice subsequently before its final destruction some centuries ago. The ruins of the three phases of the city, instead of being one on top of the other as is normally the case, occupy adjoining sites the largest of which was Merv, its immediately post-Parthian phase. The Parthian period city is smaller and contains the ruins of the city, including a synagogue, when it was called Antiochus Margiana. The remains are close to the modern town of Mary in Turkmenistan.

Nisa / Nissa – The site of this huge walled city is approximately 18kms from modern Ashgabat in Turkmenistan. At the time of the story it was the capital of Parthia.

Ostia – The port of Rome at the mouth of the River Tiber, some 19 miles from the city of Rome.

Portus Namnetus – The Roman port at the mouth of the River Loire, now the site of the city of Nantes.

Ravenna – A town on the Adriatic coast in northern Italy, at the time in the province of Cisalpine Gaul.

Zhi-Zhi – The ephemeral city which was the base of the Shanyu Zhi-Zhi until its destruction by the Chinese Army.

Notes

Lens and Dioptra

Dioptra were apparently a primitive form of telescope; the Egyptians, Greek and Romans worlds it seems knew the effects of convex and concave lens, and indeed some of the early inlaid jewellery work of the Ancient Egyptians would not have been possible without a magnifying lens of some kind. Several Roman and early lenses now in museums are mentioned and enumerated in a recent book called The Crystal Sun. The earlier examples of these lenses were made of rock crystal, but by Roman times clear glass was being used. The dioptra, a Hellenistic instrument apparently used the hollow stalk of the giant fennel, a plant now extinct, as the vessel into which two lenses were fixed the correct distance apart to form a primitive telescope. The Zoroastrians used to light the fires on their sacred altars by focussing the sun's power through a lens.

Blood-Sweating Horses

This was the evocative term given by the Chinese in the Han dynasty (206BC-220 AD) to the magnificent horses bred in the Ferghana Valley in what is now Uzbekistan using the rich alfalfa grass native to that region. These horses were far superior to any horses bred in China, and they were extremely prized mounts both in China and elsewhere. They provide the model for many of the finest Tang horse ceramic sculptures. Their stamina was legendary. The fact that they appeared to sweat blood was something noted by many Silk Road travellers into the 19th and 20th centuries. The reason for this phenomenon was only discovered in the 20th century when it was determined that it was due to a parasitic infection. The parasites burrowed under the skin in the region of the shoulder and back, and produced little swellings which burst and bled when the horse was ridden hard.

Crossbow

There is no doubt that the earliest crossbows have been found in China, with known examples dating from the 5th Century BC. The crossbow was used extensively by the Chinese as a mass attack weapon from the 5th Century on, until the invention of gunpowder in the Northern Sung period (960-1126AD). According to James Temple's recent book The Genius of China, the Romans did have a primitive but seldom used form of the crossbow.

Testudo

The classic Roman infantry manoeuvre involving the joining together of shields to form a protective shell over and around a group of legionaries.

The battle of Carrhae

Plutarch refers to the infantry being made to march at cavalry pace

Personae

Principle Ficticious Characters

Marcus Frontinius Marcellus – The Marcus whose adventures and journey to China are the subject of the novel.

Lucius Frontinius Marcellus – Marcus's father, a prosperous timber merchant and boat-builder, and a Roman citizen.

Flavius Frontinius Marcellus – Marcus's elder brother.

Eugenia – Marcus's mother, married to Lucius.

Petrus – captain of the Albatross, and a valued employee of Lucius.

Dimitri – Greek captain in the Roman Navy.

Reuben bar Ezra – Jewish merchant based in Alexandria who traded along the Silk Road.

Rebecca bar Ezra – Daughter of Reuben.

Luana – famed courtesan.

Gaius – fellow centurion serving with Marcus.

Titus, Appius, Servius, Gnaeus and Caius – legionaries serving with Marcus.

Tyluxes – Yuezhi noble, fighting with Surena against the Romans.

Tomacles – Macedonian assassin employed by King Orodes.

Melchior, Vardanes and Olthar – Parthians in charge of the Roman prisoners at Merv.

Liu – Xiongnu woman who becomes Marcus's partner after the death of her husband.

Principle Historical Characters

Aetius – Tribune in Rome who tried to prevent Crassus leaving for the East.

Gaius Julius Caesar (100 BC-44BC) – commonly called Julius Caesar one of the Triumvirs, a renowned General and author.

Gan – General leading the Chinese Army.

Jason of Tralles – famous Greek tragedian actor.

Marcus Licinius Crassus (c.115BC-53BC) – another of the Triumvirs and the richest man in Rome.

Publius Licinius Crassus – younger son of Marcus Licinius Crassus. He was a military tribune.

Gnaeus Pompey Magnus (106BC-48BC) – commonly called Pompey – one of the Triumvirs and a successful General.

Orodes, King of Parthia.

Ptolemy XII – the Egyptian ruler.

Cleopatra VII – the daughter of Ptolemy XII.

Surena – Parthian leader and aristocrat who was in command of the Parthian forces at the Battle of Carrhae, later assassinated by King Orodes.

ZhiZhi – the leader of the Xiongnu federation.

ROMANS ON THE SILK ROAD

About The Authors

Brian McElney OBE was born in Hong Kong, educated primarily in England and worked for 35 years as a lawyer back in Hong Kong, meanwhile gathering what has become a world famous collection of Chinese antiquities. He now lives in Bath in southern England where he founded the Museum of East Asian Art.

Andrew Hoste Primrose read English Literature at Bristol University and spent almost a year researching *Romans on the Silk Road,* in Hong Kong, Italy, Turkmenistan, Uzbekistan, Kyrgyzstan and China. Andrew has worked as an English teacher in Japan, Italy and Norway, in addition to assisting with the writing of a number of other books, both fiction and non-fiction.